PRAISE FOR
VOLUME I

Hemingway ... [places] a very human Jane into a vibrant, turbulent England that is seeking new ideas but also fighting the Napoleonic Wars. ... He captures the energy of the times, while also writing with the irony and sly humor of Austen herself. ... Truly a worthy addition to the Jane Austen legacy.
—*BlueInk Starred Review*

A skillful portrayal of an early nineteenth-century literary icon takes this historical romance on an imaginative journey of the soul. ... These fascinating people step off the pages in lifelike form.
—*Foreword CLARION Reviews, 4 stars*

Hemingway has a talent for witty banter and wry observations that would make Elizabeth Bennet proud. An enjoyable first novel in an imaginative, well-researched series.
—*Kirkus Reviews*

PRAISE FOR
VOLUME II

Here again is a strikingly real Jane Austen fully engaged in the turbulent times. ... She is a living, breathing presence.
— *BlueInk starred review*

A well-researched work of historical fiction ... [with] sweet moments and intriguing historical insights.
—*Kirkus Reviews*

The adventure of a true romantic partnership and all the excitement that the nineteenth century had to offer. ... [The] novel invites you to linger, to savor, and to enjoy.
—*Foreword Reviews*

The Marriage of Miss Jane Austen

A Novel by a Gentleman
Volume III

Collins Hemingway

—"This beautifully constructed book transports the reader into the constrictive social roles and expectations of Miss Austen's life while also displaying the grace and determined manners of the time. This is a delightful book, beautifully researched."

—"This lovely novel about Jane Austen's reimagined life is so well-researched and respectfully written ... that it's easy to imagine how she could have found love and a partner as intelligent, talented and passionate as she was."

—"How delightful to read a novel so creatively written which explores what many JA fans have wondered—did she ever fall in love? This author ... makes her come alive—her quick wit, intelligence, eagerness to learn new things, and thoughtful reflections are well crafted and kept my attention."

—"A gorgeous romantic tease that ultimately made me laugh with delight. ... Highly imagined, playful, and it is writ close to Austen's own voice."

—"Well written and probable tale, with lovely ending. ... It is not too far from Austen's life story—with a twist that intrigues. ... The ending is quite lovely—not contrived, impossible or out of character."

—"An intriguing and engaging, romantic, historical fantasy about the unknown part of Jane Austen's life. Leaves you anxious for the sequel."

—"I loved this book! ... I enjoyed being transported in time and into the mind and heart of the Jane Austen that might have been. I couldn't put it down."

—"A delight ... with amazing detail and accuracy. ... The characters jump off the page. ... Even those unfamiliar with the 'real' Jane Austen will find this novel a great addition to their library."

*To the sweetest flower that ever bloomed
in the garden of John and Priscilla,
Wonderfully Always Herself*

I consider everybody as having a right to marry *once* in their Lives for Love.

—*Jane Austen*

PART I

April 1807–February 1808

Chapter 1

"K-k-kiss me, Jane," Ashton whispered as they walked arm in arm toward the nursery. "If you love me, k-k-kiss me." This was their catchphrase for affection, and in the past often a prelude to intimacy.

She kissed him, but added: "I was up most of the night with George. He has never been this fussy." This was not Ashton's first overture since the baby, of course. Her response was never to rebuff—but rather, as she thought of it, *to defer*, to an indefinite time, one less exhausting and chaotic. The months of recovery from the dangerous delivery, of illness, of living uncomfortably away from home, provided all the sensible reasons a woman needed for delay.

"Perhaps something to think about?" he ventured. "I hoped you were feeling better."

"Do I sound as though I feel any better?" she snapped, with immediate regret. "My headache may be worse than yours."

"Our meetings seem to give you headaches. Are you sure you're able to carry on as secretary, on top of everything else?" They were returning from a business meeting related to the French embargo, one of several assemblies scheduled in coming days to deal with that emergency.

"I must have something to do beyond caring for a child and making unnecessary suggestions to the housekeeper. Much as I love my little boy, at times I want to scream for an adult conversation. And he is only four months old!"

"I thought perhaps one of us might be on the mend," Ashton said. Everyone in the house had been passing a respiratory complaint back and forth for weeks. In addition to general illness, the baby, George, had also been suffering colic, so that Jane was managing on even less sleep than usual for a nursing mother.

"Any hope of my feeling better has been overwhelmed by the lack of rest. This was the one night I could have used your company."

"Why didn't you wake me?" he said with a trace of defensiveness. Early on, he had sometimes risen with her, until her insistence for privacy and quiet with her baby, and his own fatigue, overcame his need to make a statement of support.

"No reason for both of us to be exhausted." After months of round-the-clock nursing, however, she could not avoid in the tone of her words a modest amount of bleary-eyed irritation at *his* being able to sleep.

As they had arrived at the nursery, and Jane was settling herself with the baby, Ashton let the comment pass. She felt momentarily annoyed with both her husband and herself, for she felt their conversation had led her to express dissatisfaction with her maternal role. As if to illustrate the restlessness she had described, little George disputed her efforts to have him nurse before at last resigning himself to the breast.

"I must sleep when he is done," she said. "Mother called on me just before the meeting. Mary's labor has begun. That is another reason I am anxious. I will go over later." As their home in Hampshire was being renovated, Jane and Ashton were living in close quarters with her sister-in-law, her brother Frank as he dashed back and forth between Southampton and his new posting, and the women in Jane's own family.

"You're too ill to be around a newborn. Mary will understand."

"I will keep my distance, but I will be there for her. I doubt her labor will be any easier than her pregnancy. A woman a-bed wants

4

to know someone is near who has been through what she is going through."

"Send Frank this way. I'll calm him with liquor. I'm glad he could slip away to come home, though he'll be as much in the way as I was."

"You may have no doubt of that," Jane answered. Her brother was relieved to finally receive his new command, the 64-gun *St. Albans*, and return to full pay. His wrangles with the Admiralty over properly re-outfitting the aging ship had had the positive side effect of delaying his departure until after the birth of his child.

"Balance your loving concern for Mary with your husband's loving concern for your own health," Ashton said. Turning his attention back to his son, who was now nursing lustily, Ashton added: "No quarrel for him, anyway. Happy—very much so!"

"Yes, well—" Their tendency to speak privately with frank humor caused her to almost remark about a general male propensity in that regard, but she did not want to take the conversation in that direction.

She was tired at nothing more than the idea of visiting Mary; more so, perhaps, because it was an obligation—an important one, to be sure—as much as a desire. She was not sure why she struggled with fatigue. Physical exhaustion was common for anyone who lacked a household of servants for most of her life, and mental exhaustion was common for someone who wrote seriously. But there was always a sunburst of energy in her core to overcome weariness. Now she felt the contradictory sense of having far too much to do while having no inclination to act—even as, every day, she trudged from chore to chore. Instead of contentment, or exhaustion, she felt frustration. She remembered what her mother had written to her about, that in early childhood each day lasted a year but each year flashed by in an hour. Only four months into it, she wondered whether she would ever accomplish that first year. ... Yet here she sat, comfortable before a fire, husband fondly at hand, baby at her breast. She should be content but felt only settled; and not the usual sort of settled. When one speaks of *settling in*, the image is of one falling back into a comfortable chair. Yet Jane felt that she had fallen so far into her chair she was suffocating: falling through the chair into the depths so that the powerful love radiating outward to her husband and child might fail to reach them. At that thought, of course, she felt terrible. It was her task as wife and mother to continually generate enough emotional heat to keep them all toasty.

"Have you heard from Mr. Wilberforce?" she asked, seeking to shake her ennui by shifting her thoughts from personal to public concerns. As with other correspondence to the abolitionist, it was Jane who had written the letter of formal congratulations on behalf of the Dennis family on the overwhelming vote in Parliament to end the slave trade. Wilberforce was too proper to respond directly to a woman (though she was sure he was bemused at her gentle prods to his conservative nature); Ashton would have received any reply.

"No," Ashton said. "I'm sure he'll get around to it. They must now establish the enforcement mechanisms, which you can be sure the slavers will fight at every step."

"Then he must keep busy rather than acknowledge our compliments. After all, we were late to join his party, and we will have little involvement going forward."

"It will take months—years, most likely—to effect any real change in the lives of the enslaved," Ashton acknowledged. "More reason to start sooner than later. But—your information was critical. Don't forget that."

"It is not as though we expect or deserve a parade," she said, "but I do feel let down. All that effort—and then it's done. A monumental triumph might trigger other successes, or it might set in motion a contradictory swell that washes away not only the victory but the victor."

"I don't see either happening here," Ashton said.

"No—my point. It seems that the most common conclusion to the big events in life is nothing at all. Ordinary disappointments and pleasures, ordinary setbacks and advances, the positive and negative ripples from the action—everything cancels out."

"By their nature," he replied, "big events come seldom and last little. That is what makes them a big event."

"After a surprisingly short time," she said thoughtfully, "the singular joy of our glorious success is being worn away by the scrubbing sands of ordinary life."

Ashton had been immediately overwhelmed with business he had neglected in the final months of the abolition campaign, work that was compounded by French actions to disrupt British trade. Jane was similarly swamped with domestic duties that had lagged, her work compounded by the need for additional rest as she continued to heal from George's birth in December. The overall situation was further wrapped in a series of colds, coughs, and infections that had beset the family during the most dismal months of a damp clime.

Ashton stroked the baby's hair, as thick and black as his own, his glance wandering over her figure. She caught in her husband's expression the faintest distaste at her looks. Under the pressure of nursing, her figure had begun to slim, but her body felt slack, the lumpen form of a new mother that had lost the robust fullness of late pregnancy but was nowhere close to the slim, lithe shape she had carried most of her life. Is that why he had bought her a machine for exercising? A chamber-horse, as it was called; of need because the cold weather kept her inside more than she would like. This, at least, was Ashton's breezy justification. She found the device useful for airing clothes.

Though not realizing she had noticed his reaction toward her figure, Ashton leaned over and kissed her gallantly on the cheek—a gesture she recognized as a sop to his own guilt for the fleeting *ungallant* thought about the physical appearance of the woman he loved. She made a note to forgive him—later.

"Are you sure you don't want a wet nurse?"

"I will do what my mother did."

"Your mother sent her children away to be nursed. After a few months, you said."

"She had a houseful of other young children to attend! A farm to run! Without the legions of nurses and servants at my disposal.

No, this means too much to me. George likes being with his mama. We will muddle through."

They sat together for some minutes.

"Jane, do you think all is well with him?" He did not say *George* or *our son*; just *him*, as if to obscure his identity from the universe's prying; and he spoke tentatively, as if this quiet moment might be the only opportunity to discuss something that had been bothering him for some time.

"He is as well as any baby in the world! Fat—happy—always smiling."

"At times he seems—a little—lethargic—"

"You would too—if you had the colic—if your aunts and uncles brought you every cold that passed through Southampton."

"I mean—he lacks—attention. When he is well, feeling good."

"He has not been well in a month—none of us has!"

"He still lacks—I don't know. I'm worried."

Jane tried unsuccessfully to quell a rush of protective anger, simultaneously irritated that exhaustion and anxiety could drain the heart yet fuel the spleen. "No eyes are brighter or more attentive than when he looks at you! There is nothing wrong with my child."

Fatigue affecting his judgment, Ashton ignored the warning signs and pressed on. "He doesn't seem to notice very much around him. Until we show it to him."

"He is a new-born! He did not emerge at birth full-grown like Athena. Every child takes his own good time to develop all his senses."

"Yes—but—"

"You are upsetting me. I cannot nurse if I am upset. Now I won't be able to nap before seeing Mary. See, George is fussing again. I must have my quiet. Please, go—now."

Hurt, he stood to leave. She took his hand and smiled at him with the full happiness of a new mother and wife. "I have never been more tired in my life. Who knew I would go from being a delirious bride to the happiest pregnant woman ever to the grumpiest old mother in the world. I hope one day to be rested enough that my eyes can focus. Then all will be well. Whatever storms may be blowing across the North Sea, spring is coming here. Once we can get outside and breathe the fresh air, we will throw off our contagions—the baby and I shall be fine. Ashton—I miss Hants! *I want to go home.* Then we shall all relax in the sun and be happy."

Chapter 2

Musings about their situation, and thoughts about Mary's imminent delivery—Jane had slipped away from her side for a few
hours—occupied her mind during the business meeting the next
day. She came out of her reverie only when Ashton was particularly
aggressive in his interrogation of underlings of the affiliates of the
Dennis family businesses for which she served as secretary.

"What's the damage?" he asked. "Can anyone determine the
degree of harm to our business?"

All those present shuffled papers, made the facial movements
preparatory to speech—and sat dumb. This—silence—had been
the predominant theme of the hastily convened meetings, held in
Southampton because of the renovation of their home still under
way in north Hampshire.

"Surely, an estimate? Mr. Jarrett?"

By far the most senior man involved in the Dennis enterprise's
international trade, Mr. Jarrett referred to a sailing schedule on
the table before him. "No wish to hazard a guess, sir—it would be
only a guess. Too many ships are still at sea."

"But you k-know the number of sh-ships! That should give you
a g-glimmer." Ashton's stutter, barely noticeable after more than
a year of steady remediating practice, emerged with his frustration. "Why m-must I remind my employees that I am n-not seeking

scientific accuracy, only reasonable estimates? Enough to inform our d-decisions."

Ashton's associates avoided his dark searching eyes. Even seated, Jane's husband dominated the physical space around the table. He no longer sought to project his strength and formidableness, as he did only a few years ago. Ashton now compacted himself as much as possible to reduce the intimidation factor; but that compression created an energy that caused others to lean away out of caution.

Mr. Jarrett was the one exception. A slim man whose glasses framed honest eyes, he responded quietly but without diffidence. "The number of ships we have inward bound is down by half a dozen, spread across several ports. We also have cargo on a dozen ships we do not own. The bigger question might be: How many ships were able to load or unload their cargoes, and how many were not? We have no way of knowing. Communication is too fragmentary."

"Over the period of?"

"Five months. The embargo had an immediate effect."

Ashton shook his head in dismay. "What do we actually know?"

"In England overall, trade is already down by a quarter," said Jane's brother Henry, who along with the banker Mr. Thornton managed their affairs in London. "Based on reports from the Ministry, the reduction in textiles is even greater. Fortunately for us, our Government and military contracts are unaffected."

"But the weather has been dreadful all over Europe," Mr. Jarrett added. "We have no way of knowing how much to attribute to the French embargo and how much to the gales of winter."

"It is never a good thing when a shipping concern is counting on storms for salvation," Jane observed.

"You know as much as I of the vagaries of sail," Mr. Jarrett said—this, to everyone in the room. "Ships routinely show up long after they're expected. Our profits in 1802 came almost entirely from two merchantmen that wandered in months after they were given up for lost."

Mr. Jarrett, an elderly widower, preferred to come to work each day instead of poking a lonely fire at home, as he had recently confided to Jane; his long years with the firm gave him a level of comfort with Ashton that most others in the meeting lacked. Indeed, Ashton's occasional severity toward him was understood to be a measure of respect. If a person's actions did not achieve at least one challenge by Ashton, there was a good chance the individual would not be invited to any consequential meetings in the future.

Mr. Jarrett smiled now in a way that made Jane wonder if he was thinking of the time, that same year of 1802, when Ashton had come close to dangling him out the window over his reluctance to report to Alethea when Ashton abruptly decided to decamp for the West Indies. That event had moderated Mr. Jarrett's views on women, and when Ashton's sister proved an adept in business, he developed an avuncular relationship with her. Alethea sat next to him today at the table.

"If I must guess," Mr. Jarrett said, "a third will never complete their deliveries. The rest will, but only after substantial delays." After pausing to see if anyone else had anything to add, he concluded by saying: "It puzzles a simple man as to why the British thought we could embargo Boney and Boney would not embargo us back." Buonaparte's Berlin Decree, which defined his "Continental System" as one that excluded English goods, had been as surprising in its effectiveness as it had been in its proclamation.

"The thinking," Ashton replied with some annoyance—he being one of the advocates of the action against the French the previous spring—"was that the Royal Navy could impose our will through blockades, while the French navy could not. It never occurred to us that the French required no naval power at all. They could stop cargoes on the docks. Coming or going."

"We have applied for special licenses," said Mr. Knollman, the former naval officer who oversaw the Dennis textile operations. "We are bound to have some of them approved."

"Those are intended for home weavers and other small crafts," Ashton replied.

"The government is being very generous in its definition of *small*," Mr. Knollman replied. "The French are doing the same. Neither country can afford to have their farmers and weavers bankrupted."

"The definition of *small* had best become *inverted* if it is to have any benefit for us," Ashton answered. Jane's attention faded for a few moments as Ashton talked. If anything, her illness was becoming worse. Her head was congested; her head hurt; her body ached. She occasionally felt a passing chill. Her body desired to sink into slumber beside the crackling fire in the cozy book-filled room. Like Ashton, she had the numb perseverance of the sick parent with no choice but to carry on.

"We need to do something," Henry said. "Our financial strategy presumed a certain level of income. We are sound today, but the embargo will put considerable strain on our reserves by the middle of summer. I suggest we pull back our investments until we have a better understanding of the future."

"Can we not borrow?" Jane asked.

"As you might expect, rates are outrageous now," Henry said, rubbing his spectacle lenses so hard with his handkerchief that they squeaked. He had the brains for the banking profession, along with a banker's innate distaste for risk. "We must reduce expenses, or increase sales."

"Any ideas?" This from Ashton, again penetrating the room with his eyes from under the disheveled mass of his dark hair.

"We are maintaining our pace with fireplaces and stoves," said Alethea, who had succeeded in making their high-efficiency Rumford appliances a matter of fashion with the *ton*, "but with all the uncertainty, I doubt we can do much better. It does not matter how much in the way of savings our improvements will provide. Hesitation is the watchword in all strata of society."

"And we are coming out of the heating season," Jane said.

"There are military textile contracts up for renewal," Mr. Knollman said. "We have won the last several bids." This was the result of the improved productivity of the Jacquard looms, the installation of which he had overseen in the last half of the previous year. "We had not planned to pursue these, but the reduction of work makes the projects feasible."

"Do it," Ashton said.

"Though I am assured we can provide the lowest price, other considerations sometimes intervene," Mr. Knollman warned. "Certain associations are known to lead to irregularities."

"We will not meet bribe with bribe," Ashton said. "Our advantages in price should be sufficient that a penniless Government will not be able to let favoritism intervene."

"Earlier," Jane said, "there were references to the Baltic, and Malta. Could someone speak to these possibilities?" She used a deferential tone that befitted her role as secretary, to ensure that Ashton had the opportunity to address matters that had been left unsettled when the talk shifted in a new direction. Her ability to keep meetings on topic, as well as the precision and thoroughness of her documentation over the last year, had solidified her position. Mr. Jarrett had thanked her because he, the former scribe, was now free to participate more fully in the business discussions.

Mr. Jarrett explained that the Baltic island of Heligoland was turning into a major smuggling outpost, along with other northern ports, while contraband goods were being offloaded to neutral ships in Malta and Sicily. The extra steps added time and cost but allowed traders to circumvent the embargo. "Being the farthest from Buonaparte's reach, the northern countries are particularly lax. Hamburg's specialty is false-bottomed containers—something of a specialty of ours, as well—but we have the fewest connections there. I recommend we move quickly, as it will take time to establish relationships. Russia is another possibility. We can trade for carpets and other goods, probably out of the Crimea—but this puts us very far afield. It could take a year to establish this route."

Ashton said nothing, though the fatigued silence of illness was something Jane took as assent, and she made her notes accordingly.

"With our mills working at less than capacity, we have developed a way to reduce our inventory of raw cotton," Mr. Knollman said. "We drop bales just offshore of France, attached to buoys. Our French affiliates come out and pick up the cotton. They claim the bales as salvage from a wrecked ship."

"And the customs agents buy that?" Ashton said. "Bold, even by our standards."

"How much could this effectively deliver?" Jane asked. "Are we doing something out of the ordinary because we can, or because it works?"

"A bale here, a bale there," Mr. Knollman replied with a smile, "pretty soon you're talking real cotton."

"A few financial incentives, and a few nice stockings for their ladies," Henry added, "and customs agents will not inquire diligently into the large number of wrecks in which cotton is the only survivor. And prizes, too—from English ships that toss cotton overboard to avoid capture. The authorities in Paris find such reports irresistible." His voice resumed its usual animation, for any tangible idea restored his natural enthusiasm.

"Proceed," Ashton said.

"There is another possibility," Mr. Knollman said, "though I hesitate to bring it forward. Woolen merchants in West Riding are in league to bid on the production of winter clothing for the French army—in Poland, where they are not likely ever to face British troops. That, at least, is the justification."

"British mills are making greatcoats for our enemies?" Holding his head, Ashton cursed to himself.

"The contract is worth forty thousand pounds," Mr. Knollman said. "Enough to keep a mill busy the rest of the year. Deliveries are to be completed within a twelvemonth."

"About the time we could launch our next expedition to the continent," Ashton said. "Is this your recommendation?"

"I am doing the duty you demanded—to speak of every opportunity," Mr. Knollman said. "But—no. A Frenchman who survives this winter could kill a British soldier next."

Even though their French customers produced only stockings and petticoats, it occurred to Jane that the floating bales of cotton could also serve the purpose of war; she puzzled at the many ways the cargo might be diverted to the French military and how they might thwart such redirection. Unable to solve the problem, her mind lurched like a broken loom and she held her peace.

"Are the Lovelaces involved?" Ashton said, after thinking about the issue of the contract for winter clothing. The Lovelace family were one-time friends of Jane and Ashton who had betrayed them in a business venture.

"I am not certain," Henry said. "I can find out."

After a moment's pause, Ashton added: "Jane, draw up a letter to Wilberforce to see if we can stop this madness. He must know the men who matter up there." Mr. Wilberforce was as ardent a supporter of the war with France as he was an opponent of slavery.

"Coats for the French," Ashton said a second time. He cursed again and started to shake his head—stopping because of his headache.

Mr. Trevithick, who had been silent for most of the meeting, spoke up. "We should halt our work on cannons," he said. "That will cut probably a third of my costs immediately."

Mr. Trevithick was responsible for the iron works for all the Dennis enterprises, from kitchen stoves to their nascent rail-road venture to large cannons intended for coastal defense. He had also been the biggest advocate of the cannon project, so that the others reacted with surprise at his proposal to stop work. He explained further: "At present, we try any new iron compounds with the cannons at the same time as we try them for boilers and rails for the rail-road. This means we double the number of tests. Until we find the right combination of strength and compressibility in the iron for the engines and rails, there is no reason to try anything else. It is a waste."

"If you're sure," Ashton said.

"We can move much more rapidly if we focus on the rail-road. When we succeed, we can quickly turn our attention back to the cannon. A decision for another time."

"And we must quit the idea of a steam-ship," Henry said in a voice as even as possible.

"No!" Jane cried. "This was promised—the Royal Navy—Frank—Charles—we cannot abandon *them*!" The plan had been to develop steam-ships as a follow-on to the rail-road project, but differences in design requirements had led Trevithick to move ahead sooner, commissioning preliminary studies for steam propulsion for water-borne vessels.

"The Royal Navy does not want—or need—a steam-ship," Henry replied. Jane could tell from the exchange of looks between Henry and Mr. Trevithick that her reaction had been anticipated, and that Henry had been delegated the task of broaching the subject because he was as loyal to their naval brothers as she. "The destruction of the enemy fleets at Trafalgar has washed away all interest."

"They cannot give away the future—!"

"There is no threat to justify the expense," Henry said. "Nothing that requires any advances in design. The Government is too far in debt with the war. The future must wait."

"The man to do the job has already returned to America," Mr. Trevithick said. "His disgust was the equal of yours, Mrs. Dennis. I wouldn't trust anyone who's left."

"And then you have objections from an entire industry—the men who build sailing ships," Henry added. "They have no idea how to compete with steam. Not to mention experienced captains who would have to give way to younger officers better able to adapt to the new machinery."

"Yes—Frank and Charles—and other men equally deserving!"

"Exactly why the old salts will have none of it. The entire Navy would be upheaved. The pressure is enormous to stay with the tried and true."

"A terrible shame," Mr. Trevithick said. "Our colleague Mr. Bramah invented a water screw that could propel ships. It was similar to ones we used to lift water from mines. Unworkable, though—it required horses in the hold turning the apparatus—rather like a grist mill. But connected to a steam engine—that could be a marvel!"

"And what if the next time we meet the American Navy, they are able to go faster?" Jane demanded. "If they can maneuver their ships without regard to wind?"

"Then British sailors will die," Ashton said, "and the Admiralty will reconsider its position." He touched her hand, lightly and briefly, to let her know he had been unaware of the plan to drop this bombshell on her. "It appears we have no choice. We cannot invest in a product this complex and expensive without a customer. No matter the potential."

Jane sat silent. On the sheet on which she was taking notes, she sketched the outline of a sailing ship—and obliterated it with black scribbles so angry she broke the nib of her pen.

Half an hour later, after action on several other cost-reduction measures, the meeting was adjourned. As the rest filed out, Ashton and Jane reviewed the outcomes. Tired as she was, she looked forward to writing up the notes from the meeting. She had recognized that the person who controlled the meeting memoranda gained considerable power in shaping the direction of the company. Every meeting left matters undecided or unclear; the secretary could logically draw the summary in a sensible direction based on the trend of the arguments. She had also observed, in the many months of assisting Ashton, that it often did not matter which of several paths a decision took, provided the rationale was clear and everyone was motivated to act together.

"Don't be too specific about the cotton," he said to her, leaning back in his chair. He had not bothered to shave, the shadow on his face adding to his overall posture of illness and fatigue. "Make it something on the order of *innovative methods of delivery*." She agreed. "I wonder if it would be simpler if I wrote the notes and you signed them," he added, "seeing that you write with the authority of the managing director, and I conform to your decisions."

Her protest was unapologetic. Though it was true she had occasionally added to the documents some actions that occurred to her on subsequent reflection, such embellishments were so tightly and logically woven into the commentary that Ashton had regularly approved her notes. He responded: "Ignore me. I feel too awful to attempt to jest. It's good to have a second set of eyes observing the meeting. I'm glad you take things forward to a sensible conclusion."

"I have learned the value of framing an issue in a tangible fashion," she said. "Even if you disagree, you are better able to judge the matter clearly."

Something about the decision on the new ports of call, however, nettled Ashton, as indicated by his querulous disputation of her characterization of the ways the Dennis enterprises might avoid the French embargo. "It must always be difficult to develop a new network of business relationships during war," she said. "But is it a bad thing to seek out new avenues of trade?"

"Of course not," Ashton said, "but there is something wrong. I can't quite put my finger on it." They would be adding enough business to overburden Mr. Jarrett and his men, Ashton feared, but not enough to justify the hiring of more people.

When it became clear that his concerns would not be quickly resolved, they began to walk. Both were better thinkers on the move.

"With a small project, you try to make it happen with the people you already have," Ashton continued. "And you fail—or struggle. It does not bode well. This happened during my first year home when we expanded our farm operations—productivity went down. We put thirty more acres into production, but afterward Mr. Fletcher and I realized it should have been a hundred."

"Your people being already fully taxed, you needed more help whether you increased the work by a great deal, or a little. That is why you added more acreage last year?"

"Precisely. We were at a crossover point. Which is why taking on a small project is sometimes more trouble than a large one. That's where we are, I think, with our trading business. Mr. Jarrett is a good man, but he cannot bear to admit he needs assistance. He will work harder and harder, no matter how much he falls behind. I would find him keeled over at his desk from overwork."

"Then increase the scale," Jane said. "Seek a dozen new ports instead of three. There must be more cities in the North hostile to Buonaparte. More coastal towns in Italy. What about America?"

"Possibly. America's tricky. We could be at war with them again. The Government believes the best way to encourage good relations with our former brothers is to intercept *their* trade with France and steal their ship crews for our own. Now would be a good time to have a monopoly, like the East India Company."

"George may get a monopoly. Or our grandchildren. We, however, are as upstart as the Corsican. We must rely on our brains."

"There you have it!" Ashton said, stopping, taking Jane's face in his hands, and giving her an enthusiastic kiss. "America, it is!"

"But—"

"Not El Norte. No!—America the Sud. The Sur. The Sul. *South* America! Spain has collapsed. Their Fleet is out of the picture. No one in England has any significant trade there. We're already established in the West Indies. That's the answer! We'll use the necessary expansion into the Baltic and Mediterranean as the foundation for additional staff, and take the excess capacity to develop trade in South America. Ha! You're a genius!"

His excitement over trade easily transferred into another kind: He put his arms around her and nuzzled her neck—this was but a passing fancy, for his mind began to whirl with projects and process, schedules and cargoes, routes and winds; his eyes moved as if working down a list of items to take to Mr. Jarrett. She was pleased in two regards: that their interplay of ideas had led to a better one than either would have achieved separately; and that her contributions as companion and helpmate had offset the lack of those intimacies which for months had suffered from benevolent disregard.

Chapter 3

Finally, everything was done. It had taken several days but at last the baggage was unloaded and sorted for use in the big house or placed in storage; the latest contrivances that Ashton had collected were distributed to sometimes doubting employees; and the inhabitance had passed the white-gloved inspection by the butler, Mr. Hanrahan, and the housekeeper, Mrs. Lundeen.

Hants House thus secured and the baby napping, Jane made her brisk way up to the Greek temple from which she would have a clear view of the estate's immediate environs. Her lifelong preference was to meander among the fields. She had been back to the top of the hill only a couple of times since their fateful confrontation there—an argument whose ferocity could only have led to marriage. Twenty months ago, it was: an eternity in terms of life lived and changes undergone. Today, for some reason, she needed elevation, as if by gaining the purer air of altitude she could rise above her sooty mood.

Her route took her through the hedgerows and the park, through deliberately casual arrangements of trees—each of which had the same unlikely combination of oak, birch, and ash—around the manmade lake, and up the rise to the Ionic temple. This fashionable *folly* was the work of Ashton's parents, as leading Hampshire landholders were required to have at least one rustic ruin. Her husband would have planted trees with commercial value and used the lake to water them. Even now he spoke of how he might justify the expense of converting the temple into an astronomical observatory. She smiled to herself, though, knowing very well it would remain sacredly untouched as the place their life began together.

She did not sit inside on the stone slab, which always felt cold, but walked slowly around the building, taking in the lands and sky. Though below her by a hundred feet, Hants House itself sat on a small rise to the south of her position, fronted by the lawn, the brook, and the meadow. Their lane paralleled the brook in curling around several large irregular tree-covered mounds before angling down a sharp slope to the village. Behind the main building were the pond, the stables, and the usual out-buildings needed to support a country house and working farm. Because Hants had grown by acquisition over more than a hundred years, it had inherited rather than constructed many of its larger buildings. The dispersion of these—the oat, wheat, and barley barns, the fodder house, cart barn, and chicken houses—lent an air of disorganization in contrast to the neatness of a typical estate. This layout, however, meant that many buildings lay close to the fields and livestock, lessening the work for laborers. Beyond these, farmlands rolled east in soft undulations planted in grain and hay, and holding many varieties of livestock. To her left, many more fields stretched up the green valley northward. Some were worked by tenant or yeoman farmers, but this area also included their own lands-in-hand, on which grazed the many horses bred and trained for the Army.

Everywhere, men worked, as signified by the occasional shout or command, the heavy movement of wagons, or the ringing strike of the smith. Everywhere, fireplaces smoked, the women already preparing supper. There were the fresh, orderly strokes of green as spring thrust itself out of the tilled ground. Trees were in that state just beyond budding such that their leaves seemed less blooms than green vibrations in the air. The air *smelled* of the green of the season. In the distance, on both sides, she could just discern the sharp quick movements of newborn animals, and the jostling of the older animals as they tried to avoid the unpredictability of prance and buck. Somewhere came the startling sound—part whinny, part scream—of a horse that had lost sight of its favored companion.

From here she could also see the coal-gas manufactory, tucked behind a small outcropping that served as a shield against any inadvertent detonation. It sat in a bed of new wood chips that, fresh as a bird's nest, softened the determined jaws of the building. It was this project that had decided the Dennises to relocate to Southampton with Jane's family at the first of the year. Their removal had enabled the renovation of Hants House to incorporate the modern Rumford fireplaces and kitchen stoves, under Ashton's edict that he would not sell what he himself did not use; and the installation of coal-gas lamps in place of candles, which required the manufactory close at hand.

Because only a handful of servants had been needed in Southampton, most of the staff had received temporary outdoor assignments with Mr. Fletcher, the steward, well away from the potential danger zone of the developing gas mechanisms. Jane was satisfied that the staff was put to good use, as her farm-girl eyes could discern subtle improvements in fencing, hay storage, and weed removal—the last of the many chores that are seldom fully completed over winter.

The Dennis entourage had returned after the difficult but ultimately safe delivery of Mary's baby, a girl named Mary Jane. Worry lingers over every pregnancy and birth, but Jane had been particularly concerned about Frank's wife. Mary had been ill, sometimes violently, and suffered fainting spells all during her pregnancy; and her delivery, just a few months after Jane's own, reminded Jane vividly of the complications she herself had suffered. Mary's confinement had, in fact, been so difficult as to alarm them all extremely, her safety and that of her baby hanging in the balance. Like Jane, however, Mary made a rapid recovery. This somehow seemed to bode well as much for Jane as for her sister-in-law, and her spirits freshened with the breeze that drove away the clouds that had sulked over the Southampton port for weeks. Within a few days, they felt free to start for Hants.

The sun accompanied them on their journey north and had been shining ever since. Every corner of the house was now dry and warm, in contrast to the musty damp it exhaled after prolonged disuse of the previous rainy weeks. By the time she reached the top of the hill today, she felt that she had climbed completely out of her despondency.

And now, finally, she felt safe enough to address her fears about the baby. She could not believe there was anything wrong with George, who had filled out as plump and strong as a piglet; but simultaneously she could not fully dispute the indications, subtle and otherwise, that some things were not quite right with him either. He lagged. He was not lethargic—Ashton's word—but he lagged. She had no definitive knowledge of the speed at which a baby developed, but she had the experience of a lifetime caring for the children of her relatives, as well as her own instincts as a mother. She had the knowledge of the nurse, who occasionally looked from George to Jane with concern, as if something might be amiss that she was not entitled to point out.

Jane could not consider the possibility of what might be wrong without initial consideration of the litany of things that were right. George was happy; he smiled and gurgled with pleasure whenever his mother or father played with him. He made the requisite smacking noises, though with less of the fullness of the mouth that would soon turn sound into vowels. His sense of touch was superb, and so was his sensitivity to pain. The slightest pinch brought a howl of protest. His taste was acute—he loved honey when she dabbed it on his tongue and pulled the most awful face when she experimented with something sour. His sight seemed fine—he lit up whenever he saw her, as if it were a game when she suddenly appeared. When they were together he stared so intently he might have been trying to penetrate her soul.

His hearing, she had to admit, was problematic. This is what Ashton was reacting to, the general lack of responsiveness. There were times, as she took George from the nurse, that he turned to her expectantly, as if he recognized her voice when she approached from out of sight. Yet at other times, he did not seem to react to sound at all. This circumstance was such a contradiction to his violent response to noise in the womb that she could not reconcile the difference. Though suffering chronically for months—as did the entire family—George did not seem to have anything but the ordinary respiratory infections that came with the clammy smoke of closed winter quarters. She knew of one or two children who had lost their hearing as the result of disease, but she had every reason to believe that his hearing problems must be temporary, an inflammation. But then the thought struck her: What if, when he turned to her when he could not see her, he was reacting to her scent and not her sound? Would a baby know his mother's smell? Perhaps—she was certain she could pick out George by smell, even if she were blindfolded.

Just in case, she had begun privately to make the gestures to him, what little she could remember. He was too young for this action to have any immediate effect, but she suspected this physical reinforcement would hasten learning when he recovered from whatever impairment to his ears he suffered. Intellectually, she reached a satisfactory conclusion as to the situation involving her child. Rationally, she could explain the issues to herself and expect that they would all come good in time. She sighed, looking about her at the beautiful spring day, the patterns of pleasing green, the shadows of clouds creating a gentle shifting mosaic over the land, the breeze caressing her arms and face. This was the land she would show her little boy. She would ask him about the shapes he found in the clouds and teach him the names of flowers. With her next intake of breath, she hated the beauty and peace around her. How could the world be so unaccountably bright when her fears and worries were so dark?

Chapter 4

"He'll be fine."

Ashton's voice, materializing from an atmosphere that had so abruptly drained of its warmth, produced the effect of a slap. He was standing beside a tree about fifteen feet away, a vantage point from which he must have been observing her for some minutes. She wiped away a stray tear.

"Did Mr. Fletcher send you?" The reference was to the steward's assignment to track her whereabouts during her long rambles while she was pregnant, which task he had renewed when she walked alone with the baby on their first day home. "Or did you think it proper to spy on your wife?"

"I saw you start in this direction from the library. The temple had to be your destination." He stopped, his thoughts seemingly poised to go down one of several paths. As can happen in a moment of tension, her eyes darted to a welter of details about him. His own distracted air. His disheveled hair, which he seemed determined not to comb until something important was resolved. The once-beautiful clothes she had bought him last autumn, now shabby with hard use—a way of repudiating the shopping expedition with the aristocratic Lovelace family, friends they had learned did not deserve the title.

"If you are here to talk about George," she said, "I will not. I cannot."

"But that's why you're crying, isn't it? Not because you miss your husband's attentions?" There was not a hint of malice in his words, yet they stung.

"You cannot raise worries about our son and then blame me when I succumb to them."

"I don't blame you at all. Worrying is half the job of a new parent."

"Then why are you here? Must every conversation we have in this place be disagreeable?"

"Our last conversation here set us on the path of happiness."

"Speak, then. If you want conversation." Yet before he could, she retreated into the *folly* and dropped hard upon the cold stone bench in an act of seeming defiance. He stopped at the entrance. "Athena's temple?" he said. "Women only?" When she made no reply, he added: "It's been a hard winter. On you. Our baby. We'll all be better now that we can—what did you say—bask in the sun? You're right. We should give George time. All babies develop in their own way. He's no different. I didn't mean to surprise you just now. You seemed so troubled—working through something in your mind. About us, the baby—I don't know. I feared to interrupt—that if I disrupted whatever resolution you were working toward, it might be lost forever."

"I resolved to carry on. What other choice is there?"

"To carry on in a way that brings us joy."

She sat, silent.

"Jane, why won't you be with me as my wife? There, I have put the question."

"I love you, Ashton. You know that."

"Which makes your avoidance of me all the more painful."

"I am not ready."

He started to say something but thought better of it; she read in his expression, however, some biting rejoinder—*our grandchildren might be ready before you are*—which justified her being equally sharp.

"A woman does not require a reason to consent to anything. Especially when it concerns her physical self."

"A woman who loves her husband might, however—*might*—wish to give him a reason. If only so his heart won't break."

"They say the only reason a woman ever goes through childbirth twice is that she forgets how much she suffered the first time. I remember. And Mary's delivery, with all its difficulties, restored the original pain."

"I know, but—"

"I nearly died, Ashton—*died!*"

"I was outside—heard every scream. I pounded the wall with each one."

"To suffer vicariously is but a ghost of the actual."

"The second baby could be much, much easier."

"Or fatal."

"Other women," he ventured, "have suffered … in childbirth … and returned to accept their husband's embraces. … And have other children."

"I was betrayed!" she screamed—losing her composure so unexpectedly that he jumped. Words flushed from her in a torrent. How, before their marriage, her body had meant nothing to her—was an externality to contain her mind and bring her to new experiences but otherwise was of no concern. How their relationship—their passion—had in some way integrated her corporeal and psychological self into the oneness of a mature identity. How pregnancy, for a while, had created a dissociation of one part of her physical self from the rest, while the quickening had turned around and restored that physical integrity. How, while immersed in the alchemical phenomenon of creating life, her body—when this new life arrived—came within a heartbeat of delivering her destruction. Here she stopped, struggling to continue the description of her half-formed conception, that her body had committed treason against her soul. "Childbirth was not a delivery but an assault—the vulgar probing of my body—hands, cold steel! I suffocated in my own blind panic. I learned that the frailty of my human form could annihilate my mind—my essence! I cannot—cannot—never again!—"

Ashton stepped forward to comfort her. She raised her hands defensively as if even now she feared a violation.

"Death, Ashton, is final! I have seen the black abyss—"

"But you believe in the afterlife. It's a fundamental tenet of your faith."

"I am not so ready to depart the world as you seem to be to have me gone."

"I meant only that—well, I don't know what I meant." Stunned by her words, he stepped back and held himself by one of the pillars of the ruin. After a few moments, he stepped forward a single step, lowered himself to the ground in the least threatening manner, and sat before her in a suppliant position.

He began carefully. "Even the most fervent Christian would not claim that death is easy. The mind cannot conceive its own extermination. It must invite panic. You did not cross over—you experienced only the beginning of the transition. Christ himself must have quailed at that moment."

"I have come to that understanding myself. But the comforts of religion cower before the coldness of death. Faith will carry me over—that's why I most fervently hope you will find your faith. It is only faith that can keep the soul from perishing in that infinitesimal moment between death and rebirth. I can face that moment when it inevitably comes. I refuse, however, to hasten its arrival."

"The doctor told us both … it may not be possible … after the injuries … for you to bear another child."

"I might still become pregnant. I might still suffer—every way a woman can—by losing the baby before its time. I could die of complications."

"Are we to live in fear? To abstain from the best of life because we fear the worst? Fear what might never happen?"

"You show great courage to risk my life instead of yours."

"I would trade if I could—easy to say, but you know I would. I have no answers. I treasure you, I cannot abide—my ears still ring with your screams. I can't conceive of losing you. And yet I already have lost you—in one important way."

"Not the only way, nor the most important."

"It is something that binds us dearly. I don't know how we can proceed in a marriage without love—physical love commensurate with the emotional. I cannot accept that a woman of your courage is unable to face the risks that every woman faces."

"I see those risks more clearly than most women. They are afraid to see them. Afraid that it will … "

"Tear apart their marriage? Life is risk, my love. To end risk is to end life. Would you never ride a horse—or take a carriage—because of the many accidents?"

"I have not ridden since Mrs. Lefroy was thrown and killed."

"Yet you have done many other things as risky."

"No, in truth, I have not. Except to bear a child. And that devastated me."

"I have enough sisters, Jane. I need a wife."

"And if I choose not to resume? Will you impose your will?"

"Of course not. But that doesn't mean I'm happy."

"Nor am I."

"But you—" He regarded her for a moment, then spoke with a sliver of a smile. "I am a master of sweet nothings. You shall not be able to resist."

She laughed. "You, who have the subtlety of a rock fall?"

"Who sits, collapsed like a mountain, at your feet. Pleading for your love."

"You have my love. We are speaking of something else."

"If you will not have me, I shall abandon you and take up with Camilla"—the wealthy, voluptuous creature that Ashton's mother had tried to marry her son to years before.

This remark coaxed from her a mirror of his own small smile. "I thought an excess of *female benefaction* interfered with your ability to enjoy a woman's personality."

"If I can't have you, I'll take any woman. No—I won't say that, even in jest. I'm more like to cast myself off the nearest bridge. That would solve the problem for everyone."

With this exchange Ashton rose from the sitting position, moved forward, and kneeled before her. He was within arm's reach, but he made no move to touch her. "Can you tell me that you do not want me? That our lot is to share a life of lovelessness?"

"Not lovelessness. Not that, ever." Yet she could see in his despairing visage the image of an empty—or at least lifeless—marriage bed, of their heretofore joyful marriage as a gray, lifeless plain stretching beyond the range of sight, God's green earth degraded into the bleakness of the moon. She felt the cold that would sweep over them from years and years of physical neglect—a cold nearly as severe as what she had experienced in the near-death of the birthing bed.

"It strikes me," Ashton said, "that a woman might want—need—certain things that convention forbids her to acknowledge—or even think about. And that the longer she waits, the more difficult it becomes for her to express those thoughts. Until she is stuck between what she really wants and what she is able to admit."

"It strikes *me* that the less a man knows a woman's mind, the more eager he is to explain her thoughts."

"You have not lost your desire for me, Jane. You have lost your sense of humor."

"When are sexual relations a subject of humor?"

"Since our first night together."

"You woo me with our blunders?"

"Our early, *tender* blunders. You're never more amorous than when I make you laugh."

They remained close to each other, neither one speaking.

"Words are not my friend," he finally said. "I don't know what to say except I miss you, painfully, physically. I venture to believe you miss me in exactly the same way."

Ashton's words were deliberately quiet—rehearsed, she realized, but not with any artificiality. His goal was not to avoid emotion but the opposite, to ensure he conveyed his meaning in a gentle manner that was seldom achievable with his voice. Speech, she had long known, served different purposes for the two of them. To her, it was a way of encouraging companionship, a form of entertainment, a way of passing the time, engaging the senses, pleasing others. She took words seriously, of course; she labored over every word, every turn of phrase, in her writing. But spoken words were meant to be enjoyed, played with, embraced. Good conversation was a playful pet that bounced along at one's heels all day long. To him, speech was a chore. It was more than his difficulty with the physical act of language. Caught up in responsibilities for the estate, his businesses and overseas trading companies, his manufactories in counties from Kent to the Midlands, his orders relayed through multiple persons across countless miles of road and sea, he had to be precise and direct in the projection of his will. To avoid misunderstanding, his words must always land like a punch.

As he waited silently for her response, the contrast between his brusque speech and his gentle physical expression of love turned this mental detour back to his statement that he believed she desired him as much as he desired her. Though she could not say so, she suddenly yearned for him. She pulled him tight against her bosom.

"I have developed a resistance to touch," she said. "I feel that I am being clawed all day by our son, by the demands of others. My body needs a respite. But at night, you are always touching me."

"I have honored your request to keep my distance!"

"Deep in the night, when you sleep. You lay your hand upon my shoulder or my waist. You stroke my thigh. You weave your fingers into my hair as a mouse might snuggle a nest. Sometimes you envelop me and cup my breasts. When the baby has been possessive of my body at every hour, I feel suffocated by your need to wrap yourself around me."

"I have awakened a few times to discover I was holding you. You didn't push me away. I had no idea you found my touch offensive."

"A few times I have come awake—annoyed—thinking you were making advances, and realized you were still asleep. You were not even encroaching upon me with somnolent need. You merely sought my touch. You act as though physical contact is all that keeps me from disappearing from your life."

"Can you blame me?"

"No."

"I can't say what larger meaning may encompass my desire to hold you," he said. "All I know is that it comforts me. Enables me to sleep. Is that wrong?"

"It reminds me of what I am denying you. It is little enough, your caresses, during the absence of our relations. Yet I feel guilty, and that guilt increases my resistance."

"I couldn't stand having separate rooms, separate beds. I couldn't."

"I do not mean to criticize. I mean to explain. I am not always annoyed. Not *always*. Your face, innocent in sleep, reminds me of the sweet but very rumbustious boy I knew years ago."

He pulled away so he could look into her eyes. "That boy loves you now as then."

"And I, you. I need to know you are there. But that is all I need for now. I implore your patience."

"For how long?"

"I do not know."

"You speak of patience." His voice firmed up. "Yet when I am away, you show little patience with our boy—and you are cross with the staff."

"How could you know that?"

"You're not the only one to treat our servants like human beings. They speak as freely to me as to you."

"And this must signify physical desire? The fact that I miss your company?"

"The fact that my absence makes you physically out of sorts—drives your behavior opposite to your sweetness—yes."

She should have set him down with a stinging rebuke, but she realized he was absolutely right. Though she could not declare it in words, her lowered brow and blushing cheeks were all the confirmation he required.

"We have—learned things—tried things—that might alleviate the danger," he said, voice quiet again. "Minimize it, at the very least."

She remembered how, some time ago, she had shifted his perspective by reminding him of his desire for her: Thoughts of romance threw him off balance enough to open his mind to new thoughts. She perceived that he had done the same to her through nothing beyond his willingness to listen. And to speak, now, with respectful insistence.

"I do not trust our passion to moderate our behavior in any consistent way," she said. Yet the way she expressed the comment made it possible for him to believe she would be willing to give certain things a try.

Chapter 5

Ashton rose groggily from the bed. Trying to put on his breeches, he tripped. Seeking to recover, he hopped once and, being unable to extricate his foot from the legging, surrendered to the inevitable and rolled onto the floor to avoid a hard fall.

"I do not believe you can walk," Jane said, just able to raise her head to admire his dexterity. The room, half-dark from the closed drapes, encouraged a lethargy equal to his. "I have done my duty."

He laughed, stood, put on the breeches with exaggerated care, and went to the wash basin. "I must have done mine," he replied, rinsing his face. "I do not believe I can *t-t-t-t-t-talk*."

She laughed in turn, resisting the urge to throw a pillow for fear of knocking over the porcelain pitcher. After he put on his shirt, Ashton returned to the bed and took her hands. "Thank you once again," he said. "From both of us."

"You are welcome," she said. "You had a point—the longer I waited, the easier it was to continue to delay."

"And, now that we have begun, it will be easier to return to something like our original routine."

"Our original routine was whenever we were alone together! But yes—as often as fatigue and schedule enable us to." She yawned. "As an ancient matron, I enjoy the indolence *after* almost as much as the intensity *during*."

It had not taken them long to make up at least a little of their lost time together. Some of what they did was commonplace and some—like today—was exquisite. It was one of the few approaches that enabled them to relax completely. The majority, which necessitated care, had changed their interactions. It was one thing to plunge oneself fully into a wild and raging stream; another thing entirely to wade in carefully so as not to slip and fall. Caution cannot be compatible with abandon and abandon had always been the definition of their love. What was the phrase he had used once before, in a different context—for the most part they now enjoyed the *ordinary* pleasures of marriage. There was, indeed, an ordinariness to match the naturalness because the need to avoid danger too often subsumed intimacy within practicality.

It was true that the restoration of touch and caress, and the release for them both from the stresses of the day, had diminished the fissure that had opened between them. This closure was significant but not entire; that the tiniest gap remained, barely perceptible, was as maddening as a splinter in the thumb. It was, in some strange way, a correlative of the sensation she had experienced when she was newly pregnant, that she was joined with a new life at the same time she was estranged from some essential element of her own. Physical intimacy still had the power to transport her, to be sure, only now it was not so far. Their life had not suddenly transformed into a shower of rose petals. She still rose at least twice with the baby each night, sometimes meeting Ashton as he stumbled to bed, red-eyed from paperwork completed in the glare of the new gas lamps; and her dawn feeding often coincided with his departure to attend to agriculture. Consequently, their ecstasy came as much from infrequency as from the male appetite that roused her own and the feminine appetite that satisfied them both. Watchfulness was the reason for the minute residual distancing: Watchfulness made the shared experience of lovemaking more of a pleasurable skill to be exercised than a co-immersion of their souls.

Ashton, himself fully dressed to begin the remainder of the day's work, had stayed his movements as she drifted in these thoughts. Used to her reveries, he waited until she began to paddle back to the shore of mindfulness. "Speaking of indolence," he said, "you planned to spend the afternoon with Cassandra?"

"Oh, no!" Jane said, glancing at the clock on the small mantle over the fireplace—"late!"

———

Jane rushed into the drawing room more than twenty minutes after she had planned. Cassandra was already there, diligent at her needlework. Jane noticed that her sister's dress was faded; the dullness of repeated washings did not present well against the shimmering blue-green wallpaper, the golden wood panels, and the lush rose-colored rug. Jane absorbed this image without judgment but rather as a woman who would wish—if it were possible without awkwardness—to gift her sister with fabric that might breathe more comfortably among the finer things at Hants.

Quickly taking up her own basket, which contained the beginnings of some work for their niece Fanny, Jane cast her eyes about as Cass often did when she first arrived, as if to confirm that the room had not in a sister's absence been transmuted into the sturdy but inexpensive furnishings they had grown up with. Jane kept the writing desk, her father's gift from her earliest efforts at authorship, in a far corner as a reminder of her origins. Writing memoranda for Ashton was a poor substitute for composing stories, but any effortful writing exercised her skills when she had neither the time nor energy to pursue her work with dedication. In her odd moments she would insert new material in an existing scene, or edit an old chapter by writing it afresh and watching the extra words fall away. Though she sketched a new idea here and there, her life was too harried to pursue anything original in depth. It is not that she did not have time. A woman of leisure has a surfeit of time. What she lacked was *uninterrupted* time. She would write a paragraph and Mr. Hanrahan or Mrs. Lundeen would need a decision about upcoming guests. She would write a page and George would need to be fed. She would begin again and Mrs. Shelley would need a consultation on groceries. Interruptions had caused her to lose more thoughts than she had written in the last year. Composition was impossible with her head full of joints of mutton and doses of rhubarb. In her present circumstances, Ashton's admonition was correct. One could live, or one would write—but one could not do both.

Still, a single sentence newly polished would keep her happy for a week. With such small actions, the slant desk anchored her feelings against the sofas, tables, china, and clocks, which had a fragility that belied their brilliance and a way of accusing her with their luxury. (Though—if she had to admit it—she no longer felt out of place in Hants' splendor.)

"Frank is finally off," Cassandra said. She shook her head sadly. "Eighteen months. Two years, it might be. What kind of absence is that for a new father—or a wife by herself with a babe!"

"Mary is not alone. For that Frank is grateful. Given the close quarters, though, she may wish she was—as may you all."

"She has her own way of managing the household and seems not to notice its inefficiencies."

"Mother's help—and yours—will more than compensate for the occasional disagreement. Mary's disposition is one that feels appreciation, though it is not one that can express it."

"He was eager to be on his way. Relieved to be engaged again, to have his pay restored—but dejected, naturally enough, over leaving his wife and child."

"His way to advancement now runs through India."

"Frank never said whether he stopped at Portsmouth at the Admiralty's behest or whether it was a clever arrangement on his part. But it gave him another precious week or two with his family. We saw him off, then climbed the hills to see if we could espy his departure. But the port is so busy, and there was such a clutter of ships at Spithead. I am sure we waved the wrong one over the horizon."

"Was he stoic as always?"

"The closer he gets to his ship, the more formal he becomes. By the time he boarded his launch, it was 'Captain Austen wishes you all a fond farewell.' "

"Only a man of roaring passion can display rigid self-control."

Their needles moved as the two sisters tried to imagine the mixture of excitement and remorse that attend a man when he sets out across thousands of miles of ocean. The breeze in his face, adventure bearing him along on the waves—his future stretching toward the horizon—while love, his family, languishes at home.

"And Charles!" Cassandra added wistfully.

"Our baby brother—married! To a woman we have never met—and may not for years!"

"A child—sixteen! But his letters are so affectionate. He cares for her, of that there can be no doubt. Good family."

"Little money."

"The only reason, I am sure, her father could be induced to accept a naval captain whose only prospects involve prizes—and the enemy without a Fleet."

"Still, consider how much more pleasant it will be for Charles," Jane concluded, "to know when he leaves his family on the docks it is only for a few days or weeks, not years."

The sisters simultaneously sighed.

As they worked quietly, the nurse brought George. Before Jane settled in for the afternoon feeding, Cassy held the little boy, who greeted his aunt with an energetic display of movements and noises and smiles. Jane felt an ache at the potential for this sweet young life and a pang at anything that might thwart it. She was reassured by his receptivity to Cass, whom he saw on and off but never with any consistency.

"And how is my young nephew?" Cassandra said. "By the time I unpacked, you were done nursing and he was having a nap."

"He is good—finally past all the colds and coughs. I had begun to believe that colic was a permanent condition."

"And everything—else?"

They shared concerned looks. Having helped raise a dozen children among their family, Cass had a knowledge of the young possessed by few mothers; and she and Jane had glancingly discussed George's situation while in Southampton. Neither wished to make the condition worse by describing it in detail.

"I am optimistic. He is still—some delay of maturity—somewhat slow in developing—but—one cannot think—actually *slow*. He does not speak well—which is to say, he is behind, I believe, in the sounds he should be able to make. But, Cassy, look at the intelligence in his eyes! Such—benevolence! No one could see the expressions on his face—the emotions, the way he responds to other people—and not believe he is the smartest little boy ever born!"

Cass had to concede that his reaction to her proved he was the cleverest baby in all of Hampshire—and far beyond its borders.

"Ashton and I both agree our little boy needs nothing more than to grow into himself. If he is behind at all. Who can know? I am trying to encourage him." She showed Cass the gestures. "I have no idea if it helps, but I cannot imagine it hurts."

Cass sewed and Jane fussed over George for some little while.

"You must have run all the way," Cassandra observed. "When you came down. Your face is still a little flushed."

Jane's face came all the redder for the comment.

"I hurried as fast as I could. Having lost track of the time, I did not wish to keep you waiting any longer. Ashton enjoys a midday nap but professes not to be able to rest unless I join him."

"I am certain you provide him all measure of comfort."

"It is a small comfort for a hard-working man."

"Though one does wonder why a man of such vigor should nap as often as a child."

Cass's face had undergone very subtle changes during the exchange—a raised eyebrow, a smile that flickered like a lamp—but she did not actually look up from her needlework.

"It is because Mr. Dennis attends to his rest that he maintains his vigor."

"Everyone in the family will be reassured that the two of you have reclaimed your footing."

"I have no idea what you mean."

"There was a strain between you in Southampton. Love, affection—as before. Yet there was also restraint. As if the honeymoon had come to an end rather precipitously."

"A sick child will do that. And it took us longer to readjust—after George—than either of us expected. We are just now—finding our way."

And so they were. Her mind jumped back to those still-fresh moments with Ashton in the half-light of the curtained bedroom.

"I am reassured by your smile," Cassy said. "But if you insist upon smiling to yourself, you must let me in on your secret." Though sternly committed to her duties with their brother's family at Godmersham or their mother's small entourage at Southampton, Cassy noticeably lightened whenever she could steal away for a few days of relief. Just now her voice was positively forward.

Jane did not know how to respond. Her private life was the only aspect of her marriage she had never shared with her sister, and this was the first time Cass had pressed the point.

"You have never been too shy to speak of me about any delicate matter," Cass said. "Why do you hesitate—always?—when it comes to you and Ashton?"

"I do not wish to flaunt my happiness in your face." Jane halted, seeing where her words might lead her. "Especially about the particulars ... of husband and wife."

"You think it cruel to regale me with tales of marital happiness because I am single and always likely to be?"

It was impossible to think of Cassandra and her continually contracting prospects without feeling anxiety about the gulf between them. Her sister was not only a spinster, but she was three years older than Jane, herself now one and thirty. She had no one to share a life with, not even Jane anymore. Cass would have, Jane believed, warmly returned the physical affections of Tom Fowle, but she otherwise lacked a native sensuality. Cass's intelligence and honesty could still charm any man she might wish to charm, but with Tom's death she had lost the demonstrable spark that would draw a man's attention and alert him to those qualities. This is what Jane felt but could never say to her beloved sibling.

"—Because it feels disloyal—Ashton could not abide the idea that I would share with you anything related to *that* aspect of our marriage. Or anything truly important between us. You might as well ask him to stand naked before you."

"That I understand. I do not ask you to share the details. Well, I would love to hear the details!—but I am really interested in how *that* aspect has changed you. What it means. How it affects your view of life, the world."

"There is something else that holds me back—I found my love after you lost your own."

Cassandra sometimes slipped into the mists at any reference to Tom, her fiancé, who had died of a fever while serving as a clergyman on his cousin's ship in the West Indies. Today, however, her response was brisk.

"I miss Tom as I have missed other people I have loved and lost. But we never married. He was dear, and his memory hurts. But I do not feel his loss as a wife feels who has lost her husband. Not as you would mourn Ashton. Imagine I was orphaned when I was too young to remember my parents. I would wonder what it was like to have parents. I would feel an ache to see another child in her parent's arms. Yet, never having had a father's love, how would I miss it—or a mother's? The loss is there, but indistinct. And who knows—we cannot expect my experience to have been identical to yours. What if, despite our affection, Tom and I had been at odds in our personal moments? We all know of couples who left on their bridal tour as the happiest of people and returned with their hopes destroyed."

"Your genuine love for Tom, and his for you, would have carried you over any obstacles. That is what happens with caring couples, I should think."

"I believe so too." Cassandra seemed only now on the verge of tears. "You must consider me the most heartless sister alive if you believe for one minute that I in any way resent your happiness, or begrudge you a moment of love or affection."

"I would never think of you as anything but the kindest person alive."

"Tell that to our nephews and nieces when I discipline them!"

Cassandra looked away thoughtfully for a few moments. Jane saw in her face an older, more somber, version of her own. "I am happy, Jane. You must believe that. What my life has become, is all I want or need. I seek nothing more. It would make me miserable to my core if you withheld one ounce of your feelings for Ashton out of concern for me."

"Can you really stand our enthusiasm? I seem to recall a wise father, and wiser sister, who cautioned a young woman about getting carried away."

"I have come to believe that the world would be a better place if more people were carried away in the manner of you and Ashton. I bask in your love for each other. It warms me to know that—indeed—Tom and I might have turned out as well. It warms me to know that you are happy. And Ashton too, that bluff rascal. I am also a practical mercenary. Your happiness will provide for me and Mother if worse should ever come to worst!"

"I am relieved. We are so ostentatious in our love. I always feel as though I taunt you with an array of jewels—"

"Which the pauper envies? No. One can never be too rich—or too ostentatious in love. Now, show me all your trinkets!"

"Cassy! You are too wicked to speak!"

Cass worked, Jane gave those small attentions to George that occupy a mother as she nursed, and the sisters discussed elements of her private history. No particulars of any moment, but the way her intimate life with Ashton informed the rest, and the way the interplay between the emotional and physical reinforced one with the other.

Soon after, Ashton came by on his way out from the library, where he had been finishing contracts for the new shipping ventures. He was going to meet Mr. Fletcher about the latest irrigation project, which was to begin soon, before the drying of the ground made for difficult digging. Ashton still moved with that mixture of sloth and concentration that implied overindulgence of a particular sort with his wife. He came halfway toward them, stopping when he saw that George was nursing. It seemed inappropriate for him to approach too near when another woman was about. He bowed and said to the ladies: "I shall be gone for the rest of the day. Is there anything I can do for you before I go?"

"No, you have done quite enough for today," Jane said.

"Enough for us both, I should hazard," Cassandra said, low enough that only Jane could hear. "Have a good afternoon, Ashton," she continued aloud, waving him out the door. "Stay busy!"

They listened as his lethargic footsteps sounded their way down the hall. Listening expectantly, they heard the distant outside door open. When it closed with an almost funereal yawn, the sisters burst into laughter that would have puzzled Ashton had he heard it from the lawn.

Chapter 6

A few days later, after Cass left to return to her auntly duties, Jane and Ashton came around the side of the house, discussing an expansion of greenery in the elegant but spare front lawn. They saw, beyond the brook, on the meadow just where the slope began to fall toward the village, a horse grazing. They advanced slowly, thinking that a neighbor's animal may have escaped and not wanting to startle it. Even from a distance, however, the horse looked familiar. As they approached, they saw with some astonishment that it was the black mare—hugely pregnant!

She did not shy from them in any way; she nickered in recognition and came to them the last few yards. Ashton rubbed her head and ears—she had always enjoyed her ears being scratched—and they marveled at her presence.

"The last I heard, Lovelace's encampment was more than fifty miles away!" he said. He went to her legs and hooves to ensure that she was neither injured nor lame. "Sore, I'm sure, from the distance," he said. "A small crack on her left forehoof, but no permanent damage I can see."

Jane smoothed her hands along the swollen sides of the horse. As she did so, muscles rippled along the horse's back. Jane felt the foal move within the body, and she sighed in sympathy as the mare leaned into her as if recognizing their bond. Standing beneath the clear sky, the mare's black hide warm on the sun side, the situation was a picture of calm. "Your time will be easier than mine," Jane said quietly. "No bloody intervention, of that I am certain."

"She must have come all this way alone," Ashton said, shaking his head in wonder. "A *long* way."

"How did she find her way back? She was never out of Hampshire before."

"Horses navigated the steppes for thousands of years with no one to show them the way. There's one horse every generation who shows the same ability."

"Look," she said. There were signs of abuse: the apricot signature of a bruise; abraded strips on the coat, where ropes had been too tightly bound or whips too eagerly dispatched; reddened areas around the mouth, where the bit had been applied not for discipline but for pain.

"Yes," Ashton said. "Some of the scrapes must have happened on the journey, but not this or this"—pointing out similar evidence on her legs. "That villain Sawyer. He would rather compel a horse than lead one."

Sawyer, a foul little man who served as overseer for the Lovelace estate, was undoubtedly assisting Lovelace to prepare the cavalry for the season. "I cannot believe he would risk harm to such a valuable horse—never mind the foal."

"He knows how to hurt them without doing damage—until he loses his temper. A sad claim for superior equestrian knowledge."

The mare was not bridled—she carried no tack at all—but came along as Ashton put his arm under her neck and indicated the direction he wanted her to go. "I'm sorry," Ashton said to her. "You paid the price for my conceit." He was speaking of the prideful bet he had made the previous autumn, his mare against Lovelace's stallion, in a winner-take-all contest that Colonel Lovelace had won with superior riding skill.

"She came home," Jane said. "The only place she felt safe."

It took only a few minutes for them to walk the horse around to the barn and have her settled in a stall. Sending the groom for Mr. Fletcher, who was as wise in the matter of equine health as any veterinarian, Ashton gave the mare water and hay and brushed her himself. The best way to understand the state of any animal is to run one's concerned hands over every inch of its body.

"She must remain here, of course," Jane said. "We cannot let them take her back."

"I don't know if that's possible, Jane."

"Until she foals. She is too far along to make the return. Even Lovelace would agree to the sense of that."

"Don't bet on it. Control means more to him than any other consideration."

"Then we shall not let them know. Once the foal is born, we can give them proper notice."

"I am honor bound to send her back. At least, to give the owner that choice."

"You are honor bound to protect an innocent creature from abuse. One you love nearly as much as you love me!"

"Would you have your husband hanged for a horse thief, dear?" His voice lacked the mischief inherent in such a remark, though it brought a grim smile to his lips. "A horse comes halfway across southern England—avoiding capture or even notice. Arrives safely at her natal home. Every worker on our estate will tell the tale—and make himself the hero of it. It will become the story of every tavern for twenty miles around. How long, do you suppose, before every passerby through Hampshire knows? How long before word reaches Lovelace? No, he must hear it from me. And soon."

She heard his words with dismay and regret proportionate to their truth. "I will write the letter, then. Perhaps I can phrase it in a way that makes him believe it is to his advantage, not ours, for her to remain at Hants."

Chapter 7

So it was that the letter to Lovelace was composed and dispatched. There was no eloquence, for the communication must come from Ashton rather than Jane. There was only the humane consideration of one horseman to another about his property: The mare had somehow escaped and found its way back to Hants; a hasty return would aggravate injuries suffered along the way and possibly lame the mare and endanger its offspring; Ashton would provide for the horse until its recovery and delivery; and of course, the horse and foal would be delivered in good health when Hants made its next deliveries to Lovelace's regiment in the autumn. The words about the injuries were not exaggerations; Mr. Fletcher's more careful observations revealed that the crack in the forehoof was deeper than Ashton could tell and inflammation was setting in.

The response from Colonel Lovelace was neither an appreciative acceptance of their offer, nor a polite rejection and counterproposal of when a transfer might be effected. Rather, it took the form of a dusty skirmish, which came to Jane's attention when she heard a commotion toward the barn and looked out the window in time to see a flailing body flip over the rail of the arena. By the time she reached the scene, Sawyer and two companions stood outside the fence, hurling imprecations but otherwise hesitant, while Mr. Fletcher and several of his men formed a resolute barrier to their advance. The mare walked agitatedly back and forth behind them, but not in a panic and apparently suffering no direct harm.

"Watch your language, Mr. Sawyer," Jane said as she came up. "There is a lady present."

He turned to her in anger and surprise. He had lost his hat and was covered in dust. Grains of sand sparkled on his forehead, and blood caulked around a split lip. "Your men are keeping me from my duty," he said.

"These men seem to be protecting our property from thieves," Jane said. "What have you to say for yourself?"

"I've come for *my* property," he replied, his natural arrogance swelling with the indignity of having been thrown over the fence. "I'll summon the magistrate if need be."

"My husband being the magistrate, I have no doubt he will welcome the call—and have you *whipped* for the bother." Her sudden anger was for the horse and more—for what she had seen Sawyer do to the poor black servant months before. Responding to the flare in her eye, he took a grudging step back and spoke with more civility.

"The mare is ours. I'm here to reclaim it, nothing more."

"And what do you intend to do with her?"

"That does not concern your lady."

"Your lady has every reason for concern. If any harm comes to that horse before its safe return, the Colonel will hold us responsible."

"Not if you turn it over to me, ma'am."

"So you and your men can drive it too hard for seventy miles?"—They had learned the regiment was stationed outside Stanmer, even further than they had believed.—"So the horse is ruined, or loses the foal? My responsibility is not to you, Mr. Sawyer, but to the horse and the family who owns her. We will maintain the mare until proper steps are taken for her recovery."

"I'm the *proper steps*. I've come in the Colonel's name." Sawyer uneasily rubbed his short hair—sand colored and sand filled—as if recognizing that his effort to take the horse, rather than ask for it, could well send him home empty-handed. The two men with him began to shift uncertainly as well—not only in response to Jane's forcefulness but also to the other workers who had congregated behind them wielding all manner of farm implements. One of Sawyer's men acted as if he had wandered in by accident and might wish to wander away.

"If you had come with suitable authorization, you would have called at the house, announced your intentions, and produced documentation for your claims."

"Ha!" Sawyer said, as if no honest man had to bother with such particulars. Looking around at the reinforcements, however, he added loud enough for all to hear: "I've a letter of reclamation from Colonel Lovelace."

"And that gives you the right to simply—*invade*—our estate and take whatever you fancy?"

"You know that mare belongs to us."

"When Ashton and I arrived unannounced on your estate several years ago, you were pleased to hold us with your pistol until matters could be sorted out. We had as much right to be there then as you have to be here now. Very well, I shall accord you the same courtesy. Mr. Fletcher, lock these men in one of the stalls. Retrieve our weapons from the storeroom. If they attempt to escape—shoot them."

Though the men of Hants were not, in the main, hard men, Jane knew they would act as severely as needed to handle the intruders; for nothing roused the protective instincts of the estate workers more than being asked to protect the lady of the landholder who treated them justly.

She sent off two missives. One was to recall Ashton instantly from Thor Place, where he was reviewing the latest rail-road developments with Mr. Trevithick. She sent a rider rather than await the post, as if the energy used in the gallop would somehow dispense her own excess. The second was to Lovelace himself. Seldom had she written in such fury, recognizing that Sawyer's arrogance proceeded directly from his master's. The only difference was that Sawyer's cruelty lacked the polished sheen of the well-to-do.

15 July 1807

Colonel Lovelace—

    Your man who came today acted in a reckless and pre-sumptive manner that does no credit to your family's ancient name or its social standing. Rather than treat us as a family who had voluntarily taken your misplaced mare into our care and commenced the effort to restore her health, his approach was that of a man assigned to recapture a stolen horse from a band of highwaymen. He was repulsed in like manner.

    Having no confidence in Sawyer's ability to safely restore this valuable creature to your possession, I promise you Mr. Dennis and I will take that responsibility upon ourselves. Re-gardless of ownership, however, the mare is too damaged to be moved today. Whatever the protestations of you or your overseer, the Dennis family shall not be put in the predic-ament of acting negligently toward her health—only to be castigated by fair-minded people later for bringing her to harm. Whatever our differences on other matters, both sides must be accountable for the safety of this fine animal at a time of great danger to her. I assure you that we will return the mare in much finer condition than she arrived.

    You will be informed when she can travel safely.

    I am, sir, yours—

Mrs. Ashton Dennis
Hants House

Jane took the letter out to the stables, bringing Mr. Fletcher and several others along. There two field hands sat on separate stools. One had a pistol, the other a stave. Both rose when Jane entered.

Sawyer and his compatriots were sitting on bales of hay in the extra stall. Upon seeing Jane, the two men meekly stood. Sawyer rose as if doing her a favor. When the door was opened to the impromptu jail, she handed the letter to him. "Deliver this to Colonel Lovelace. These men will see you down to the village."

Sawyer began to reply, but she turned away so that his objection was addressed to her retreating back.

His continued insolence, however, was more than she could bear. She turned to him a final time. "Do not come back. If you personally ever set foot upon our land again, I will have you taken as a common poacher—for common you are."

Chapter 8

Ashton was home the next afternoon. A conference in the library with Mr. Fletcher confirmed what all of them already knew: The mare could not be immediately moved. It would be weeks before the horse could attempt a long journey, assuming that Lovelace's regiment had not decamped even farther away. The timing would be further complicated by the birth of the foal at about that same time.

"Lovelace will not wait that long," Ashton said. "We need another solution."

They considered adapting a hay wagon to carry her so that the mare would not have to walk, but a cart would undoubtedly take longer than a steady walk and the ride over rutted country roads would cause more discomfort than she would suffer under her own power.

"We need a way to whisk her over the hills," Jane said. "It is unfortunate your experiment with the balloon was unsuccessful."

"But it wasn't," Ashton said. "Not entirely. The balloon was impractical for largescale movement of livestock. We're speaking of one horse."

Ashton consulted a map. "Here!" he said. "Horsham! Perfect! What better place to halt than at an ancient horse-trading town?" Before Jane could interrupt, he added: "If that's too far to go in one day, we can stop at Guildford or any number of places. I think we can do it—thoughts?"

Jane had any number of thoughts; it was the organization of them that was the difficulty. The hot-air balloon, it seems, would remain an unlikely but dangerous complication in their lives. It was an apparatus he had brow-beaten an impoverished French-man into selling several years before. That incident had led Ashton and Jane to be carried away in the vehicle before crash-landing on the Lovelace's estate. The meeting with that family had led to the development of a likely relationship that had, however, ultimately ended in disaster. In the years since, Ashton had sought—unsuc-cessfully so far —to use the aerostat in some practical venture.

"It seems rather a grand leap from shuttling an unhappy cow around the fields to hauling a pregnant horse halfway across south-ern England," she said.

"You and I made sixty-odd miles in an afternoon. We could easily move the mare in two, don't you think? Three at the most. It's not the distance. It's keeping her quiet. If we can do that for several hours a day, the distance will take care of itself."

"What if she panics? She could tangle herself in the ropes, kill herself thrashing around. It is far too dangerous."

Ashton was already sketching a design. "We won't have her dangle. No, we'll build a second basket, like what we already have. Two decks. One for the man and the stove. One underneath for the horse." He continued to scribble. "We could even come up with a couple of cinches for her body to keep weight off her foot."

"How will we navigate? That was the main difficulty. She could end up in Ramsgate as easily as Stanmer."

"She'll be tethered at all times. We'll pull her along. If the wind is too strong, we'll bring her down until it eases off." Ashton was so infatuated with his idea that he did not see Mr. Fletcher's grim negative shake of the head to Jane. That, at least, gave her hope. Regardless of Ashton's enthusiasm, she knew the steward would do nothing to endanger the horse—or her husband.

Ashton's grand dreams of aerial transport came crashing to the ground several days later when Mr. Fletcher used numbers to convince him of the reality that the hot-air balloon would be unable to lift the pregnant horse, which was many times the weight of human passengers, and that the additional compartment, which in his designs had come to resemble the superstructure of a man-of-war, was an impossibility.

"Why not attach a steam engine to the whole device and paddle along with that?" was Jane's only comment before Ashton finally conceded.

But Mr. Fletcher was man who would say *how* rather than *no*, and in further conversations he and Ashton developed a much simpler concept that used a modified haycart along with the balloon. The cart would hold the horse. The balloon, tethered to the wagon instead of the animal, would ease the strain on the wagon's primitive leather suspension, thereby cushioning the ride. Mr. Fletcher would pilot the balloon. A young groom would tend to the mare. To his annoyance Ashton had to accept banishment from both vehicles because of his heft.

Ten days later, the mare's hoof much improved and the hay wagon suitably refashioned, the ungainly circus pitched into motion. A regular haycart led the way, carrying supplies for an expedition that might take as few as two days or as many as seven. Next came the carriage for Jane, George, and their attendants—though Jane, carrying the baby, walked nearly as much as she rode. Then came the special wagon, over which the balloon swayed like a gigantic oriental umbrella. With much less resistance than normal, the four horses pulling the conveyance started off smartly. As it began to roll, the mare, who had loaded quietly, stood with her ears pricked, her eyes bright, and her nostrils wide, as content as any queen on her litter. Behind came an additional horse-drawn cart carrying every conceivable accessory related to balloon support and repair. Ashton rode front to back on his stallion in an unceasing inspection of it all.

The weather remained fair, the wind no more than a quiver, and the roads dry. Encountering few troublesome passages, they made surprisingly good time. One fear, that the county's uncomprehending livestock would be stampeded by the creaking parade, proved to be unfounded. Cattle observed their passage with the ruminating dullness of their kind; sheep worried much more about their own shepherd dogs than the disturbance on the road; horses chased along to the end of their fences as if hoping to come along. Humans did take notice, one farmer after another pausing the plough to watch them pass. One family removed their hats as if viewing the funeral procession of an important dignitary.

At the scheduled change of horses, they had no difficulty bringing the balloon down in an adjoining field for fuel resupply. The mare, allowed to stretch her legs, gave no more trouble upon reloading than she did the first time. She seemed curious at the goings on around her and eager to see what lay ahead. At the next stop, several hours later, she grazed contentedly while her caretakers picnicked beside the road. The Dennises felt obliged to offer a repast to the half a dozen or so residents who had followed on horse and foot, explaining to them that this loaded-down group of travelers was not a troupe of actors who would be putting on a show at the next village.

"Your arrangement seems to be working," Jane said to Ashton as they shared savories Mrs. Shelley had packed for them. "I stand corrected in my concerns."

Ashton shrugged. "If we get her even halfway, I think she's healed enough to make it the rest of the way on her own."

"At this rate, we could very well make Horsham by nightfall."

"Unless there are problems with the horse stations further along. But Mr. Fletcher has his best men working ahead of us. From there we could easily make it on foot."

"Is this project working because of the cleverness of the idea," Jane asked, "or because we put the effort of the entire estate behind it?"

"Both, I should think."

"Most elaborate schemes fail because of their elaboration."

"True enough. But sometimes you don't have to solve a problem all the way through. Sometimes a partial solution is enough. We knew the mare was well tempered. We just had to make her as relaxed in the wagon as in her stall. For every hour that rolls by, we close the distance to something manageable."

"Yet how complicated! The number of people involved!"

"The only problem we had to solve was improving the suspension. We could have had fifty men carry her on their backs."

Jane laughed. "So your solution, whatever it was, would have required the effort of all our people."

"Compared to other possibilities, the balloon is a simple solution. We only had to get her so far without unreasonable distress."

Jane did not pursue the topic further. There were times when Ashton had to be free to pour his energy into an idea, to weave some abstraction into the physical cloth of production. That was as intrinsic a need for him as writing (even if reduced to memos) was for her. There were many other elements as well. Given their history, the meeting with Lovelace could go badly. Even if the meeting went well, it would be tense. She could tell by Ashton's distracted mannerisms that he was working through in his mind the many ways the conversation might go. His need to create and execute a complex project was partly a statement of his concern for the mare, partly a declaration of the degree to which he would go to honor his earlier commitment to turn over the horse to Lovelace, and partly a necessity to occupy his mind until he had to confront a former partner who was now a formidable adversary.

Chapter 9

The second day became problematic because the aerostat's brazier, which had never been used for extended periods, began to vent heat sideways rather than up, and because the wind became as inconstant as a rogue's heart. Surprisingly patient with the starts and stops, the mare eventually had to be walked to sustain her composure. Her hoof seemed improved by the exercise, leading Ashton to surmise that the injury was at that point at which rest can make it worse rather than better. Despite that observation, he called a halt for the day as twilight neared when they were barely two leagues short of the regimental encampment. "More harm than good could come from pressing on," he explained, "and this"—a wide field near a quiet stream, flanked by beech—"is as pleasing a spot to camp as we're likely to find." Jane's thought was that Ashton wanted to meet Lovelace in the full light of day to offset the Colonel's shadowy behavior.

As the road turned busy in the morning with military traffic, only three groupings continued: the carriage, the mare cart with its uplifting companion, and Ashton on horseback. High clouds streaked the sky in the direction of their progress. When they were perhaps a mile from camp (the distance provided by passing soldiers), the assemblage pulled over. Ashton intended to continue alone, but Jane objected with an unassailable assertion:

"She is in my care."

Her meaning was conveyed by her eyes as much as by her voice. Not only had she been the one to fire off the bristling letter to Lovelace, which put the responsibility for their meeting squarely on her shoulders, but her being a new mother gave her the prerogative to protect the prized animal in its vulnerable condition. There was the other matter, as well—her sense that a feminine presence would dampen the antagonism between the men.

Theirs had been a promising friendship, beginning years before on the evening of the balloon crash on the Lovelace estate, where the appealing Colonel and his beautiful wife Kat entertained the wind-blown fugitives from Bath. Once Ashton returned from his nearly three-year absence in the West Indies to marry Jane, they rekindled their acquaintance with the Lovelaces. Robert, too, had been away, on assignment to India where he had earned military renown. The women quickly became breezy confidantes, the men enthusiastic if competitive friends and business partners. The relationship ruptured as the result of Kat's brutal treatment of a negro servant and Lovelace's use of confidential information to undermine Ashton's rail-road venture. Ashton and Jane responded by using their own private information to destroy Lovelace's pro-slavery testimony in a parliamentary hearing, clearing the way for passage of Wilberforce's bill to abolish the slave trade. The debacle not only harmed Lovelace's reputation but also his finances—his wealth coming from Kat's sugar plantation in Jamaica. It is a matter of small regret when the taking of a moral stand provides the ancillary benefit of retribution.

"We have been careful not to express our apprehension," Jane said to Ashton as they walked along, the mare between them.

"Robert and I should be able to keep things civil," Ashton said. "I have no desire to start any new dispute. He has a military campaign to prepare for." Ashton seemed to relish the opportunity to speak of something other than the impending transaction. "You know, Wellesley has returned to the Army. Parliament was not enough for him when he scented another war."

"We talked about it. You said his return indicated we would be embarking on a major campaign."

"This business about the Danes has the whole country in an uproar."

"Pity them—trying to remain neutral between two powers, both of which believe the other will steal their Fleet."

"Either will, given the opportunity."

She paused for a few moments before returning to the primary subject. "But is there no way to transfer your duties to someone else? Whenever I think of the Lovelaces, I grow sick to the depth of my stomach. I cannot imagine dealing with them on a regular basis."

"The contract for stock and supplies was signed long before the falling out. If I canceled, I would end up in a lawsuit with the Army, and I would lose any potential business with other regiments. I would not give Lovelace the satisfaction." Before she could respond, he added: "Most of the work is handled by others. This is my only dealing with him since the hearing."

This was his way of saying *enough*.

She came around the other side and held his hand as they walked.

Military cantonments popped up around southern England like fields of red poppies, fading away and reblooming in a new location whenever complaints reached a certain level about the imposition of the troops on the stores of local food and the honor of local women. This camp, spreading across half the wide valley, comprised a mix of artillery, infantry, and horse. To the left, artillery was being assembled and disassembled while unimpressed sergeants yelled for greater speed. To the right, small groups of soldiers marched or practiced weapons drill, to the cadence of Scottish-barked commands. Behind, in the distance, a line of cavalry wheeled and charged, ghostly in the dust of their exercise.

"This is proof of an action this summer," Ashton observed. "Combined maneuvers here, from the looks of it. You don't go to the expense of bringing together all the different arms unless battle is imminent."

Ashton and Jane walked the mare through the disorganized tents and wagons of the camp followers, which served as the preamble to the story of the Army just beyond. Children and dogs raced about in joyous abandon, and women, most of them reputable if poor, evaluated the well-to-do gentleman and lady as they passed. There was no formal separation between the ragged outskirts and the official camp; Ashton and Jane merely stepped from irregular openings formed by lean-tos and tents to straight lanes created by neat rows of military tents. Off-duty soldiers loitered about, smoking and hurling good-natured insults at men in other groups. Judging from the coarse laughter, they were trying to outdo one another in stories of their exploits with the nearby ladies. Though it was mid-morning, several campfires still banged and scraped with the sound of breakfast cleanup.

Occasionally, soldiers indicated with a gesture of their heads the direction the well-dressed horse purveyors needed to take, though the command post was obvious from the larger if temporary structures, the flags, and the systematic confusion of which it was the center. Only now did sentries bother to make themselves known, the single question being whether the Colonel was expecting them and their answer being that they had sent a message ahead the evening before.

As they neared the headquarters, Sawyer appeared from their right, saying: "I'll take that." Ashton and Jane walked on without acknowledging his existence. At last they stopped an aide de camp—one who appeared efficient rather than officious—and asked if he would let Colonel Lovelace know that the Dennis family had arrived with his long-expected property.

They waited, as they knew they would, that period required to signal the relative importance of the requestor versus the requested; for if Lovelace were free, he would have come out soon; and if he were truly occupied, he would have sent word of a delay. In the interim they chatted about an unusual crossbreed of South Down sheep that had caught Ashton's eye on the way down and whether the balloon-and-wagon combination might be able to transport a sampling of the herd quickly to Hants. Sawyer hovered, close enough to expect to annoy them by his presence.

The mare's ears flicked with curiosity whenever a line of soldiers marched by in one direction or a caisson clattered by in the other. Responding to the nearby cavalry, she nickered and occasionally started to step toward her brethren, though tolerantly obeying her mistress's gentle restraining tug on the halter. Realizing the mare would soon be gone again, Jane leaned into her for one last inhalation of the warm, slightly pungent smell unique to a horse, just off-putting enough to separate the lovers of these animals from people without souls. The scent took her back to her first meeting with Ashton—their first as adults, the first that mattered—when he had burst into the Upper Rooms at Bath, fresh off a twenty-mile ride, and leaned into *her* to invite her to dance.

This agreeable memory dissolved when Colonel Lovelace emerged and strode over to them. Tall and athletic, lean as Ashton was muscular, blond and blue-eyed, with a full but neat moustache, he wore his immaculate uniform with natural authority: a man of bold looks and bold disposition. His smile and demeanor were so appealing that one immediately understood him to be a man of frank and engaging disposition. This is the advantage society graciously accords attractive individuals. There is an immediate dispensation toward their behavior, some inborn belief that anyone who looks so noble will conduct himself nobly toward others. Indeed, when matters aligned with Lovelace's interests, no one could be more gracious or solicitous to those around him. It was when matters failed to align with his needs that one learned his manners were more a façade than a matter of principle.

For all that had gone before, Jane's reaction was surprisingly neutral.

"Dennis," he said. He scarcely acknowledged her at all.

Ashton took the reins and fell in beside Lovelace as the Colonel started toward the corrals a quarter of a mile distant. Ashton described firsthand the damage to the mare's hoof and other incidental injuries that had occurred during her travel back to Hants, explaining the care and feeding provided by Mr. Fletcher.

Signaling to Sawyer, who had come along on the opposite side of the horse, Lovelace said: "My man will reimburse you for any costs."

"No need," Ashton said. "I'm concerned, though, about her treatment. Some of her injuries preceded her escape. A horseman of your caliber would never resort to the severity implied."

"No," Lovelace said, giving Sawyer a sharp glance, "but I am in no position to work exclusively with one horse, or even to spend time with the horses. That is the concern of Sawyer, the quartermaster, or others of that sort. My job is to train the officers and men. In addition to my own regiment, I devote a considerable amount of energy on another—the individual who purchased that command cannot be trusted."

"Yet a horse in advanced pregnancy should not be worked at all," Ashton said.

"Your point?"

"If she is subjected to similar methods again, she could very well bolt again. Only this time she is so far along she might lose the foal—or her life."

"That is my concern, not yours."

"It is my job to provide you with quality stock," Ashton said. "This is the finest mare in Hampshire. Whether she is with you, or you return her to Hants for breeding, she is too valuable to waste out of carelessness or"—he glanced at Sawyer—"a temperament ill-suited to the business."

"I can afford the loss, if it comes to that."

"Financially, perhaps. But can you afford the loss of the well-bred mounts she will provide your cavalry—provide, perhaps, directly to you? You will face battle in the next year or two—perhaps much sooner." Lovelace examined him as if he had been privy to information that he should not have, then recognized the obvious deduction from the scale of the maneuvers. Ashton continued:

"Do you want carelessness—or contempt—to put your men on inferior horses?"

When Lovelace seemed to be considering his argument, Ashton pressed his point: "She's worth more as a brood mare than as a warhorse. I'll buy her back for twice what she's worth. You'll still have the foal, as we previously agreed."

Jane subtly pulled on Ashton's arm. Though keen to confront any man in a test of wills, he was protective of any creature at an inherent disadvantage—women must be put in that category, along with children and animals. In contrast, Lovelace would see Ashton's attitude as a weakness to exploit.

"All this because of your love for a horse?"

Sensing his mistake, Ashton backed off. "One appreciates a horse one has raised, but I am thinking of your investment in the animal. It is to your interest to keep her healthy. To make a profit."

"Yet you propose returning her to Hants—a trip you have already said would kill her?"

"We took it easy coming this way. We'll take it easy going home. And we have a contrivance that eases the strain."

"Another of your inventions."

Ashton shrugged. "An advantage of constant tinkering."

"You are prepared to offer me twice what she is worth to avoid her running away?"

"A benefit for both sides."

Lovelace looked to Ashton and Jane—both now trying to keep their faces neutral—and then to Sawyer, whose expression reluctantly indicated that the representation made eminent sense.

"It's your decision, of course," Ashton added. "I propose no more than what common sense suggests."

"Of course," Lovelace said. He pulled his pistol from his belt, cocked it, and shot the mare through the head. The horse toppled, sending dust billowing sideways. Sawyer jumped clear, gore having spattered his face.

"There," Lovelace said. "She won't run away again."

Jane had the strangest reaction, which was seemingly no re-action at all. She knew that Ashton roared in fury and she was screaming in outrage, but she was certain the impression came be-reft of any sound. Everything collectively increased in speed, while each individual action slowed to distinctiveness. She knew that a squad of infantry was running over at the shot, but she was not sure how the impression arrived, as she had looked down to avoid seeing what remained of the mare and was noticing that the blood had contaminated her boots without a drop being wasted on her dress. She looked up only when Ashton grabbed a musket from the closest man, who was so surprised by the sudden movement he had no chance to prevent the taking. Ashton turned the musket to Lovelace. The long, thin bayonet pierced the air under his chin. Lovelace presented an instant of surprise, an instant of fear, an instant of calm recovery. He glanced at the soldiers who, though confused, were beginning to raise their weapons against Ashton's threat. Lovelace smiled a thin ironic smile, as if curious whether he, Ashton, or both would end up dead in this moment of absur-dity. Ashton swiveled from Lovelace and stabbed repeatedly into the belly of the mare. Though the act was the only way to prevent the foal, writhing within the dead mare, from slowly suffocating, Jane clinched herself to avoid any further response until Ashton's violent thrusts left the fetus as still as its mother.

Chapter 10

"Did you find out whether Lovelace was involved in that scheme to clothe the French? Have you failed again? Must I do everything?"

These words, and the venom they contained, caused Henry to blanch. Ashton's questions were normally abrupt; he seldom coated a phrase with the sugar of civility. This, however, was something altogether different. Under the sting of this attack, Henry sat up straight, gathering time and his thoughts by removing and examining his spectacles. "Excuse me?" he responded at last.

"You heard me. My orders were simple enough. Why do you think I sent for you?"

As they began to regroup their assemblage at Stanmer to make their ragged way back to Hants, Ashton had dispatched a rider to London arranging for Henry to meet them upon their return to Hants. Ashton had not, however, explained in his cryptic message what had happened with Lovelace or what the purpose of the meeting was to be.

Jane's brother had no context, therefore, by which to understand this extraordinary rudeness. His normal deference to Ashton related to his position as advisor, not to his position as a human being. He responded with words that, while carrying the implication of an apology, were conveyed in a firm and uninflected manner that displayed anything but. "I ascertained that the Lovelace family was not involved with the greatcoats. In fact, Lovelace and

Wellesley have also raised the alarm with the men of London. That being the case, I went no further. Did I misunderstand your directions? Or possibly—your intent?"

His failure either to cower or to respond with anger left Ashton with nowhere to go. It was as if a fencer had begun a match with a lunge at his opponent's breast, missed, and the other man merely walked away.

Jane was herself so appalled at Ashton's verbal assault that she was not immediately able to form her own admonishment. Seeing that Henry had learned from Mr. Jarrett, she learned from Henry, and eventually gathered her words in as calm a voice as she could manage. "Lovelace killed the mare we had been caring for, the one I mentioned to you in a letter. Having been unable to prevent that act of barbarity, my husband is having difficulty keeping his emotions in control."

Ashton shoved away from the table, in a corner of the library by the wide set of windows. The windows normally provided an excellent location for reading, but their exchanges appeared to drain the energy from the light, leaving the leather books on the shelves pale and out of focus. Indeed, the entire room seemed stunned at Ashton's opening.

He walked over toward the globe, an elegant apparatus standing near his desk, set in a half-spherical frame upon a wooden tripod. He slammed the globe with the intent of spinning it angrily, but his blow was so hard that the tripod tipped and he had to grab the globe and its stand to avoid them toppling over.

"It is a good thing you did not use the telescope to register your anger," Jane said, referring to the instrument close at hand by the window. "It would have spun around and knocked you senseless."

Ashton now stood with their eyes upon him in the ludicrous position of being wrapped around a wooden and ceramic ornament that his mother had placed in the library as a show of scholarly ostentation. In his embarrassment, he looked very much like a greengrocer struggling not to drop an armload of vegetables. After carefully reestablishing the mechanism on the floor, he returned to the table, stiffly bowed to Henry, and said: "I have said very little since the confrontation, for fear of losing my composure. I was trying to cool my anger, but all I did was bottle it. My apologies, brother."

Ashton sat in a movement that combined the violent with the contrite. Jane explained how, after they had restored the pregnant mare to health and used *scientific transport* to take her carefully to Lovelace's camp near Stanmer, the Colonel had drawn Ashton into displaying more concern for the beast than was wise and then destroyed the mare and foal in an act of casual cruelty.

"I would be equally upset," Henry said, with more kindness than was warranted.

"I'm sure humiliation constitutes a goodly proportion of my reaction, but I want to believe that most of my fury concerns the death of an innocent creature," he said.

"A wise man would let it pass," Henry said. "What is there to be gained?"

"A reckoning for an unconscionable bully."

Henry continued to fidget with his spectacles before setting them down and running his hands through his hair, which was beginning to turn gray and to slightly recede in the same fashion as their late father's. His high cheekbones and thin face added to the resemblance. Reminded of a meeting with her father a few years before about the balloon incident, she apprehended that they might be in for a lecture. As if responding to her thought, Henry said: "I must stop and ask you to consider the situation in its fullness." He looked from one to the other. "We have actions at our disposal that would cause them harm. In some cases, they will not know who has brought it. In most cases, they will. My estimation of the Earl and his son the Colonel is that neither of them will shy away from confrontation. In their position in society, they have no concept of loss. Consequently, they will proceed until they win. Whatever we may do to retaliate, they *will* counter. Then the question is whether we will let *that* response be, or whether we will respond again. Further, while you have more direct wealth, they have a greater number of friends and associates in their own positions of power. If I were to ask our banker Mr. Thornton of the odds, he would say that—even after a series of unpleasant exchanges with our adversaries—we are likely to do no better than stand even. And could very well fare worse." Mr. Thornton was a cousin of Mr. Wilberforce and the man who had put together Ashton's group of investors for the rail-road project.

"I will not turn away from that arrogant bastard Lovelace—excuse my language."

"No one ever went to Heaven for vengeance," Henry said.

"It may be wrong to retaliate for a wrong," Jane said, "but is it not equally wrong if we, through inaction, let a man without principle obtain whatever he wishes? What does it teach an evil man when no one is willing to stand up to him, except to bully even further?"

"Evil men do not learn. That is why they are evil."

"They have no trouble learning how to expand upon their wickedness," Jane replied.

"I understand that these steps could well have consequences, both moral and practical," Ashton said. These were the first words he had spoken that represented thought rather than emotion. "I do not wish for war. I wish only to let them know there are consequences to *their* actions. Give us whatever advice you have, and we will try to develop a response—something *symmetrical*, let us say."

"It remains highly probable that they will reciprocate and escalate. Can you live with that?"

"When I cannot, I will stop," Ashton said.

"Ever since we humiliated Lovelace in the Parliamentary proceedings, I have been expecting some response on their part," Henry said. "I did not expect an affront as nasty as shooting a horse. Assuming they would attack our businesses, I have been compiling information about the Lovelace family holdings."

"Continue," Ashton said.

"You recall the conversation in which Mr. Knollman spoke of several military contracts coming up for renewal? These are contracts held by companies in which the Lovelaces have interests. I would take great satisfaction in taking those contracts away from them. It would serve them right for deceiving us on the rail-road project last year—joining our competitors. Not to mention the ugly business with the mare."

"I should not have to repeat: I will not stoop to bribery. Even here."

"No need for bribery. However, we will have to go so low in our bid we will not make money. We will be lucky to break even. This approach may not be perceived as a direct attack, for in these uncertain times every man is desperate to win what business he can."

"Better I'm breaking even than Lovelace is turning a profit," Ashton responded. "It's not much recompense for what he has done, but at least our people will have work."

"Then we are doing this for the right reason," Jane concluded. "We will not require absolution for our behavior."

Chapter 11

After Henry returned to London, Jane found herself spending more and more time in the nursery with George. Even a firm decision on a course of action with the Lovelaces did not immediately relieve Ashton's state of high agitation, and she did not want to become a target of unwarranted complaints—or he the recipient of her deserved retorts. Herself grieving more about the mare than she let on, she had Cassandra return for a few days. Though Jane remained mostly to herself, her nerves began to settle once she knew her sister was somewhere nearby. Cass's presence also seemed to hasten Ashton's return to equanimity, as his generosity toward her mother and sister immediately softened him.

It was not the avoidance of the negative, however, that was the primary reason for her dedication to the nursery. A quiet, airy room just off her own, the nursery held all the joys that hurry a mother hither. It was decorated in bright colors and full of eye-catching toys—stuffed animals and dolls from her and mechanically inclined devices from Ashton that for safety's sake must, for now, remain out of the reach of a baby who was trying to crawl.

The domestic nurse was new. Not just an abigail, but a young woman by the *name* Abigail, she had dark brown hair and eyes, a thin but pleasing smile, and expressive eyebrows that revealed her moods. Despite her youth, Abigail had been recommended by Mrs. Lundeen for her sweet disposition and for having helped her mother, who was raising a large family. The most favorable recommendation, however, was the scene that greeted Jane as she entered today. Abigail was down on the floor with a basket of small things for George, who was pulling them out one by one and testing their validity with his mouth. Whenever he would throw one—a block, one of several wooden soldiers, a miniature locomotive crafted by Mr. Trevithick—Abigail would exclaim with astonishment at the baby's athletic abilities. She also spoke to him nonstop. A nurse should be able to talk nonsense in abundance!

When she noticed Jane, Abigail laughed. "Good morning, ma'am. Little George is in fine spirits today!"

The baby smiled, drooled, and waved his arms at his mother to be held. Jane picked him up. They set him in his chair to continue the introduction of solid foods; today's menu featured highly pulped peas. Disgust was an easy reaction to judge, though when the food flew as far as the toys Jane took it as a sign of enthusiasm for the new diet. In either case, Abigail was quick to assist with the cleaning.

The girl was an augur for a positive future. Though diligent and warm-hearted, the nurse who had preceded her was too closely aligned with the earlier illnesses, which like the alternating bitterness and damp of winter had left them feeling as if all were a dispiriting deluge. While grateful for her service, which had included the sufferance of the same contagions that had subdued the rest of the family, Jane felt that when she left it was possible that George's difficulties had departed with her. Abigail, at least, had no knowledge of any of the earlier issues concerning her baby. Having a fresh start with her, he would bloom!

After Abigail left with the infant's laundry, Jane worked with George as he strove to synchronize the opening of his mouth with the arrival of the mashed peas on a spoon. Jane was mildly bewildered at the scene before her: Ashton's face and bright eyes set upon a chubby body, and this image working with feverish determination to master an elementary skill. "Eat?" she indicated between each mouthful. "Eat?"

"What are you doing to my grandchild!"

The exclamation so startled Jane that she nearly dropped the spoon.

"I am feeding him. What does it look like?"

"No—that!" Mrs. Dennis made a series of angry movements with her fingers, mimicking the gestures with similar ugly movements of her mouth. Had either been words, they would have cursed Jane as a mother. Mrs. Dennis was short and barrel-shaped. Heavy bags under her eyes concentrated the unpleasantness in her gaze. As she stood silent and demanding, her lips remained pursed as if momentarily holding in a stream of criticisms.

At first Jane thought to demur; the few other times someone had happened along, she was able to disguise what she was doing. She had not expected her mother-in-law, however. Because George had wailed the last several times his grandmother tried to take him, Mrs. Dennis had resolved to stay away until the boy learned better manners. Having let down her guard, Jane had no way, now, to arrange for Mrs. Dennis to un-see what she had seen, and no way for Jane to explain her actions as anything but what they were.

"I was teaching him to say *eat*."

"*With your fingers?*"

"Yes, with my fingers. A common gesture." She replicated the action, her fingers pinched together toward her mouth.

"Why would you need to do that?"

"I believe it will help him learn to speak."

"What kind of *normal* child needs help to speak?"

"George developed some complaint of the ears. I mean to help catch him up."

"He cannot hear?"

"He struggles—at times—there is no reason to suppose it is serious."

Jane's inherent honesty, however, caused her expression to implicate a possible contradiction to her words.

"He's deaf! Oh, my God! My God!"

Mrs. Dennis ran into the hall. Jane grabbed George and followed. Weaving and giving out heart-rending cries, Mrs. Dennis in her disturbance drew servants out from different rooms. By the time she reached the bottom of the stairs, Jane hurrying behind, Mrs. Lundeen and Mr. Hanrahan had come to investigate and Cassandra had emerged from the sitting room. Mrs. Dennis stood, swaying, until Ashton arrived from the library, at which point she made a heartfelt though overly dramatic exhibition of despair.

Upon surveying the scene, Ashton motioned for all but the family to depart. As the upper servants shepherded the rest away, Ashton led his mother into the sitting room, where she swept Cassandra's needlework to the floor and collapsed onto the sofa in a continuing display of shattered nerves. Ashton, Cassandra and Jane stood around her.

"Tell them," Mrs. Dennis said. "*Tell them.*"

"I was explaining to Mrs. Dennis that George had picked up some ailment over the unseasonable months. It seems to have affected his hearing. He will be well soon enough."

"You don't use *sign language* to communicate with a child whose ears are stopped up. He's deaf, Ashton—deaf! She won't admit it. The shame! All we've worked for! Your heir—deaf and dumb!"

"I spoke with my fingers to reinforce my words." Jane bounced George nonchalantly to indicate the insignificance of Mrs. Dennis's comments. "I thought it might help if he had fallen behind. I should think it a very pragmatic thing for a responsible mother to do."

The room was silent for so long that Jane began to hear beyond: glasses and plate rattling in the direction of the dining room, patient instructions from Mrs. Lundeen to a servant in a nearby hall, a gardener afield speaking in a thick Hampshire accent. Then Ashton spoke in a voice that seemed louder than it was because her ears had become attuned to the distance:

"W-Where d-did you learn s-sign language?"

"I—"

The ensuing silence collapsed even deeper than before, a sinkhole for all emotion.

Eventually, Cassandra ventured an explanation, her voice having the same disproportionate effect in the quiet as had Ashton's.

"We had a brother," she said, linking her arm with Jane. "George. He was deaf. We all learned a little sign language."

Ashton crashed back into a chair. "You had a brother? How could I not know this? George? My son is named for a deaf-mute? For some impaired individual?"

"He is named for my father," Jane said. "As was my unfortunate brother."

Mrs. Dennis, murmuring a quiet ululation, rocked forward and back. "A brother! A brother!"

"You never thought to tell me of this?"

"He was sent away when we were all young. To a lovely family, the Culhams, near Monk Sherborne. We never think of him."

"Monk Sherborne." Ashton was too astonished to raise his voice. "I could be there in a brisk day's walk."

"We understand he is very happy."

"How would you come to that understanding?"

"James visits him—not as often as he would like, for fear of disrupting his life. Edward makes certain he is provided for."

"Let me be sure I understand this correctly. Jane Austen Dennis, the kindest, sweetest woman ever born, has a brother living nearby she has never visited? An unfortunate brother—damaged—that she never sees, never thinks of—*never mentions to her husband?*"

"I think of him," Jane said. "And yet—not."

"We all think of our brother," Cassandra added. "Daily he is in our prayers."

"I hear your prayers regularly. Never a mention of any *George*. Not that one, anyway."

"We think of him, but we cannot speak of him," Jane said. "A matter of pain, not reticence."

"You understood the shame!" Mrs. Dennis cried. "You knew this was the one impediment to marrying Ashton you could not overcome! You deceived us—deliberately, wickedly."

"I have five brothers who are as healthy and gifted as any men in England. I never thought of George as being of any consequence—not to my marriage—*our* marriage. He was an exception—a very rare one. A sick brother."

"You lie! You knew!"

"Cease, Mother," Ashton said, but his tone warned that it was only so he could delve further into the facts. "Tell me more about George, the uncle my son is not named for but seems to resemble in a monumental way."

"We did not try to hide him away, not intentionally," Jane insisted. "We were a family of modest means. My mother had seven other children to raise. She could not care for George without taking time away from her other children."

"He became more difficult as he grew older," Cassandra said. "He did not understand things. He would become confused, angry. After he left, our mother cried for weeks—months."

"When we named our son George—even then—you never thought to say to me, 'By the way, dear husband, I have a brother of that name? He is *not quite right?*' "

"I thought of the honor to my father. ... But, yes, at some level I must have thought of him, the other George. The matter was too unbearable to bring to mind."

"*You knew!*"

"Is there anything else that *I* should know?" Ashton said. "About your family? About anything? Now is the time. Whatever I do not know to ask—I demand of you. There will be no secrets—no more. Never again."

Jane and Cassandra stood with their heads bowed, cheeks inflamed.

"We have ... ," Cassandra began.

Jane took the responsibility on herself. "We have an uncle named Thomas. My mother's brother. He suffers as George does. Possibly worse."

"Another one—worse?"

"He was called an imbecile. He is also with the Culhams. Very nice people, as I have said."

"*It runs in the family. It runs in the family. Imbecility runs in the family.*" Making her fists into small balls, Mrs. Dennis repeatedly slammed herself in the lap as she spoke. "You have ruined my son. I said you would do this. You have ruined my family. All I have worked for!"

"Your letter," Ashton said, remembering. "When you were visiting Stoneleigh. The baron and his sister both died insane—that's what you said. All on your mother's side."

"You cannot use distant relations to disparage my mother! Every family has someone with—problems."

"Not our family!" Mrs. Dennis said. "We were poor stock but healthy—firm of mind as well as body. As far back as anyone wants to look!"

"I am trying to understand what is happening with my son," Ashton said. "An uncle, a great-uncle, other relatives—all suffering serious impairments." He sighed heavily. "Any other pleasant news?"

"Eliza's boy Hastings," Cassandra said. "He was damaged too. He died relatively young."

Ashton put his hand to his forehand. "Eliza. On your father's side."

"Both sides! Oh, my God! Both sides!" Mrs. Dennis laughed hysterically. "Lucky there are only two."

"It does not signify," Jane said. "This is history. We had one sad brother in a family of eight. The rest are as fine as can be. George is fine too. You will see." She bounced him again and he smiled, looking around at all the attention directed toward him. "He could hear perfectly well in the womb. Ashton—you recall. When I banged the metal spoon and bowl. He jumped! He could hear! It is some minor thing now, some temporary distemper."

"Why is he not upset now," Ashton inquired, "considering the agitation in the air? My mother's laments? Her howls of anguish?"

"He has always had the sweetest disposition, the pride of us both."

Ashton rose and crossed over to a table, where he fingered a fine Wedgwood vase. "The last time I went down to Winchester to see Trevithick about the rail-road," he said, "I learned something very interesting." He manipulated the vase in his hands as he returned to them. "We have built out the line six or seven miles. Quite an achievement. One of our problems, we learned, is that the underlayment needs to be built up and compacted until it is quite firm. To reduce the flexing of the rails."

The women stared at him in alarm and confusion. Had the revelations about George unhinged him, sent him staggering to a technical lecture to avoid the implications?

"At one point, they started the locomotive well down the line," he said in a calm, reasoned way. "We could see the smoke in the distance, over the trees, but not the engine itself. Nor could we hear it. Long before the locomotive came into sight, I began to feel the tracks vibrate. I kneeled and pressed my cheek to the rail. I could feel the machine very strongly—the wheels, the weight, the steam engine working—all one big vibration coming down the rails. And then I knew."

He continued to pace. "Jane—put George on the floor, there on the rug, facing the windows. Yes, away from the rest of the room. Give him something to distract him. Just for a moment." She did as she was told. George was happy to investigate her household keys with his mouth. "Step back," Ashton said. As she did, he hurled the vase against the nearest wall, not ten feet away, where George could not see. The vase smashed with a *bang*. George took no notice of the noise, though he turned toward the women when they jumped.

Jane rushed to pick up her child as if he would be Ashton's next target. "A temporary affliction," she said. "I told you."

Ashton came over and held her as she held the baby. Normally this would have been far too intimate for a public setting, but his action was natural considering the extremity of the situation. "How did you hold the bowl and spoon? You had the bowl in the crook of your arm, tight against your abdomen—remember, you showed me when I came home? The baby didn't *hear* the clang of the spoon on the bowl—he *felt* the vibration through your skin. Like me and the rails. That's why he reacted so violently—it was the first time he had experienced anything like that." He put his head next to hers. "Our baby is deaf, Jane. Deaf. Dumb, we must assume."

"But we would have been able to tell by now," Jane said. "We would have known long before."

"We couldn't have told when he was younger—no baby is attentive enough. The older he got, the less either one of us *wanted* to understand. You made excuses for him. I made excuses for you."

"How long have *you* known?" she asked, distress constricting her voice.

"Three weeks, the trip you recalled me from."

"You knew and did not tell me?"

"I felt it was best to let you reach the same conclusion on your own."

"You lacked the courage."

"If I had been the one to tell you, it might have become my fault."

"This is all a very pleasing domestic scene," said Mrs. Dennis, rising from the sofa with purpose and gesturing at their tableau. "But it is time for hard decisions. We must get rid of it before anyone else knows. I'm sure that family would be delighted to have another Austen to care for. They'll soon have enough for a cricket team."

Jane was so shocked that her only means of protest was to point out the advancing age of the Culhams.

"Then some other worthies at Monk Sherborne. Anywhere far enough from here not to create an association. In time, it will be convenient to forget about him. That should be no trouble. You Austens are quick enough to ignore the idiots you spawn."

Sensing that Jane needed all her energies to survive this exchange, Cassandra slipped in to take George.

Mrs. Dennis added: "I thought ill of you from the beginning, Miss Austen. When marriage became inevitable, I prayed that, however poor you might be, you would prove hardy English stock. You gave us a son—but not one that any grandmother could wish for."

"But one that any grandmother should love," Jane shot back.

Despite her protestations about the temporary nature of George's disease, she had not been able to fully escape the possibility that George might share the afflictions of his uncles. Over many weeks, just on the edge of her consciousness, she had prepared herself to argue for her baby. It seemed impossible that she could keep him. Removal was how it was done, the proper and precedented manner by which society swept away every act and evidence, every hint, of shame. She understood that there would be no way she could talk her way around *these* strictures, any more than if she had given birth to an illegitimate child—for a deaf-mute was as illegitimate as any bastard. She could, however, argue long and eloquently for possession and in this manner wring concessions for the delay of his departure. The longer her baby was with her, the better she could prepare him for a world he would have to face alone.

Ashton mooted the argument before it began.

"George is not going anywhere. He is my son. He stays at Hants."

"He is irreparably damaged!" Mrs. Dennis asserted. "You will humiliate our family! A disgrace—"

"The more he is damaged, the more he needs the protection of his father."

"Even the Austens had the good sense to rid themselves of such a *thing*!"

"It might have made sense for a struggling family to send the child away. It might have even been best for the boy—to give him a quiet place away from the tumult of a busy home. It does not make sense for us, with all our resources. Hants can provide anything George might need."

"You will never again be able to take your place with the best families. Not while you are parading around an idiot."

"The best place for him is with his family. His mother, father."

Jane fell against her husband. For the first time in public she forgot restraint, dignity, forbearance: She gave herself over equally to the wretchedness of grieving tears and the recognition of the heart of the man beside her.

"But—!" Mrs. Dennis began.

"I will not turn out my child. I *will* turn out anyone who cannot accept the decision."

"Lunatics! Imbeciles!" screamed Mrs. Dennis, storming from the room. "Defectives! The lot of them! Defectives—all!"

Chapter 12

"Come, the baby is down. Let's walk."

Jane relished her husband's invitation as an antidote to the strain in the household. Since the confrontation, Ashton's mother had done Jane the courtesy of avoiding her as much as possible. Yet one must always remain steeled lest one blunder around a corner into the teeth of a malicious glare or muttered barb.

The couple began in the formal garden. After several rounds, Ashton asked whether she would prefer the hedgerows, or the path from there cutting up to the temple, or the bower he had refurbished for her the previous year. "None," Jane said. "The fields"—indicating the rolling landscape toward the east. "We could ride," he suggested. "Too hard," she replied, thinking of having to stop and summon the grooms and the effort to be courteous as they prepared the mounts. "Walk."

"Normally, you prefer the bower when you're in a contemplative mood," he said.

"Restless," she said.

"Normally, I'm the one speaking monosyllabically. Which raises the question: Why isn't the word for speaking in single syllables itself a single syllable? Like *short*. There's a word that sounds like what it is."

"Onomatopoeic."

"Another word that's too difficult for the meaning it conveys. One can't pronounce it, never mind spell it."

"Greek," she said.

"Must be why they switched to Latin. So English speakers a thousand years later could make sense of important words."

"Sesquipedalian," she said. "A word that means long. Or someone who uses long words."

"Finally!" he said, as if all were right with the world.

"Thank you for asking me for a walk," finally conceding to his effort to draw her out. "I have too much on my mind to be hemmed in by the hedges. And the bower—"

"—long your sanctuary—"

"—feels too confined. As if I were trapped."

"Our landscaping reflects your mood."

"Which is why I must be out here in the fields. To give me some relief. I cannot breathe."

"Worry does that."

"I am no longer worried about George. At least, not in the way I was. I am relieved that his illness—condition—is in the open. The sooner we—I—admitted it, the more likely it was that we would be able to help him. It is you, Ashton. I feared your reaction when you found out—I feared you would send him away. Your love—your generosity to my son—caused my heart to nearly burst."

"A man cannot accept praise for loving his son. I love him for the same reason the sun comes up: a function of the universe."

The route they took was agricultural, a gap in thick growth that was wider than a path and narrower than a country lane, through which workers traversed the fields on foot and in conveyance. Scattered trees, which served primarily as shelter from the elements for mid-day meals, shepherded the creeks and ditches. Without this rough and irregular border, the lush acres of barley, wheat, and rye might have slumped off the sides of the earth. The view, as handsomely plain as an unadorned English maid, pleased her. The songbirds exchanging sentiments from tree to tree did not necessarily lift her spirits, though, for she noted how the common brown birds darted out from time to time to keep watchful eye on the ancient elm in case the rooks there adjourned their parliament in search of their own repast.

"Your warmth toward George will be recorded by the bards," Jane said, "but you have remained cool to me. Despite my best efforts to make you—*happy*."

It was one of the few times Ashton ever blushed, for he understood that her efforts—prodigious as they had been of late—were more for *him* than *them*. "I am aware of your labors—pleased, beyond measure—and understood them to be at least partly an expression of your thanks. I would say any thanks is enough—except I do not wish to discourage that particular method!"

She smiled along with him. "It is out here where I feel your distance. You stand away from me. You no longer reach for my hand. You accept my presence but do not delight in it. You speak less and—"

"—monosyllabically?"

"Ashton, you cannot blame me for bearing you a sickly child. There are Georges in our line going back to the very first Austen. One or two of them are bound to be weak. You cannot attach significance to a name. You cannot blame my baby."

"I would never blame a child for anything adhering to the parent," Ashton growled. "Any child, any parent. Most particularly—*not mine*."

"Then what, my love?"

"You cannot help what happened to George. It was not the result of any carelessness or misbehavior. It happened. He is who he is, and we shall take care of him. There is nothing more to say on that account. But, Jane—you lied to me. You hid from me something important about your family. I rely on your honesty as much as your love. Both failed me."

"It was not to hide the risk of having a damaged child."

"It does not matter why! Our George could be as brilliant and compassionate as your father—as strapping and bright as your nephew of that name. I would still be outraged. *You hid it!* You kept furtive something fundamental from the one man from whom you should hold no secrets. And you did this out of doubt about my character. How I would respond when I found out. Forget my money, Jane—all I own is my character. Which—as you just admitted—you lack all confidence in."

"I have no answer, Ashton. What I expressed as doubt about you was really doubt about myself." Jane felt like crying but tension squeezed her feelings in such a strange way that no tears flowed. "This was something within my family—my Austen family—something within me. There was shame, embarrassment. We had all hidden it for so long, agreed not to address it. By not speaking of it, we almost forgot it was there: evidence that, despite the intelligence and character and hard work of every one of us, we were still in some fundamental way—lacking. Not good enough. Unable to stand head high. Among those many people who would react exactly as your mother did. Not merely high society, but ordinary people eager to look down on others."

They stopped mid-lane.

"I will make mistakes, Jane—have made many. But if you ever doubt me—doubt who I am in my heart—we are done. I am done. My belief in myself is a fortress against the world. But you are inside those walls. If you disbelieve—gates will open, walls crash, barbarians swarm. I am lost."

"Ashton, listen to me." She took his face in her hands to direct his eyes fully into her own. "The shame is mine. The dishonor—mine. My silence had nothing to do with you. I was a convenient hypocrite—silent not for any advantage with you but for the comfort of not having to deal with the uncomfortable. For the comfort of not being *different*. For the pride of convention."

"Then you and I are together—still one?"

"I have never had more love or respect for you than I do now."

"Then we must take our youngling to see his new uncle."

Turning to retrace their steps, Jane gave him more background on her brother and his needs. According to James, they should not visit too often, nor stay too long. George must have a regular routine, and visitors—however closely related or well intended—too easily disturbed his serenity. "I cannot imagine what it will be like when my little George is running about!" she said, already opening her mind to the disorienting but sweet thought of meeting again a brother she barely remembered.

It was a companionable walk home. The exercise, the flowers, full in bloom, as well as their clarifying dialogue, enabled her to relax for the first time in weeks—months, if she were to be honest. Their talk flowed with commonplace matters. He brought her the news of the attack on Copenhagen, launched when the British had word that the French were massing on the Danish border. "Lovelace is part of Wellesley's brigade," he said. "That battle will keep him out of our hair for some time." She brought him news of Mary, Frank's wife, who would arrive in a few days on the way to Godmersham and then on to her family in Ramsgate. With Frank en route to the Cape of Good Hope, the experiment in Castle Square—to reduce expenses by sharing living space—was in suspense and likely at an end. Because his postings would likely still originate from Portsmouth, she would need to remain nearby, but when Mary returned it would probably be to separate lodgings. Despite the support for Mary during her pregnancy, no one had been happy with the arrangement, but it kept her close to his station for as long as possible before he put to sea. "It was well worth it, considering her difficulties."

"I have no doubt that his being with Mary as much as he could before their daughter's birth made everything go a good deal better."

"I suspect that her mood will be much improved compared to the months she remained in cramped quarters with her in-laws. As I suspect their moods will be at her departure."

"Mary Jane. I like Jane as the name for a daughter," Ashton said. "Jane Cassandra or Cassandra Jane? The latter rolls pleasingly off the tongue, and would honor your mother. And sister, too."

"You are not worried?"

"One in eight? That gives us seven more!"

"Too soon, my dear. But let us talk seriously when we better understand what we face with George."

They were now back in the gardens, where they inspected an expanse, about an acre in size, that Jane had never cared for. It wore neither the bright uniform of a formal garden nor the colorful dishabille of nature. The area seemed to have been planted with the aim of offending the eye—vegetation too dense here, too sparse there, colors at war. Under her guidance, Mr. Hayes, the gardener, was redressing arrangements to better resemble the ones she once admired at The Vyne. The elimination of some species and the shifting of others had decongested the space; the impression was that the plants could better breathe. The colors shone forth in attractive gradations by the addition of pinks, carnations, and geraniums, and the scent enlivened by the sweet lilies of the valley and Cassandra's ambrosia-scented mignonettes. Her sister's touch showed too in the addition of several beehives tucked away on the side, insisted upon on her last visit as a necessity considering the number of plants that required pollination and the number of people who treasured honey.

They lingered the last few minutes before her gathering fullness required her to return to George.

"There is one more thing, Jane. You must pay your penance for the secret you kept."

"Name your price. I have done nigh onto everything."

He returned her smile. "Another kind. After Mary leaves, I think it best that you should go away. You and George. Didn't you say something about a family trip to Chawton—Edward inspecting his holdings?"

"I will never hesitate to join an Austen adventure, but why?"

"Our happiness is more likely to hold if there were a respite."

She considered. "Your mother?"

"Her ability to adjust to another dramatic change is hampered by the constant reminder of the reason. I fear our baby's presence is a provocation. If she were to have a few weeks—"

"I am to be banished—instead of her?"

"Temporarily."

"It distresses you that my dear child provokes her, but it bothers you not the least that her nastiness provokes me? Let her be the one to go. *Forthwith*. Ashton, you cannot. Do not let that woman come between us. When we married, we cleaved together. No one should cleave us apart."

"I am hoping that a little distance, for a little while, will make all the difference."

"My departure will convince her that she has won. I either will not come back—or I will come back alone."

"I cannot banish her to the island, Jane. It's as simple as that. It is too far away and across the strait. She has not been to that house in a dozen years. She has no one there. No friends or family. No society. Unfamiliar in every way. It would kill her—I mean that. She would be dead in a year. Alone and forgotten, or at least ignored. I may not love her as I should—she may not deserve to be loved as she should—but you cannot cause me to abandon her any more than she could cause me to abandon my son."

"Then banish her a little closer—Monk Sherborne, perhaps."

"Jane."

"Mrs. Knight, Edward's adoptive mother, has a much more pleasant relationship with her son, yet she voluntarily withdrew from Godmersham to a lovely home in Canterbury. All to give Edward and *his wife* space to breathe."

"They have ten children. She fled for her life."

"Ashton."

"I will not put her before you. I am, however, trying to find a middle ground."

"There is no middle ground. One submits—or resists. If it were just me, and this were the only way to make you happy, I might—but not at the cost of my child."

"We are already decided on that."

Jane saw that Ashton had been struggling with the matter for some time—possibly even before his ultimatum to his mother in the sitting room. The occasional jokes about exile to the Isle of

Wight had never exactly been jokes. Jane understood further that this subject was not intended to convince her to abandon the field to Mrs. Dennis; nor its opposite, to convince him to dispatch the elderly woman to a distant shore. It was for Ashton to accept the need to remove his mother—*that*—and for Jane to accept that her removal was not the same as remote and permanent exile.

"If you put distance between us, I will not begrudge the amount. I even have some servants—those more comfortable under her than me—I would gladly part with."

"We must act quickly, then," he said. "I must find a suitable house. Smaller, of course, but at least as grand. Winchester? Basingstoke? Soon—it would not do to remove her during the dismal months."

"Every month is dismal in her presence."

"Jane, the right decision is seldom the easiest."

"You are right. I apologize. My dealing with her tends to make my response of a kind. I understand how hard this will be for you. Ashton, know this: I will always welcome her as your mother and one-time matriarch here. She will not lack for respect. Even if she is not forthcoming with hers."

"Then you will understand what I say next. You really *must* leave. No, don't—you must go before I tell her, and remain away until the transition is complete. This will reduce her ability to blame anyone but me."

"It will not eliminate her blame of me. However, it will reduce her humiliation—and your pain. Very well. Banished after all, but for a reason I can accept."

Chapter 13

4 September 1807

Dearest husband

I must tell you the three words above all others that every man yearns to hear: You were right. Though I understood and agreed with the reason for our departure, I still felt at some level that I was, for reasons not of my doing, being ousted from my own home. However, I am compelled to admit that time in Chawton has brought me the most remarkable relief. After months of illness that overwhelmed the household, after all the worry over little George and his health through the spring and summer—the culmination of all these aggravations in the malice of your mother—I am most happy to be at Chawton with my people—the only others besides you that love me without question. Mother and Cassandra are here; Edward and his bustling charges; and 'the Steventonites,' as my niece Fanny calls James and his family. Though we are not twenty miles away, it feels like a happy two hundred. I do not exult in my absence from you, but I do exult in coming down to breakfast without any worry of being set upon by someone muttering about my heritage. I have broken the news to everyone about George, and they are sad but most supportive. As the youngest and least-often seen, he would have been the center of attention anyway, but now his aunts, *his uncles, and especially his cousins consider him to be their special darling.*

This familial conviviality, however, fills me with guilt—or perhaps regret—at the situation with your mother. Seeing my mother, rootless since my father's death in Bath, cheery yet somewhat lost, keeping a brave face to the uncertainty of her next inhabitance, must give anyone with feeling, pause. I remember, as well, your mother's own crushed spirits last year when she decided—for no reason other than her own distrustful nature—that we were going to ship her off to Wight then. On reflection, even Basingstoke might be too far, though I agree it may be the closest town in which a suitable house may be found. My requirement is tempered to be: far enough away that she cannot surprise us with her presence but not so far as to create any more discord than necessary. I have no way of knowing whether this pronouncement will provide any flexibility in your choice of domain, but it will provide some relief to my conscience.

It is a shame that our village is not as long established or as prosperous as this one. Everyone is acquainted with Chawton and speaks of it as a remarkably pretty village. It has two dozen houses, most of them timber and thatch, along with a few handsome brick homes, along wide, graveled streets. Several of the nicer homes would be fitting for the dowager Mrs. Dennis, despite the noise and dust of the stage coaches. You will remember the intersection that brings together the roads from Winchester and Gosport on the way to London. At regular times of the day, dogs, children, and chickens run for their lives.

As we discussed, I broached to James the subject of joining him the next time he sees our brother in Monk Sherborne. He was as doubtful as he was surprised. He asked that we wait. He will go again in several weeks. He wishes to raise the subject with the Culhams, as well as to see if George remembers the rest of his family. He wishes to ascertain whether our coming with him, or possibly separately, would cause a disturbance for that family. There is Thomas to consider, as well.

I even offered your suggestion, that Cass or I go alone with him, but he demurred. I admit to disappointment; now that I have opened my mind to the possibility, I find myself rather eager to see my lost brother.

On the subject of our Godmersham royalty, my brother Edward implies that his preference would be to slowly—over years—shift his interests from Kent to Hampshire. I had not realized that the Knights own more land around Steventon and Chawton than they do in Kent, so a return to his home county would make sense in many ways. Godmersham, however, is far more luxurious than the Great House here, and the former is where his benefactor lives and where Elizabeth has borne and raised her boisterous brood. Edward must therefore tread lightly at any thought of a move. He wishes me to say nothing about it to her or his children. For now, he speaks of the necessity of coming to Chawton more often as a "man of business" engaged in farming and timber. Already owning several houses in Chawton, each one within walking distance of the Great House, he has let it be known to Cassandra and me that he might one day offer one to our mother. The news is not to be given her, lest anticipation spoil her enjoyment of Southampton. It could be months or years before a vacancy arises. I would not be opposed if a similar situation were to arise at Hants, with your mother only a mile away instead of eight or ten. Of course, she would need a carriage to come up the hill to harangue us, walking being the resort of the poor and desperate.

I have held unhappy news in reserve—one is never sure whether to begin with it, and put a pall on everything after; or close with it, and leave the reader sad.

Elizabeth comes from a large family. With her many relatives coming and going, and our few trips to Godmersham, I cannot recall whether you ever met her youngest brother, Brook George, known as George. Like Frank and Charles, he joined the Royal Navy. Elizabeth learned just before she came here that he had been wounded in battle and taken ashore. It has now been confirmed that this fine young man, a bare three and twenty, has died of his wounds. You can imagine the shock for Elizabeth and her family—he was more of a brother to the older children than an uncle.

For the first day or two, I failed to respond with the compassion I normally feel for someone who has suffered the loss of a loved one. I strove to make my behavior *as sympathetic as possible so that my moral indifference was not exposed. I struggled in my private moments to understand my inability to relate. I concluded that it must do with the wealth and position of the Bridges and Knight families. Now, if someone had died of disease or ordinary accident, I would have been entirely supportive. But the Austens have made the Navy a career out of necessity and have demonstrated superiority in the performance of its duties. It has been our only claim to achievement and fame—when "Austen" could appear in the chronicles on equal footing with the most respected families in the land. (Or "Austin" as it is regularly misspelled in the notices!) It is at the heart and soul of our generation, the only thing that might bring us renown. If Frank and Charles continue to advance, there is the possibility, however slight, that our name will be written in the annals of history—the next Nelson! A dream, I know.*

It is this—the central importance of the Navy to our lives—that provides the contrast to Elizabeth's family. Their George entered the Navy just a few years ago—a man, not a lad of twelve or fourteen like my brothers. This laggardness caused me to think of his commitment as an afterthought for a well-to-do Bridges, as if he were playing at this career for sport, a dilettante rather than a professional. Yet, he was the youngest of half a dozen sons, with neither the title of the oldest nor the calling to the clergy of the rest. Though of *wealth, he did not* have *wealth. He had no more prospects than Frank or Charles—or even Lovelace. Would any of us have been content to accept a modest competence from a father while living a life of indolence?*

In fact, George admired my brothers; he asked about them regularly. It is likely their success in the Navy and the place it has provided them in the world shaped his own decision to join. He did no more than seek useful and honorable employment in the world, a chance to prove himself. Why should I begrudge him a path that might prove his worth and bring him honor? Why would I consider a naval career as exclusive to my family? Would his achievements cause my brothers' stars to shine less brightly?

Elizabeth is as stunned by the death of her youngest brother, as I would be by Charles'. The equivalence of the two situations should have been enough to make me weep, but I did not feel until I was reminded that George served as a lieutenant on Frank's old ship, the Canopus! *I shuddered to realize that Frank himself had walked the same quarterdeck; that it could have easily been his blood spilled on the oaken planks instead of George's. Then, and only then, did my heart open to my dear sister-in-law. Must tragedy be personal to be understood? Refusing to recognize another's misfortune is a form of jealousy. I am adult enough to admit that failing.*

I was left to wonder at the condition of the ship. Frank had spoken of its difficulty in handling—crazily, he said—its need for complete refitting after two hard years at sea. Do you remember Frank's complaints about the condition of the St. Albans *when he took his new command? It is another older vessel that had been taken in for repairs, yet he had to write forceful letters to all the principal officers and commissioners in His Majesty's Navy to make it seaworthy for his India assignment. Would the new captain of the* Canopus *have had the credibility or courage to fight that hard? Had young George put aboard a leaky crate because a contractor had put more money into his pocket than into the ship?*

I hope this latest unhappy family connection to the name George does not mean that it is now cursed. ...

—With that—

A return to more pleasant thoughts—

The entire family sends their love and best wishes. We will remain at Chawton for another week or so, after which the entourage will shuffle down to Southampton. This is where you should plan to pick me up once your mother is fully settled.

The baby and I do miss you terribly. When one of my brothers comes near, George first responds happily, then with displeasure as he realizes it is not whom he expected. He turns to me with a look of disdain as if I have tricked him. ...

Y^r loving wife,

Jane
Chawton

———

7 September 1807

Dearest wife

I was sorry to hear of Elizabeth's loss. I do not remember meeting that brother, but I know how—in a good way—you mothered young Charles, and I have no doubt she felt the same protectiveness. The war was bound to strike the family directly at one time or another. There are too many uncles and cousins and brothers in service for the odds not to catch up with us. The longer the war drags on, the greater the risk becomes. Though I know it is not the best for their careers, I am well satisfied that Frank and Charles are serving where there are apt to be few engagements. As I said when we were waiting to hear about Frank at Trafalgar, I would rather your brothers come home poor and unacknowledged than martyred heroes. It was a shock to me to read of George's position on the Canopus. *I cannot imagine how the news must have affected you.*

Please do not be too hard on yourself about your initial reaction to the news of this young man. You had just experienced the most terrible recognition about your own child. And had experienced the most miserable mistreatment at the hands of my mother. Do not confuse numbness with a lack of feeling. We all have only so much to give. Your spirits were depleted. It was nothing more than that.

95

Like you, I have been casting about in my mind for a suitable dwelling for my mother that would be close enough but not too close. The only one on any of our properties would be the steward's house, but I would not turn out Mr. Fletcher for Mrs. Dennis, for too many reasons to count. There was the one large Tudor house in the village, but inspection showed general disrepair and too much damage from a leaking roof. It would take months for restoration, and its proximity to Hants would lead too many gossips to understand the reason for her relocation.

Mother herself set off—alone, at her insistence—to inspect several homes in Basingstoke. She found one she likes, and I am finishing the lease as we write. Like Mrs. Knight, she has finally recognized that her state of mind, as well as ours, will be improved if she lives elsewhere. Besides, the main reason for her to remain at Hants was to promote the interests of her grandson. She now sees that role as irrelevant. ... It is, as she would think of it, a respectable distance from us, one that she herself might have insisted upon. The building is traditional and very stylish, in a matronly way. Painters are at work. Footmen are cleaning. She rejected, with either real or mock horror, my offer to install gas lamps. I am finding it more difficult to ascertain her actual revulsion from her fake. If one practices upset enough, it must become ingrained.

Mother has already chosen her carriage; I could not grudge her the nicest one. Judging from the pile of furniture being positioned for departure and the number of vehicles being arranged for transport, she will not stint in making her new accommodations comfortable. Mr. Hanrahan assures me, however, that she will not make off with more than half the furniture or more than fifty of our servants.

I will arrange to fetch you from Southampton when she is established, likely in two to three weeks. As we had discussed, I was planning to stop at Thor Place to show you the progress on the locomotive, but I no longer believe it would be worthwhile. We are still seeing too much damage to the rails. After thoroughly reviewing the results, Mr. Trevithick told me he did not believe it was possible to move ahead unless we could substantially reduce the weight of the machine. With the thickness of rails now required, the cast iron cannot be cooled quickly and consistently enough to solidify the melt. He rode up to show me new designs that reduce the number and complexity of parts. The cylinder is now to be mounted vertically and will drive a pair of wheels directly with the connecting rods—no flywheel or gearing. It's difficult to explain without your being able to see an illustration, but you wanted me to give you all the details. Suffice it to say there is nothing worth seeing now. Trevithick believes he will have the new prototype ready early in the new year.

We will still plan to see Mr. Knollman's new textile manufactory. Even without a stop at Thor Place, we might still be best to go direct and spend the night on the road. Hants is just enough out of the way to make the detour inconvenient. I think you'll be pleased with the new system that's been installed. With no concerns about weight for a fixed machine, the installation of the new engine driving the looms has gone smoothly.

Y^r loving husband,

Ashton
Hants House

Chapter 14

"Hampshire lacks industry not simply because it has no coal but because it has no water."

Ashton spoke teasingly, as if presenting a charade. Abigail blushed because the master was speaking to her rather than to his wife. He had been instructing the women on industrial matters during their journey to the remodeled woolen mill near Sherfield on Loddon. Jane, having listened to this disquisition before, was not as attentive as an expansive husband requires; consequently, he showered explanations of the latest developments in business and science on the rapt if overwhelmed maid.

Jane looked up from George, who previously had rotated among the three willing adults in the carriage and now sprawled, soundly asleep, his head on his mother's lap and his feet on Abigail's. "Now you must ask," she said to the maid, " 'Mr. Dennis, how can you say we have no water when we are making brisk time along the river?' "

Ashton blushed nearly as brightly as Abigail. "I speak to her as a person fully capable of understanding ideas," he protested. Jane's glance caused him to throttle his enthusiasm, however. Any man in his mid-twenties might be forgiven for trying to impress an intelligent and attractive lass, but this one, in addition to being young and susceptible, was also in his employ.

"Is it because the water is flat?" Abigail asked, looking out the window. The carriage was making better time than the sluggish River Loddon, which they had picked up at its source at Basingstoke. "There's not enough—what did you call it, *drop?*—to power a really large machine?"

Ashton roared with laughter and clapped his hands. "There, my dear," he said. "This one is paying attention!" Jane gave him a look, but that was for fear of his waking George; then, remembering that the noise would have no such effect, she sank back, crestfallen. Ashton blanched twice, the first for having made enough noise to wake a child, the second for having caused his wife distress of a sadly different sort. She shook her head, however, and pulled herself into a positive mind: "It will not be the last time," she said. "We can both be forgiven old habits. Now, continue with your education of our fledgling engineer."

"I believe I am done. She answered correctly." He had been describing to her the historic need to site mills along fast-moving streams so that water power could be used to grind grains and flour and, much later, to power manufactories. The Dennis woolen mill would utilize the next advancement, steam power. Steam-driven mills existed in the north—Boulton and Watt again—but none had been tried in the southern counties with their dawdling rivers. Ashton's eventual goal was to establish a mill untethered to any water source.

Abigail asked several more questions, her dark eyes lit with pleasure, more for the understanding they all had reached than for correctly surmising the answer to Ashton's interrogation. Jane's pleasant challenge to her husband meant that there was nothing to fear from Ashton's playful address. A maid must worry if the husband were forward in his wife's absence; or, if he spoke in her presence, and the wife remained sullenly silent. This interchange meant that Abigail was under Jane's protection and that Ashton expected no less. He could entertain and educate a willing young woman while keeping a respectful distance; she could enjoy her employer's intelligence and his generous inclinations without any danger; and Jane could take a few minutes to herself now and again while observing their interplay with amusement.

The discussion reminded Jane: "Why are we building a rail-road when we have the Basingstoke Canal?" The canal, which they had passed earlier, took a more easterly wander toward the Thames.

"Same problem. Not enough fall. Oxen must pull the load in both directions. When steam-boats are perfected, it will not be large enough. Cheaper to build a rail-road than to widen a canal. " ... One goes *up* to London," he mused, "by heading *down* the river. Curious."

"For a man who struggles with words, you are certainly enamored with them," Jane replied.

"Like a man around wasps. One is more alert when one has been stung."

They passed the largest mills on this stretch, two brick structures around Old Basing, after which the river paused like an asthmatic pensioner, for it seemed to have forgotten the way to the Thames. The Loddon had nearly as many mills as mileposts. The network of dams and weirs had the contradictory effect of speeding up the stream to power the wheels while also creating slack water farther behind.

Shaded areas beside the road, Jane was pleased to see, were full of snake's head, a benevolent little flower, purple and speckled, that was undeserving of its sinister name. The hay meadows had been cut and given over to grazing cattle; only the cows knew where the meadows ended and the peat moors began. They passed pond after pond cultivating watercress, hoverflies caressing them in a cloud.

"If you were nicer to me, I might buy the stocking mill in Wokingham," Ashton said, apropos of nothing. His eyes wide, he pantomimed stroking a smooth fabric. "*Silk*." He carried on in exaggerated, seductive tones: "Or, even more enticingly—the paper mill at Arborfield!" The maid, who had turned away again in full blush, stifled a laugh. "Every fine lady needs a paper mill, don't you think, Miss Abigail? At least one who writes—"

—Jane kicked his shin—

"—who writes enough letters to fill a library."

From time to time Jane had to remind Ashton that her work must remain private until *she* was ready for its disclosure. Not even the housekeeper was exactly aware of her fiction, only that she was often at her desk long after the accounts should have been balanced. This Austen foray had related to Ashton's mother, but he regularly encouraged others, possibly thinking that being away from the house would give her more time to write. It would—were she not carrying a baby along with her writing materials.

"You are the lord of this household," Jane said, "not the court jester." Yet she could not begrudge her husband's boyish spirits. There was the pleasure of their being together again after nearly a month's separation; his anticipation at showing her his latest adventure, which he himself had not seen since the final installation; the knowledge that his mother was now ensconced at Basingstoke, her defiance at a blessed distance. They had passed within a quarter of a mile of her new abode but forgot to call in.

"You will learn, Abigail, that when Mr. Dennis is most jocular, he is most serious. This mill is designed to provide jobs for the people. As you have understood, only steam gives us the opportunity to make the mill large enough to achieve that goal."

Abigail turned to Ashton as if Jane's remark was a prelude to a speech. "We shall empty the poor houses!" he said. Embarrassed at the self-promotion, he added: "Or try."

They saw fishermen plunking bait through sun-shimmered insects into green-sheened water. Maggots, she wondered in regard to the bait, or worms? She had occasionally fished as a child, though more commonly she observed Henry and Frank matching wiles with what Henry called their "piscine opponents." Today, one young man, sitting on the opposite bank, waved a proud string of fish for their appreciation. Another boy, on this side, sat quietly, waiting for the sign of a bite. "If he is after chub," she said, "he should fish farther out. Frank said they loiter where the water begins to move."

"At least he's in the shadows," Ashton said. "I never understood people who would stand on the bank at midday—sun at their back—and wonder why they caught no fish."

"A blind man assumes sightlessness is the rule," Jane said.

They rocked quietly with the carriage for a while. When the maid was distracted by the outside view, Ashton pulled a face and feigned another stroke of luxurious silk.

"I wish the mill had been done last year," Abigail said into the quiet. "Two of my brothers had to join the Army."

"I would encourage any man to join the military," Ashton said, "but not just to fill his belly. I hope to change that—I do." After thought, he asked: "Were they deployed to Copenhagen?"

"No, sir. Their regiment is still at home."

"Good. I wish them well."

"Thank you, sir."

"Only a few went ashore—including Wellesley's troops," Ashton said to Jane. "Nothing like bombarding a defenseless city to compel surrender."

Jane nodded. The news of the capture of the Danish ships had been greeted with patriotic fervor in England, though more recent reports of the thousands of civilian casualties had tempered celebrations. The Danes, after all, were not at war with England; they were simply caught between the two large belligerents.

Below the Hartley mill, beyond the point where the Lyde River added its meager ration of water to the Loddon, Ashton pointed out the diversions that built up the head of water to their mill. At the same time, they heard a rhythmic thumping, like a giant stamping its foot. They had no clear view of the cause, but over the trees lining the river Jane could see great puffs of black smoke—she feared a fire almost instantaneous with the realization that she was seeing the steam engine at work. The noise grew louder, as if they were being warned away.

When the carriage halted in the sweep where they were preceded by cargo wagons, Ashton stepped down to assist Jane once she gently disengaged from George. The thumping was worse, enough to worry the horses. The carriage, carrying Abigail and the sleeping baby, was directed to wait in a shady spot beside the river, a short distance back the way they had come.

Mr. Knollman greeted them in his formal but friendly manner. He pointed out the original mill, which had made coarse products such as grain sacks and workmen's garments, along with its companion fulling mill, which beat and cleaned the wool, shrinking it with water to thicken the fibers. He showed them earlier expansions as well as the improvements he had recently overseen. The mill was at least three times its original size, from possibly hundreds of years before. The steam engine had its own building attached to the back of the mill. "We'll stay away from there," he said. "Too loud." Neat stacks of wood were a complement, lined up like rows of tents. For now, the mill ran on firewood rather than coal, another effort to employ the locals and obtain the goodwill of landowners. Until the rail-road came, they would not be able to obtain enough coal for steady use.

Where the river curved right, Mr. Knollman pointed out new cottages to house workers from more distant parts. Among these were a one-room school and a small chapel for Sunday worship. They would view the little community later. The company had also leased lands to ensure that workers' families could graze animals, as the estate-holders had enclosed the commons.

When Mr. Knollman opened the heavy door to take them into the mill, they were battered by a barrage of sound. The steam engine pounded, wooden frames slammed, shook, and rattled, the entire building vibrated with noise. When Jane covered her ears, the noise felt like a detonation against the skin, one explosion after another accompanied by an ongoing deep vibration that caused one's teeth to ache. Mr. Knollman quickly walked them through the large weaving room and the smaller carding rooms, shouting out the operations over the din. They had to take an irregular path, evading metal machinery that lunged for them and wooden frames that slammed forward and back and up and down. Through this maze of perilously fast equipment, the employees—mostly women—worked at the looms, handling whatever tasks the apparatus did not, while a select few moved about to free jammed mechanisms. It was late afternoon, and Jane could read the exhaustion on their faces—they would have been at work since dawn. What if fatigue caused one of them to momentarily lose her concentration? Under several of the most frenetic apparatuses, Jane saw a scurrying underneath—young boys and girls dashing in and out, grabbing tufts of loose threads, unsticking fabric that had caught in a machine, treating as a game of dodge the most dangerous of activities: serving as human grease to keep the machinery of business moving. Noting her astonishment, Mr. Knollman hustled them through ancillary rooms, where in a slightly less abusive atmosphere more women, assisted by children, pieced garments together. Then the visitors were out of the mill, their sense of hearing disturbed by the sudden cessation of aural assault.

"Ashton!"

"Say nothing—we will talk. Mr. Knollman, thank you for the demonstration. We must—"

Mr. Knollman removed his hat in a gesture of chagrin and addressed them both. "Unsettling—I know."

"Unsettling is not the word, sir!"

"Jane, let him speak."

"Noise is a measure of inefficiency, Mrs. Dennis. I have been in manufacturing for many years. I have seen wondrous improvements. But to leap forward is also to fall back. Almost always, the first generation of a new machine is worse than the last generation of the machine it replaces. It takes three times to get anything right. I have found no way around this predicament. That is the sum of my experience with mechanisms."

"Then skip this horror and move to the next!" Jane cried.

"If only we could. It is impossible to know how a machine really functions until it is on the floor. Only then can we see its flaws. Things that look elegant in design turn out to be complicated or dangerous. Parts do not work as they should—break too often—and we must make additions and corrections—more controls, brakes, guides. The added complexity introduces new failures. It is a miracle we can make new apparatuses work at all the first time round! But we learn, we simplify, we improve. Eliminating one set of problems, however, uncovers still more. We repeat the process over and over. By the time we can enjoy the full potential of the machinery—and operate the mill long enough to recoup its costs—someone has come up with a new idea and we start all over again."

"Engineers sound more and more like Sisyphus pointlessly pushing his rock uphill."

"We feel those frustrations, yes, but, unlike the rock—we do see improvements in time. Very substantial ones."

Mr. Knollman bowed, restored his hat, and turned from them with the expression of a man who is guilty of a crime he does not know how not to commit.

Jane and Ashton walked toward the carriage. They stepped off the lane to let a wool-laden wagon pass. "You cannot allow this to go on," she said. "These people need to be working out of doors—in the fresh air."

"They used to. And they starved. I pay them well!"

"Not enough!"

"I am doing all I can, Jane. Everything to improve the lot of my people."

"Children work here! Do you not comprehend the danger? They could lose their fingers!"

"We will work on that." Ashton's frown showed that he understood the inadequacy of his response. "We'll make enhancements. Do more to protect the young. A few things were obvious even to me in our quick walk through the mill."

"Hire the fathers and let the mothers stay home with their children."

"Their husbands were killed or disabled by the war. That's why I built this place—to give the women work!"

"This is what comes when you take God out of your equations—treating human beings like cogs in your machines! *Mercy,*

Ashton, Mercy! There must be a choice between starving on a farm and working to death in a mill!"

"*When you figure out the answer—tell the world!*"

<hr />

Jane stared out the window of the carriage, a knot in her stomach. Her frustration was more intense for having no outlet, for she could see very well the contradictions surrounding Ashton's efforts. His intentions were humane; his methods wrong or precipitate. Was Mr. Knollman correct? Was there no way to improve something without taking painful, preliminary measures that were often worse than what came before? She had never operated any machine more complicated than a churn. She had never designed anything more intricate than a plot. When a story went awry, one had to back up and revise—frustrating labor, to be sure. But altering a mental edifice was not the same as dismantling and rebuilding a factory at a cost of thousands of pounds—and putting employees out of work for months. She could not be angry at Ashton for circumstances that seemed intractable.

She was further torn by the anguish he himself displayed, sitting silent across from her—holding back further explanations, she could see, in the recognition that more rationalization would bring more recrimination. But they had been apart for nearly a month, and she could not allow an argument to nullify all that Ashton had done for their marriage, his protection of her and her child from the viciousness of his mother. While she had spent weeks resting in the bosom of her family, he had endured daily conflict with Mrs. Dennis to enforce the decision Jane needed most.

In the confines of the carriage, there was also the effect on Abigail, who had seen them off all cheerfulness and smiles and saw them return grimly at odds.

They were not two miles down the road when Jane took Ashton's hand. "It will be much improved on our next visit," she said. "Of that I have no doubt. Nothing will motivate your engineers more than knowing that the mistress might involve herself in their affairs." Her tentative smile indicated that she understood the complexity of the situation and would afford her husband some measure of grace.

"It might be some time before that visit is advisable." His frown of regret acknowledged her offering, promised that he would throw himself into the task of improving the manufactory as rapidly as possible—but cautioned of the difficulties involved.

"As long as you make it a priority." The timbre of Jane's voice made it clear that she had not withdrawn her concerns, merely put them into abeyance. Time was the solution, they both understood; the argument now was whether that time might be months or years. To reassure the now nervous maid, Jane said: "Abigail, Mr. Dennis found his operation was not as advanced as we had hoped. We were both sorely disappointed, but he has pledged to improve it as quickly as he can. Now, tell me, husband—beyond the obvious—what is new at home?"

"If it is possible for a large country house to exhale a huge sigh of relief, Hants has done so. Not only because sunshine now blazes where my mother's shadow used to loom. But also because of the departure of those older servants who had helped impose the *Ancien Régime*. I calculate that Mr. Hanrahan and Mrs. Lundeen are giddier than you." Realizing he had said too much about his mother in front of the maid, he fixed a faux glare upon her. "Abigail, you will not repeat what I have said to anyone, for we will trace it back. And you will be packed off to Basingstoke too."

Abigail's laughter enabled Jane to relax.

This is what she had missed while away. After all that time in a female establishment, she desperately required thoughts outside the commonplace of a household, outside the bright but conventional judgments of her relations. As the collapse of Mrs. Dennis's musty reign allowed Hants to take a collective breath of fresh air, she needed to escape Southampton and enjoy Ashton's bracing and outrageous observations. She needed to think when challenged, to laugh at absurdity, to show the agility of mind that comes from the interplay with another who is as happy to exasperate as to offer a new point of view, who sees his duty as shaking her out of a propriety that easily shaded into prudery. She needed, that is, to re-establish intellectual and emotional intimacies with her mate after their weeks apart, after the confrontation about the baby's health and the restructuring of family arrangements, to re-forge the bonds of marriage that had gone unattended.

They spoke of other matters of the estate—the latest cutting of hay, the child of a first-time mother safely delivered, the health of an aged widow (it seemed to be holding). Her smile grew as they approached their home and took the sharp turn that began the upward climb. A rush of memories elevated her spirits: her youthful visits for the balls, her dash to Alethea when they feared for Ashton's safety in the war; her first entrance as the mistress, when the last half-mile rose with both power and fear like the climax of a symphony; and now, her arrival in peace, with no residual worries about matters dearest to her heart. At the home safely cleared for her and her child.

After being greeted by Mr. Hanrahan and Mrs. Lundeen—if not giddy then well on the way—Jane and Ashton remained outside in the sun as the baggage was being unloaded. They both felt the need to savor the moment, for once they crossed the threshold the change would be accomplished and anticipation would soon solidify into a new but ordinary status quo. She drew her husband aside. "I know you care about your people. I know you respect my beliefs and will do all you can to accommodate them. These are some of the reasons I love you as I do."

Chapter 15

Normally, the cook would come to the madam to discuss the menus, but Jane enjoyed the walk across the bright chambers of the house to the warm and cheery kitchen. She enjoyed the reaction of George, her hip-riding escort, to Mrs. Shelley's effusive greeting, and to the kitchen help who welcomed him as their special charm. The walk became a weekly activity.

It was Jane who, nearly a year ago, had crossed the divide to establish a level of familiarity with the girls. On that day, as a pregnant woman overwhelmed with the responsibilities of a great house, she had needed to reconnect with ordinary people—as she still viewed herself, a person without airs or pretensions—with the ordinary routines she herself had followed before her marriage. She had never repeated those intimacies, but her continuing informality reaffirmed the humanity of the girls and reassured them that that first morning had not been an error in judgment. Now, after enthusiastic but respectful greetings, the staff returned to their work.

Along with the pleasure of the kitchen and her conversations on future dinners with Mrs. Shelley came the reminder that here she had caused her unborn child to jump by clanging the metal spoon on the metal bowl. Everything wretched about her boy seemed to resonate with those metal implements, giving Jane the impression that George's deafness had originated here, in the warm bosom of Mrs. Shelley's aprons. Fortunately, each happy visit reduced

Jane's continuing if illogical guilt at having been so wrong—so vain—about George's hearing. Today, her concerns about her child were more immediate. He had been running a fever for two days, and he protested beyond soothing when his mother sought to leave him to come here. Today, the visit was as much about helping his tranquility as it was hers.

When the planning was done, George accepted a soft treat that magically materialized from Mrs. Shelley. The girls returned to watch, pleased for him and expectant for their commensurate shares upon Jane's departure. It was fitting that the spoon, which had once launched her into a panic, had metamorphized into a vessel of pleasure for her boy. After George had licked off the concoction of honey and softened bread, she played hide-and-seek with the spoon. It was a game he never tired of. When she stopped, he signaled "more, more," which in this context was interpreted to mean "keep playing!"

At last, when she had convinced him they really must go, George began to try to stand on her arm and push off. This movement she recognized as a common one brought on by a diet that was steadily growing in complexity. Quickly saying her goodbyes, she stepped into the hall where George could relieve his distress privately. When the cramping did not subside, she began to wonder about other remedies. At that moment, however, his arms and legs pulled in; he squeaked as his breath was squeezed out of him; his head and eyes rolled back. His body attacked itself.

Jane's flight across the full width of the house was a tragicomic repeat of the year before—the same footman detouring out of her path, the same maid with linen sidestepping into an alcove, Mrs. Lundeen hurrying along behind at a safe distance, available through her uncanny sense for whatever help might be needed. For the entire length of her run, Jane's tears spattered the floor like transparent blood. She burst into the library, calling her husband's name in a tortured voice, heedless that she was interrupting his meeting with Mr. Fletcher. Ashton rose and started toward her, his face ashen. Simultaneously, the steward removed himself to the far bookshelves.

"Seizure!" she cried.

———～～～———

The best of England's physicians began a pilgrimage to Hants, repeating the same wise apprehension of the symptoms and the same rituals of examination, dispensing the same sage though largely unaccepted medical advice. No, they would not bleed George, even in reduced proportion to his size. No, they would not blister his back with miniature cupping. No, they would not treat him with emetics or purgatives without proof of the need and efficacy. When one priest of the medicinal arts recommended that they take the baby to a resort for a regimen of sea bathing, Ashton dragged the distinguished physician out to the pond on a cold, bleak late October day and threatened to toss him in.

"How would it feel?" he asked, corralling the worthy until he replied. "To go in today?"

"Dreadful," said the physician. "As one would expect."

"You tell me that we should not take George out in the rain for fear of his catching cold"—a reference to one of the precautions earlier submitted—"yet we are to plunge him repeatedly into the freezing ocean?"

"The sea has recuperative powers," the man said, with considerably less assurance in front of a pond than in front of a fire.

"Go—before I drown you like a rat!"

Chapter 16

During the many weeks in which the physicians shuttled in and out, George's health took a decided turn for the worse. He had always been robust. At six months, one could begin to speculate that he might one day proudly rival his father in size and strength. At eight months, he was crawling with an energy to show they would soon be chasing him about. Now, at ten months, the on and off seizures changed everything. George slowly lost interest in everything around him. At times, he would not eat. The food would simply sit in his mouth as if he did not know what to do with it. At other times, he ate ravenously in compensation. The inconsistency of feeding caused Jane to attempt to reinstitute his earlier, more vigorous schedule at the breast. His marked lack of interest, either for sustenance or comfort, alarmed her on many levels. She was unable to relieve her own anxiety and worry through compensatory grief, for much of her emotional energy went to console the young nurse, who feared that George's setbacks were bound to be her fault.

Whether George's seizures were the result of the fever that rose and subsided, or whether these were the opening spasms of the epilepsy that ran in the family, no physician could be sure. For some reason, the seizures increased with his teething. When Eliza came down with Henry, she told Jane that a similar thing had happened with her son. The doctors, however, would have none of it. There was no credible relationship between whatever was causing his convulsions and his teeth. The whole idea was ludicrous. The experience of two mothers was irrelevant. Jane, meanwhile, had the insane notion that her son's teeth were growing upside down, the sharp daggers being the source of his excruciating pain.

Whereas before he had greeted the women in the morning with bouncing energy in his crib, alert and ready for the day, on too many mornings George was to be found on his back, looking about in confusion. Upon realizing he must be suffering seizures in the night, Jane extended the now erratic nightly nursing periods, rotating vigils with Abigail. In these dark moments, she worried about her ability as a mother. It was axiomatic that if a mother loved her child deeply enough and did everything possible for him, all would be well. That George, instead, suffered terribly, left a sense of inadequacy that no amount of objective thought could overcome. Every cross word with her husband—inevitable in their distracted state—struck her further as a rebuke for the neglect of her duties as a wife. She knew that, even with maids and nurses, the first year was often hard. She had seen new babies pull parents apart, but she had also seen other couples—Edward and Elizabeth sprang to mind—who had child after child with joyful regularity. Ashton apologized whenever they had a spat, even when it was not his fault; yet the loss of their easy companionability, however understandable given the baby's debilitation, left her adrift. She knew that a conversation with Ashton might dispel such fears, but she did not speak because in the light of day she was afraid that whatever she might say in this vein could sound not like a concern but like an accusation.

Ashton took his own watch over George or stayed awake with Jane. Occasionally they talked and occasionally they watched the fire. A few times, Ashton tried to work, but fatigue precluded productivity. She asked him about improvements in the mill, but waved away his answer before he began. Exhaustion muffled whatever concerns about the struggling classes she ought to have. She did let him expostulate on the newest concepts in natural philosophy and business. He turned out to be interested in a new form of musket that had spiral grooves in the barrels—"rifling"—to improve its accuracy. If someone could produce the weapons with sufficiently close tolerances, these "rifles" would render muskets obsolete. Ashton was certain that Mr. Bramah, their quality-control professional, was the man for the job. Muddled as she was from fatigue, even Jane knew that they had neither the men nor the money for an enterprise so out of sorts with their other projects, and told him so.

Nor did she wish him to be one of those men who became wealthy by manufacturing weapons. Though it invariably did, war should not produce riches. When he pointed out that nearly *every* business of the Dennis family was related to the war, she countered that their products supported soldiers in the field with food and clothing; they were not implements designed to kill. "I appreciate your moral aversion," he said, "but nothing helps a soldier in the field more than being able to kill the enemy before the enemy kills him." Jane countered again that if his experts could not produce a *cannon* that did not explode, it was unlikely they could produce a proper *rifle*. Truer than he would admit, Ashton conceded, then asked—"What about a brewery? Henry has brought forth a proposal. Your banker brother wants to invest in beer. And you think I'm scattered!"

The most sensible advice about George came from Dr. Parry, whom they were finally able to bring over from Bath. Though celebrated among the fashionable, he had also been recommended by the sensible, including their friends, the astronomers Dr. Herschel and his sister Miss Herschel. In addition, Ashton remembered the physician favorably from a lucid talk on sheep breeding at an agriculture meeting the previous year. Dr. Parry heard their words; unlike the others, he seemed to listen as opposed to waiting out their description of the baby's ills as a prelude to issuing a predetermined set of instructions. Dr. Parry had a way of inclining and turning his head, so that he did not look directly into one's eyes but peered sideways over the bridge of his nose, asking questions in a skeptical but not imperious way. His parrot-like mannerism seemed a way of slipping up on a problem unseen.

He told them they were doing everything right—at least, all that any prudent parents could. Soft food, nursing as he would, fresh air, regular schedule of rest and exercise—these were just the thing. Parry's advice seemed more to calm them than to aid George, for there was little directly he could recommend. No doctor could tell them whether the seizures were febrile in nature or endemic, but the source made no difference, for there was no specific countermeasure. "Care and comfort," the doctor said. "And time. The child may improve, or the symptoms may manifest in something treatable. Watch and wait—I wish I could offer more."

He further advised them that the approach of winter was bringing with it the usual onset of virulent disease. Typhus and scarlet fever were taking hold in outlying districts, from where they would ramify to strangle London. Measles was always a problem, and smallpox continued a scourge in the many areas where vaccinations were still uncommon. He suggested that they keep George away from crowds, limit the number of staff who went into the village, and further isolate those people from anyone who might encounter the boy. The doctor also strongly recommended that they vaccinate him against smallpox, which he was prepared to do immediately.

"Absolutely," Ashton said.

"No!" Jane said. "Rather—doctor, would you excuse us while we discuss this matter? I am not convinced vaccination makes sense. Not for our boy—not now."

"I can explain the procedure and the benefits."

"I appreciate both—I am versed in the subject. The matter, however, is between me and Mr. Dennis, not between us and you."

"I understand," Dr. Parry said. "It is important that both parents agree on a course of action." He withdrew with a bow.

"You know vaccination works," Ashton began. "Mrs. Lefroy led a campaign to inoculate the children of the parish."

"Mrs. Lefroy was an insufferable meddler. She risked the lives of children to promote herself as the center of knowledge."

That her words were stingingly unfair did not make it possible for her to arrest their speaking. Too much was happening, too fast. Too many puzzling, damaging changes in George's health—too much unexpected and confusing decline. Too much contradictory advice—too much absurdity packaged as knowledge—too much unknown about his condition—too little known about any solution. If only they could jump ahead a hundred years to the marvelous cures Ashton promised would exist—but these tantalizing possibilities were as far beyond their reach as the moon.

So much to consider—so many avenues—opportunities—possibilities—and yet—

—Nothing—

This nothingness seeped into her mind, filled it with black ink, leaving her unable to comprehend the cumulative impact of all these unknowns. Confusions and contradictions collapsed her will. It was an easy thing to say—her precious child was sick and no one knew how to make him better. Yet it was difficult to think these thoughts, and impossible to feel. The result was that the one action which might make sense seemed the least conceivable. The most measured and reasonable conduct—*reckless.*

"It works, Jane. We don't know how, but it's been proved repeatedly."

"We know it has worked a few times on a few children—older children, mostly. They were all healthy. George is too ill to be vaccinated. His weak constitution will not support it."

"He's too weak and ill *not* to be. Smallpox kills one in three—that *one* will surely be a weak child—our child."

"Only the insane could believe that sticking the poison from one disease into a baby would protect it from another."

"D-d-damn it, Jane!" He stood there, so angry and frustrated he could not say more.

"You will *not* raise your voice to me!"

"I will do whatever I please to protect my son!"

"He is *my* son. I carried him, birthed him, nursed him. You stood by looking proud."

"I have given way to you more than any husband alive. I have given you freedom, let you overrule my wishes. I am laughed at by other men, I assure you—but I have not been deterred. I have done all I could to treat you as an equal."

"Yet on the most important issue we have ever faced—you do as you wish."

"On the most important issue—you are making no sense! Have faith!"

"My faith is in the power of God—not the conceit of man."

"God gave us brains—we need to use them! It will work, I assure you."

"You parrot the claims of others. You have no direct knowledge yourself. You are too impatient to actually study. You defer to others who may not know any more than you. It is too great a risk. If you love me, Ashton, you will listen to me now. We have no idea how cowpox will affect a child who suffers seizures—who has a fever!"

"He has no fever now! Enough! If you are afraid—I will act on his behalf."

"I will not let you."

"You have neither the authority nor the ability to stop me. On this one matter, Jane, *I* will decide what is right."

When she moved to block his way, he picked her up, put her aside like a ladder-back chair, gathered the doctor in the hall, and stood beside him until the vaccination was complete. Jane retired to the bedroom, where she threw the washing pitcher into the fireplace out of frustration at the danger to her child.

———

As a conciliatory gesture, Ashton agreed for them to return to Southampton during the most dangerous months. Hants House was within the outer eddies of the swirling cesspool of infection that was London, whereas the port town, thirty miles farther south, had the bracing winds that blew pestilence away and the salt water that Jane thought of as a natural preventive. In this instance, it was Ashton who felt that the action—travel in dirty weather—might be detrimental to the boy's health, and she agreed to turn back at any sign of trouble. George, however, seemed no more bothered by travel than by remaining home. Indeed, the gentle rocking of the carriage seemed to soothe him. He was soon soundly—peacefully—asleep. After joining Cassandra at Manydown for a few days with friends, they continued. Wherever they settled too long, though, the baby's seizures increased in number and duration. This aggravation caused Ashton to lament that he must build his rail-road in a large circle around southern England so that his son could live out his life in peace through the continuous rocking of the rails.

Southampton was also where Ashton's trade expansion was under way, with wool, both raw and finished, being scheduled for delivery to Portugal and the Baltic. The shift in location enabled him to more actively supervise the changes in load and route. One day, while Ashton was tied up in meetings, and George having suffered seizures through most of the previous night, Jane found herself, almost without thinking, in a wheeled bathing machine, her baby in her arms, being gently pulled by a horse into the choppy sea. When the rear door opened and the dipper sought to coax her from the wagon down the steps into the seawater, the bracing winds shook Jane from a kind of mental slumber. She realized that the only person in the frigid water along the entire beach was the heavyset dipper, a woman whose weight acted like the insulating blubber of a whale, while she, Jane, had regained her slim form and George was already shivering in the cold. "Take us out!" she cried. "Out! Now!"

Neither Ashton nor Cassandra ever learned of her seaside undertaking, though she was hounded by guilt whenever bad weather hit the area—near-gales in January, heavy snow and wind in early February. It was as though Nature itself was meting out chastisement over Jane's irrational need to seek some kind of treatment for her son.

But they rode out the storms in the snug harbor of Southampton—nursing, encouraging, praying for her son. When the weather cleared, Jane was ready to go home. There, a short but intense frost struck Hants. She welcomed the condition enthusiastically in the belief that contagions would fare no better than people exposed to the freeze. Her common-sense view seemed to be substantiated by reports from London that the deadly winter sicknesses were breaking up along with the ice. A few days later, however, measles erupted almost simultaneously in half a dozen villages in northern Hampshire, including their own. Despite all their precautions, two of the girls in the kitchen came down with the gagging coughs, skin eruptions, and sweating fevers.

As epidemics went, this one was mild. Only a grocer and a scullery maid in the local parishes died, and no more than a dozen of the young.

Chapter 17

Mama—

I lost my Dear George Maurice at 12 o'clock last night. Pray for me, my dearest Mother, take me in your arms. Your prayers will be heard though mine were not listened to. I have lost my George, my angel George—my soul doted on him, I was wrapped up in my child. From the moment of his birth, to the fatal night it pleased God to call him, I have devoted myself to him. I am resigned to the Will of the Almighty, but my happiness is destroyed forever. My George, my adored George is gone—gone—and left me here.

Jane
Hants House

PART II

March 1808–October 1808

Chapter 18

Several weeks later, Jane and Cassandra were far out on one of their long loops across the Hants estate. All the workers kept their distance, for the walks were not a typical long-striding Austen promenade but more of a stately funeral cortege. It was that clear and mild weather of middle March that teased flowers from the moist soil and birds out of shelter. The sun, filtering through the branches, offered hypocritical cheer, for Jane felt there was never any place that deserved life less than this one did today.

"If an entire estate could weep, Hants would be flooded."

Since the baby's death, the sisters had walked, in good weather and bad. It was Jane who spoke and Cass who listened. If the older sister provided any consolation, it was not by seeking to soften the blow—occasionally, when the younger sister struck out emotionally, she absorbed the blow herself.

"Everyone tells me it is a blessing—the most despicable thing anyone can say to a mother! Why do people come pretending solace? All they want is to enjoy my pain."

The pattern was for Jane to speak, then lapse silent for several minutes as they carried on.

"Two years I had him." At Cassandra's quizzical look, Jane explained: "He was with me from the start. Nine months within my body, fourteen without."

They walked, and she spoke.

"He told me, after we found out about George's condition, that I was to be excused for feeling numb. I had no idea what numbness meant till now."

They walked more, then she spoke again:

"Little George looked so much like Ashton, I think I buried my husband too." It was not the first time Jane had said these words, and each time Cassandra gave her a sharp look.

Later, still again:

"Though I make no effort to avoid him, I find his company best when it is absent. I am not certain he feels any differently about me. I moved into my own bedroom. I am not certain he has noticed."

Jane was vaguely aware of the wide spacing of her remarks, recognizing that a thought welled up in her at some peculiar object—a tree with a sharp branch, a rock with a pointed edge, a stream with a jagged metal gate. It was as though the landmarks meant to pierce her heart, hoping to drain the anguish. Or did they call for a reckoning?

As they closed upon the house, they could see Ashton waiting for them near the stables. He paced back and forth near the rear fencing, gesticulating as part of a mental debate that, she could tell from a distance, must have to do with *them*. First the cane came up in one hand, then the other hand shot up in counterargument. She could see in his expression his remorse, his questioning of his judgment and his decisions, his desire to somehow make matters right. Back and forth Ashton went, arguing with himself, spinning on his heel with each rejoinder. No—it was not an argument. It was a plea and rejection, repeated in various forms. Nearby workers were careful not to appear to be eavesdropping, while horses registered their concern whenever a point was contended too intensely. Becoming aware of Jane and Cassandra, he abruptly ceased his pantomime, standing contrite yet defiant in the pretense that he had not been talking to himself.

Seeing Ashton there, a vital young man in his middle twenties, looking as George might have looked at the same age, she was reminded of how much of life her little boy had lost. It was a half-thought prayer or curse that wondered how a grown son might appear in place of a husband who seemed to have usurped him.

The vicinity of the stables being inappropriate for conversation, by unspoken consent they all turned toward the gardens. The rustling, civilized movements of a gentleman and two ladies, the pleasantries—however strained—about their walk, the beckoning presence of blooming flowers, might have promised a softening of what lay between them. They stopped at an intersection of several paths, at a bench next to a topiary and stone cherub. Despite his invitation, neither lady sat.

If Ashton believed that Cass would serve as a moderating influence that enabled the introduction of difficult thoughts, he was right—but not in the way he had intended. Her sister's presence gave Jane the courage to speak.

"I am going with Cassandra. Back to Southampton."

Though Cass expressed surprise, Ashton turned on the sister: "I should have known you were enrolled in the conspiracy. Every time you come, you take my wife away."

"It is the same as when you sent me away over your mother," Jane snapped. "You said there had been too much change too quickly and we needed time apart to adjust. The same is true now."

"I cannot adjust to the loss of my son by the loss of my wife! We cannot heal our wounds if one of us runs away."

"I am not running away. I am stepping away before anger overcomes us."

Ashton turned to Cass again: "You would take her away from me—I, who have loved and protected all of you!"

"I am not certain of the best course."—Cass looked at him pleadingly—not wanting to become his antagonist but unwilling to act against her sister. "Except that—perhaps a break might help. No one being held against her will can be expected to forgive—"

"Forgive what—protecting my son?"

"You killed my son! You gave him that poison!" Jane leapt at Ashton, her anger and grief spilling over. Cass's intervention could not prevent Jane from digging her fingernails into his arm.

"He died of measles, Jane. Not smallpox. Not cowpox. Measles. Cassandra, help me, please. Make her see reason. I did what I did to keep my son alive."

"But he is not—*alive*—, is he?" Jane said. "You did what you wanted, and he is dead."

"The vaccination did not kill him!"

"It weakened him! Made him more susceptible! Complicated the measles!"

"You cannot know that. Or believe it."

"You gave him a vaccination. He fell ill and died. *Quod erat demonstrandum. Your* science killed *my* boy."

Tears welled in his eyes. He had risked the life of her baby in the furtherance of his ideas, ignored her most profound fears in order to prove himself superior. She hoped the remorse would tear his soul to shreds.

"If I accept your belief that he had a weak constitution, can't you accept the likelihood—the possibility—that a weak constitution needs all the protection possible? Most likely, the vaccination had no effect at all. If anything, it might have helped."

"You ignored his weakness."

"Whatever other issues our son may have had, he was physically strong."

"Not after the seizures began."

"*If it was w-weakness that k-killed him, it did not come from m-my side! There—if you want to assign b-blame—accept your p-portion!*"

Holding her head high, she waited until her emotions settled enough to speak in a way that nullified all he had said. "I want a divorce."

"You cannot have one!" His fury having been roused, Ashton made no attempt to rein it in. "Never! You are stuck with me—until death, remember?" He pushed Cassandra aside. "George has been—gone—barely a month. You cannot make such a decision in haste. Give yourself time, woman—give *us* time."

"How much time do I need to know I cannot stay with the man who took away my child?"

"Jane!" Cassandra said.

"The man who saved your son from smallpox will not grant you a divorce because he died of something else."

"Then I will seek divorce on my own."

"You have neither the money nor the connections to obtain one."

"I shall find someone to help—Mr. Wilberforce would be sympathetic."

"Mr. Wilberforce believes in the sanctity of marriage. To him, unhappily married Christians should experience a Hell on earth for all their natural lives."

"What kind of marriage is it when the only means of happiness is to separate the principals?"

"The kind of marriage we have. For now, at least."

"You can have children with another woman, all the healthy heirs you want. You can keep your fortune together and the estate intact."

"You argue on behalf of heirs I do not have or want—unless with you. If I am not with you, I care nothing for what happens to the fortune. I'll be pleased to make a distant cousin happy when I am gone."

"I will find a way to make our separation permanent. We will be divorced in fact if not in law."

"Do you love me, Jane?"

"Jane is dead. Only the brutal Mrs. Dennis lives. Now you have two."

"Do you *not* love me, *Mrs. Dennis*? Tell me now, in front of your sister, that you do not love me."

"I have asked for a divorce. That is all you need to know. An honorable man would grant it."

Ashton looked from Jane to Cassandra and back. "You may go with her." As the women began to turn away, he stopped them. "Provided one thing. You challenged me once to declare my love publicly in front of your family and friends. I make the same challenge to you. You may go to Southampton—Godmersham—anywhere you please. You may have your divorce—an enormous settlement. Only this: Disavow me to your family. I will go down with you, and we shall dine with your lovely mother. Send for Henry and Eliza, the Steventonites—the entire Austen clan. Declare publicly at the table, before all you know, that you do not love me, and I will let you go. I will give you anything you want."

"I have no need to parse words with you, Mr. Dennis. Nor to prove myself to you in any way."

"Then you, Mrs. Dennis, will go inside. And you, Miss Austen, will pack your things and leave my home."

Chapter 19

It being the start of the tax season, Ashton spent the early part of the day with Henry, who had come down from London, and with Mr. Fletcher, who was reconciling the final income and expenses for the farm. After emerging from the library, Ashton joined in the activities as the tenant farmers and laborers rapidly assembled, having camped in the fields or found a nook in an outbuilding, gathering in small clusters of acquaintances, and occasionally succeeding in having a friend among the staff slip them an early mug of beer or ale.

Around these important social functions, the farmers engaged in earnest conversation with Mr. Fletcher, who at Candlemas had been pleased to accept their signatures or marks on the contracts for the new year. Today was when people moved to their new farms as the result of those contracts, but the reputation of Hants was such that tenants and laborers seldom left. This year there was only one: the McLendon family, which was moving to care for an elderly relative whose farm was to be their inheritance. Their fields were passing to the Mathis family as recompense for a tenancy near Headbourne Worthy, the most productive parts of which had been plowed under by Ashton's rail-road.

With so few changes among the people, the main activities were the renewal of friendships, the endless comparisons of milk production among favored cows, and calculations of last year's harvest totals for the new Swedish turnip. The discussions with Mr. Fletcher involved requests for improvements that might with some persuasion fall to the landholder instead of his tenant. Mr. Fletcher was not ungenerous in his response, often agreeing to work that would benefit multiple farmers for the cost of one, or obtaining agreement for the farmers' help in some other mutually beneficial labor. Chief among these was the renovation of a small, centrally located grain mill. These deliberations were not about improving the terms of the agreed upon contracts but about obtaining some other consideration that might make the difference between a passable and a successful year. Chief among *these* was the growing pressure by Hants on the hay harvests of the farmers, occasioned by the large increase in the number of horses now being provided to the Army. Hants had agreed to give more for hay this year, and the tenants were successful in also asking for the proportional increase in fertilizer produced by said animals, permission to glean Hants' lands-in-hand, and the right to keep as firewood any brush they cleared for Mr. Dennis along the roads.

Mr. Fletcher did not quibble because these gentle negotiations had as their real goal the confirmation of the estate's ownership of the land and leadership on matters agricultural, along with simultaneous acknowledgement of the value of the people who did the hard labor. Though he indicated with a subtle inclination of his head the support of these requests, Ashton stood more as observer than referee. His primary task was to greet the tenants and workfolk and express gratification for their continued partnership in the husbandry of the land.

All this time, Jane was supervising the preparation of the food and social activities. She was dutiful in her role and spoke with suitable condescension to the men and women who came to ask a question or to respectfully greet the mistress. It was difficult for her to maintain her composure as these people, in their simple and deferential way, expressed by a look or gesture their grief on her loss. Any words they might have dared to offer would fail at the memory of their own loss of a Jenny or a Sam. It was with immense relief that the preliminaries were at last concluded and everyone could turn to food, drink, and games. Jane sat, able to relax and enjoy as best she could the Lady Day festivities and cheer on the participants of the games.

Before their marriage, Jane had learned, Ashton had done little beyond the required on the quarter-days. His dealings with his tenants then were the same as they were in every other way: terse, strict, and fair. Since their marriage, he had begun including donkey, sack, and wheelbarrow races and providing local musicians, dancers, and jugglers. The noticeable rise in song and laughter came from his increase in the supply of food and drink. This had not been Jane's idea but his own. The increase in happiness of a principal has a way of benefiting those in his employ or operating under his protection.

One of the things he most enjoyed was involving all the children with the horses. Under the supervision of Mr. Fletcher and the stable men, the older, more experienced youths had the opportunity to undertake trotting and cantering exercises while those less experienced took the gentlest horses (including a thirty-year-old gelding on whom Ashton had learned as a child) through a simple obstacle course. Ashton himself gave rides to the youngest children, walking beside the ponies in the small arena. Some were so young that Ashton walked on one side and a parent on the other.

Several times as he walked beside the children, praising them for their horsemanship, Ashton's eye caught Jane's. She smiled a small but unforced smile at the sight of the gleeful sprite next to him, and he smiled in return, and then she was reminded that George was not among this happy crowd, that he would not go up in the saddle next year, or any year. Jane's smile faded, Ashton's smile faded, and she turned away to gossip with Mrs. Liebman, the wife of their primary tenant.

As the festivities wound down, the farmers and workers dispersed to their temporary encampments, where they would settle around fires for more private merriments in the evening. It was important that the work-folk had time with one another as well as with the landed proprietor. Jane saw to the taking down of the tents and tables, more to keep herself busy than for any assistance required by Mr. Hanrahan or Mrs. Lundeen. Ashton brought out a horse to work in the small arena. It was young, and it must have been new, for Jane did not recognize it. The light ground work being something more suited for a groom than for the master, Ashton must have had the same need as she did to keep himself occupied. The horse was agitated, for no apparent reason; nervousness is as natural to a horse as playfulness is to a child.

Jane had seen her husband work young horses out of their nervousness through work and patience: The work would burn off their excess of energy while the patience would convince them that the human was in control, giving them the confidence to relax. When he mounted today, however, and the horse resisted, Ashton rode roughly, seeking to control it through power and fear. At every mistake, he punished the animal with the spurs and crop, rather than using them as guides. The more the horse acted up, the rougher Ashton became, to the point that the horse panicked and began to buck.

Ashton leapt off and began to whip the horse while cursing its intransigence. His actions sent the horse even more out of control, rearing against the reins. Mr. Fletcher came out of the stables to see what the disturbance was about. When he viewed the abuse, he jumped the fence and tackled Ashton. The horse circled them, white-eyed, kicking randomly, knocking off a crosspiece of the fence. Ashton roared up, ready to do battle. Jane stood paralyzed at the possibility of a physical confrontation between the two good friends. Fear struck the steward, too, for he was half Ashton's size and could be felled with a single blow. If Fletcher survived the battle, Ashton could fire him for the attack, have him jailed—hanged—for assault. Yet Mr. Fletcher stood his ground.

Ashton threw a wild punch that did not appear intended to hit the steward so much as to rake the sky. Fletcher took him down again, keeping upon him as one accustomed to waiting out an unbroken horse. Ashton cursed and threatened his man, but directed no more violence his way. Finally, Ashton's fury subsided, the dust settled, and Fletcher stepped off. The steward began the slow process of calming and containing the horse, which during the row had continued to race and buck around the arena. Ashton rolled from his back to his stomach, rose to his knees and crawled to the fence. He leaned against it and wept shamelessly. She could see the lines of tears on his face.

Recognizing his grief, it struck her that there was an equivalence after all between the love of a father for his child and a mother for hers. Her own father had loved her at least as much as her mother had done, because he had a distance from his children that her mother did not and the ability to see a child for who he or she was, unentangled by the apron strings. While her mother had the ability to appreciate the general intelligence and kindness of her brood, her father had the ability to identify the best specific qualities of each child. He had not just praised the endowments of her mind, he had nurtured them in a way her mother never thought necessary among her other more generally supportive actions.

In the same way, she saw that while her love for George was enveloping, Ashton's was particular, a response to the personality of the child and the actual way he behaved and was developing. Where she wanted to hold and protect, Ashton wanted to prepare and set free. George had been just a babe, yet already the parental dichotomy was clear in many of the smallest things. She had felt an unwillingness to acknowledge Ashton's contribution out of fear that it meant she was not doing enough, that she could not do everything for her child.

She saw instantly the torment that the death of their child was causing him—*that* death, and *her* alienation. A woman must love a man who feels that depth of agony, especially when the cause of it was not provably his fault. At the deepest levels, closest to her soul, she identified with him and regretted the way she had been treating him, her husband, George's father. As this emotion welled toward the surface, however, it became diffused within the many other emotions she had carried over the last weeks. She lost the cause of the violence and registered in her mind only the violence itself. As he had seen the weakness of George's mind running back generations in her family, proof that it was congenital, she now marked the viciousness of his father and mother and no doubt many generations of Dennises before—the kind of anger a family needs to claw out of poverty into wealth. Her dislocation with the world became particularized in this one man, her husband. Who was this embodiment of rage? How could she ever trust in what he thought, in what he believed—about anything? This sorry dusty man on his hands and knees in the arena was a stranger to her. She could not understand how she ever could have been intimate with him; their bedroom was now a gray shadow, an obscuration that led to nothingness. As she had begun this cycle of her life—through the conception of her child—as a stranger in her own body, she now was a stranger in her own marriage. And her marriage was her life.

At last Ashton pulled himself up by the railing and tried to apologize to Mr. Fletcher, who brusquely rebuffed his remarks. Jane slipped inside, hoping to avoid Ashton entirely, but he caught her in the hall.

"I see you have adopted the Sawyer school of training," she said. "Must you extend your cruelty to every creature?"

"You should not have seen that."

"It is not the sight of the act which repudiates but the act itself."

He nodded as if to accept her judgment but looked vaguely about. Her heart seized when Ashton's gaze reminded her of George's vacuity after a convulsion. It was as though Ashton could not let her come into focus without his brutality coming into focus as well. "Henry's here still, correct?" he said. "He hasn't left?"

"You told me he needed to stay at least another day to work on the taxes. Did that change?"

"No, no. But the taxes can wait. You must go with him. To your family—wherever you feel safe. I will stay in the village to-night. You and Henry can leave in the morning. I love you, Jane. I'm sorry. You must go."

Chapter 20

7 May 1808

Dear Jane

I have desperately wanted to write to you from the moment you left. I thought to have a letter waiting for you at Southampton to express my sorrow—thought better of it. Whenever I sit at my desk, I feel the need to communicate with you. The number of weeks I have waited is a measure of the constraint I have placed on my impetuosity and my respect for you. I hope that time and distance might enable you to accept my apology as being one of honest reflection and remorse and not the "I'm sorry" of someone who has been caught in an outrageous act. I hope the weeks may also have softened or provided some perspective on the other issue that divides us.

Mr. Fletcher has forgiven my violence against that poor animal. He has also told me in explicit terms that he will leave if he ever sees anything like that again. My sin continues to be visited on me, though. The horse still shies whenever I am around.

Considering your other indictment against me, I cannot imagine what my actions on Lady Day must have caused you to think. Whatever else you may feel, I hope you will recognize that the action—the beating, I've said it—was out of my character. Certainly nothing like the way I've ever treated any animal. You have observed my behavior closely for two and a half years. You have watched it from afar since my days *as a youth. Have you ever seen me abuse any creature? You might upbraid me for a caustic reply to my fellow man, but I challenge you to identify an incident in which I mistreated anyone who was at a material disadvantage.*

I see that I am working up to a list of reasons or excuses for my behavior. I did not intend to do that. My actions were terribly wrong. They were also in no way typical of how I act or what I think or believe. You of all people must know that. I beg you to recognize the enormous strain we have both been under ever since George fell ill. The worry about his illness. The agony his death imposed. Even if you continue to think me wrong in what I did with our precious child, I hope you can somehow bring yourself to see that I never intended anything but the best—to help him in every way—even if, as you believe, my actions caused his death. I can barely stand to write that word.

I cannot argue such a difficult matter in a letter. Nor do I wish to argue it at all. I mean nothing more than to state my love for you. To plead with you not to let our horrific loss destroy our marriage. I believe you still feel love for me. Or at least that we are not so estranged that we cannot find our way back to love. Or if not love, a peaceable understanding. I have no idea how we might proceed. I cannot believe we are better off proceeding separately than together.

I ask that I may come to visit you. Under whatever terms you deem acceptable. I ask nothing more than that we talk. Let us see where conversation takes us. Even if we sit and stare at each other for an hour—that would be worlds better than our current situation. I beg to say that with all we have been through we should do that much—meet directly—before we make irreparable decisions about our future. Or allow them to happen through inaction. Love does not enable us to skip merrily through life. Love helps us get through the times when we otherwise are destroyed.

Yr husband,

Ashton
Hants House

11 May 1808

Dear Mr. Dennis

Thank you for your letter of the 7th inst. Assuming that the interactions will be civil, a wife cannot reasonably deny a request for a visit by her husband. I expect that Cassandra or one of my brothers would join us for any conversation. We are now at Steventon and will soon be traveling to London to visit Henry. Perhaps it would make the most sense for you to wait until we are established at Godmersham, where we plan to spend the latter part of June. We expect to be there through the first part of July.

J—
Steventon

13 May 1808

Dear Jane

As you have suggested, I will plan to visit you at Godmersham. Please write to confirm the dates that best suit you and Edward.

Abigail is settling in as a regular maid. Having lost half a dozen servants to my mother's departure, and under your instructions to hire only when we could find the best, Mrs. Lundeen was ready to receive a bright, energetic girl to fill the breach. Abigail, certainly, needed something. You were wise to keep her on. Even though her only tasks those many weeks were to arrange and rearrange George's toys. I can't imagine the effect of sending her away, as disconsolate as she was. She remained unaware of your idea to groom her to be the governess—more to educate her, I know, than to saddle her with that "odious occupation." Thus, she expressed an interest in working at the big mill at Sherfield on Loddon! She sees more opportunity there. At least, feels the excitement of being involved in the newest thing. Her curiosity about work puts a different light on our improvements. It is one thing to have a workplace for laborers in general. It is another when someone you know might be placed in that environment. My goal now is to improve the manufactory until I would not feel uneasy in sending Abigail—any of our people—to Sherfield to work. I can hear your rejoinder—that you have better things in mind for her. I agree. But the thought provides me with a useful way to view the improvements.

We have made progress in reducing the danger and the noise. It is by no means quiet, but the din is diminished. We have accomplished this through additional insulation and through hurried changes to some of the apparatus—fewer parts mean fewer things to clatter and bang. We have set the schedule to include a regular halt to clear out the thread, the fibers, and other debris. This reduces the number of times children must pluck away material while the looms are running. These stoppages give us time to make other small adjustments, which have a similar positive effect. We have identified the most dangerous areas and keep the children completely away. For the rest, I have directed that only the quickest boys should be employed. But the quickest boys are the ones to take the greatest risks. Mr. Knollman has put the fear of God into them. If they take any unnecessary chances, their mothers *will lose their jobs. Boys are naturally protective of their mothers. They understand what the loss of employment means to food in their own mouths. This has led to some harshness by the mothers whenever one of their sons becomes too venturesome. Better they have their ears boxed than lose a finger.*

You need not tell me this is inadequate. Is it enough that we have reduced the danger by more than half? I realize I am bargaining with the welfare of children. It is the best we can do for now. I felt wretched about the situation before. I doubt that a word exists to describe the diminution of wretchedness, but that is where we are.

Except—we moved ahead the opening of the school. Now children go for several hours in the middle of the day. No teaching is yet being done, but they have a respite from the work. For the moment, we have older women who look after them. We are trying to recruit a teacher. (If she still wanted to be involved with the mill, this would be the perfect job for Abigail in a few years, once she has received the semblance of an education herself.)

Further—I shortened the work day by thirty minutes and gave them half of Saturday off. Imagine when Mr. Knollman's reports arrived to show that productivity had increased! A capitalist can be surprised to learn that, when employees are rested and in better spirits, they work faster and with fewer errors than when they are worked to an extreme.

My sister Alethea has demonstrated her business acumen again. No shock to you, of course. This time with the rail-road. Given all that has happened since, you may not remember that Mr. Trevithick completed his redesign of the locomotive last September. The new machine arrived (in parts) in the following months. Satisfactory testing led us to again extend the tracks. The result is that early in the year we completed a twelve-mile run in exactly an hour—on successive days! The wagons were lightly loaded. But Mr. Trevithick believes that a few alterations will yield more power, enabling us to maintain the speed while carrying a substantial load. We have not resolved the problem of the rails failing after a limited number of runs, but we are making progress.

To Alethea—You know from your last meeting in the summer quarter that we have the funds to carry forward. But not as rapidly as we would wish. To lure more investors, my sister suggested we take the rail-road to London and put it on display! An entertainment for the young! "Entice the children, and the parents must come along!" She found a location in Bloomsbury for the installation of a circular track. On her advice, we will charge a shilling a ride. Though anyone can watch, the fee will ensure that only the affluent will climb aboard. Among these, perhaps—adventurers! The *locomotive is named "Catch Me Who Can." I'm sure Henry would take you to Bloomsbury to see the demonstration, if you wished.*

Your brother may also have mentioned to you several matters related to the rail-road and other business. The Love-laces, in addition to their earlier duplicity toward us on behalf of our competitors, were attempting to obtain the rights to land in Hampshire that would have blocked our access to Southampton—or greatly increased our costs by forcing us to go around. Much of this came to light during the months of your preoccupation. Dennis monies and Austen connections enabled us to thwart their efforts. Be sure to thank the Chutes when next you see them. It helps when a Member of Parliament lends a hand! We were able to secure the remaining rights-of-way to the north end of Southampton. Though the effort cost more than we would have liked, it needed to be done. We were lax not to have acted earlier. Too trusting.

This latest interference gave momentum to our carefully developed plans to undermine our aristocratic friends. I suspect they had taken our inaction as another expected victory of the nobility over the commoner. Through Henry's connections as an Army agent, we captured a few contracts of theirs. These were relatively small. More annoyance than damage. Of greater consequence: We have used these many months to buy up substantial amounts of their debt—both personal and business. We then broke the gentleman's agreement by not refinancing the debt when it came due—except on onerous terms that they declined. It was only after the third or fourth of these transactions that the Earl began to catch on. The cash he needed—and his desire to prevent any future traps—has forced him to liquidate several large holdings (properties as well as paper) on inconvenient terms. I do not speak of these attacks with pride, only determination. Everything we did was aboveboard. And fair, considering their past behavior.

Making matters worse (for them), Robert is on fulltime duty with Wellesley. The youngest son, who feigns ignorance and uninterest in business the way a spider lies motionless in its web, cannot for the moment bring his energy and ability to maneuver into the fray. He must be stewing in his juices.

Wellesley, as you may have heard, has been made lieutenant general. The promotion is well deserved and long overdue. It portends something bigger, however. Would Buonaparte be smart enough to ask: Why has England's finest young officer been promoted now? I have taken to locking up my account books and have directed Mr. Fletcher and all of our suppliers and partners to do the same. A clever spy could look at the accelerated schedules for delivery and the demands for additional equipment and goods and very quickly come to an important—correct!—surmisal.

I am involved in another project that also supports our military efforts. For the reasons above, and others, I cannot discuss them in a letter. It is something that will involve all of Hants, and you—directly or indirectly, depending on circumstances. This is one of the reasons I wish to speak with you face to face.

This letter had more news than I expected when I began. I hope the detail is not unwelcome.

Please pass on my regards to Henry and Eliza and the rest of your family when you see them. I pray you have not related to most of them, the worst of me.

Y^r husband,

Ashton
Hants House

---

24 May 1808

Dear Mr. Dennis

Thank you for the latest information about the rail-road. I am certain of Alethea's pleasure in continuing her remarkable contributions to your family enterprises. One hopes that the demonstration in London will broaden the exposure for your business. At a shilling a ride, I should think you will recover the costs of setting up the track there. We are very busy here, as I am sure you can imagine.

Henry had mentioned that you were taking steps against the Lovelaces but did not provide particulars. As I am no longer directly involved, his discretion is probably wise. Whatever you can do, legally and ethically, to thwart that nasty family has my full endorsement.

I can confirm that we will arrive at Godmersham no later than Tuesday the 14th. Edward indicates that any time from the 20th on would be fine with him. Please let one of us know your preferred date.

J—
London

Chapter 21

At dinner, Edward repeated one of his favorite jokes, that Ashton had had to work for his wealth, while he, Edward, had had the discernment as a young man to be taken in by childless relatives and made their heir. Ashton's rejoinder was always the same, that the wealth on both sides had been created by their progenitors and that the two men carried the same responsibility, which was not to find amusing methods by which to fritter it all away.

Today, Edward felt the need to dispute with his brother-in-law on the nature of progress, expressing *"quelle horreur!"* at the belching smokestack of Ashton's locomotive. He had suffered the bellowing of the beast while traveling to Winchester.

"It will modernize England!" Ashton responded.

"Surely there is a difference between modernization and turning bucolic England into Birmingham?"

"A rail-road cutting through the countryside is music to my ears. And whatever the ocular equivalent is."

"Equally offensive to the eye. Noisy, smoky, intrusive. Sheep and cattle were running for their lives."

"Next you'll tell me the hens won't lay."

"I would not be surprised. All this disruption—why?"

Despite their different backgrounds and temperaments, their jocular exchange typified an easy familiarity. Though Ashton had a propensity for more complicated schemes, Edward in his good-natured way was as practical as his brother-in-law. Jane had observed that his stewardship of Godmersham was slowly building a foundation for the future, while his actions the previous autumn in Chawton—her first time closely observing his work there—showed him to have a grasp for an orderly sequence of improvements that would unfold over years. He was a tortoise to the slapdash hare of Ashton, who had the confidence that one or two of his ten bold strikes would win.

The two men recognized in the other a fellow who had mastered the complexity of wealth without having succumbed to its excesses. The result was that, like Ashton's argument with Wilberforce the previous year about the political system, there was jockeying, ripostes, vigorous criticism—and a healthy respect on both sides. Their banter was also a way of dealing with the latent uneasiness that honest men have about unearned good fortune; their public acknowledgment of the situation reinforced a commitment to do something positive with the opportunity that fate had bestowed upon them both.

"You're a business man," Ashton continued. "A rail-road will take your timber, your oats and barley, to more markets."

"I sell all of my produce within twenty miles. I never take timber unless I already have a buyer—one at an advantageous price. Otherwise, why cut?"

"A very limited market. In London or Southampton, you could get much more."

"And put my local customers out of business? Leave my tenants and workers without food? Come, come, man. I know you ensure that your local partners thrive."

"I'm a manufacturer. Few of my goods are perishable. Nor can Hampshire by itself support large mills producing clothes or carpets. Much of what I buy or sell goes overseas—or did, before the blockades. Our needs are different. I assure you, every day I save in delivery makes a huge difference in my success."

"First it was canals. Now your rail-roads. What else will carve nasty scars across our beautiful land? It is all moving too fast!"

"Not the canals in Hampshire!"

This and a few of Ashton's other comments felt strained to Jane's ear. Though normally at ease with her family, he spoke now as if trying too hard for bonhomie. At the same time, she felt relief that ordinary topics occupied the men during the meal. Henry and James were also present, and they chimed in from time to time. James and Mary were staying here, and Henry had slipped down for the day. At intervals, Ashton gave her a preparatory look as if wanting to speak, and she responded by engaging Edward's wife, Elizabeth, in conversation about the dining parlor's new pink and white décor or the excitement at her latest pregnancy, the baby being due in September. That the conversation with Ashton was inevitable did not mean that it should cause the lobster and duck to become indigestible.

"Think of the travel, then! The ability of ordinary citizens to go about our country. To see and enjoy its pleasures."

"Wonderful," Edward said, as they finished the meal. "More riffraff to join the ones falling off the coaches."

"Riffraff who often become your workers!"

When they adjourned to the blue drawing room, Jane caught Edward's wry expression at Elizabeth's animation over the redecorations under way at Godmersham. Here her brother was hoping to nudge his wife along the road to Hampshire, and she, anticipating her eleventh child, was happily feathering her elegant nest in Kent. After a dozen years of marriage Elizabeth and Edward had come to resemble each other in an easy-going, doll-like way. Yet Jane knew through her handling of the children and her husband that Elizabeth had an underlying firmness that served as a keel to steady the family's blowing softness.

"He cannot very well complain," Elizabeth said, referring to the new drawing room, which presented pale blue wallpaper with dark blue flower patterns and oriental-style Chippendale furniture in a matching satin design. "I have given him all the children a man could want." In a wife-to-wife whisper: "And have entertained all the things that *deliver* children."

Jane smiled, thinking of their new canopy bed, which featured a silk tester and curtains in the same patterns as here. They must share an enjoyment of these colors and textures and perhaps took advantage of an oversupply of material, yet she also wondered whether the appointments in the drawing room were a subtle reminder of the more luxurious moments in bed. As she walked about with Elizabeth, admiring the new furniture and cabinets, she also recognized the subtle effort to keep up with Hants, the refurbishment of which Jane had overseen when *she* was nesting in preparation for the birth of *her* baby.

It had given Jane pleasure to equal Edward and Elizabeth's situation, as she had long been the recipient of their generosity, while also becoming a dependent. Until she had her own home—it need not have been as large—she could not fully erase her envy. It made her feel less small to acknowledge that this thought *was* small of her, for never were there two people more generous; yet an aunt in residence must help with the growing household. That it was treated as a courtesy made it no less a requirement. She and Cassandra alternated, effectively, as nurses and secondary governesses. One could not resent a welter of loving, obedient children, yet one could feel a suggestion of despair that this was the only outlet of work or accomplishment for a single woman, paid or not. And however pleasant each visit was, each one ended with the embarrassment of her leaving the maid Sackree a tip of shillings instead of pounds. That was the main difference of Hants—the ability to finally pay a proper vail.

Cocking an eyebrow, Elizabeth indicated that Jane and Ashton might wish to share the sofa; Jane subtly indicated no—indeed, Ashton took up a chair directly opposite, in keeping with his desire to address Jane and, as it would happen, the room. The sisters-in-law settled next to each other and the other men in facing chairs. Drinks were served. One had to look about to remember that Mary was there.

All but her sailor brothers were present (all but they and George—she must now include him in her thoughts whenever Ashton was about). Henry and James had remained largely quiet and observant during dinner. Each came for ostensibly different reasons, but the death of the child—the second of Jane's long absences from

Hants—the hardness of her references to her husband—the relegation of Ashton to a separate room upon his arrival here—confirmed that something was fundamentally amiss. To what degree or for what duration, everyone must learn. The demeanor of her brothers showed that they were prepared for a business-like conversation in which they would need to understand and ratify whatever was afoot in a way that protected their sister's interest.

Before this came Edward's children. As well-behaved as they were, it was impossible for this many, with a governess and two nurses in tow, not to thunder onto the scene. They scattered to every available seat. Several contested for Jane's lap as the favorite, Elizabeth serving as referee. The previous week, the entire clutch had suffered sore throats; today, despite their mother retaining mild symptoms of the Godmersham Cold, ruddy health beamed throughout the room.

In the warm effusion of the young, Jane felt the most tender pain at the loss of her own child. Fanny, as much a younger sister as a niece, had shepherded the giggle of girls. The boys, reminiscent of her own brothers, jostled with one another despite the force of manners. The baby, Cassandra Jane, not a month older than—. She was eager to be taken up, and Jane feared to suffocate her with a hug. She teared up; glancingly she saw Ashton, watching, doing his best to maintain control. They managed to shield their discomfort from the children until they could recover. "A little something in the eye," she told the inquisitive Lizzy. The children showed off, according to age, their smears of paint, their crooked letters, their half-learned lines of poesy, all with the deserved pride of achievement. Edward's offspring were sweet as could be, pleasant and respectful. Their only failings were a certain satisfaction shared among the older siblings in their status and comfort and a lack of the fire that motivated their elders—a fire their father courteously hid. She had been less attentive to her nieces and nephews than normal on this visit, however: a restlessness related to all that was unsorted in her own personal circumstances.

As the two ladies shared small talk and Elizabeth occasionally directed the children, Edward tried to convince Ashton of the
bloat-free merits of sainfoin as livestock feed.

"I would bet my globe against your orrery that sainfoin would
rot in Hampshire—at least in my soil," replied Ashton, whose own
envy was expressed in joke: He regularly threatened to abscond
with the mechanical replica of the solar system, which took pride
of place in Edward's entry. The orrery was much superior to Ashton's simple globe, though the globe was a gift from his father, one
of the few that had not required some accomplishment for Ashton
to earn—as he had once explained in better times.

The other thing that regularly drew her husband's covetous
humor was the carpet at their feet, which may have been what
triggered his remark about the orrery. The primary rug pattern was
an elaborate multicolor flower motif featuring recently discovered
flora—magnolias, tiger lilies, cacti. Ashton could not understand
how Edward—not he—had snagged this artistic rendering of the
latest in natural philosophy.

With an occasional opinion offered by Henry or James, the men
carried on about agricultural operations and other concerns of es-
tates. Beyond the details of the conversation, Edward was trying to
establish a rhythm that might encourage an easy transition to the
topic at hand, leavened with a pleasantness that might smooth its
expression. Ashton waited for the children to conclude their visit
and bustle out before he began. As they were leaving, and she saw
the seriousness on her husband's face, Jane knew she could not reveal the contents of this meeting in one of her breezy letters home.
Any exchange of confidences with Cass would require a tête à tête.

With more hesitation in his speech than Jane had heard in
some time, Ashton began to explain the purpose of his visit. "You
all k-know that o-one of m-my primary b-businesses is to s-supply
the Army. Y-you know, too, that the Army plans an expedition. In a
m-month. Two at most. It's b-become almost an open s-secret that
the adventure w-will be to P-Portugal and S-Spain—but k-keep
this to yourself anyway." As was his pattern, the more he spoke
the less pronounced his stutter became. "It s-seems my interests

have combined with those of the m-military. I am not only to s-supply horses and provisions—I am to d-deliver them. Later. In the autumn."

"You will go to the continent?" Edward asked.

"Yes. And stay."

Jane swiveled her gaze to and from Ashton and Henry: Her brother studiously toed the carpet's flowering cactus. *Stay?* It was irregular enough that a civilian would be required to escort military livestock and provisions across the Channel, but what further irregularity would necessitate him to *stay?*

The question held in the expressions of surprise by everyone—barring Henry.

"My brothers, I hope I may call you that,"—a nod to Edward and Henry—"you have served in the Militia. James, your ecclesiastical position prevents your bearing arms, but you have recruited. I am attempting to serve my country. As all of you have." He stared into his wine glass, took a deep breath—a memory floated into Jane's mind but did not resolve itself before swirling away—and said hurriedly: "I am raising a company of men. We are to deliver goods to the Army as part of a normal resupply operation. After that, we are to be taken into one of the regiments at the front—whichever has the greatest need." (Jane heard the last phrase as "whichever has sustained the greatest losses.")

"Splendid!" Edward said. His exclamation was at the boldness of the plan, yet afterward he settled back in his chair with a look of concern. James nodded in approval, for one could not oppose an action of open patriotism. Henry looked warily toward his sister, for of course he would have known about the plan because of the financial components.

"The Militia does not go overseas," she said. "Your company would be stationed here—in England, I mean. Along the Hampshire coast? Southampton, Portsmouth?"

"It's regular Army. Well, it's Army but not exactly regular. One of the experimental Rifle regiments. The 95th, very likely. The approach is very much in keeping with my own experience. Limited as it was. Skirmishing. Sharpshooting. Irregular actions. The Rifles fight more like the Americans than the British."

So you will have your rifles after all, Jane thought. At least these will be manufactured by a company that knows what it is doing. The men were silent, absorbing the news. "Oh, dear," said Elizabeth, putting her hand on Jane's arm as if to ensure she did not miss the import of the remark.

"Mr. Dennis, this makes no sense," Jane said. "You are no soldier. You have no training, no background."

"I served with Maurice, Jane. Two years."

"As a civilian! A few exchanges of gunfire when you were crouched in the rear. You told me so."

"And one battle, large enough to suit anyone's desires. When I was not in the rear but in the front with my men." He unconsciously touched the scar on his face.

"A fixed position!" she said. "You were on a rock. You would be lost on a battlefield. Your ignorance would cost your men their lives!"

"The purchase of commissions means half our regiments are led by boys or idiots—a common expression among the troops. I saw combat. I served under a magnificent officer. I am a significant improvement over most."

"A merchant pretending at war! Bullying people over contracts has nothing to do with battle. Its hardship, dangers."

"The only difference between me and Frank is fifteen years of service and a dozen rounds of shot!"

The men laughed, for their sex was supposed to encourage any preposterous disregard of danger.

"Frank will soon be home to correct your foolishness. He will tell you all you need to know. He will sober you out of your delusions of glory!"

Ashton pulled a letter from his pocket and laid it on the table in front of her. He punched it with his finger. "The endorsement of Captain Francis Austen."

She flushed with the sense of betrayal that Ashton would write directly to Frank—even though they were long since friends—and that her brother would support his wild idea without any consideration of his sister's feelings. Her look toward Henry could have blistered his face; for in having just told her that Frank was unexpectedly coming home, he had somehow failed to mention correspondence among the men that her husband was about to join the Army with the consent of everyone but his wife.

She pulled away from the letter as though it were a confession of adultery.

"Craziness! This cannot possibly be within the regulations."

"It's amazing what is possible when a Government is in desperate need of men and supplies. And a man is willing to offer both. A gentleman who provides volunteers can obtain a commission. Same as a purchase. The only exception is that I made the service of my men specific to this campaign. I would not have it that I could retire whenever I wished through the sale of my commission, while my men would be forced to stay on. As it happens, *anything* can be authorized if it involves the necessities of war. The lawyers produced enough paper to cover this room, but I prevailed." Jane looked to Henry again, because as an Army agent he must have handled most of these machinations.

"Then you *must go?*" Elizabeth asked. "You, personally? How long?"

"Until the expedition concludes. A year, perhaps two? The requirement is that I provide an officer to lead the troops. I assume that officer will be me." He looked at Jane. "I have several qualified candidates who would go in my place. Young officers without the wherewithal to buy a higher rank. Eager to prove themselves. But I would need a reason to stay."

"What am I to do?" she cried—as if his departure would leave her dispossessed.

"I understand you would prefer to remain with family. As Mary does when Frank goes overseas." He added: "If the current arrangement is insufficient, I can do more."

"Your generosity is not in question. Your sanity, however—"

"Do you not care about the danger, Mr. Dennis?" Elizabeth asked softly. "You have a family."

"A man feels the danger most acutely when another person feels the danger for him." He looked again at Jane. "Otherwise, he does not really care."

"But you have served before on behalf of God and Country, Mr. Dennis," Jane said in a more persuasive tone. "I did not intend in any way to demean your earlier time. I meant only that you have demonstrated your love of England. Your loyalty. Surely it is someone else's turn."

"I'm not sure the war operates on political equity among the well-to-do. Those willing to stand up—already have. Besides, I assume you would feel the same pride for me as you do for your brothers. To serve—like them. As an act of deliberation. Not an accident of fate. As before."

"Even if all these things are true, you cannot possibly be ready in time. Not at harvest time. Not with all the changes in your business. How can you possibly prepare a hundred men—more—in a matter of months?"

"We were given an experienced sergeant and several of his best men. Mr. Fletcher, as it turns out, is from an Army family. Learned the business at his father's knee. He is now the oldest lieutenant in the service. I would have made him my superior, but he insisted on a rank below mine. Recruitment is complete. We began training months ago."

Jane caught a visual exchange carrying the implication that James' most recent recruits might have been directed Ashton's way. Which might also explain why there had been no rumblings of Ashton's plans from Hampshire. She was aghast. Had every brother turned against her?

"And you did not think to tell me!"

"You happened not to be around. ... I did not wish to distress you ... at a distance."

She could think of a thousand reasons to oppose Ashton's plans, but he had already knocked down the most convincing. She sat, thwarted. He gathered his remarks in a summing up.

"Some men go to war with a purpose. Lovelace is among those, and should draw our admiration. Much as we detest him for other reasons. Others go to war because they have no reason—*not to go.* I am of that persuasion. My estate is running beautifully. Mr. Jarrett and Alethea have the businesses well in hand. What is to keep me from going, my friends? Give me one deterrent. One reason that would keep the uniform in the closet. One reason that would keep me here at home, safe and warm. I shall be glad to stay."

"Our affection would hold you here, dear Ashton," Edward said, "but not at the expense of your duty."

Her thought was the opposite of Edward's: that their affection should hold him here—regardless. Yet she could not speak those words.

"I have given you all the reasons a rational man should want," she said. "And more. As always, you do not care. You wish only to disturb your family, to disrupt their lives with an extremity of action. For attention—glory—I know not what. Your wildness will have a bad end. Recklessness and regrets are all you have ever given the world."

"Secondary. Every reason you have cited—secondary. To any meaningful response. Tell me why that humblest of men, your husband, should stay at home. At peace. In safety. One reason, and I shall gladly stay."

There was a silence of many, many breaths, after which Jane bravely announced:

"I shall wear a riband, or cockade, or whatever it is that ladies do, to signify my husband's service."

Chapter 22

After watching Ashton ride away, Jane remained in her bedroom looking out upon the vast expanse of lawn. Godmersham had always been too manicured for her, lovely but artificial. She walked here for exercise and refreshment but not for pure enjoyment, not as she did in the woods of home. She wondered if Edward felt the same as she, if that was one reason he sought to shift his attention from Kent to Hampshire. Barring some childhood horror, did one always feel nostalgia for one's nativity?

She could not vent her thoughts until Ashton disappeared from view. The rage that had fueled her emotions for nearly half a year had softened when she saw him ride up the sweep two days before. She knew what she had missed—and then remembered why. She had to concede that the anger seemed independent of the person she saw dismount. There was Mr. Ashton Dennis, the man seared into her mind as the perpetrator of the decision that destroyed her life, and there was this man—sad, distracted, uncertain—who greeted the servants kindly and looked about with half-hearted hope that he might be received by someone closer than his brother-in-law. However much her feelings may have tended to ameliorate, though, his being here still reminded her of George, and George represented the hole in her life, her heart. Ashton's presence was itself an act of alienation.

Everyone told her she was too hard, too unforgiving, too petulant. A year of mourning was standard, yet she was to let go of her emotions in half that time? How can one grieve if one does not feel? She was not even certain the emotion she carried was anger. When anguish is intense enough, how could there be a difference? She swam in misery. The only way not to drown was to push another beneath the surface. No, that was not exactly true. Ashton remained a part of her; her actions were the only way to ensure his misery was the equal of hers.

His joining the Army was an act of desperation, she knew that as well as anyone. An effort to return his wife to his side. It would have been all too easy to swoon in his arms, to declare her love, to plead for him not to go to war. But his was also an act of domination. Not deliberate, perhaps, but one that compelled her to submit as she was required to do with the smallpox vaccination. Here was another lifechanging decision on which he could ignore her wishes—or agree to a secondary wish only after she capitulated on the significant one. That Ashton was as reasonable as any man could be did not change the fact that he ultimately was the only one able to choose. In marriage, every decision required the consent of just one partner, and that partner would never be her. Not because the husband was smarter or better informed but because he was not the wife.

The social structure was not Ashton's doing, and he pursued a more equitable society; yet he did not hesitate to use the status quo to his advantage when he and Jane were at odds. Just as he had overridden her beliefs as their baby's life hung in the balance, he could override her views on any other decision of moment. This distinction left them in different places psychologically on both the general and the particular. On the general, she must despair of ever prevailing when in fundamental disagreement with her husband—whom the law considered her master—whatever the merits of her case. On the particular, Ashton had acted, and by acting he had somehow closed the matter. She had waited and hoped and prayed that God would take the cup away. She had not acted, for there was nothing for her to do—Ashton already had done it. Her inability to act—not by choice but by role—left the matter open and her wounds still weeping. She understood why Ashton had done what he had done and logically understood it was a reasonable course. Yet understanding was not the same as agreement; recognition was not the same as reconciliation.

Ashton had once said that the more emotional she was, the more intellectualized her arguments became. That may be so, but it seemed to her that women were forever being accused of petulance when they were standing against injustice. Whatever—her son had died for reasons out of her control, for actions out of her control. Someone had to answer for that. She must forgive God but in doing so she could not forgive her husband.

Chapter 23

Frank still had bright eyes darting out from under his dark, fly-away hair—the look Jane associated with his youth—but at thirty-four her brother was finally beginning to show the weather-blasted face of a man who had sailed the seas for more years than he had lived on land. Though he now resided almost within hailing distance, his hectic sailing schedule and young family made it difficult for him to make the dash up from Portsmouth for dinner.

"It is likely that Captain Austen and the *St. Albans* will stay busy indefinitely ferrying troops and supplies," he said. "Not as lucrative as foreign trade, but I will be home every week instead of every year." The *St. Albans'* first tour on the China routes had gone well in every regard, including the East India Company's special remuneration for the successful return of bullion and opium along with their merchantmen. The gathering force of the expedition to Portugal, however, had caused Frank to be reassigned to convoy military transports on their way to the Peninsula.

"And Mary Jane is doing well?" asked Mrs. Austen of her newest grandchild, concluding her questions about how he and Mary were faring on Wight. Her lack of teeth gave her a habitually stern expression that made it look as though she were subjecting Frank to an inquisition, but her words and eyes sparkled with good humor.

It was ironic that Frank and Mary had ended up on the island, which because of Mrs. Dennis had all the associations with exile. Their settlement there served the same purpose as the settling of Ashton's mother in Basingstoke, which was to establish a minimum safe distance between the couple and an attentive mother-in-law. Wight was also less dear than Southampton for an economy-minded officer.

They discussed the military campaign, which had made a confounding start. As General Sir Arthur Wellesley was deftly maneuvering toward a major victory at Vimeiro, he was superseded—not once, but twice—within little more than a day. Frank, who had watched the battle unfold from his ship (and later ferried the wounded and captured home), offered his view that only the Government would think that a veteran of multiple wars required the oversight of two generals with no combat experience. When the French sued for peace, the terms agreed to were so favorable to them that all three generals were recalled to explain themselves. General Sir John Moore was left in charge. Contrary to public opinion, Frank supported the controversial convention, as the French under Marshal Junot still held all the strong positions in the country, while the British had insufficient troops and artillery. Under the agreement, the French would be out of Portugal, and England would establish a strong base from which to liberate Spain.

Everyone ate quietly. Several times Jane thought to frame a question but could not come up with the appropriate words. Frank watched as if expecting a resolution to the dilemma but feeling uncertain as to what it might be. Finally, it was their mother, who had been observing both, who spoke:

"This home has reason to wonder where the Army might advance—and when." Mrs. Austen's gesture included herself and her two daughters, as well as their friend Martha Lloyd, who had, as usual, contributed more to the preparation of the meal than to the conversation over it. Martha herself was helping establish Mary and Frank on Wight.

Frank laughed: Mrs. Austen had probably never ventured a military comment in her life. "If I knew," he said, "it would mean everyone knows—including our foes." But her question served the purpose of bringing up the topic.

"There is no way to learn where Ashton may end up serving. We have troops in ports up and down the coast. We could launch from any of them. To dislodge the French from Spain, we will have to strike into the interior—Madrid. General Moore is busy organizing his forces, waiting for more men and materiel. We in the Navy might be able to deduce the departure point from the convoy schedule, but troops are being spread around to ensure that no one area exhausts local supplies—and to keep the French off guard."

"Ashton—all of us—will be kept in the dark until the very last minute," Mrs. Austen deduced. This time, her expression matched the severity in her words. "For security."

"Security, certainly," Frank said. "But this campaign has been dogged by last-minute actions. It will be the Government ministers who decide, and their behavior has so far been both dilatory and contradictory." To Jane: "When I endorsed Ashton's plan, I did not understand your resistance. I would have been more cautious in my response."

"As an officer, you expect every man to do his duty," she said, unwilling to allow herself to meet his eyes for fear of how she might respond. "I expressed alarm at the irregularity of the enterprise. Will his company—unattached, it would seem—be treated properly? Will they end up standing in the corner with nothing to do, or worse—thrown into the worst of battle with no guidance or support—to be butchered?" Though studied coolness was her signature, she could not avoid a hitch in her voice.

"If every wife had a veto on her husband's service," Frank said, "there would be no soldiers overseas."

"To the advantage of the world, I am sure. If armies would not fight the wars, princes would not bother to start them."

Her comments, Jane could tell, left her brother perplexed. Though never an advocate of violence, she had always treated opposition to the French—Buonaparte in particular—as the necessity of every loyal citizen.

"We all must strive for peace—unless it brings subjection," he said. "This war will end only when English troops march into Paris—or French troops into London."

"If Ashton must go," Cassandra said as if musing aloud, "perhaps it would be best for his wife to be with him until his time. They are training at Hants."

Something in her movement just before she spoke gave Jane the sense of what she might be about to say. In that half-moment, she had time to manage her response, for she had been required to hear her sister's observation more than once. Speaking in a voice that matched Cass's nonchalance, Jane explained: "He must accomplish in a few months what a normal commander has years to do—create a fighting force out of a rabble. Our Hampshire men are good and true, but they are not soldiers. They do not respond naturally to discipline or the need to think and act as one. It was agreed, for his own safety—for that of his troops—that Ashton needed to bring *all* his energy to bear on training. To waste not a moment. This is best accomplished if he is not distracted by ordinary domestic cares—or by a wife who sometimes occupies more of his attentions than is good for him. It matters not whether he sleeps in his own bed or a tent. No commander has his wife to pester him while on maneuvers."

"Yet every soldier receives a leave," said Cassandra, ignoring Jane's visual hint to leave well enough alone, "when a wife and her *attentions* would be very welcome, I should think."

"If Ashton felt the need to be with me, he *could* come to Southampton," Jane insisted. "They are drilling seven days a week. I would rather miss my husband than divert him from the purpose on which his life will hang."

Cassandra's exasperation was impossible to contain; and Mrs. Austen frowned at such a close parsing of words, for while it was true that Ashton *could* in theory come to town, Jane had made them both to understand he was not to be welcomed in the *house* without an invitation.

"No one argues that," Cass said. "However—"

"This topic has been discussed before, to no conclusion," Jane said. "Let us drop the subject. I am too tired tonight."

"The maintenance of umbrage requires all the energy a person has," Martha said.

The other diners turned toward her. She was voluble enough when it was just the privy council of women at table, but she almost never volunteered an opinion when anyone else was present—even family. To Martha, being forward with opinions in public would show presumption that might appear to negate her thanks at the Austens' generosity, while also calling attention to her position. The spinster sister of Mary, James' wife, Martha had been taken in as the result of equal parts love and pity, for she was nondescript in every way except her feelings.

Surprised, Frank waited for her to say more, but she did not. Mrs. Austen and Jane were in fact astonished, for Martha had repeated Cassandra's words verbatim from several days before. Since Ashton's announcement, Cassandra's attitude had shifted from commiseration to challenge. That their mother and friend had sat silent during their arguments did not—evidently—indicate either a lack of interest or neutrality.

Carrying the huge weight of her sister's judgment, Martha's remark oppressed Jane nearly as much as the modest dining room, whose deep red color further constrained the space by making it dark. Though it had been renovated before their occupancy, the house at Castle Square felt as faded and tired as ancient wallpaper. Such is the impact of *comfortable* after one has lived in *luxury*. Mismatched possessions too small for this room or too large for that hall. The barely noticeable, *but noticeable*, scuff or furniture scrape. Beds a little tight in the attic. A smattering of prints insufficient for the expanse of walls. The only thing that beamed with pride were the miniatures on the mantel, particularly those of the two young naval officers—looking like twins—challenging the room—undaunted, even, by the living, full-sized counterpart who had come by today.

It was hard to believe that only a few months ago this room had been jammed with the four women, Ashton and George, Frank and Mary and their Mary Jane, plus James—when the laughter had expanded the walls and ceilings into a happy space for all (except, possibly, for James, whose unhappy loyalty to Steventon made the oldest brother *act* unhappy even when glad to be away).

Today, the cheery sun of Frank's personality could not burn away the saturating fog that constricted her emotional view. Everyone, it seemed, was content to see her husband take a musket ball.

"Jane, if you are angry with me for supporting Ashton," Frank said, "you should not take it out on others."

"She supports his plan with the same level of patriotic enthusiasm," Jane said. "Cass, I mean. The one who instigated these rebukes of her younger sister."

"I do not support Ashton's plan. I support Ashton. As a sister might. As a wife should."

"I must be honest, Frank. Ashton and I are not on the best of terms. He made the decision to go to war without consulting me. Without considering the consequences for me—for any of my family."

Her brother made a disarming remark, but Cass refused to let her comment go unchallenged: "You had been gone—of your own volition—for months! With no communication—your choice!"

Jane replied as a person maintaining civility toward another who is guilty of deliberate misunderstanding. "I had gone away from him to protest the fact that he had previously made another important decision—a life-and-death decision—without my involvement. It had devastating results. Yes, with George. I left to recover my composure, to gain perspective. To *regain* my belief in us as a couple."

Cass: "You left to punish him."

"The result?" Jane concluded. "He made *another* decision—as potentially fatal as the first—without considering me, without giving my feelings the least concern."

"Your argument is composed to be as complimentary to you as it can, and as derogatory as possible to Ashton," Mrs. Austen said. "In fairness, should you not be equally kind, or equally harsh, in your interpretation of both?"

After letting their mother's words resonate—Jane gave no inclination to respond—Frank spoke: "I have seen you relatively little, to be sure, but Ashton always seemed inclined to involve you in decisions. Even you must admit he acceded to your requests more than almost any other husband. More than I do with Mary, if I am to be forthright."

"My requests are more reasonable than hers."

Here Frank showed a little steel of his own: "Few would agree with that."

"He gave way in the little things in order to exclude in the big." Jane was going to say more, but the expostulations of the last few minutes had exhausted her. There was the energy required to avoid her sliding into despair at each reminder of her lost child, a ghost in every fleeting shadow of Castle Square. There was the energy needed to maintain the force of her complaints against Ashton. There was the energy expended to justify the belief that his own grief over George's death had turned him violent—had, perhaps, exposed a vein of violence that had always been present. There was the anger summoned to obscure this riot of feelings so that all she experienced was a violent thrum in her head.

In the middle of this discord among the women, as honest as it was unheard of, Frank hesitated to proceed. Cassandra took a sip of water. Jane did the same. As if the actions served to douse a few of the sparks of anger—to acknowledge that Jane was beyond further argument—the brother chose amelioration. "This will be a difficult expedition. The time of the year—approaching winter. The need to cross the mountains to reach Madrid. The uncertainty of support—the local population will cheer the army in residence—whichever one it is. Ashton does have his work cut out for him."

Chapter 24

Jane went to Cassandra as she was packing to leave for Godmersham to help Elizabeth, whose new baby was soon due. Hoping to reconcile but unsure how to begin, Jane dithered by asking her sister to relay the usual compliments to Edward, to give Elizabeth her best, and to hug the nephews and nieces for her. Cass nodded but did not let her focus waver; a practiced traveler, she knew that an item forgotten in a moment would be missed for a month. Jane sat on the bed, silent, hands folded, until Cass finished.

"Now—what?" her sister asked. She did not sit across from Jane as she would ordinarily, to establish the cozy camaraderie that marked their usual talks, but stood over her in a position of authority.

"I have felt your absence, while you have been here, more than I have ever felt when we were apart," Jane said. "You cannot add distance to the separation I already feel."

"Be pleased I was gone much of the summer, or you would have felt my distance more," Cassandra replied.

"Why must you be so cold? You know how I rely on you."

"I commiserated with you on the loss of your child. I supported you when you first became estranged from Ashton—I thought I could help you find your way back. I am far less cold than the ice you serve your husband."

"I must lose my sister along with everything else?"

"You suffer from your own device."

When Jane did not challenge the assertion, Cass said: "Look out the window. The war is here! Regiments choke the streets of Southampton and Portsmouth. Does that mean nothing to you?"

"We have no one to care for particularly among the troops—no one in fact nearer to us than Sir John himself."

Cass now did sit—reaching across and pinching the back of Jane's arm so that she cried out in pain. "*What—!*"

"My temptation is not to pinch but to slap—what you deserve. You know Ashton's regiment has arrived? That he is camped not twenty miles from here? Expecting to shortly leave for Spain?"

"I saw the same letter from James as you."

"Your husband is about to go to war, and you mark yourself clever for mocking him? While you wallow in this pig sty of your creation? He is the one to be pitied, not you."

"He left me—chose the war—"

"He lost his son. He lost his wife. He did not *choose* to go—you *sent* him. As before! He leaves because he has no reason to stay—or to live. You will never convince anyone of anything different. Not your brothers. Not your mother. Certainly not me, who knows what you have done." Cass spoke before the protest could be lodged: "Ashton did not kill your baby. Life killed your baby, as it kills half the babies in Hampshire—in the world! *Look at me!*" Cass took her by both arms and shook her. "At least you had a baby. At least you held him, nursed him, loved him. Treasure that. And the man you have."

"Do not bring up Tom Fowle to me. Your betrothed has died a hundred times for all the mentions of his revered name."

"I bring up Ashton Dennis. Your husband. Very much alive. The man you pledged to honor, for better or worse. But since you mention my betrothed, do you really believe I am better off to have lost him, before we ever began? Because it would hurt more once we had a life together? Am I content not to have had a husband or child, because one of them—possibly both—could have died? Would I have rather wasted away than bear the risk of childbirth?"

"Must we always compete in our catastrophes? You live the abstract pain of what might have been. I suffer the very real pain of what is."

"Only because you abuse the man who loves you. You seem to think that, when there is so much love on one side, there is no occasion for it on the other."

Jane remained still, too shocked to wrest herself free of her sister's anger. Cassandra let her go and stood ramrod straight. "If you will not go to him, then I shall."

"And what will you say to him," said Jane, laughing, "when you go to him?"

"That he is respected, admired, missed—*loved*!"

"You love Ashton?" Jane said, shooting to her feet.

"Of course I love him. How could I not?"

"You would go in my place?"

"Only if you are too stupid not to go yourself."

"You *love* him?"

"I love him now as anyone in my position must. If necessary, I will love him as someone else *should*." To Jane's shocked regard, Cassandra added: "I will not send him off to war unwanted. I will not give him a reason to die."

"You do not know how. To *love* him."

"It cannot be hard if one such as you can master it."

"Your effort to goad me is pathetic."

"Ashton will know he is loved by an Austen sister. At this point, he may not much care—which one."

"You will not touch my husband!"

"An unclaimed husband is no husband at all!"

"Then go—if you think that will make him happy."

Without a moment's hesitation, Cass grabbed her bag. She pointedly explained the conveyance and route she planned to take to reach Ashton's encampment and the servant who would escort her. This information shocked Jane even more than Cass's original pronouncement, for it proved that her outburst had not come in the heat of the moment, nor was it only an aggravation to spur Jane to act.

Jane fell back on the bed as if into a confessional. "I would not blame you at all, Cass," she said in an entirely different tone of voice. "I am not avoiding Ashton out of anger. It is out of hurt."

"His hurt for George is as great as yours."

"I do not mean that. I mean I cannot open my heart again. If we were to love again—and I lost him. Or another child. I cannot let myself be wounded that severely. Not only emotional pain—physical pain. Every thought, every feeling—about George, Ashton—sears my every nerve."

"The result is that Ashton suffers instead of you."

"I am brave about everything except what matters."

"Will you see him, Jane? At least to say goodbye? To give him hope?"

"The pain, as I said—"

"You are hopeless! If you are afraid of pain, why do you live?"

Cassandra swung her luggage within inches of Jane's face and stomped down the stairs. "To Godmersham!" she exclaimed to the man waiting in the hall. "Against my better judgment!"

Chapter 25

6 October 1808

Cassandra

I have sent you a chatty letter and will soon begin another. I repeat my felicitations about Elizabeth. She bears children with such ease;—her recovery is so rapid! Ten children in fifteen years—another one shortly!—and she looks younger and brighter than either of us! It is a wonder the doctors cannot patent her methods and make them available to all women.

The longer and gossipier my normal letters are, the shorter and deeper my other ones must be. It is a form of compulsion. Knowing that you will pass around the general note to the family, I fill it up with all kinds of talkative nonsense. The purpose is the same as having someone dominate the conversation in a sitting room while the real business is happening over in a corner. Our private communications are the ones that truly matter.

I have considered everything you said during our last conversation—if conversation it can be called. I understand that your intent was one of provocation, to shock me out of my own self-regard—my complacency—to bring me, as you would see it, to my senses. Before I can go further, however, I must ask you to tell me honestly what you meant about your feelings toward my husband. You and I cannot go on until I understand these emotions, and I certainly cannot approach Ashton until I know what complications exist between you and me. (We have the time—a reprieve—for Frank now tells us that the expedition will not leave until the end of the month. We have more troops than ships, and more transports are still to arrive from Cork.)

You have always had the strongest sisterly affection for Ashton. You have always shown the deepest appreciation for *his kindness to you and our mother as well as to me. I have seen you fingering the necklace of your cross as he has spoken to you. These things are not only acceptable but a mark of your own appreciative spirit and kindness. Yet surely you must understand how your comments have affected my mind, which was none too settled beforehand. More than once, my thoughts and fears have brought me full awake in the night. To realize that you had already planned how you would see him—I reel!*

And so I ask you to communicate frankly and honestly: Did you speak those words to wound me, to galvanize me into action, or did you mean them? Did you create this threat to force me to act—or something entirely different?

Jane
Castle Square

---

9 October 1808

Jane

My temptation is to wound you as you have wounded Ashton. My temptation is to say to you such things as—

"Did you create this threat to hold over me until I act—or do you love my husband?"

—Do not ask a question if you are not prepared to hear the answer.

—You cannot abandon your husband's affections and then claim possession of them.

—You took a vow for him. Honor it—or another woman—sister?—will.

But I will not repeat to you the cruelty you show your husband. Therefore:

I did not develop the plan to see Ashton for myself, you simpleton—it was for your benefit! I thought by now, with him soon to leave, you would at least be willing to see him off—with your deepest concern, and hopefully love.

As for me, I have held Mr. Ashton Dennis in the highest regard since I first recognized that his feelings for my sister were both generous and sincere. This recognition came before your own, as he did not resemble the dutiful clergymen you felt compelled to encourage even when they lacked the fire to sustain your interest.

My feelings for that man are as deep and kind as he deserves. These feelings are—I must add, though I need not—entirely appropriate to a sister.

Open your eyes! That you claim his affections for yourself means they are reciprocated! *You still love your husband—you never stopped. The pain you feel is the torment of one who has torn herself needlessly from the man she loves. I love him because of how he has loved my sister—nothing more—but that compels my fury when you are so fully in the wrong. If you do not change—and soon—you will bitterly rue the day when another woman equal to Ashton's merits comes along. He is an honorable man, but he will not be without feelings for the rest of his life. You will obtain the divorce you so arrogantly sought—and recognize at that bitter moment your foolishness to seek it.*

Y[r] *sister*

C. Austen
Godmersham

------

11 October 1808

My dearest Jane

We must put all else aside—Elizabeth is gone!

Our dear sister-in-law! Suddenly, unexpectedly, unbelievably—died! After eating a hearty dinner, she was taken violently ill and expired—may God have mercy on us!—in half an hour! The baby is fine—the rest of us—thunderstruck.

Edward, as you may suppose, is devastated but, out of habit and concern to set an example for the children, he displays his usual gentle manners. He sees to everyone, he issues orders to the servants and nurses, and yet he is not with us in any meaningful way. Mr. Whitfield's visit seemed to settle and to some extent organize Edward's mind, for the vicar prayed with him—and for him and the family—which gave him solace, as well as comfort over Elizabeth's soul. Fanny, bless her, is beyond grief. She retired to her room and has not come out. I sought very gently to encourage her, as the oldest child, to take a few small burdens off her father's shoulders. I expected nothing more than to keep her busy. All I achieved was to send her into greater paroxysms of grief, by reminding her of the many household accomplishments of her mother.

Except for Fanny—who, we must remember, was as close to her mother as any daughter who ever lived—I have been able to set the older children to useful tasks and to follow up with the nurses on Edward's rather indeterminate directions. The babies cry constantly—they do not understand what has happened, but they absorb the anguish in the air.

Henry is coming down, though the openness of his heart may make him receive more of our support than he provides of his. The one chore he must do is to deliver the unimaginable announcement to Lady Bridges about the death of her daughter. James and Mary are dispatched to Winchester to break the news to Edward's sons there. It is expected that James will take young Edward and George from college back to Steventon for a few days.

This house—always full of lively children—how are we to manage?

Dear Elizabeth—can you believe she is gone?

C. Austen
Godmersham

---

13 October 1808

My dearest Cassandra

I have received your letter, and with most melancholy anxiety was it expected, for the sad news reached us last night, but without any particulars; it came in a short letter to Martha from her sister, Mary, begun at Steventon, and finished in Winchester.—We have felt, we do feel for you all—as you will not need to be told—for you, for Fanny, for Henry, for Lady Bridges, and for dearest Edward, whose loss and whose sufferings seem to make those of every other person nothing.—God be praised! that you can say what you do of him—that he has a religious mind to bear him up, and a disposition that will gradually lead him to comfort.—My dear, dear Fanny!—I am so thankful that she has you with her!—You will be everything to her, you will give her all the consolation that human aid may give.—May the Almighty sustain you all—and keep you my dearest Cassandra well—but for the present I dare say you are equal to everything.

You will know that the poor boys are at Steventon, perhaps it is best for them, as they will have more means of exercise and amusement there than they could have with us, but I own myself disappointed by the arrangement;—I should have loved to have had them with me at such a time. I shall write to Edward by this post. We shall of course hear from you again very soon, and as often as you can write.—We will write as you desire. As for Lady B.—but that her fortitude does seem truly great, I should fear the effect of such a blow and so unlooked for. I long to hear more of you all.—Of Henry's anguish, I think with grief and solicitude; but our brother will exert himself and be of use and comfort.

With what true sympathy our feelings are shared with Martha, you need not be told;—she is the friend and sister under every circumstance.

We need not enter into a panegyric on the departed—but it is sweet to think of her great worth—of her solid principles, her true devotion, her excellence in every relation of life. It is also consolatory to reflect on the shortness of the sufferings which led her from this world to a better.

Farewell for the present, my dearest sister. Tell Edward that we feel for him and pray for him.

Y*rs* affec*tely*

Jane

Castle Square

  P.S. Perhaps you can give me some directions about the clothes you need for mourning.

  I will write to Alethea and Catherine.

———

14 October 1808

My dearest Jane

  Emotions ebb and flow but have not yet begun to subside. Edward will be soothed by prayers and his spirits will improve for a while; then he will wander about the halls, lost, the rawness of emotion leaving him tender to every experience. The cook preparing her usual good dinner has him proclaiming her worth to the dining room; his receipt of hot tea leaves him nearly in tears at the kindness of a footman. He is genuinely grateful for James arranging to take care of young Edward and George, but do not be surprised if they come your way. James will do the required, but Mary's generosity can be measured in cups, not bowls.

  Fanny remains in seclusion; she will come down to dinner but only to demonstrate that her grief is superior to anyone else's—including her father's. (Like many girls her age, she feels all severe emotion as rage.)

  Lizzy worries me the most, however. She is old enough to truly comprehend what has happened—to know that her mother has died—yet she is not old enough to have any mechanisms—such as Fanny's dramatic exits—to help her cope. Lizzy experiences the loss, fully, with neither innocence nor sophistication to shield her.

  Henry was a good help, but one responsibility fell to me I had not expected. The men concluded that Lady Bridges and Mrs. Knight should hear the news from a "senior, respected female member of the family." Henry accompanied me, and stood as solemn and forlorn as I know he felt, but it was left to me to explain to both elderly ladies what had become of their Elizabeth. They took it as well as could be expected—we use that expression all the time, yet I have no idea what it means. Lady Bridges cried at the loss of her beautiful daughter, Mrs. Knight at the loss of her beautiful daughter-in-law. Only the experience of age, and the loss of other loved ones in the past, inured them in any way to the pain. It was agreed that Edward would pay his respects later, when it is hoped all parties will be able to survive through the meeting without collapse. It will be as difficult for Edward to speak to his adoptive mother as it would be for him to speak to our mother. I cannot tell you how grateful I am that you and Martha have been there for her!—

I cried all the way back to Godmersham.

The service for Elizabeth will be on the 17th. Edward cannot decide whether to attend or, if he does not, who he should send in his place—whether Henry would be enough to indicate the proper level of respect. I have never understood the custom that older boys away at school remain away, because none of the other boys is old enough to attend and Edward cannot imagine leaving his children during those desperate hours when their mother is laid to rest. Would that funerals accepted the entire family instead of a few stately males. Edward could take his children and they could weep together and be done.

This is a good family. Elizabeth taught them courage along with manners. They are close to the low point, but one can sense in them the strength to rally. They are taking it as well as can be expected, which means—we will all get through it somehow.

I should have thought to mention the baby—they had already arranged a wet nurse, of course, and the boy has taken to nursing enthusiastically. He thrives!

Y^{rs} most affectionately

C. Austen
Godmersham

P.S. Please send whatever you think is suitable in the way of mourning; you know what clothes I already have here.

15-16 October 1808

My dear Cassandra

Your accounts make us as comfortable as we can expect to be at such a time. Edward's loss is terrible, and must be felt as such, and these are too early days indeed to think of moderation in grief either in him or his afflicted daughter—but soon we may hope that our dear Fanny's sense of duty to that beloved father will rouse her to exertion. That for his sake, and as the most acceptable proof of love to the spirit of her departed mother, she will try to be tranquil and resigned. Does she feel you to be a comfort to her, or is she too much overpowered for anything but solitude?

Your account of Lizzy is very interesting. Poor child! One must hope the impression will be strong, and yet one's heart aches for a dejected mind of eight years old.

I suppose you see the corpse—how does it appear? We are anxious to be assured that Edwd will not attend the funeral; but when it comes to the point, I think he must feel it impossible.

Your parcel shall set off Monday, and I hope the shoes will fit; Martha and I both tried them on. I shall send you such of your mourning as I think most likely to be useful, reserving for myself your stockings and half the velvet—in which selfish arrangement I know I am doing what you wish. I am to be in bombazine and crepe, according to what we are told is universal here; and which agrees with Martha's previous observation.

I have written to Edwd Cooper, and hope our cousin will not send one of his letters of cruel comfort to my poor brother; and yesterday wrote to Alethea, in reply to a letter from her. She tells us in confidence, that Catherine is to be married on Tuesday sennight.

I am glad you can say what you do of Mrs Knight, and of Goodnestone in general;—it is a great relief to me to know that the shock did not make any of them ill.

But what a task was yours, to announce it!

Sunday. We know that you must have been informed of the boys being at Steventon, which I am glad of.—Mary wrote to ask whether my mother wished to have her grandsons sent to her. We decided on their remaining where they were, which I hope my brother will approve of. I am sure he will do us the justice of believing that in such a decision we sacrificed inclination to what we thought best.—The poor boys are perhaps more comfortable at Steventon than they could be here, but you will understand my feelings *with respect to it.*

Tomorrow will be a dreadful day for you all!—Mr. Whitfield's will be a severe duty!—Glad I shall be to hear that it is over.

That you are forever in our thoughts, you will not doubt. I see your mournful party in my mind's eye under every varying circumstance of the day; and in the evening especially, figure to myself its sad gloom—the efforts to talk—the frequent summons to melancholy orders and cares—and poor Edward restless in misery going from one room to the other—and perhaps not seldom upstairs to see all that remains of his Elizabeth.

Dearest Fanny must now look upon herself as his prime source of comfort, his dearest friend; as the being who is gradually to supply to him, to the extent that is possible, what he has lost. This consideration will elevate and cheer her.

Adieu. You cannot write too often, as I said before. We are heartily rejoiced that the poor baby gives you no particular anxiety. Kiss dear Lizzy for us.

Yours most truly

Jane
Castle Square
P.S. Mother is not ill.

———

18 October 1808

My dearest Jane

*The first order of business is to hie thee to the Coach &
Horses, where two abandoned nephews may be standing for-
lornly in the rain. Though the rectory at Steventon once burst
at the seams with a dozen riotous children, James has let it
be known that the addition of two older boys to a household
with three existing children presents more difficulty than
his hard-working wife can sustain. The boys are better off
crowded into a small home in town with older women for
their entertainment. Nor would our brother wish to deprive
his family the opportunity to express their* love *in person to
their nephews as they grieve.*

*The disentangled sense is plain. Mary has had enough of
them—expect Edward and George on the coach to Southampton. Now, of all times, the dear boys require the open
arms of their family—not ones folded in exasperation.*

*Our brother, I believe, is finding his footing. Edward re-
mains overly solicitous to everyone, whether it is Thomas
helping him with his coat or the groom saddling a horse; but
his mind unfolds in orderly thoughts for an hour at a time
until lapsing in charming confusion; which is rather the opposite of the previous week. He was able to talk Fanny out of
her room to join us in a discussion about Chawton.*

*At first I was worried because settling the Austen women
in that village seems to begin his plans to shift his interests
from Kent to Hampshire—something that would not have
happened with Elizabeth alive, considering her family here.
Nor will it happen with Mrs. Knight still alive, as he is too
kind and shrewd to offend the woman who made him her
heir. Premature, to say the least! However, Fanny is unaware
of his thoughts in that direction, and the idea of helping her
grandmother with housing has animated our niece in a way
that nothing else has since—*

*Her father was careful to speak only in terms of Mr.
Seward's death last February and the availability of the bailiff's cottage. The advantages are plain even if Edward remains*

in Kent forever. Chawton is thirty miles closer, and most of the properties in the area belong to him. The only connection to Elizabeth is that her death seems to have stirred in him a desire to see his mother settled for good, as well as being a project to occupy his time. "Better in the bosom of our lands than in a lonely city by the sea," he said. You can be sure the mother of the landed proprietor will be shown every respect in that neighborhood!

I did not initially remember the house he has in mind, but it is the large, two-story cottage at the foot of the village, where the roads come together from Winchester and Gosport. The cottage has trees and a shrubbery. There is a pond across, between the two roads, and small worker tenements on the far side of the pond, in the trees.

Edward indicates the need for renovation, which he expects to take several months. Very likely we will need to visit and walk through the cottage with him. We would not have demands, of course, but he is determined to make it as comfortable for Mother as possible. I suspect we will have one of those conversations in which he will suggest more changes than any of us want, and he will think we are demurring out of modesty or concern over cost. Still—what a lovely conversation to have!

He gave Mrs. Seward the cottage through December, yet he is concerned about dispossessing her at this time of year, and whether it would be best to uproot all of us in the coldest, dirtiest season. If we wait until next summer, he will be able to prepare this cottage, as well as another place for Mrs. Seward nearby. Yet he knows how desperately our mother wishes to have her own home, and will leave the decision to her.

Another thought: We will be close to the Digweed farm and their house in Alton. The Digweeds always have the freshest fruit and vegetables. It will be nice to be a pleasant walk away from a family we know, and Harry will sprawl across the kitchen to regale us with the latest in sheep and cows.

A home again, after all these years of sooty, crowded apartments! Only fifteen miles from where we grew up! I can breathe better already.

Yet, I will be staying at Godmersham longer than planned. I cannot leave this family now under any circumstances. I will come home when a new, motherless routine has been established and Fanny has fully assumed the role of the elder daughter for a single father—his helper and hostess. You will understand the extent to which I miss you, Mother, and Martha, as well as you understand the necessity of my remaining here.

Y^{rs} affec^{tely}

C. Austen
Godmersham

24-25 October 1808

My dear Cassandra

Edward and George came to us soon after seven on Saturday, very well, but very cold, having by choice traveled on the outside, and with no great coat but what Mr. Wise, the coachman, good-naturedly spared them of his, as they sat by his side. They were so much chilled when they arrived, that I was afraid they must have taken cold; but it does not seem at all the case; I never saw them looking better. They behave extremely well in every respect, showing quite as much feeling as one wishes to see, and on every occasion speaking of their father with the liveliest affection. His letter was read over by each of them yesterday, and with many tears; George sobbed aloud, Edward's tears do not flow so easily; but as far as I can judge they are both very properly impressed by what has happened. Miss Lloyd, who is a more impartial judge than I can be, is exceedingly pleased with them.

George is almost a new acquaintance to me, and I find him in a different way as engaging as Edward. We do not want for amusements; cup-and-ball, at which George is indefatigable, spillikins, paper ships, riddles, conundrums, and cards, with watching the flow and ebb of the river, and now and then a stroll out, keep us well employed; and we mean to avail ourselves of our kind papa's consideration, by not returning to Winchester till quite the evening of Wednesday.

Mrs. J.A. had not time to get them more than one suit of clothes; their others are making their way here, and though I do not believe Southampton is famous for tailoring, I hope it will prove itself better than Basingstoke. Edward has an old black coat, which will save his *having a second new one; but I find that black pantaloons are considered by them as necessary for mourning, and of course one would not have them uncomfortable by the want of what is usual on such occasions.*

Fanny's letter was received with great pleasure yesterday, and her brother sends his thanks and will answer it soon. We all saw what she wrote, and were very much pleased with it. Tomorrow I hope to hear from you, and tomorrow we must think of poor Catherine and her wedding. Today Lady Bridges is the heroine of our thoughts, and glad shall we be when we can fancy the meeting over. There will then be nothing so very bad for Edward to undergo.

The St. Albans, *I find, sailed on the very day of my letters reaching Yarmouth, so that we must not expect an answer at present; we scarcely feel, however, to be in suspense, or only enough to keep the plans about Chawton to ourselves. We have been obliged to explain them to our young visitors, in consequence of Fanny's letter, but we have not yet mentioned them to Steventon. We are all quite familiarized to the idea ourselves; my mother only wants Mrs. Seward to go out at midsummer. What sort of a kitchen garden is there?*

Mrs. J.A. expresses her fear of our settling in Kent, and, till this proposal was made, we began to look forward to it here; my mother was actually talking of a house at Wye. It will be best, however, as it is.—

I hope your sorrowing party were at church yesterday, and have no longer that to dread. Martha was kept at home by a cold, but I went with my two nephews, and I saw Edward was much afflicted by the sermon, which, indeed, I could have supposed purposely addressed to the afflicted, if the text had not naturally come in the course of Dr. Mant's observations on the Litany: "All that are in danger, necessity, or tribulation," was the subject of it.

The weather did not allow us afterwards to get farther than the quay, where George was very happy as long as we could stay, flying about from one side to the other, and skipping on board a collier immediately. In the evening we had the psalms and lessons, and a sermon at home, to which they were very attentive; but you will not expect to hear that they did not return to conundrums the moment it was over. Their aunt Mrs. JA has written pleasantly of them, which was more than I hoped. While I write now, George is most industriously making and naming paper ships, at which he afterwards shoots with horse-chestnuts, brought from Steventon on purpose; and Edward equally intent over the "Lake of Killarney," happy enough to lose himself in an Irish romance and twisting himself about in one of our great chairs.

Tuesday. Your close-written letter makes me quite ashamed of my wide lines; you have sent me a great deal of matter, most of it very welcome. As to your lengthened stay, it is no more than I expected, and what must be, but you cannot suppose I like it. All that you say of Edward is truly comfortable; I began to fear that when the bustle of the first week was over, his spirits might for a time be more depressed; and perhaps one must still expect something of the kind. If you escape a bilious attack, I shall wonder almost as much as rejoice.

The day began cheerfully, but it is not likely to continue what it should, for them or for us. We had a little water party yesterday; I and my two nephews went from the Itchen Ferry up to Northam, where we landed, looked into the 74-gun under construction, and walked home, and it was so much enjoyed that I had intended to take them to Netley today; the tide is just right for our going immediately after noonshine, but I am afraid there will be rain; if we cannot get so far, however, we may perhaps go round from the ferry to the quay. I had not proposed doing more than cross the Itchen yesterday, but it proved so pleasant, and so much to the satisfaction of all, that when we reached the middle of the stream we agreed to be rowed up the river; both the boys rowed a great part of the way, and their questions and remarks, as well as their enjoyment, were very amusing; George's inquiries were endless, and his eagerness in everything reminds me of his Uncle Henry.

Our evening was equally agreeable in its way; I introduced the game speculation, and it was so much approved that we hardly knew how to leave off. Your idea of an early dinner tomorrow is exactly what we propose, for, after writing the first part of this letter, it came into my head that at this time of year we have not summer evenings. We shall watch the light today, that we may not give them a dark drive back to Winchester tomorrow.

They send their best love to papa and everybody, with George's thanks for the letter brought by this post. Martha begs my brother may be assured of her interest in everything relating to him and his family, and of her sincerely partaking our pleasure in the receipt of every good account from Godmersham.

Of Chawton I think I can have nothing more to say, but that everything you say about it in the letter now before me will, I am sure, as soon as I am able to read it to her, make my mother consider the plan with more and more pleasure. We had formed the same views on H. Digweed's farm. A very kind and feeling letter is arrived today from Kintbury. Mrs. Fowle's sympathy and solicitude on such an occasion you will be able to do justice to, and to express it as she wishes to my brother. Concerning you, she says: "Cassandra will, I know, excuse my not writing to her; it is not to save myself but her that I omit so doing. Give my best, my kindest love to her, and tell her I feel for her as I know she would for me on *the same occasion, and that I most sincerely hope her health will not suffer."— Love to all.*

Yours very affectionately

Jane
Castle Square

Chapter 26

The next morning, Jane took Edward and George to Mr. Wise at the Southampton coach stop for their return to Winchester. She could not be the fussy aunt smiling through her tears unless she saw that they sat inside the coach, and they could not be her lively nephews unless they climbed outside as soon as they were out of view.

From there, following Cass's directions, she went directly to Ashton's cantonment, which was several miles to the southeast, on the outskirts of Portsmouth.

She found her husband finishing up the morning's drills. He was conferring with Mr. Fletcher, himself now trim in a smart uniform, along with several young officers—two of them boys. The enlisted men were standing informally, chatting, their rows not yet fully dissolved, a few standing aside smoking pipes or drifting back to their tents. Mr. Fletcher, observing her first, called the company to attention; the men, seeing the approach of the mistress, quickly regrouped, dressed ranks, and snapped their weapons to. That she recognized many of the men from the estate and the parish, and that they hurried to organize themselves in sharp, proud alignment at her presence, caused her heart to swell. Ashton turned in puzzled annoyance at the unauthorized call to arms, saw Jane, and stared.

When she came to the distance at which an aide-de-camp might relay instructions from headquarters, she called to him: "Captain

Dennis! You once challenged me to declare my love for you in front of the world. Very well."

Imitating what she had seen officers do in parades, she swiveled to her left with as much precision as possible. "I hereby announce to the good men of Hampshire that I love my husband—deeply and truly. That I respect and admire him. That I repeat my marriage vows here for all the world to hear. Let us hear a cheer for our handsome Captain Dennis!" She whipped off her bonnet, thrust it into the air, and led the men in a military salute to celebrate their leader, concluding with all the company's hats being tossed into the air. The complete breakdown of discipline left Mr. Fletcher and the sergeants bellowing for order. Their dire threats of punishment brought riotous laughter. Ashton turned three shades brighter than his scarlet—except, Jane noticed, his uniform, and those of all the men, was green! He dismissed the troop, shouting above the din: "An extra ration of rum tonight!", bringing the loudest cheer of all.

It took more than a few minutes for the demonstration to subside and the soldiers to disperse, for, in addition to the disruption of military etiquette, many wished to pay their respects to Mrs. Dennis; and one young private—a footman in his former life—came with a bow to return her bonnet, which had sailed away along with the other hats. This show was more than their respect for Ashton or affection for the mistress: It was the sudden appearance of someone from home, a reminder of family, of wife and child, of a cottage snug—of all that they, very shortly, would leave behind in the wake of a tossing ship.

Eventually, Jane and Ashton could get away and walk into the fields surrounding the encampment, which contained several regiments as well as their own company. Alone at last, she stepped back to admire the way her husband looked. He had grown a moustache in the dashing Army style. "If we were not married, the sight of you in uniform would be enough to make it happen."

He smiled as he might at any woman's flirtation. "You realize that in two minutes you destroyed all the discipline it took six months to create. They will require a hard march tomorrow to return to the proper mind."

"It was worth it. For them and you. Their last chance to have fun before they leave. The last chance for you to show a little humanity."

"No doubt."

There was so much to say that neither could speak. She covered by asking about their uniforms. Rifles wore green, he explained, to blend in with the flora, as they skirmished among the woods more often than they exchanged fire in formations. The Redcoats did not have much use for the Rifles, and saw their uniforms as a sign of inferiority, but he was certain his men would prove themselves when given a chance. Their walk took them back to where Portsmouth began to pull itself together from scattered cottages and farms. One estate featured a home built of the honey-colored Bath stone in the style of a typical Bath residence; beside it was a large barn on which had been painted an image of the Royal Crescent. A bench had been situated so that passers-by could sit and enjoy the feigned view of the fashionable resort.

"A strange apparition in the suburbs of a grimy English port," she said. "We should all prefer to be seventy miles away, sipping tea at the Sydney Hotel."

"I was sorry to hear of Elizabeth," he said, brushing a strand of hair from her eyes but, upon becoming aware of his action, pulling back. "She was an exquisite thing. How is Edward—Fanny?"

"Devastated—crushed. But they are struggling back. Cass is there."

"Do any of you realize how hard it is for her to always be the rock?"

"I am beginning to. Her letters hurt to read. Edward and George came down—the boys."

"I saw you on the shore—George running about, chasing the gulls. Edward tried ever so hard to be an adult—but had to join in. You aching to wrap them up in your arms."

It ached now for her to think of Ashton watching them from a distance in his solicitous, protective manner, then slipping silently away.

At her look, he said: "Business in Southampton. Dashed up for the day. More problems with the rail-road." He laughed. "I swear this war will conclude before we have that thing functional. The circus in London is running. It's become a tourist novelty, but nothing more."

"I thought you might come by—to pay your respects."

"To Mrs. Austen, you mean? Goodness knows I wouldn't offer them to my wife."

She smiled, acknowledging the justice of remark, which because of its soft tone she could accept as a tease.

Looking into the distance—beyond "Bath"—he said quietly: "No. I would not come. I am done chasing."

Something in his words chilled her.

"W-we are d-different now, Jane—y-you and I."

The import was like a sentencing.

"Am I too late? Did I wait too long?" As full as her heart had felt at the welcome by the men, it shriveled now at the thought that her despair had infected Ashton, causing his love to collapse like a rotten squash. "After my proclamation—humiliation enough for us both—can you doubt my love?"

"We were everything until you had a baby. Then you were gone. We were everything until the baby died. Then you were gone. It's a pattern with you."

"Each event was different, impelled by different motives—" She stopped, recognizing that, regardless of how she might rationalize her behavior, from his point of view it did form a pattern.

"What kind of marriage is it when a partner leaves at every trouble?" Ashton said. "Isn't that when a marriage should hold most firm?"

"It was never a fault of yours. You always believed. You fought for us."

"I was as disconsolate. As heartbroken. As lost. You did not care—or notice."

"I was the coward. By thinking of us as one—I lost you. It was not until Cass provoked me—" Jane saw his reaction and set

him straight—"*she stood up for you*, Ashton. She made me understand what I had lost—thrown away. Earlier, she supported me in
the hope she could ease my way back. She loves you, Ashton. She
is your champion—a better friend than your wife has been." Indicating that he would accept her evaluation for now, he told her to
continue. "Cassy shook me up. I came to understand that I could
forsake you because you would never forsake me. It was more than
taking you for granted. It meant we were still tied together—by a
single thread instead of two, but together still. That kept me alive
through all my grief. … I was alone and yet you held me."

"I am not capable of holding you anymore. I cannot do the
work of two. Never again."

"I know. Cass's intervention had me glimpse a world in which
your heart was free to love whomever you chose—there was no
requirement that it be me. I realized I did not want you to love anyone else. I wanted you to love me. But I had to earn it—and that is
what I am here to do."

"I understand what you say. But, dear … we have got in the
habit of living apart. Thinking apart. Feeling apart. … *Grieving
apart.* … What is there to do together? Loneliness is the most
comfortable of lives." He spoke with less energy and more consideration than usual, the reflection of a man who has had nothing to
do for months *but think* in the light of a soldier's fire late at night.
"Certainly the easiest."

"You will never be lonely again. I promise you."

"As you've promised before and reneged—going all the way
back to my first proposal. You know, I threatened once to drown
you and your sister if you ever broke your word to me again. I
should have carried out my threat. Enough cold water, at least,
to make you feel *my* unhappiness. They matter, you know—the
feelings of people around you." These were the first words that expressed anger rather than resignation.

"The loss of you was obscured by the loss of my son."

He stared at her until she corrected herself:

"The loss of *our* son. O! Ashton—*I miss you both dreadfully.*"

She tried to explain what Elizabeth's death had helped her see. Compared to friends who lost many of their siblings growing up, Jane had lived a charmed existence. The number of people she knew who had died was relatively small, and only two—her father and Mrs. Lefroy—had lived in her heart. There was her aunt who came as a nurse during the typhus outbreak and her daughter, years later in a carriage accident; James's first wife; Tom Fowle, of course, Cassandra's betrothed; a young friend in Bath; Eliza's son, Hastings; her sea man, who might have made a husband; and Elizabeth. One or two others, likely, that had slipped her mind—because they were not of central importance.

All of them belonged to more than her; every relationship, including that of her father, had been secondary to that of someone else. "Our life—yours and mine—had opened me to absolute joy, and that gave way to absolute pain. George had been mine alone—*wait!*—that was my mistake. By failing to acknowledge your loss, I doubled our—your—pain. And then I saw Edward's agony *open* him to the smallest kindnesses. And my nephews instinctively opened to me—nothing more than a generous friend who offered them consolation. Anyone with any sense reaches for another—except for the haughty Jane. I did just the opposite."

"In retrospect, my willingness to always come to you did nothing but encourage you to leave," he said. "I try never to display any weakness to an opponent, for I know it will be used against me—as Lovelace, with the mare. It never occurred to me that I would need to stand *against* my own wife, to protect myself. Knowing I would always reach out, you felt free to walk away. You did not take my love as a comfort. You used it as a weapon."

"People who are afraid will use anything as a weapon. Even the love of their life."

"You are not afraid anymore? By my reckoning, you found that every kind of love was the path to death."

"I thought life was all sunshine, with the occasional rain. When I learned it was the other way around—I was destroyed. I thought God had abandoned me."

"You have not become a godless cynic like your husband?"

"No—but when life is easy, one is apt to think it is religion that makes it so. Self-satisfaction is the trap that seduces the pious—myself along with the rest. I took God for granted, along with you. I have not become hard, but I have become realistic. You are going to die, Ashton. And so am I. The Afterlife is for the Hereafter. The question on earth is how much love we give each other before we go. That is the sum of my wisdom."

"God will always exist where there are ones like you to believe," he said. He pulled her to him. She relaxed into his embrace, smiled at the scent of wool and sweat. *Husband.*

"I've missed you, love," he said, reestablishing the distance between them. "But I cannot carry you anymore."

"I will carry us both! It is my turn. Time to start afresh! You can play with your inventions. We shall have a laboratory where the greenhouse is. You can blow up all the things you want. I will give you a dozen babies. We will be happy."

She spoke with the lilting charm of their early love, and he responded with equal zest: "Babies and books—I'd settle for half a dozen each."

"Then come!" She stood and pulled him up. "To paraphrase my sister, hie thee to Hants!"

His expression was one of genuine confusion. "Jane, we leave momentarily. I cannot abandon my men!"

"But you said others would take your commission—if I pledged myself to you!"

"Months ago! We have worked and trained to exhaustion. Days on end—weeks! I know what they can do. They know what to expect from me. You can't replace that trust—not in a minute! You saw how they responded to you. Imagine if we drove off now in our fancy carriage. Sent them off to fight a miserable war while we went back to lounge in comfort! Their confidence would be wrecked. *Betrayal, Jane, betrayal!* How could they face the enemy, knowing their Captain had fled? I would rather run away in battle. Panic is understandable—but not *intent*. I could not send off my men without me. Nor would you let me!"

"No," she said. "I would not." She felt in her own blood the heat of his pride—not in himself but in the entity he had created with his company. "So this is your purpose. Not your gadgets and apparatus. To lead the rag and tag, who in the spring did not know a pitchfork from a roundshot."

"Two things have made me a man. Your love. Their respect."

"If my husband will not abandon his men, I will not abandon him. We will find each other again, Ashton. We will find our way. I know it will not be easy—I know I am mostly to blame—but I know equally well that we will succeed. I ask only the time to prove myself."

"Thank God." He pulled her close again. "Hants would love to have you home, but I understand if you prefer to stay with your people. We will have all the time in the world when I come home."

"That is not what I mean—I go with you."

He laughed. "You will *not.*"

"I saw the wives—*children*! The camp followers."

"Of the enlisted men. Not the officers. The women who have no place else to go."

"I have no place else to go."

"I will not take you back only to put you in danger!"

"Nor will I, you!"

"There are enough irregularities about this group as it is. A lady does not go to war."

"Mr. Ashton Dennis, the knocker-down of social barriers, cowering before the idea that *it is not done*! My, how the mighty have fallen."

"We are at our limit—twelve women for ten score men. Those are the rules. Weight and space constraints. We have been full almost from the day we formed."

"Then pay some private to send his family home. Hants will see after them until we return. Send them all home—and take it from my budget! Mrs. Lundeen can put them to work. There is a precedent for a lady at war, I have no doubt. Where there is a lawyer, there is a way. You said so."

"This is not a game, Jane. Even if we are stuck in a garrison, it will be the most miserable experience of your life."

"You have shamed me—properly so—for having abandoned you at every difficult point. How am I to prove myself if I stay home while *you* go off? I would be doing to you, what your conscience says you cannot do to your men!"

"No—I would go willingly. Knowing you were safe."

"And come home also knowing I had conveniently walked away again! You cannot have it both ways, Mr. Dennis. You demand proof of my love—here it is. No fancy proclamation. No public display. I go with you. I help you. I support you."

"You will worry me to death."

"You will have me at your side—or strapped to the mast. Choose."

"You will get only half the rations of a man."

"I am only half your size."

"Obstinacy is not a Christian virtue. Meekness. Resignation. *Obedience.* Those are the Christian virtues."

"If I have made you a Christian, then I have won. Now, come. Your men will not begrudge your time with me now. They would think it terribly ungallant for you to leave your wife languishing on the nights before we sail."

They *were* together, but their time more closely resembled their first nights together than those nights in which they displayed their mastery of physical desire. It is the easiest thing for an experienced couple to fall into those satisfactions that can mask fundamental difficulties; difficulties that, when they finally emerge, strike both people as a hateful betrayal. But Ashton did not, as he would have ordinarily, demand marital relations as a natural expression of their feelings; nor did Jane unloose the passions she had discovered within herself. Instead, they talked, and sought to understand what they really felt about the other, now, after all their trials; they confronted the things, big and small, that had come between them. He would not use the force of his personality to overwhelm her sensitivity. She would not use the subtlety of her mind to take advantage of his feelings. These and other promises, easy to make and one day perhaps all too easy to fail to observe. Yet a commitment made in good faith is the only honor we have. When they *were* at last together, Jane was struck by her repeated failure to understand that love was not a thing isolated in a moment but a series of interactions that solidified and strengthened under the pressure of time.

Chapter 27

It was a gull-soaring, sail-flapping day that cheered the men as they boarded the transports for Spain. Insults and jokes hid their nervousness, as few had stepped aboard so much as a fishing boat and likely none of them could swim. The transports, mostly civilian vessels of varying sizes and designed for everything from cargo to fish, spread across the Solent. The warships lay at anchor beyond, one or two of which would escort the fleet on the next morning's tide. General Sir David Baird's fine expedition, some fifteen thousand strong, was ready to go! Jane kept an eye out for the *St. Albans*. She might not have recognized Frank's ship from this distance, but it was due; any man-of-war dropping anchor was likely to be his.

Small boats came and went, the harbor as raucous as London Road. The harbormaster and his men were checking off their paperwork with a jaunty, self-important air, directing the sequence in which designated ships would pick up weapons and gunpowder—the latter in a different depot, both for safety's sake and to deter any thoughts by the odd radical. The air had a salt tang, but the general smile turned to a frown when a shift in the wind carried the stench of the prison hulks.

Despite his sincere and protective desire to keep her safe in Hampshire, far from war, it was not until Jane joined him on the dock, nervous but determined, that Ashton could finally believe that her fine words about commitment were more than pretty vibrations of the air but the foundation of their relationship going forward.

"You were correct," he said. "I hate that you will not listen. That coming with me might bring you harm. But if you had chosen safety now over danger, I could trust you only when everything about us was safe."

"Going to war, I find, is more nerve-wracking than promising to go."

"Still time," he said, though they were both smiling.

"No."

They had already filled one transport with equipment and supplies and were busy separating the men and horses for embarkation on two others. A few minutes later she noticed something. "Ashton, look—those horses." Not far away, on another part of the Portsmouth dock, they saw blue roans—the horses they had provided Lovelace for the last two seasons.

"What now?" Ashton wondered.

His question was answered later in the day when Colonel Lovelace sauntered down with his adjutants—and *Sawyer*—to inspect their progress.

"Captain Dennis! And Mrs. Dennis. What an absolute delight to see you." He looked Ashton up and down, finding nothing amiss in his dress but registering amusement at his moustache; and glancing at Jane as if to remind himself that his Kat was far the superior skirt.

"Colonel, I thought you were already in Spain?" Ashton said.

"I returned with Wellesley. Sir Arthur wanted someone he could trust to see to the resupply. Particularly for the cavalry. Rough going over there."

"Shame to lose any, then."

Ignoring the barb about the mare, Lovelace observed: "As cavalry are our greatest need, the Army has seen fit to deliver them last. The 7th, 10th, and 15th all at once, though any one of them could have left in September! Unfortunately, more horses perish in war than men. We require more fresh mounts than riders. I have no doubt the commissariat will be hopeless in providing the necessary provisions; still, we require all the stock we gather—including, I am afraid to say, a boatload or two of nags."

That explained Sawyer: an inferior trainer for inferior stock. Ashton's response was: "I hope you're not including Hants in that assessment. The ones over there look like our newest horses, and they appear to be in fine shape."

"No, no—I refer to almost all the horses *except* yours. Your quality is impeccable. The Hants brand is all a trooper needs to see. Other regiments sought to outdo our officers in their procurement efforts, but we raised the bids—'Keep them at any cost!' was the cry. I daresay I might have turned a profit." His shining smile served to indicate that profit had been the last thing on his mind but he was too much of a gentleman to turn it away.

"If you are here to inspect our latest offerings, most of the horses are already loaded."

"I have the utmost confidence in your stock. Forage is the big concern—and shoes." He called for the transport documents, consulted the itemization, and asked more in confirmation than question, "You bring two thousand shoes?"

"Two thousand and ten—a baker's dozen, as it were. Plus nails. Hammers. And several farriers. The Army seemed to have overlooked those necessaries. That transport, unfortunately, has already begun to take its position offshore."

"No matter. You have never failed to deliver."

"Rather a mundane matter for a senior officer, is it not, sir? Shoes—even for your cavalry? Sawyer here could have probably puzzled out the documents, and he's much more suited to crawling around a rat-infested hold." Ashton smiled genially at the overseer.

The Colonel laughed, to his man's disquiet. "How very true. Yet. There were other items that drew my attention." He consulted the bill of lading again. "A hot-air balloon. A large basket. Boxes of ropes and miscellaneous equipment. Surely, this is not *the* hot-air balloon? The French machine in which you and the lovely Mrs. Dennis so charmingly condescended into our lives?"

"The very one."

"Much as Sawyer might enjoy the opportunity to shoot it down again, I am afraid it is not suitable for a military expedition."

"The space was available. I'm paying for it."

"And what, exactly, is the British military to do with a hot-air balloon in the mountains of Spain?"

"Observation, was my thinking. It could be tethered well above a garrison to improve surveillance. At sufficient height, it could increase our warning of an enemy approach by a day. In an emergency, it might be useful for delivering messages."

"Yes, if the wind happened to be blowing in the right direction. If we were able to fill it in the middle of a battle and avoid a thousand puncture wounds."

"I honestly don't know. My intent was to determine the feasibility."

"I admire your ingenuity, Dennis—I always have. But this is not a science experiment. It is a military venture. A real captain would focus on the lives of his men, not some mechanical inamorata."

"My men will have my full attention. And I will abandon the device the moment it becomes a burden."

"I am afraid I cannot take that risk. You will *not* bring this equipment aboard."

"You are my senior, Colonel, but you are not my commanding officer. We are not even in the same regiment."

"Oh, but you are mistaken, Captain." He signaled for another document from his adjutant. "Your regiment—the 95th, is it not?—is already abroad. Yours is the first truly detached detachment I have ever seen." He laughed at his little joke. "Sir Arthur admired my initiative at requesting to take you on. The otherwise purposeless company from Hants will add infantry support for my hussar regiment until we reach your own—which could be days or weeks, depending on where we land. The least experienced soldiers in Spain will come under the wing of the most experienced command. *Much* to the general's satisfaction. I look forward to educating you in the art of war. I see it as my duty to assist your men in every way I can to overcome the inevitable jitters before their first battle—and of course that horrific shock the first time they see one of their friends blown apart. We would not want your little ducklings to scatter at the first sign of rain."

"My men will stand."

As Ashton read the order, the men around him positioned themselves as if warned of possible resistance, and the Colonel, while surveying the harbor, idly put his hand on his saber. Looking up, Ashton noticed the preemption and smiled. "A good day for a swim," he said, nodding at the filthy dockside water. He made a sudden movement that led everyone to jump—but it was only a salute. "Excuse me while I locate the boxes, sir," he said in a respectful, even tone. He turned away to call the nearest dockworkers.

After noting more carefully how she was dressed, Lovelace said to Jane: "You are going?"

"Yes."

"It is not for most ladies, but you will do."

Chapter 28

They lay becalmed for several days. After the first, the novelty of watching the many small boats skitter about like water bugs began to wear off, and after a while no number of visits from curious seabirds or truncated strolls around the small deck could forestall the onset of boredom.

At last, of an early evening, when the moon glowed over the water, the wind began to freshen and the passengers hurried forward. The crew assembled at their posts, attentive. The master pulled out the glass to monitor the headquarters ship, which, except for the stature of its occupants, was undistinguishable from the rest of the freighters. Everyone milled about, eager to be on their way, wondering who would decide whether the wind would likely hold. After many minutes, during which they saw an exchange of signals between the headquarters ship and their military escort, they saw flags run out on the freighter and its sails promptly billow. The masters of forty ships rang out orders; the crews sprang into action; forty anchors weighed; forty sails blossomed in a series of gentle cascades that swept across Spithead.

There was a surge, and then a settling of motion, and because all the ships were moving together it did not appear they were making much progress until one noticed the change relative to land. "We go!" Jane said. It was an easterly breeze that took them out past the Needles on the Isle of Wight. As the flotilla came around the rock formations and began to tack against the wind to the south, the varying speeds caused the ships to begin to separate. A few small gunboats, which had paralleled the civilians, slipped into the holes in the groupings. "A sheepdog for every dozen sheep," Ashton noted. The largest naval vessel, the only true warship, flanked the convoy on the ocean side.

The same wind that took them out brought Frank in. The *St. Albans*, softly illumined by the cross-lights of late sun and early moon, stood off while the ships passed. When perhaps half of these had crossed its line, the *St. Albans* fired a salute, flames rippling from the barrels and reports echoing along the hills, bringing cheers and the waving of hats from the passengers and sailors crowded upon the many decks. Jane started to tell everyone that the salvo was courtesy of her older brother, but Ashton indicated she should treat the action as a private message. Frank knew that Ashton would be somewhere in the mass of bobbing transports. Would he suspect that Jane might be there too?

Big swells in the Channel brought the first onset of distress to the transport; the Dennises congratulated themselves on the strength of their stomachs while other landlubbers rushed to the side to disgorge their meals. The weather set fine on Friday and Saturday, a light northwest wind pushing the transports along (according to the master) at a steady four knots. Jane took it as a fine omen that their frigate was the *Endymion*, on which Charles had served several times.

Night came. Nothing ever delighted her senses as much as the nearly silent progress, on a bright moonlit night, of these whispers of ships, neatly ordered to the horizon; the synchronous rise of the forty on the waves, the synchronous fall; the rustle and ripple of the sheets; the murmuring of the divided sea. She understood the dangers; she knew that a broadside more usually signaled death than celebration. Yet she felt a certain tranquility in knowing that her brothers, on many other nights, had served their watch under the same soft light and twinkling stars; that they had felt the same rapture; that they could pine for home and yet never wish to be anywhere else. As much in communion as they had ever been, she and Ashton stood by the rail until after midnight, when the moon and constellations could relax and begin their drowsy downhill slide to America.

Before dawn on Sunday they were awakened by a violent shudder, almost as if the ship had collided with another in the dark. Orders barked. Sailors shouted with alarm. Hatches slammed. Sails rattled down as lines screeched through block and tackle. By the time they got up top, the wind was blowing hard and rain was pelting down. Within the hour it was blowing a fresh gale. The ship pitched and rolled: two pitches forward and three rolls—left, right, left—followed by two more pitches. The sequence was as regular as a metronome that measured the beat of nausea. They learned that having greater fortitude *early* meant only that they had more to heave into a bucket *late*—by now, with waves crashing to the beam ends, it was too dangerous to be on deck. There was nothing to do but sit and use the bucket or lie until one felt able to sit and use the bucket. The passengers developed a progression not unlike a dance in which people moved up and down the line in keeping with the level of their distress. The horses and mules became confused and dizzy. They did not suffer human biliousness—their colic might prove dangerous later—but they expressed their distress in ways that were even more severe.

After several hours of thrashing seas, a large cask of wine broke loose. As its movement in the compartment was both capricious and unsafe, the cask led Ashton and the other men in a fine game of chase for nearly an hour before they re-secured it. After that, it was a return to the effects of the boat's motion in the mountainous seas and unrelenting rain, which did not diminish until early afternoon.

Monday opened wet and cold, the ocean itself dispirited from its excesses of the day before. The storm had blown the fleet quite literally to the winds, for nothing could be espied in any quarter. The only choice was to proceed and hope to find the English before the French found them. Tuesday was even more dismal but was still too done in to work itself into another tantrum. By now they could see a sail here and there. Most tacked warily away, but one closed on them in a decisive and ominous move. The master called for the carronades to be loaded, though the three-pounders lacked the bite to scare off a privateer. The strange vessel displayed the French flag at the last moment, when it offered the courtesy of a shot across the bow, as it was to no one's advantage for the prize to be damaged. The master slowed but did not completely stop, managing to steer the vessel clumsily and, seemingly without intent, frustrating the enemy's ability to close and board. When the Frenchman caught on, he sent a cannonball singing through the lines, a way of inquiring: *Did we misunderstand one another?* When the master at last relented, the other vessel suddenly veered away, heeling over with the sudden deployment of its sails. Everyone stared in amazement until the *Endymion* plunged past in pursuit, damaging the retreating ship with a fusillade before turning back and signaling the transport to stay close.

In the middle of that night, Jane was roused by a rustle, an exclamation by Ashton, and the glimmer of a candle, quickly doused. A cabin boy had come down in search of something in the cupboards without realizing he was poking his torch where the unused carronade cartridges had been stored to keep them out of the rain. "I ardently wish to be in Spain," Ashton said after shooing the boy away. "We are less likely to be blown up there."

Come morning, they had lost the *Endymion* again, but they avoided any further molestation by the enemy. By midday Wednesday they were in sight of the Spanish coast and by evening anchored outside Corunna, waiting their turn to go in. Despite problems with the lines that caused delays, they warped into the harbor on Thursday. Being very nearly the last to arrive, however, they were not able to commence unloading until Monday.

That morning, as he had every morning, Ashton gave his men the freedom to walk about the town. He checked every day in the hope of finding orders, but none were to be had. General Baird, heading the expedition, had already left. The 95th was with Moore, and the rest of the infantry was marching out; there was no other regiment to be attached to.

Lovelace's ship, though arriving after, was given priority. They were standing beside the street halfway up from port when they saw their nemeses emerge. Lovelace rode his white stallion. Already, the Colonel's fair skin had reddened from the cold wind and spattering rain. Though mostly covered by his greatcoat, what could be seen of his uniform was immaculate, the buttons shining, braid glistening. Directly behind him came Kat upon a black horse, dressed more as though she were on a Sunday ride in Hyde Park than embarking upon a military outing. In addition to the protection offered by her hat, Kat also had the benefit of an umbrella. This was held over her head by Philip, the negro servant they treated as a slave, who rode beside her on a mule. On Kat's lap rode a small King Charles spaniel. This was new, perhaps a required addition to the inventory of a lady accompanying her man to war. Behind came her maid—the young one, not Mrs. Ormsby—on a donkey. Trailing the maid, attached to the donkey's saddle by a blue ribbon, came a small goat, there to provide fresh milk for her lady. Several attendants accompanied a light wagon carrying her things, including a teakettle and a cage of canaries, both swinging with the wagon's motion. Last in the caravan was Sawyer, positioned to keep the auxiliaries moving along.

None of the animals looked in good shape; the enforced idleness before their departure from Spithead and the delays in unloading had undermined their legs. Ashton and Mr. Fletcher had directed that none of their stock be ridden for at least two days after disembarkation, and only after restorative exercise. This was a luxury compared to the regiments, of course, because all of Ashton's mounts were spares. Still, Ashton noted that the other hussars were walking their horses up the hill. The plan evidently was for the Colonel to rendezvous with his troops beyond the narrow streets of town.

Lovelace nodded in passing to Ashton and Jane, while Kat acknowledged them as the queen might acknowledge her subjects.

"Noah had less baggage on the ark," Jane said.

"We'll see how far they get," Ashton said.

"I feel as if I am letting down Hants," said Jane, who wore sturdy if handsome clothes, "dressed for a march instead of a parade."

"At least now we know why there wasn't room for the balloon."

PART III

November 1808–July 1809

Chapter 29

Cassandra

As you will have read in my hasty dispatch from Portsmouth, I have at last taken your advice and gone to claim my husband. You may not have expected this assignment to take me as far afield as Spain. The reasons are too deep and complex to explain by letter, but you will believe me when I say that this was the one way to save my marriage—not that Ashton was happy with my coming. I will let you decipher the sense of that last statement.

I will begin by telling you about the ancient city of Corunna. It is dominated by the citadel, but its most striking feature is a lighthouse, here since Roman times, of a design unlike any I have ever seen. It is called the Tower of Hercules, as the locals ascribe the building of it to the Greek hero. Ashton and I designed to walk out to the lighthouse and, judging by the surrounding windmills, estimated it to be a mile or more away. We walked over the first hill—and there it was! The windmills, being only eight to ten feet in height, provided a false perspective.

Corunna itself is as one imagines an old European town to be—a very unfortunate old European town. For someone with the English standard of cleanliness, it is difficult to describe the conditions. The stone fortress, old houses stumbling *drunkenly down to the sea, wretched quarters for the poorest (for everyone is poor). The Pescaderia sells every kind of produce along with fish; it is disordered rather than bustling. The main streets have flagstones, the secondary streets are dark and narrow. I agree with one officer, a Captain Walsh, who said the place was "something like a miserable Welsh village, but to describe the filth and dirt that incommode the streets would be impossible." The people themselves are so wretched that one supposes they do not notice the nastiness around them. The men cover themselves with heavy cloaks and cocked hats, as much to protect the streets from their grime as the other way around. The women are dressed worse, if that is conceivable. Bad teeth, all!*

Cart drivers push their oxen through the crowds, yelling commands over the screeching of their wooden axletrees. The story is that a well-greased vehicle once silently ran over a cleric whose head was "fuller of wine than devotion," and the junta passed an act insisting upon noisy carts rather than sober priests. The din, compared to which London is as quiet as the grave, compels everyone to communicate in loud voices and wild gestures that seem to token violence. Our men express their disgust and treat the people as inferior creatures. Their misery must *require them to be lazy and useless. Yet I see a castle town torn from the Dark Ages—something like feudal rule is evident today. The people have been so poor and depraved for so many centuries that they are blind to any other possibility.*

We tried the theater, which was poorly acted but well-danced. Some officers and a few of their wives—I am not the only wife here!—expressed outrage at the sensuality of the female dancers, but I found them fascinating and their use of castanets—small, wooden shells, played as accompaniment by the fingers—to be enchanting. Ashton, of course, loudly demonstrated his rendition of the steps on the street afterward. There was a ball which the Lovelaces and other officers attended, but we chose not to go. Yes, Colonel Lovelace and his wife, Kat, are here with the hope of making our campaign a difficult one. We hope to find asylum in a regiment out of his purview.

On a personal note, Ashton and I are adjusting to being together again. There is a tranquility between us that is difficult to explain. We lack the novelty of the newly married, but we equally lack the continuity of couples like Frank and Mary, who have also been separated for many, many months. Theirs, however, was because of circumstances rather than the choice of one or the other. In some ways, we are like newlyweds: Privacy of that sort must be stolen, but that is part of the fun. In other ways, we are as comfortable as an old shoe. It is not expectation, or belief, or hope—or even passion!—that holds us now. We are together because we want to be. That is all we have; that is all we need. He is such a fine man! Cranky, clever, fine—mine. Grief makes us hurt. It makes us helpless. I never thought it would render me stupid in the treatment of my love.

General Sir David Baird began moving troops forward before we even arrived. The last of this first contingent is still waiting to leave. We will follow within a few days, but beyond that we know nothing. The officers serving in the last detachments are scheduled to meet tomorrow on the operational details. I will plan to write at least once more before we set out.

Y^{rs} affec^{tely}
Jane

Mrs. Ashton Dennis
Corunna, Spain

Chapter 30

There was little in the way of food suitable to the English taste, so that Ashton's men preferred to eat onboard until space opened in the St. Lucia barracks overlooking the harbor. The wait was brief, but Ashton paid the ship master over his complaints that the soldiers were nibbling into his profits. For the officers, there was only one hotel that catered to foreigners, Hotel d'Ingleterra, though the "*English* Hotel" was rightly referred to by the Army as the "*British* Hotel." Its food was plenty—meat, game, fish, poultry—highly spiced, and almost passable. The bread was gritty and sour and the diluted wine was more sour than the bread—one must add sugar and spice until it was mulled to one's satisfaction. The officers grew infuriated with the servers for their inability to understand proper English—spoken, naturally, in the dialects of a dozen counties, not to mention Irish and Scots. They were further mystified that Ashton and Jane received their food promptly and in better proportions because they used the word "senor" instead of "muchacho" and had learned such complex phrases as "por favor" and "muchas gracias."

After inspecting the rooms, in which from the correct angle one could observe on the beds the bounding contests of athletic fleas, the Dennis family found lodging with a physician on the outskirt of town. This house, built in a square, contained a courtyard within, and had spacious though nearly empty apartments.

Whatever other ills they might suffer, the Spanish must be hardy, for they required neither furniture nor fireplaces.

There being little else for her to do, and seeing the other ladies escorting their officers about town, Jane joined Ashton as his formal duties began. Ashton's men came with them part of the way with the last of their cargo—the extra food and equipment he had brought on his own initiative. Their large group jostled with the natives through the filthy flagstone streets. English and Spanish cart drivers cursed their opposites in their native tongues, the sense being as plain as the words were unintelligible. The crowds at least expressed their gratitude for the British presence along with intense declamations against the French. The beggars had a little ritual involving the Upstart's name. One would shout "Buonaparte," and another would smile delightedly and correct it to "Malaparte!" This cry was expected to earn a financial reward, and Ashton was happy to oblige. Jane wondered, however, whether a similar ceremony, involving deprecations of the British, occurred when the citizens found themselves among the French.

The regiment's heavily laden carts went one way with Mr. Fletcher to the commissariat, while Ashton and Jane turned the other way to report to the municipal building where the military plans were to be outlined. Upon arrival, however, they found the office nearly as clamorous as the streets outside. A beleaguered set of financial men and clerks, led by the Army agent, contended with the regimental commanders. General Baird's expedition had gone abroad with the design of tapping into the immense cache of money already delivered to Spain, but the agent was refusing to release any funds, insisting that he had received no authorization from London.

"The Army is here!" Colonel Lovelace shouted above the rest. "You cannot send us away penniless! We have a war to fight, you fool!" Lovelace, another dozen colonels, their wives (exasperated on their men's behalf), and a swarm of adjutants pressed upon the finance men. The agent, one Mr. Frere, was a corpulent man who used his girth in conjunction with a heavy wooden table to keep the besieging officers at bay. A military guard stood ready to aid the agent but looked none too happy at the possible necessity. "General Baird and General Moore have given you all the authority you need," Lovelace insisted.

"We explained the circumstances to General Baird," said Mr. Frere, his jowls shaking. "Neither he nor General Moore control our finances. We report to the Government, which has sent us no directives regarding the new expedition." He expounded at some length with vague assurances that, when parsed, were nothing but an evasion: The requirement for paperwork stood before all.

"That London sent you an Army should be instruction enough," Ashton inserted. "Do you—or they—expect us to turn around and go home?" Mr. Frere began to respond but, seeing that he was only a Captain, turned away. Each layer of his jowls was a different shade of red.

"In the last weeks, you have sent tens of thousands of dollars to the Corunna junta," Lovelace remonstrated. "The result is that they have failed to provide either provisions or transport as agreed. Now you refuse to give us money to obtain them on our own."

"The Government was very clear about our duties," said Mr. Frere, who was sweating through his shirt. "We are to fund the partisans, as they issue requisitions. They will do the bulk of the fighting. Our purpose is to support them. Your task will be incidental."

"Where are they?" Ashton demanded. "No soldiers—no weapons—no wagons!"

"You gave Sir David the money to start out with the first half of our Army," another officer said. "You can't believe that London intended the rest of us to rot in port."

With some exasperation, Mr. Frere explained that about half of what he had released to General Baird had been held on account for General Moore—all that remained of *those* funds—and Sir John had authorized a transfer. That action was perfectly in order. The other half, Sir David had signed for personally.

"You're seriously telling us that a British general had to take out personal loans from you in order to fight his country's war?" Ashton asked. "Still—if Sir David signed for the money, release it!" Mr. Frere again sought to ignore him because of his rank, but the last point led to more outbursts by the senior officers, forcing a reply.

"We need more collateral before we can release the last of the silver. General Baird signed for only so much."

"Perhaps the easiest solution would be to shoot you all and take the money we need," Colonel Lovelace said. This comment caused Jane to shudder, as she well knew what he was capable of. "We would certainly put it to better use than your purchase of phantom arms for phantom soldiers." This remark caused the shouts—along with Mr. Frere's perspiration—to reach a crescendo. Finally, he made a loud protestation for quiet so that he could make a proposal.

"I invite your representatives to read our very strict directives from London and the contract with Sir David. Our company will be held directly accountable for any spending not authorized by London. Physical threats will not force us to act—not if we're thrown into Newgate upon return to England."

Lovelace, acting as *primus inter pares* among the Colonels, sent the rest of the officers to the other side of the room while he inspected the documents. He invited Ashton—strange as that request struck the Dennis family—to join him. After their review, they grudgingly conceded that Frere was not only within his rights but had no other choice, for he faced fearsome penalties for any release of any coin not specifically approved *in writing, in advance*, by the Government. "General Baird apparently miscounted the number of men behind him," Lovelace said, "or felt uneasy at signing for more loans than he felt he could bear."

"With more collateral," Mr. Frere said, "I could alleviate your distress." He looked about at the mostly aristocratic officers, appeared to be calculating the wealth of the room, and announced that he could release whatever amount of Spanish dollars required, provided that, like Baird, the officers personally vouched for as much. "If what you say is true—and common sense says that Government orders are on their way—I will soon receive the proper authorization and the loans will be released. Very little risk."

"That is far too much to put upon the officer corps," Ashton said. "You give us what we need—now—and we will give you surety for half. Or we will guarantee that this is the last Government contract you or your firm ever win."

"Impossible," Mr. Frere avowed.

"An Army can't fight if its leaders are worried about losing all they have because of a paperwork problem in the rear," Ashton said. "A soldier putting his life at risk cannot also risk his fortune."

"I can act only if you sign for every Spanish dollar."

"Under your proposal, you are neither helping the Army nor taking any responsibility—which is your job as Army agent," Lovelace observed. "If that is the best you can do, then we face less risk by taking the money and facing a court-martial. And we will be glad to put you in chains until we return to London to settle the dispute." He added with his glorious smile: "I suspect that will not be anytime soon."

After seeing that the last exchange had only provoked more hostility of the military force about him, Mr. Frere threw up his hands in a gesture of defeat, agreeing to the terms proposed by Ashton.

"Captain Dennis and I will each sign for"—Lovelace named a generous number—"which should leave a manageable amount for the rest of our gentlemen." Though Jane gasped at the size of the commitment, Ashton readily agreed. The documents were instantly drawn up and the formalities concluded. The officers moved to a conference room to discuss the deployment and Mr. Frere left to change his shirt.

---

19 November 1808

My dearest Cassandra

It is my pleasure today to describe to you the British strategy in Spain, which is to throw huge bags of money at any beggar who claims to have a Spanish army hidden in the trees, while leaving the British Army penniless! Ashton and

I have only just returned from a very frustrating day dealing with the bureaucracy that surrounds our Army, astonished that the very men sent to support our soldiers are acting in ways that endanger their lives! The Army agent here, one Mr. Frere—though no brother to the military!—would not release funds to our regiments, while lavishing hundreds of thousands of Spanish dollars on our allies to purchase arms for nonexistent soldiers! The ignominy: Not only Sir David but all of his officers had to take out personal loans in order to mount a military expedition! My detestation of the Colonel has dropped a notch, as he and Ashton stood for the greatest part—and were the first to sign.

Where is Henry when one needs a competent agent, who understands that the purpose of the job is not to impede the Army but to help it?

We had no more finished that confrontation when word came from Mr. Fletcher of problems at the commissariat, where he was delivering extra supplies. First the commissariat officer refused to accept them; then he attempted to requisition them without payment. After we hurried over, it became obvious that the people in charge of managing the supplies for a huge Army have no more logistical skills than you and I require to ship a box through the post. There were more drivers, standing about gossiping, than there were animals to drive or carts and wagons to be pulled. There were more supervisors than loaders; yet judging from the shouting—which had a tone of alarm rather than excitement—these supervisors lacked the authority to respond to new orders, which were coming in from the field by the minute. To the lack of overall movement, Ashton asked: "Are the men to carry a winter's provisions on their backs?" No answer. The loading strategy consisted of jamming onto a cart whatever fit—no thought of putting like with like. Ashton reclaimed the horseshoes because we found they had put the nails in with flour boxes and had already lost the hammers! He was so frustrated he withdrew our additional supplies along with our own carts. He signed a separate note for the misdirected farrier cargo, which he also reclaimed; the commissariat seemed glad to be rid of even a small pile of materiel. "The imbeciles will either lose the note along with everything else," he said, "or they will cook it in the flour."

Drama enough before we even begin! We have been given a departure date. The plan is to move in small detachments. One reason is the lack of conveyance for the supply trains. Wagons must go back and forth to ferry supplies and equipment. The other is consideration for the stock, which need more time to recover from their confinement onboard. Even with rest and light work, Mr. Fletcher fears that some may be permanently ruined.

Finally, then—every preparation has been made for our departure. The Army runs a regular post system from the front, but ships depart for England at irregular times. Do not be alarmed if my epistles are few and far between. Dispatching a letter from deep in Spain is not the same as sending one from Hampshire. As we do not yet know which regiment will accept us, it is not possible to reply. For now, the communication must be one-sided.

Do not worry about me, sister—this is the adventure of a lifetime!

Y^{rs} affec^{tely}

Jane

Mrs. Ashton Dennis
Corunna, Spain

Chapter 31

28 November 1808

Cassandra

In four days, we have walked the distance from Steventon to Southampton. We rest for a day here at Lugo. ...

We covered only a couple of leagues each day at first. As I explained, we needed to rest the horses, and we lacked transport and supplies to do much more. One part of the brigade would move up, the carts would go back, and another part would come, & etc. We at last have sufficient transport—pulled by oxen, mules, asses, horses—and the question to mind now is: Where did Spain get so many beasts of burden? We have thousands, the French have thousands, the Spanish army—when we find it—must have thousands. Were all these animals standing around in a pasture waiting for war to start?

I imagined that, beside my gallant husband, I would ride into battle astride a charger, England's Joan of Arc. Instead, I struggle along on icy, muddy roads behind miles of baggage train, moderating the querulous chatter among women who seem more eager to fight with the wives of the other regiments than they do with the French. ...

I could ride with Ashton—other wives join their husbands—but these, like Kat, are the wives of the cavalry officers. I am the only infantry wife, and he is a lowly Captain.

I have neither the elegant riding clothes nor the grace—nor the expensive mount!—to match the other ladies. In a saddle, I look what I am: a plain farm girl who can competently ride a farm horse. Which makes me neither fish nor fowl: not stylish enough to ride out proudly but "better" than one of the ordinary wives who wonder if I rattle along in the rear to keep an eye on them—which, as it happens, I do.

The women are supposed wait until after the soldiers march off each day, and they are to remain behind the supply wagons, to prevent interference with the movement of the Army. The first day, our women ignored this stricture, and Lord Paget, the overall cavalry commander, sent back a stern reproach about followers clogging up the roads. (I can report that our contribution was women only, as the three wives with children took our offer to return to Hants for the duration. The other women insisted they would rather be with their men on the campaign than in Hampshire alone. I cannot very well argue with that logic! This leaves us 10 women for 190 men—180 infantry and 10 to care for the horses.)

To make certain our female company obeyed, Ashton put me in charge of the "reserve." Much to the complaints of our ladies, which I heard all day, we followed protocol and marched behind. The result was, we had the worst camping location of anyone in the Army, and the men sat around cold and hungry for an hour—every other regiment had ignored the order! This created an uproar among our people. Their job—the women's—is to provide good camp, good water, good food. They cannot do that if they remain in the rear. A conference among the officers led to an agreement that each regiment could have an "advanced guard of skirmishers" go in front to set up camp and begin cooking, while the majority remain out of the way.

We send ahead our toughest crew. Among the Hampshire recruits, I am glad to say, are perhaps a dozen previous soldiers and five or six wives. They know what they are about, especially Sergeant and Mrs. Stout. The men have helped Ashton and Mr. Fletcher shape up the company from the start, and now their women have taken charge of the rest. That most of the others are cavalry emphasizes the social stratification, and several of these wives informed our women that they needed to shift to a less advantageous location as hussars, being the elite, should take precedence over mere infantry—the men who had ridden all day above those who had walked. I will spare the details, but our women quickly disabused the other ladies of that notion, and everyone now understands the wisdom of giving the "Redcoats of the Rifles" a wide berth. The name comes from the fact that our female veterans wear redcoats from previous tours—stripped from the dead on the battlefield—shabby now, but a more serious badge of service than any campaign medal.

We are led by the redoubtable Mrs. Stout, the sergeant's wife, a woman as fierce as she is round. Her personality, along with her position, works to everyone's advantage because the ladies generally defer to one another according to their husband's rank. I thought this strange at first but now see that it makes sense. An established hierarchy provides immediate stability in an uncertain environment; and a severe dispute between two women would involve the men anyway, and rank on that side would be a deciding factor. I am like a young lieutenant who—I hope—has the wisdom to rely on an experienced soldier in my ranks!

I have been assigned the general oversight of the women and children in the rear, for lacking any central authority they tend to become disruptive, or aggravate the locals by excessive foraging, or otherwise become scattered and strung out for miles. A few families have a donkey, but mostly everyone walks. The babies are usually carried on the back in a modified knapsack, while the older children walk. I keep the lot from weighing down the supply wagons—they have piled on in such numbers that they have brought the strongest oxen to a halt. I turn a blind eye to the very young children (some are barely old enough to walk) and anyone who is seriously ill. The wagon masters take this as a reasonable compromise.

I am, however, useless in camp. Ashton is often in meet-ings, and the cavalry ladies have not seen fit to invite me to their teas. Not that I am interested in being served by slaves or maids who have already walked 20 miles through the cold. (Few of the auxiliary mounts survived, and those that did were reallocated from the lesser to the superior persons.) In keeping myself occupied, I sought to assist with the mending and sewing and the laundry, but Mrs. Stout took me aside to explain that I was taking food out of the mouths of the other women, as they earned their money by providing those services to the single men. Indeed, as a lady I was expected to pay the other women to wash and mend my things! When I tried to help with the cooking—open rebellion! The Red-coats would not allow the honor of the 95th to be debased by the servile behavior of its mistress. And so I spend my eve-nings visiting with the women and offering unneeded advice and encouraging the men with smiles and niceties. That is to say, I am reprising my role here that you and I often have at home, of the genial but eccentric aunt that no one quite knows what to do with.

(I have written a little of this letter each evening when having nothing else to do.)

There are native women who provide other *services to the single men. They began to congregate before we left Corunna, and more have appeared along the way. They are tolerated provided they otherwise behave; my inclination is to intervene, yet young men about to be subjected to vi-olence—who may never have any other opportunity for feminine company—are not appropriate subjects for a lecture on conventional morality. Some of these foreign women have taken up permanently with one man because of the security this offers—two or three have joined our regiment. They talk as if they have married; they act as if they are married; yet they have not received permission from their commanding officer; nor have they had the benefit of clergy. Overall, however, they are a positive; the more women in camp, the less competition flares among the men. Wives—legal or otherwise—reduce the restlessness of the men who have them and quiets those subject to their presence. I have stayed alert for signs of jealousy, as there have been outbreaks of violence in other regiments. So far, we have had none. Exhaustion now serves to reduce that form of male energy.*

Ashton leaves it to me to keep the peace. Everyone understands that I accept the situation as an "exigency of war" but will not tolerate any misbehavior stemming from it. I doubt that any reasonable person can insist upon the scruples of civil life when we exist in circumstances so contrary to all that civil life is about.

I have made several mentions of the 95th. We have at last received an official acknowledgement that we are a part of that regiment. The Rifles, however, are with General Sir John Moore, coming up from Lisbon, while we are with General Sir David Baird out of Corunna. The hope is that we will rendezvous sometime in the next week. Meanwhile, Sir David has little enthusiasm about managing riflemen, who by virtue of being different must be trouble. But, as the 95th was the creation of his superior, Sir John, he cannot ignore us. Therefore, with a great flourish of the pen he has confirmed the singular honor of our continuing to serve the 15th cavalry until time and circumstances enable our linking up with the main body. Translated: Having no use for us, Sir David would prefer Lord Paget feed us! But having official recognition puts Ashton on better footing with the Colonels in the war councils. He can couch his opinions as those of the "Rifles" (and by implication the Commander of the Army) rather than a mere Captain.

Our mission in the north of Spain is to support the Spanish army. Their 100,000 men are supposed to be the core, and our men—about 25,000 between Baird and Moore—are supposed to be auxiliary. However, we have yet to see any Spanish army, though we hear of reverses in the south. It has become a joke that the "patriotic armies are invisible."

I want you to know that conditions have been difficult but bearable. We push ahead tomorrow. The men's excitement has settled; they are steady and seek to do their duty.

Please give my love to Mother.

Y^{rs} affec^{tely}

Jane

Mrs. Ashton Dennis
Lugo, Spain

Chapter 32

14 December 1808

Cassandra

We have marched another 150 miles since my last letter. I write these words and I am astounded. On paper, they look no different than my writing "we walked from Steventon to Alton." But how different the reality!

The terrain and the weather became much harsher, quickly. The animals have suffered terribly, and the men nearly as much. We have lost stock to lameness and lack of forage and sent others to the cavalry to compensate for their losses. We now shepherd no more than fifty horses. Sickness has been rife. Many of our men, along with sickly stock, were sent back to Lugo for convalescence. Many more of each also went from other regiments.

The march was hard but uneventful until we passed beyond a miserable little village called Nogales, about 90 miles from Corunna. To that point, we were covering 8 to 16 miles a day over bleak terrain, though we did occasionally cross through or above a beautiful valley. This was a glimpse of Heaven from Purgatory. By now, we had walked ourselves into good condition, and to this point food stores were sufficient. Beyond Nogales, we had to make a steep, seven-mile climb, cross the summit—about a mile in which we were soaked in ever-present clouds—and then descend another nine miles down a slick, treacherously narrow trail along a precipice. This occurred as the weather continued to worsen, and we have had frost ever since, and at least a skift of snow each day. We had not yet encountered the enemy—we are habituated to the rumors that the French have materialized nearby—but this crossing made us understand that even more difficult and dangerous times lay ahead.

It was after this that our animals began to fail and the men fell sick. We put up in farmhouses and barns as much as we can find. The holdings are very much the same throughout the land—one large chamber in which the animals and children huddle together in the straw, and adults sleep on benches or on top of chests. The inns, or posadas, offer the singular improvement that the entire ground floor is given over to the animals and indifferent hay lofts serve as sleeping quarters above. Most of the citizens of the region have helped us as little as possible, but occasionally a farmer will offer sopa consisting of train oil—rendered blubber!—, garlic, and red pepper. Even in our hungered state it is all we can do to force this nasty concoction past our lips. ... Since Corunna, we have had only one real meal, at a tiny place called L'Orchid in Lugo: beef, black pudding, and peas boiled together, along with stewed pears and cheese. That was more than two weeks ago, and I remember it like my honeymoon.

I wish I could report that our men carry on in a determined if not spirited state, yet that would not be entirely true. A soldier's attitude is to march, fight, and march. We have only marched (and marched). Still more, almost since the day of my last letter, Sir David has issued contradictory orders. We advance; we halt; we retreat; we press forward to regain the ground we gave up the day before. Once, the Army passed itself—half moving up, half moving back. An indecisive commander is more dangerous to his friends than to his enemy, I should think. ...

Though leaving the ordinary soldier incredulous, these actions have come as the result of conflicting information. Sometimes the French are supposed to be behind us, *sometimes approaching from the flank. As a precaution, we must move back into a more defensible position, or turn to face them, or divert to block a crossroads. The omnipresent concern, of course, is that they will cut us off before we can combine with Sir John, or strike him before we can reinforce. Whatever the value of these movements, they have created confusion and dissension in the ranks, for little is explained to the regiments. Without answers, soldiers make up their own questions. Are we outnumbered? Are we surrounded? Do our generals know what they are doing? Are we lost? (!) Ashton knows enough of the deployments to make reasonable surmises about the decisions, and he has kept our men apprised to the extent he can. The result is that they are less alarmed than the rest, though by no means satisfied. He may be the only officer here who believes a soldier will put up with more, and fight better, if he halfway understands what is going on.*

16 December. *I can announce that the final and biggest worry is now resolved. Like two blind beggars, Moore and Baird stumbled into each other—in a snowstorm!—Moore having straggled 300 miles up from Lisbon and we having come 200 miles east out of Corunna. Yesterday! Confidence rises! Now there is only one English Army wandering upon the plains rather than two, and only one General determining strategy. Our attention is now turned to the French rather than to locating the lost tribe. However, we have also learned that Buonaparte is in Spain, his new army having poured into the country, swept the Spanish aside, and re-captured Madrid. Rather than supplementing the patriotic forces, we are now their replacements. All we have seen so far is about 2,000 men of the Marquis de la Romana, who joined us at Astorga. They are even more miserable than we, and it is difficult to tell how eager they are to fight. They do not seem to like the idea of any foreigners marching through their territory. They wear English uniforms and carry English muskets: At last we see some purposed use to the silver we have poured into the country in place of men.*

Ashton's retention of the provisions proved to be a greater boon than we might have expected. The commissariat has been incompetent in placing stores close to any regiment. They had done their duty if the food wagon found its way within a league or two of a regiment. Now they are much better at coordination, but the wagons are—very nearly empty. Much of the "planning" assumed that the Army would be able to purchase provisions and feed along the way—a perfectly logical idea for a winter campaign, and great news for those of us who have been in the rear, crossing a land that has been stripped by preceding regiments like Egypt by locusts. Foraging has been worse, because the pressure of earlier troops has caused farmers to hide what they need to survive. Many soldiers and cavalry have had nothing to "dine on" but a cold piece of beef obtained earlier along the way. To stretch our supplies, Ashton has given our men but a little each night, enough to keep their strength. A very thin beef soup is our standard fare, romantic lighting provided by a candle in a potato. And (without giving any indication we have a surplus) we share what we have with any cavalry who stop to warm their hands over our fires. Our men understand the value of having friends among the mounted!

At my suggestion, at night we hid the provisions among our tents and other equipment, and kept guards—the one duty our men do not complain about. As carefully as we have measured out the food, however, we are almost done: Our surplus can now hide in a pillow. Going forward, we are no better off than the rest; but we will be stronger when hardship strikes.

I have another duty I would like to recount. Two or three of the junior officers have asked me to review their letters before they send them home. They did not say why, but I suspect they wanted to sound mature and nonchalant to their worried families at home, and, indeed, they do. I confessed to one young man that I did not know how he did it. I wake up each day anxious, I told him. I am anxious when we eat, anxious when we stop, anxious when we go to bed. I see no evidence of anxiety in anything that the young men write—or anything Ashton has written to Alethea. Everyone is showing such remarkable restraint, I told the young man, such fortitude. I expected him to make some comment about men not being as naturally nervous as women, but he confessed to the same emotions as mine. But he was a soldier and had to behave as if he was not anxious. Not being naturally brave, he said, he would pretend to be brave until he was. I wanted to adopt him, then and there! *That is what we all must do—pretend to courage until we find it. This is what I am doing now, writing a letter that is matter of fact, but only because my fingers are too stiff to write "I feel anxious ..." at the start of every sentence.*

Ashton and I have spoken about his own fears. One can see the worry in his brow and in the set of his jaw, but what the men see is determination—which is certainly there. He says he feels the fear in his belly more than his mind but also says he has a greater fear of dying badly than of dying at all. I suppose that must be true of anyone who has nearly 200 men looking to him for direction. I can also see that he intellectualizes the danger; thinking of it in terms of odds or possibilities and abstracting the risk away, at least for a little while. When it returns, I see terror hit him, causing a silent recoil. Some of our men, looking haggardly out from under shadowed eyes, look as if they know they are already dead. Others, though struggling under the same fear and privation, remain cheerful and tell jokes without any kind of haunted look. If they get their rum, they are happy. (Not that we have any rum.) Do they not see that death might await them? Do they think about it at all? Or do they jest to keep the phantoms at bay? Is it only the better educated who think abstractly enough to worry about a future dread, or are the ordinary men, who suffer more often and severely, better able to hide or submerge their fear? Mr. Fletcher, I think, is most like me. He knows that death stalks us from among the frozen fields. Though he will smile and show a strong face, he never completely lets down his guard. For that, we both believe, is when death will come.

It is not until I thought of death that I remembered George and his birthday. And my father. And Mrs. Lefroy. December was once the happiest month, the time of my birthday and Christmas. With Mrs. Lefroy and my father (whose death just after the new year I still associate with December), it became the most terrible month. With George's birth came happiness again; yet now his short life ties birth to death again. I do not think of him for days at a time. I hope this is not the end of grief. I would rather cry than lose his memory. I should feel bad about forgetting George for the littlest while; but it is fatigue not forgetfulness that is the culprit. I have not forgotten my sweet boy; I am too exhausted to feel. I am a headstrong, excitable dog that runs until it collapses on the floor.

To busy my mind on the relentless marches, I began composing a poem about Mrs. Lefroy. The trick is not to compose but to remember an hour later—cold numbs the brain as well as the feet. I jot down the lines at camp. The military environment reminds me of several of my characters. One in particular is bought off at the end, a disreputable outcome to everyone's mind but his. I am adding the receipt of a commission in the Army *rather than the* Militia; *astute readers will recognize that this will one day take him off to war, where he will face men instead of girls.*

Generally, I have been less melancholic on this expedition than I was at home. Partly it is because I have—most of the time—something useful to accomplish—or at least physical activity. Partly it is because this venture—the sheer scale of human effort and potential calamity—puts every individual life into perspective. How can my sorrows compare with those of a host of men and women, most suffering worse than I? How can my pain compare to that of a Spanish peasant, who has lost more children and endured more hardship than I will ever see?

In truth, I am trying to describe our situation honestly without displaying too much or too little emotion. I am trying to counter the impulse to make everything sound so ordinary that you imagine far worse horrors than what are here. I am

frightened but not incapacitated. Truly, we have needed per-
severance more than courage. With any luck, that will remain
the story when we set sail for home a few weeks from now.
    Y^{rs} affec^{tely}
Jane

Mrs. Ashton Dennis
Spain

Chapter 33

Consolidation of the two Armies left the military relationship between Ashton and Lovelace largely unchanged—the riflemen remaining as skirmishers for the hussars—only now both were part of the vanguard. The Colonel regularly moved among the companies, arrayed across many roads and tracks of the countryside, to ensure there were no gaps to allow French infiltration. Having noticed the difference between Ashton's victuals and his own, Lovelace happened by at mealtime more than once. He, Kat, and his squad were fed as any others would have been, and he and Ashton spoke of any likely changes in deployment according to orders and terrain.

Despite their fears, the Dennises had had few difficulties with Lovelace. If his intent was no more than to force the Hampshire men into a series of hard marches to keep up with the mounted troops, the 15th's struggling horses and the congested roads meant that the Rifles waited upon the hussars more often than the other way around. If his intent was worse, the condition of his own troops left him no time for malign pursuits.

Jane recognized that Lovelace, no fool, had come to appreciate the Hampshire men. They had handled the difficulties better than most, had never failed to muster promptly, and had out-marched not only his horse but also the rest of the infantry. Part of this was their morale (credit Ashton) and part of this was their superior food (credit again). Lovelace probably did not realize the extent to which basic sustenance affected the ordinary soldier. One suspected he could go a week without eating if he thought a lively battle lay ahead. But as he himself had observed a long time ago, the way a soldier discharged his secondary duties often predicted the way he discharged his primary one, and Hants' exemplary behavior in an Army full of complainants had given him the confidence that he could rely upon them when it really mattered.

Both men were concerned at the toll being exacted upon the animals. One reason the mounts were so knocked out was that, whenever the Army changed direction, the cavalry was required to quickly move to the new front from wherever the last maneuver left them. The rest of the vanguard was expected to quickly follow. Also, many of the recent marches had been at night, leaving everyone exhausted and disoriented. Hard on the men—much worse on the horses.

As they discussed this problem, Ashton suggested that the substitute and reserve mounts should come along easily to ensure that at least some were fresh when a battle was planned. Lovelace agreed, going a step further to relegate Hants' blue roans to the substitute pool. His reason was typically harsh: "I would rather kill a nag on the road than in a fight," he said—keeping the Hants horses as fresh as possible until required.

The men were civil and brisk with each other. There was no open animosity—for now. They were conserving their energies for the French. But Jane knew that they were not done with the Colonel, nor he with them. The more level and direct he and Ashton were with each other, the more one could expect something to happen when the last crisis of the campaign had been surmounted.

Jane was similarly polite with Lovelace's wife, her one-time boon companion. Kat's menagerie had quickly disappeared. The canaries froze, the goat became a delicacy, the pretty spaniel disappeared—into the jaws of wild dogs or, when no one was looking, into the stewpot along with the goat. Though no one at this point in the adventure was attractive, Kat carried herself as much a queen as ever—no more daunted by a snowstorm than by a slave rebellion.

She was as cold as she once was warm, but the change amused Jane—her only source of comedy here—because the weather was so frigid that one could not tell if her demeanor came from attitude or frozen muscles. A few months ago, Jane could not have imagined ever breaking bread with the Lovelaces again. The strangeness of the situation made everything normal. With no formal duties between them, and having only the trappings of a canvas tent instead of an elegant home on which to comment, the two women strained to fill the time.

At one point, Kat asked Jane why she did not join the other wives at the front. At least four other ladies rode beside their officer husbands. She described to Kat her responsibilities in the rear, keeping the camp followers off the wagons, sweeping them along to prevent dispersal, refereeing the inevitable disputes.

"That is the duty of a housekeeper, not an officer's wife," Kat replied.

"*This* housekeeper is glad to provide the service," Jane said, heat in her voice. "Discipline among the followers is as important as discipline among the troops. Indeed, a lack of discipline in the rear would destroy discipline in the front. Every soldier would deal with the distresses of his family first."

"Someone must do it, true," Kat said. "I suppose it might be appropriate for a Captain's wife—to shuffle along in the snow."

"I would rather walk than render a horse unfit by adding to its work," Jane said. "We lose one or two every day. I should ride, that a hussar lacks a mount when the French are charging?"

Kat bristled at the implication. "We ride our own horses," she said. "None of them are trained for cavalry work."

"Still, a cavalryman would much prefer an untrained horse than to meet the enemy on foot."

When Kat shrugged dismissively, Jane added: "If you are unfit for walking, you might consider a mule. We have enough of those to spare—for now."

"A lady does not ride a mule—not when her stallion is available."

The rising temper of this side conversation began to gain the attention of the Colonel and the Captain.

"Perhaps you prefer to walk because it puts you farthest from danger," Kat suggested.

"As neither of us is likely to fight," Jane responded, "the issue is the vanity required to waste the Army's most critical resource."

Before their contest of words devolved into open conflict, the Colonel suggested that Jane should join them at the front on the next operation. A single ride would not break down a mount, and she might benefit from seeing the cavalry at work. Though the offer bore little relation to the argument, Ashton and Jane finally agreed, as much to end the quarrel as anything else. Jane protested to Ashton later that she did not know what troubled her more—that Kat might be right about her fear of danger, or that she would attend a battle as if it were a sporting event.

Chapter 34

Colonel Lovelace's invitation became a reality a few nights later, when the Dennises were rousted from bed shortly before midnight. The ice on the roads, tossed up by the Army's movements, lay in hard twisted sheets so uneven they had to lead the horses out rather than ride. Once away from the village, Lovelace and Kat rode ahead with other officers. Ashton and Jane rode far enough back so as not to interfere with the command. Beyond the village, they learned that French cavalry and artillery had been discovered at Sahagun, about twenty miles east. The plan was for the 15th to go around behind to block any escape, after which General Slade, coming along with the 10th, would attack the town.

Snow continued to fall, heavy but crystalline—the cold was bitter. From time to time, a horse went down on the ice with a heavy, frightened grunt. One or two men were injured, but by some miracle no legs were broken—neither horse nor man. Jane's mount slipped so often she thought to dismount; but she could not have persisted through the snow, which in many places drifted to the horses' knees. They passed through two small villages which, despite the muffled noise of several hundred horse, showed no inclination to rouse from unhappy dreams. About halfway to Sahagun, the snow stopped and the moon glowed yellow through the vapors. They came upon a gothic edifice that could have been Walpole's inspiration for *The Castle of Otranto*. Shortly afterward came an alarm: a clash between the advanced guard and enemy pickets, several of whom escaped. The element of surprise lost, the hussars hastened along, though they had to almost tiptoe across two narrow, icy causeways.

At Sahagun, General Slade and the 10th were nowhere to be seen. "Lost!" Lord Paget said. "On purpose, I have no doubt." A reconnaissance determined that a large body of French chasseurs had formed up behind the town, on the road to Carrion, with the evident plan to retire. "Forward!" Paget said. They found the French as described, moving away but in no apparent hurry. As the auxiliaries took position on a small hill, Paget led his men out to cut off their retreat. In the half-light of first dawn, Jane picked up the silver sheen of their blue roans near the center, led by Lovelace on his white charger. She excitedly pointed these out to Ashton, who nodded, alert but apprehensive. *Their blue roans*—Hants reared and trained! She was struck with pride, worry, confusion over her mixed thoughts about Lovelace's exposure to danger. Next to them, Kat smiled. Jane's hands were so cold she could barely grasp the reins, leaving her to wonder: How could the men hold their sabers?

The two forces were separated by a neat olive vineyard several hundred yards wide, which had ripples of snow every twenty or thirty yards. When directly opposite the French, Paget gave a series of orders, the 15th wheeled, a strong *huzzah!* rang out, and the hussars began to charge. In those first moments, as the cavalry surged forward into a gallop, the French were aligned five or six deep against only two lines of the British. "They are so large—medieval knights!" Jane cried, meaning the French. "Heavy cavalry," Ashton said. "Ours are light." This could not be good, but the French did not respond to the attack. There was no time for other words or thoughts. The 15th came. When they reached the first ripple in the field, several horses stumbled and riders nearly went down—ditches! *That was why they did not charge—a trap!—they would see us disordered and dismounted, then fall upon our men with their heavy beasts!* But the 15th came. They dodged the small trees and—now aware—timed leaps to cross one after another invisible ditch. Hooves pounded, the powdery snow flew and sparkled as the sun and mist mingled. When they closed to about fifty yards, the French fired—hundreds of short muskets. Three or four horses went down; others careened sideways into other riders. Two troopers flew into the air; another flopped like a rag doll in his stirrups. But the 15th came. If one can say that entire regiments can be concurrently surprised—the French were surprised. They had barely time to brace for the impact before England struck them a ringing blow. Heavy cavalry or not, the front lines crumpled under the assault. Men were unhorsed; horses were knocked down. Screams—human and horse. Sabers clashing, pistols popping, the 15th carved its way forward through a human wall. Lovelace and his men hacked through first, turning left and half right to pincer the French. More screams—cries for mercy filled the air.

The British left was also now enclosing the enemy in a fist. Jane had read in the old books the importance of surrounding an enemy, but she had never seen the deadly consequences of a "flanking maneuver" for the defender. Less and less room to move and—in a matter of minutes—no hope of escape. As if simultaneously reaching the same conclusion, the French cavalry bolted. No withdrawal—no retreat—bedlam! Cavalry racing away in all directions, men on foot trying to reach the trees, others on their knees in gestures of submission, squadrons of the 15th chasing any group large enough to be worth the effort, receding combinations of fighters and snow swirling east—the road to *Carrion*, what a meaning it had today!

To her astonishment, a British orderly near Lord Paget raised a white flag!—then it became evident he was being sent forward to seek the enemy's surrender. Lovelace and most other commanders chose not to notice and carried on in pursuit, but large numbers of the French, taking advantage of the hesitation of the British immediately around Paget, absconded with their lives. Bugles sounded; the 15th began to reassemble; the French continued their flight; clusters of men and horses—prisoners—began to be gathered.

Suddenly, a large force of cavalry appeared on an eminence to the left, unopposed. The hearts of the auxiliaries nearly stopped as they realized that the newcomers could sweep the field of the

15th—scattered and disorganized, all the horses blown! Lovelace saw, and one of the commanders on the left saw. Realizing what was about to happen, both squadrons formed, turned, and—outnumbered ten to one—began to trot toward the new adversary—ready, everyone realized, to sell their lives dearly to save their brothers. Only then did someone recognize—*General Slade and the 10th*!

A great cry of pride and congratulations roared from the fresh hussars upon surveying the scene. Their cheers were acknowledged by the 15th as they regrouped. But the implication of Lovelace's action—and those of Gordon, the leader of the flank—was clear to every watcher of the scene.

"Was there ever a braver man!" Kat exclaimed. "A warrior for the ages!"

"None but eagles could look him in the face," Jane replied.

---

22 December 1808

Dear Cassandra

We have seen the most inspiring and terrifying event a civilian might ever see—a cavalry charge! The force—the power—the courage—the carnage! Lord Paget destroyed a French column early this morning, as we watched from a nearby knoll. Despite a disadvantage in numbers, our light cavalry overthrew the heavy French. Half the British forces arrived too late to participate: The officers complained bitterly that their General Slade gave an intentionally windy speech to ensure their lack of punctuality. Colonel Lovelace played an important part in the Army's success; he not only led the charge, but he rallied his men to face the latecomers, not realizing at first that they were friends instead of foes. Despite the severity of his shortcomings in other areas, we cannot begrudge the Colonel's courage.

We spent the rest of the day helping with our wounded, the prisoners (wounded and otherwise), and the horses. Our losses were small, but these were real men, not numbers or names in a gazette. French casualties were severe. In addition to the losses on the field, still more died in town. As soon as the inhabitants saw that we had won, they put to the blade all the sick and injured French within their walls. I cannot imagine how they thought this would ingratiate themselves to the victors, knowing the situation might conceivably be reversed one day.

Much to our consternation, our victorious hussars—to whom we are assigned—remained drawn up until dark, while the tardy 10th was sent to quarters early. The anger was salved by the immense amount of booty taken. The French had melted down religious gold and silver into small bars suitable for the saddle.

It was beneath the walls of the town that we again met Sawyer, whose task was to destroy the injured horses and, theoretically at least, tend to those that could be saved. You remember my grievances about this unhappy person, whose mood was even fouler than usual. He has suffered on the march as much as anyone and the Spanish youths assisting him disappeared before the mountains—no English coin was worth the adversity. In addition to taking orders from the Colonel and his wife, he is now also having to take direction—abuse, as he sees it—from boys bearing officer rank on their epaulets.

In the evening, we shared a stable with the Lovelaces, where we noticed that their black servant Philip was absent. Upon inquiry—indirect, for you know the tinderbox his status has created between the families—Kat acknowledged that he had gone, having stolen enough money to disappear among the wagons returning to Lisbon or Salamanca. Spain still flows with Moorish blood, and he took the risk that he could blend in well enough that he would not be recognized as an Army deserter—which, technically, he is not. "He might survive—if he can avoid being robbed," Lovelace said. "If he can overcome the lack of language. Perhaps. Most likely, he is dead. If alive, he will make the worst Moor since Othello!" With more candor than might be expected, he added:

"However, give him credit. For the first time in his life, he showed enterprise."

When we had settled—as I began this note—I whispered a question to Ashton: In view of the Colonel's bravery, have we been too harsh in our estimation of him? Surely, a man displaying such honor on the field is more likely to suffer from excessive zeal or competitiveness than a lack of moral strength and direction? "As tempting as it might be, we cannot fall under his sway again," Ashton replied. "There is physical courage—intellectual courage—moral courage. Lovelace has so much of the first that he has never seen a reason to develop the other two."

I leave you with those thoughts—

Y^{rs} affec^{tely}

J—

Mrs. Ashton Dennis
Spain

Chapter 35

Moore made Sahagun his headquarters, with the rest of the Army in motion to join him despite rain and another freeze. The Rifle companies, cold and half-starved, deployed ahead to a village toward Carrion in case of a French counterattack. Everyone expected to fight on Christmas day—a beautiful way to honor the birth of Our Lord, as Ashton observed, when he was encouraging the men about the importance of their performance in the coming action. It was a test all of them must pass, he said—himself included. At one point, the men thought they could hear other forces moving up, yet evening came with neither the French, nor the rest of the British Army, at hand.

Very late, nearly midnight, the reason for the Army's delay was revealed in new orders that left Ashton staggered. His only reaction, when he showed Jane the news, was that he would let the men sleep, for there was nothing to do till dawn.

When at first light he roused the company from their icy beds, he tried without much success to show enthusiasm. "Our orders are to demonstrate toward Carrion, to confirm Soult's expectations of an attack," Ashton said. "We must keep him busy on defensive fortifications."

When he did not expound further, Sergeant Stout asked for clarification. "To drive back their pickets so our Army can get in position?"

"No, not exactly. To push back the pickets, yes—but only that," he said. Here he faltered, for Jane knew he felt he was betraying his men. "We are not the precursors of an attack. We are the precursors of the *impression* of an attack." He could delay no more. *"General Moore has ordered an urgent retreat!"*

The formation exploded. *Outrage!* From private to sergeant to ensign, the men would not retreat, not after all they had done to get here. After all the miles they had marched, all the sacrifices they had made—they would *not* retreat when the enemy was at hand! They might not be the most experienced soldiers, but they would not run before the battle began! In the last few hours they had traded shots with the French guard; they could capture Marshal Soult themselves with a dash through the woods. If Moore was too cowardly to join the enemy, the 95th would go it alone! Ashton let them rage, acknowledging their fury, conceding the rightness of their position. When at last the anger began to subside—more from the temperature than reconsideration—he gave them the news:

"Buonaparte is on the way!"

To this the cry was unanimous:

Bring on the French bastard, and we'll bloody his nose too!

"He's not coming *at* us," Ashton said. "He's coming *behind* us. Listen—you must understand! Moore's intent from the very start was to pull the French away from the Spanish. To protect our shattered allies in the south. Give them time to regroup. His strategy worked too well. Buonaparte didn't just turn to fight us—he's turned to strike *at our rear*—with his entire army! Riding hard to get between us and the coast! To block supplies—reinforcements. *This is what has changed!* If we stay to fight, the French win even if we beat them. *Any* delay will be fatal! No food. No way home. Soult—even if we hand him a bitter loss—will still have enough men to harass us from this side. We'll be trapped. *If we stay, we die.* Either tomorrow or next week."

"Then we must go?" the sergeant asked, on behalf of all the men. He looked at Jane, as if—against the inconstancy and foolishness of their military leadership—they could expect plain truth from her.

She took Ashton's hand—a non-military movement that, however, confirmed that she stood with them even as she confirmed the worst. "We must run," she said, "but only so we can find a better place to fight."

That should have been the end, except for the extraordinary—contradictory—orders that they must move forward before they move back. Now, it was Mr. Fletcher who raised the question on behalf of the men—but as much on behalf of Ashton, whose intention was required, clear and concise, in the brittle air. "How can they ask us to attack, when we know it is a feint? No soldier wants to die in a false assault."

"Sometimes a small group of soldiers is asked to sacrifice for the benefit of the whole. We must convince Soult to dig in and wait—to give our Army the opportunity to get away. If we convince them the attack is real, we'll gain two days—perhaps three—before the Marshal realizes he's been made a fool. I go forward with volunteers. Anyone who wishes to start back now can rally round the ensigns."

"We follow you, Captain," the sergeant said. He spat. "Just not the bloody General."

So it was that as the sun made its full but feeble rise the lonely companies of the 95th plunged forward through the thick snow. The French, however, needed no encouragement to withdraw—in their exposed positions, the weather was more dangerous than their enemies. When they saw the determined lines making headway despite the icy impediments, when they experienced the first shots singing past their ears, well out of the range of their own muskets, they disappeared one way into the white powder sifting down from the trees. Upon confirming the abandonment of the outposts, the 95th vanished just as quickly in the other.

—∾∾—

26 December 1808

Cassandra

My letter was to open with the frightening news that we are in full retreat, yet we have sat at Sahagun for two days, like an Austen sister waiting for a protective brother to escort us to London. The news is frightening—we are in full retreat—but the retreat is that of a giant, slow-moving millipede whose segments consist of infantry, artillery, cavalry, baggage, and followers, lurching into motion on a 230-mile crawl to the sea. The best that can be said is that I have time to write to you—as well as to report that the Lord's birthday provided the second decent meal we have enjoyed in a month. We in the rear guard will come along tomorrow.

I mention these military secrets because, by the time a French spy has intercepted this message, we will be luxuriating in a flea-infested hotel in a coastal fortress, sipping indigestible sopa and sour wine.

I have no idea whether I will be able to post anything after today, because the whole Army will be moving as fast as any courier—once we set into motion. I will write as often as I can, and assume the mail will go out. If it does not, I will treat the letters as a journal and deliver them to you personally upon my return. Either way, you will have a record of my thoughts and feelings as I go along.

Jane

Mrs. Ashton Dennis
Spain

Chapter 36

As the Army's shield, the rearguard swung south to keep between the huge column and Buonaparte; despite this, the French
intercepted the cavalry's baggage at Mayorga and the 10th was
dispatched to retrieve it. The action nearly failed to come off, as
General Slade's difficulty with his stirrups required another officer
to take command. The weather moderated slightly so that the soldiers were cold and damp rather than bitterly cold and dry. Once
they began, they moved in stages. The starting and stopping made
the miserable conditions worse; motion was the only thing to keep
frostbite away. The women now walked with their men, for no one
except Sir John made any pretense of protocol anymore.

Being the rearguard, they always arrived last and had difficulty
finding quarters or provisions. Often, they were thrown in with
the 15th cavalry in whatever shelter was available. They were also
assigned picket duty at night; even a daylong march did not guarantee rest. Ashton's men did not resent their duties, as they had
marched out as far from potential action as one could be; but the
hussars complained bitterly about their lack of relief.

"Lord Paget seeks to save his precious 7th and the Prince of
Wales' 10th from too severe an exertion," one officer said.

"Give it no mind," Colonel Lovelace responded. "We all have
to go the same distance. The more opportunity for battle, the more
opportunity for glory."

"Glory comes at a cost," Ashton said. "The lives of your men."

"Men will die in war. I claim—this is my experience—that more men die running away than running forward."

"You're probably right," Ashton said, thinking back to the panic of the chasseurs at Sahagun. "But a soldier should have a meaningful objective before he risks his life. His superior's desire for glory does not count."

"Certainly," Lovelace said. "But his superior's desire for glory may be what turns the tide." He smiled and recited a line from Shakespeare. As he began, his men, hearing a familiar phrase, smiled with him. "If it be a sin to court glory, I am the most offending soul alive."

The snow, the sleet, and now several days just above freezing left the roads so heavy that the 95th was often detailed to help the horse artillery drag their guns through the mud. The deterioration of the conditions matched the deterioration of the Army; every settlement showed signs of worse and worse treatment. Just before reaching the River Esla, they came upon not a cottage on fire—the negligence of the soldiers set at least one ablaze at every stop—but an entire village, whose residents pelted the British with sticks and snow and *other* things, crying: *"Vivan los Franceses!"* At Benevente, just over the river, Sir John had immense stores of every kind destroyed. The Rifles saved farrier gear from a foundered forge-cart and used the shoes and nails to reshod Lovelace's regiment. Rags being all that held their footwear together, they commandeered fresh boots before the gear was burned or given to the Spanish as modest recompense for general depredations. The opportunity for self-pillage was the only advantage of being at the back.

On the approach to Astorga, a group of their German cavalry met them with the exciting news that the Army was about to be reinforced by 120,000 men—Spanish allies to the rescue! Ashton's company slept outside that night because Romana's sickly few—the source of these preposterous rumors—had filled all the rooms. Almost simultaneous with their departure, Buonaparte paraded in at the head of his Grande Armée. The British soon learned that the French leader, having just missed catching his enemy before Moore entered the passes of Galicia, left Soult and Ney in charge of the combined forces and started home.

For an emperor, Paris was a better place to spend the winter than Spain.

Chapter 37

Cassandra

We reached the town of Bembibre in time to see it descend into chaos. More baggage and stores were being burned; the logic of exhaustion and despair quickly extended the fires to any buildings at hand. Soldiers had broken into immense vaults of wine. The streets swarmed with drunken men and women, as well as Spaniards who were trying fruitlessly to halt the destruction of their shops and homes. The senior officers, including Moore, were having as little luck restoring order as the locals, while many of the line officers, drunk or sober, saw no reason to prevent their men from enjoying a respite after all they had endured.

Our company found shelter for the twenty or so horses that remained in the reserve, along with several abandoned mules we had brought along. Once the animals were secured, our men—broken down, hungry, numb from the intense cold—surged toward the riot of food and drink. It was with great effort—and not a little physical incentive—that Ashton and Mr. Fletcher diverted the company into a small warehouse, and then only with a promise that wine would be delivered to them there. The noncommissioned officers were dispatched for barrels, and the women blocked the exits: Their threats were more effective than their Captain's. He had the men break out bread and beef from their knapsacks.

We soon had the fireplaces going, upon which we discovered that the building housed tobacco, and every man received a cigar or enough tobacco to fill his pouch. Shortly after, our search party returned with sufficient casks to satisfy the men, and matters calmed enough for Ashton to speak. Before him were about 130 men; illness had sent the rest back to Vigo before Sahagun.

"After all you have been through, I understand why you want to let go," he said. "Especially when you see everyone around you letting go. You assume it's safe, or all the others would be on guard. It's not! The French are on our heels. You know that! We see their fires at night. They have not gone home!" *His words were not a chastisement but a reminder.* "It's been incredibly hard. I'm proud of every one of you. But—we are only halfway *there*. You can see how the Army is breaking down. It's the easy way. Those who break down will die. The men out there having their fun tonight—dead tomorrow. And their women—children. I don't intend to be dead. I don't intend for any of you to be dead. I'll kill you myself to keep it from happening!"

The men shook their heads, whether in recognition of his terrible joke, or despair at their situation, I could not tell.

"If we stick together," he said, "we'll make it. I'll carry you on my back if I must—you know I will. But not if you give up. You give up, you're lost."

I could see the recklessness in their eyes begin to clear, the desire to forget their horrible circumstances fade, their thoughts begin to settle into the disappointment of reality but at the same time reforming their resolve. I saw the darting worry in the women's eyes begin to ease as their men came back, relief that the chances were now good that they would not disintegrate, that the women would not be lost because their men had yielded all.

"I don't speechify," Ashton said. "I don't know how. I'm telling you the truth. You know that. Stay together. Keep your woman close. Put one foot in front of another. Keep moving. If you're too tired to take another step—take another step. Each one takes you toward freedom. We have the men to *hold Corunna. Our job as soldiers is to get there. If we can make those walls, we'll give the French a taste of English love! Then—home!"*

He had not roused the men to enthusiasm, only to a level that enabled comprehension. They nodded wearily. Beginning to warm, free of the false hope of alcohol, they looked to sleep.

"One last thing," Ashton said. "When we must fight, fight with no surrender. To lose is to die. Even if the French show quarter, they will leave you outside, and you will freeze. For tonight—we'll find more supplies. We'll be the only ones sober enough to cadge food instead of liquor. If I return and find you gone—I'll come for you—I'll kill you with my bare hands." This, he did not say in jest.

Mrs. Stout and I were in better shape than many of the men, and we need only walk in the future, not fight; we went out with Ashton and the ensigns, leaving Mr. Fletcher in charge. We retrieved several mules and sought what food we could. Every home had been broken into, and the residents gone. Where they had fled was anyone's guess. If British soldiers were present, we moved on; but we found enough unoccupied houses to satisfy our needs.

"We cannot steal their food," I protested. "The people will starve. Can we at least leave payment?"

"They will not be back before the French," Ashton said. "I see no reason to pay our enemies."

"Ashton—"

"It's horrible, Jane!—I warned you! My men won't starve. I won't let them."

"Somebody must."

"Somebody must. Not us. Not tonight."

On our way back through the narrow streets, we came upon Lovelace, exiting a house on a similar mission. He carried a lighted brand.

"You're not going to burn it!" I said. "You're no better than the common soldiers!"—pointing to the devastation around us.

If anything, the Colonel looked more haggard than any of us, yet he had the energy to dispute my claim. "I would pay, but the owners have fled, leaving me no choice. I am no villain. I do not burn because I like the sight of flames—I burn to keep the French from eating!" With that, he threw the torch into a pile of straw in the front room. We all hastened away as the fire began to taste the fuel.

Ashton and I chose to return the mules and provisions to the stables and bed down here for a few hours' sleep. Few people were about, and we would be able to avoid the disturbances and protect the food. I could not sleep—thought to write you before our small fire. Our men will be fine—safe, ready to go at dawn. But I think of what we passed on the streets—hundreds of soldiers lying in doorways, some already dead of the frost. Others piled into taverns and rooms. The entry to the vaults are full, as likely are the vaults themselves. A few people were awake if not entirely conscious, singing tuneless songs, saluting us and nursing the last of their drink.

At least once a day I think of lying down in snow—or the gutter—and being done with it along with these others. What difference will it make if one Englishwoman more, or one less, survives—or does not? My responsibility to Ashton and his men deters me, of that I am certain; but more often it is thoughts of little George that keep me pushing on. Against my depression at home, here memories of my boy's smile and bright eyes give me strength. I have sweet memories of him that no one else does—in the firelight, at dawn, in his bath. If I perish, those precious memories—all that remain of him!—will pass away too.

Thus I carry on. And try not to imagine what it will be like in the morning when the French cavalry sweeps through, cleansing the streets with their sabers.

J—

Mrs. Ashton Dennis
Spain

Chapter 38

The French advanced guard keeping hard upon them, the Rifles were occupied with repeated alarms and occasionally bothered with musket fire, but the distance was so great that Ashton would not let his men waste their ammunition with replies. Receiving reports that the French had brought up their infantry to join the cavalry, the regimental commanders invited General Slade to join a reconnaissance to ascertain the enemy dispositions. He declined, instead spurring his horse in the opposite direction to inform Sir John of the news.

"When did the General become your aide-de-camp?" Ashton asked the officers.

For the first time in nearly two years, Lovelace smiled at Ashton in a genuine way.

Repeated cavalry skirmishes had done in what was left of the 15th's horses; Ashton's few extras made little difference. Accordingly, the Rifles replaced the hussars at the very rear. The French tried to demoralize them by leading with a band, but the 95th marched disdainfully in time with the martial music and retired with dignity. Their job was not to attack the much larger enemy but to delay his advance. As they approached, the Rifles moved back in alternating ranks. Rather than lead a charge, Ashton had the job of ensuring that his men, once they began to run, did not continue to. Instead, they must drop and cover the men who had covered them. After a series of such exercises, they developed a confidence and rhythm. The riflemen also fired in an unusual manner. Instead of standing or kneeling, the soldier often lay on his back, feet crossed, and aimed the weapon through the 'X' so formed. Jane seldom saw their opponents—her responsibility was to keep the women far enough back to be out of danger—but as unorthodox as the methods were, the message from the 95th must have been compelling. After only a few exchanges, French muskets would fall silent. The British would be several miles down the road before more fighters would set upon them.

These maneuvers worked well until Cacabelos, where the Army had to cross a long, exposed area on a slight decline to reach the town. Upon reaching the rise and able to see for the first time the shockingly small number of adversaries resisting their advance, the French cavalry charged. The 15th, which had deployed in front of the bridge, came up hard, but French numbers were overwhelming. The British cavalry was driven back into the Rifles, and the men panicked. As Jane led the women across to temporary safety on the far side, some of the soldiers ran into the open streets and market areas, where they were cut down by the French who had penetrated the British ranks or trampled by the horses they had only recently provided to their own hussars. Ashton raced among them, seeking to pull his men out of the path of the mounted melee and dodging blows himself. Fletcher, Jane could see, was leading his section to the woods on the right.

It was chaos in the middle where Ashton tried to organize his men while waves of cavalry swept back and forth through them. French infantry now swarmed over the rise. Terrified soldiers shot at anything through the smoke and confusion, sometimes hitting their own men. From behind, Jane heard several loud reports and saw French soldiers bowled over and torn apart—British light artillery was now in play. Fletcher's men began to pour a steady fire from the trees and the horse artillery barked every thirty or forty seconds. At this distance, the French soldiers might as well have been ants stirred up by cruel little boys, for unable to see the path that death was taking they were crushed randomly for fun.

Through it all, the scene was bathed in a shimmering haze, for the gunfire and cannons sent a fine dusting of snow into the sky and the blood made red flower-petal designs on the white ground.

Beside her, Jane heard a joyful cry—Kat on her black horse! "Is it not wonderful? To see how men face death? Look at that one—running away! Ha, shot in the back, as he deserves. That one—a chicken after a bug. And over there—charging straight at his foes!"

The last man's head exploded in a pink mist.

"What a glorious death!"

"Dear God, Kat, shut up!"

Surprised, Kat said no more but exclaimed under her breath whenever a fusillade dropped soldiers like sticks or the artillery blew men to pieces, sending detached arms and legs rotating at different speeds into the snow. One of the arms stuck upright in a snow bank. It looked as though a buried soldier was signaling his comrades to follow. Behind her, Jane saw Moore, Baird, and their small staff scrambling to depart: If the line did not hold, the French would end the campaign today by capturing the high command!

As Ashton brought the men to the relative safety of enclosed gardens and vineyards, Lovelace pushed on against French chasseurs as brave as he, though not as fierce; all fell before his saber and the hooves of his stallion. Despite the efforts of his squadron to protect his back, however, his small pocket of victory became encircled. With the British cavalry intermixed with that of the French, the Rifles could not fire at will. At his signal, Ashton's men charged, using their bayonets and shooting at point-blank range to extricate Lovelace and his squadron. The weight of numbers, however, continued to slowly push the British line through the huts and lanes toward the bridge. Every hussar, including Lovelace, was unhorsed. Cavalry and infantry fought the French hand to hand, brother to brother. When a French general came to encourage still another cavalry charge that would have swept away the last of this thin defensive line, a shot rang out and the general dropped. When another officer rode to his assistance, another shot cracked and the new officer fell beside his leader. Jane sought the source of this remarkable display and saw a single rifleman—of the 95th but not of Ashton's company—reloading to knock down anyone else who wanted to challenge his accuracy.

Hesitating, the ranks of the enemy were decimated with another volley by rifle and gun. The front line of their cavalry felt fresh resistance. Their horses—as exhausted as the British mounts—flagged. Suddenly, every Frenchman saw that men were falling on either side of him; noticed the mounds of dead men and horse; recognized that British resolve was firm. This was not like the earlier battle in which the encirclement created terror, but an instant in which the will of one side faltered. The French did not abandon the field, but they had had enough. They retreated in order over the hill. In the time it took for the men's breath to evaporate in the cold air, the approaches to town were clear of everything but its defenders. The men were too exhausted to huzzah; nor was a salute needed to honor their deeds. The hussars embraced the Rifles for coming to their rescue. Jane wondered momentarily whether blood spilled together might be the one way to reconcile differences as profound as those between Ashton and Lovelace. But then Lovelace came into the mix of men with disputatious words, and Ashton heatedly responded. Hussars and riflemen had to pull the two apart.

Chapter 39

Cassandra

When I began these letters, I promised myself I would tell you everything; for if anything were to happen to me on this expedition, I knew you would demand the truest record of events, however terrible. I reported earlier on a cavalry charge—viewed from a prospect that magnified its glory and masked its bloodshed. I saw another battle today from close at hand. I saw death but no evidence of glory. Today was not a matter of splendid charges or spirited retreats but of who could stumble the farthest through the mayhem, through smoke and confusion and death from every angle, through awkward thrusts and clumsy shots. I saw a desperation to butcher the other fellow before he could butcher you.

Time and again, all that stood between our men and annihilation was courage and luck. This is the new definition of glory: courage, luck, survival. In these moments, I understood the fundamental difference between Ashton and Lovelace. The Colonel attacked; he slashed; he drove. Heedless of his own safety, he sought to dominate the foe with his will. If he had the enemy on his heels, the enemy could not strike! He never thought to seek a better approach or to coordinate his rushes with those of others: Everyone else must keep up. In contrast, Ashton's first thought was protection and the second *was attack. He fought with an eye to the overall board, with an appreciation of the best position and distance from which to strike. First he rallied his men, establishing order; then he moved them to the left, opposite Fletcher, to create a cross-fire. Ashton was never as conspicuously brave as Lovelace, but by thinking on his feet he did not have to be.*

I tried to keep the whole field in view, because my task was to move the women to safety. I also watched my husband while, paradoxically, trying not to. I did not want to turn away, for fear I might miss his last moments. I felt that if I were watching, he would not die alone. Yet I could not abide the notion that I might see him fall, for there is no way to absorb the sudden death of a human being. The wounded man retains some control, some coordination. He rolls, or stumbles, or tries to limp or crawl to cover. However badly hurt, the man is still there, struggling. But when life is snuffed out—as I saw today, here and there, everyone else too engaged with his own survival to notice—the body collapses as soul-less as a bag of wheat. One instant it is a vessel for a living, thinking, vibrant soul, then—instantaneously!— gone—not a vessel for precious life, not anything at all, nothing but one of dozens of soft new boulders strewn about the ground.

Somehow, we held off the French until everyone could cross a bridge to safety. Beyond the village, the artillery found a ridge from which to remind the French to wait their turn. Our defenders, helping the wounded, passed to nearby Villafranca, where further scenes of rampage waited. Did these soldiers not recall what had happened after the bacchanalian ribaldry *at Bembibre? Did they not understand that the French would be the ones to finish the wine they uncorked this night? We pushed on to iron foundries west of town, where I am writing these few lines as others try to rest. We have been told the Army marches at midnight and we are* again *deputed to form the rear. Now even the 95th protested—why had Moore not remained in the heights behind Villafranca, where a small contingent could have held off the enemy indefinitely? No one knows.*

I am not the only one whose finger-ends are frozen tonight. More and more officers are also writing home. They write, knowing the letters may never be mailed or reach their destination. However unlikely it seems under such conditions, everyone wants to leave a record in case they do not make it home. We may starve. We may freeze. You are as likely to find us with a pen in our hand as a sword. Callous as men can be in war, eager as they are to plunder the dead after a battle—any letters or journals found are let be, and are often turned over at a subsequent parley. Both sides value these last words as sacred relics.

Strange, is it not, that there can be these unexpected moments of rapprochement with the enemy, yet not within our own ranks? I had thought perhaps Lovelace and Ashton might find—not peace—but a truce as they fought together—literally side by side today. At one point, Ashton led his men forward to save the Colonel from entrapment, and our men shielded the hussars when they ended up on foot. Yet, afterward, Ashton and Lovelace nearly came to blows. When I asked what had happened, Ashton said that Lovelace claimed he had not needed our assistance, that the presence of infantry hindered the cavalry's ability to maneuver—that is why they were cut off. After his foolish attack left him exposed and cost us a dozen lives! "I replied that it was curious indeed when infantry had to rescue cavalry, and not the other way around," Ashton said. "I told him his performance deserved two medals. One for valor. One for stupidity."

Jane

Mrs. Ashton Dennis
Spain

Chapter 40

The British Army soon reached the steep and narrow mountain passes where, there seldom being a role for the cavalry, the Rifles were permanently made the rearguard. Their resolve kept the enemy from striking hard, but it did not keep them from striking. The French lost four to five men for every Hampshire man who fell, but they had four to five times as many men to give. Pushing up, the French must have believed they were winning; but Ashton convinced his soldiers that they were waging the most successful retrograde attack in history.

On they went, one day's march indistinguishable in its misery from any other; except that every day they believed the weather could not get worse and every day it did. Outward bound on a journey usually feels longer than the return. The mind records in detail every milestone, every unknown stretch or climb. Each change marks the passage of time. On the return, the mind records fewer novelties, and time hastens. Yet the opposite was true on the roads of Spain. They returned through the same uneven terrain, climbed the same summits, paralleled the same rivers, traversed the same bridges (which their sappers repeatedly failed to blow after them), skirted the same frightening precipices. Every landmark, every town represented another marker on the road to safety—another calculation of the miles and days remaining. They marched fifteen miles and it felt like fifty. They marched thirty-five and it felt like a hundred.

After the battle at Cacabelos, and after every skirmish in which they lost a man or two, Jane saw that, blizzard notwithstanding, within a day the new widow would marry someone else. Mrs. Stout put her to rights about the matter. A woman without a husband was a woman without rations—even if rations came only every third day. Nor, without a husband, would she qualify to board a ship for home.

Single women offered themselves to men for a scrap of bread. Jane's surge of indignation was not at their immorality but at the men's refusal to trade with her begging sisters. Seeing that sick and wounded soldiers were left in the ambulance wagons when the bullocks died, she was not shocked that these men had been abandoned to die. Instead she thought they would die anyway and their rations put to better use. She could not look at the men as they passed, any more than she could look back into the shadows where French scouts might suddenly appear and she risked becoming more visible to marksmen. When Jane found an infant crying in the arms of its frozen mother, she picked up the baby and carried it inside her coat. At camp, she found that the infant had died. When next she saw an infant crying in the arms of its frozen mother, she arrived at camp with empty arms. She did know whether she had reached for the baby but lacked the strength to pick it up, whether she had dropped the baby on the way without noticing, or whether she had walked on guiltlessly because she could not bury any more babies in the frozen ground.

One day, Jane and Ashton saw casks of dollars and doubloons being rolled down a hill to escape their capture by the French. "Our money," she noted. Ashton nodded and they walked on. Another day, they saw artillery being spiked and sent over the side (more dead mounts). Still another, they saw a dejected General Slade returning to his regiment. Somehow, he had wandered several miles ahead of any danger, and Lord Paget had ordered him back. They saw Paget himself, as well as their own General Stewart, both blinded by the snow, being led by their adjutants.

At this point, every person in the rear helped another; everyone on his own had already died. They saw to their wonderment Mrs. Stout pass by, carrying her sick husband, the always slim and now cadaverous sergeant. She trudged through the snow, grunting with each step, undisturbed by her burden—her man, his knapsack, his rifle. Facing backward, the sergeant acknowledged his Captain and shrugged his shoulders: Ashton had offered to carry him, so he couldn't very well refuse his wife, could he?

"Do not get any ideas," Jane said to *her* husband.

After enough cold and snow and climbs, fighting with the French subsided. Their condition was very nearly as bad as the condition of the British. By mutual consent it became understood that the march would be the battle and whichever side did not perish would be declared the victor. Still, from time to time bad weather caused the two parties to blunder into each other and honor required that a few men die.

6-12 January 1809

Cassandra

I have seen things that make a road lined with the dead no more remarkable than a road lined with elms. I have no reaction, for my conscience is frozen and starved into submission.

We press on, resisting the siren lure of rest. As the animals collapse, the troops must get around more and more burned wagons blocking the roads. Yet the sight is not without benefits; for the snow is so thick and blowing that the only way to stay on the road is to follow the dead. The pyres of ruined villages and the carcasses of beasts serve as the most reliable direction posts. The number of dead animals has become too large to count and what now marks the miles is the number of human bodies. This casual acquiescence to death has given me a new commandment: Thy conscience requireth food. This thought occurred to me after days without eating, when dreadful scenes had become routine. At home, my emotional numbness affected me physically. Now, physical inanition subdues my emotional response. My body has no physical heat; my moral fire is gone. Scenes that would have drawn screams of outrage only weeks before now barely gain my attention. It is all I can do to describe events. I have no mind for commentary. One cannot contemplate what happens in war, as it happens, or one would go mad. Nor, I think, can anyone speak of it later without relapsing.

My thoughts—if one can dignify them with that word—turn on the attitude of the corpses themselves. The animals have the glassy stare of any dead thing mounted on a wall. But each human has a unique expression; the staring or closed eyes, the attitude of the body, gives proof whether they perished in fear, exhaustion, or peace. One day, I saw the body of a well-dressed, dark-haired woman in a clump of bushes and believed for a moment that it was Kat. The attitude of the corpse was striking—as if she had been fighting off an assailant, her mouth open in a scream that would carry silently into eternity. I instantly believed that, exposed and vulnerable, she had been debased by Sawyer and murdered to keep her silent. Yet I knew that, with no more gallant cavalry charges to be admired, Lovelace had sent Kat ahead days before. A second look revealed that the woman was not Kat, and her frozen expression was no different than any other of the English dead pleading for their God not to abandon them.

This incident caused me to look hopefully for Sawyer among the dead, his smug countenance shattered by the realization that his nastiness and conceit proved conclusively to be of no account in the world. I have not found him, and I know that his innate fury and sense of self-preservation will have propelled him to the safest part of the retreat. The anger of my thoughts, however, kept me moving for another day.

Finally, the storms passed and the stars shone forth as in a poem. The clearing skies and dry wind, however, merely increased the desiccation of the soul. The moonlight had no capacity for tears. Not acknowledging what we were going through, its loveliness seemed a rebuke, as if dappled shadows on glistening frost were equally beauteous regardless of what lay buried beneath the snow. What mattered to us was not the air but the earth, for at last we escaped the mountains. At last we walked on level ground. Somehow the Army increased its speed. Somehow we made the mileposts come faster than the dead. Somehow we hobbled into Corunna on frostbit feet to cries of halleluiah and saints be praised. As one, we crested the last hill before the bay, expectant eyes searching the harbor where the Fleet was to be.

No ships!

Chapter 41

By the time the rearguard marched into Corunna, in a fair approx-
imation of military order, Moore was already beginning to deploy
troops along the ridge in front of the city. There was a celebratory,
though not drunken, air, for the soldiers did not have to pillage
to find food, clothing, shoes, or—most important—weapons and
powder. Every lock, every stock, every barrel was damaged from
a month in the snow and rain; all the powder was damp. In place
of superior numbers and a prudent disposition of force, the British
had fresh arms—the one critical element the French would lack.

When an observant person has been exposed to battle, military strategy is easy to understand. High ground to artillery. Open
ground to cavalry. Everything else to infantry. Jane recognized that
the British were exposed to being shelled on one side and flanked
on the other. It required Ashton, however, to explain that, because
the anticipated ships were more important than the citadel, Sir
John had to deploy his men in the only position that had a chance
of keeping their enemies from sweeping down to seize the harbor.

Though their situation was precarious, she took heart that the
soldiers decided to become an Army again. After weeks of march
and countermarch, of embarrassing retreats, of humiliating disin-
tegration, the British finally had a purpose that brought out their
martial temperament. They collectively decided it was time to return in kind the mortification they had experienced, to the enemy

that had brought it upon them. This grim determination was evident in every face, in every posture, in every vigorous "Yes, sir!" To survive until the winds brought deliverance, they had but one mission: to show the French what it meant to war.

For the rearguard, by some miracle or mistake, there was rest within the walls. They would be held in reserve for battle. For the 15th and the rest of the cavalry, the news was more dramatic—or less, as it might be. The rugged landscape rendering horse useless, the cavalry regiments would be the first to evacuate. Though the pride of the British Army bemoaned their fate, none of the officers accepted Ashton's invitation to temporarily join the Rifles. For a hussar, it was difficult to know the greater insult: to miss a battle, or to fight on foot.

Soult's advance came the next day, the twelfth of January, though it was the thirteenth before he had the troops to consider an attack, and the fourteenth before his artillery arrived. It was as obvious to the French as to the British that, where Moore's defense must be the strongest, the topography rendered it the most vulnerable. That exposed portion leading to the harbor, however, was also where the British could be expected to contest every inch of ground with all the blood they had. The French therefore tried feints and maneuvers to seek to draw Moore to other parts of the field, but he did not succumb to the temptation and the French redeployed. All Soult had to show for a day of movement was a wasted day.

Because of the proximity of the forces and the slope of the ground, these actions were there for all to see, from the most seasoned officers to the lowliest privates to the most obtuse camp followers, who remained close to their regiments in case the coming of the Fleet led to a precipitate evacuation. The entire arrangement had a certain intimacy, in fact, for not only were the military formations and their followers close together but the two armies had also shared common privations for close to a month. Though both sides had the requirement to destroy the other, there would have still been something like disappointment if one side awoke the next morning to discover the other was no longer present as a harbinger of destruction.

As British eyes swiveled from the unmoving French in front to the invisible Fleet behind, Sir John dispatched instructions to the reserve to further prepare for an eventual withdrawal. Lord Paget and General Stewart being still abed from ophthalmia, the honor of carrying out the orders fell to Colonel Lovelace. On his horse—wonder of wonders, still the white—and accompanied by a squadron of hussars, the Colonel came down the line, handing out assignments. Most of the tasks involved the movement of supplies and equipment from the citadel or other storage areas to the shore. Company by company, men marched off. When Lovelace came to Ashton and his men, he appeared to be considering several alternatives, or working through one alternative that might have several outcomes. In the end, he seemed satisfied with what he was about to announce. The duty was unexpected—a small number of men to oversee the destruction of a munitions magazine. The location was one that Moore did not believe he could protect once the battle began, and he had no intention of leaving his French counterpart such a generous bequest.

Expecting a punitive assignment that would exhaust his men, Ashton was naturally suspicious at what seemed the simplest. "Isn't this a job better suited to the sappers?" he asked.

"Must I remind you of their failures with the bridges?" said Lovelace, handing Ashton a hastily drawn map. "Besides, they are all at work on the trenches in front of our lines. The task should be simple enough—two or three gunpowder trains, a hundred yards in length. Light them. Stand back. Are you not up to the challenge?" After contemplating the instructions once more, he added: "Make sure it completely blows. *Destroy it all.* We cannot allow these munitions to fall into the hands of the enemy."

Leaving Fletcher in charge, Ashton took a handful of volunteers. The magazine being well away from the city, the task was expected to take several hours. Jane watched the men move across fields in the direction of several buildings in the distance and eventually disappear in trees and the folds of the land. Time passed slowly. When Colonel Lovelace left to check on other projects, the Rifles received permission to take their ease. Upon his return with his squadron, the men re-established formation in front of him.

"Well, how hard does one suppose it is to light a match?" he said, directing his comment toward Jane, who did not reply.

A short time later, an explosion rocked the town, sufficient to jitter the horses and rattle the windows. Before anyone could do more than smile with that surprise and delight that accompanies safely distant fireworks, a second explosion slammed the town and roiled the ground and buildings. Everyone in the assembly area was thrown off balance and several people were knocked from their feet. The concussion shattered every window. Flower pots and one cat came flying from window sills. A hut collapsed. A cart broke loose and banged down the hill. After an interval in which the air was so stunned it was impossible to breathe, the disturbance rumbled into the distance and broke against the hills. Half-dressed citizens rushed from their homes in panic and fell to their knees, entreating God for mercy. The hussars, having worked to control their horses, turned with the foot soldiers to Lovelace for an answer to this ear-splitting, body-quaking destruction.

The Colonel looked calmly over everyone, his gaze settling again on Jane. "I must have forgotten to tell Captain Dennis about the second magazine in the adjoining building." He smirked. "The *large* one."

The cluster of buildings—they would have been among them! *Ashton!*

Mr. Fletcher, in the few paces it required for him to reach Lovelace, pulled out his pistol, stuck it on the Colonel's heart long enough for his target to recognize what was going to happen, and shot him out of the saddle. Lovelace tumbled backward, dead on the way down. His startled horse accidentally trampled the lifeless body. Lovelace's cavalry compatriots reached for their sabers and began to spur their horses, but a company's worth of new weapons rose, the bayonets in the sun smiling their wicked smiles.

Fletcher spoke. "Too many good men have died stupidly today. Let's not increase the number."

The hussars remained uncertain, torn between loyalty to their leader and the certainty of death with another move.

So shocked that she could not respond to what the explosion meant or to what Fletcher had done, Jane acted on the certainty that the fate of many more men rested on the actions of the next few seconds. She spoke without the benefit of feeling, but she spoke: "The last month has made us brothers. You know Ashton—Captain Dennis—did not deserve his fate. You know the Colonel did. We can kill each other, or we can treat both men as casualties of this insane expedition. You have your ships to board. We have one last stand to make—to protect you as you leave. Go your way in peace, and we will go ours."

The hussars chose to ride away—slowly, so it was understood to be an act of peace, not cowardice. They took Lovelace's body with them.

As the Hampshire men stood there, shaken and disbelieving, Mr. Fletcher came up to Jane, bowed, and said, "I will take a detail out to—bury—our dead."

"No," Jane said.

"That's the only way. We cannot take him home."

"We will take him home. He is not dead."

"Mrs. Dennis—"

"He would never leave me. Not after all we have been through. The Rifles have no other assignment today. We will find him and bring him back. Or I will go alone. Who is with me?"

A hundred men stepped forward.

A black cloud, as close to oil as smoke, spewed and churned almost straight up at least a mile into the stricken sky. Lightning crackled at the very top. One could believe the explosion had ripped the earth open to the very bowels of Hell. Would that man had never found a way to create a bomb of this magnitude, Jane thought as they moved forward, for evidence of its destruction began half a mile away from its source. A farm building peppered with holes; a barn roof knocked open by a falling stone; a haystack, though covered, penetrated and smoldering. Closer, they found a series of stone enclosures; more vineyards and gardens, the trunks and limbs broken. *Please have the sense to take cover. Something heavy enough to survive the blast.* This was a faint hope, though, for the buildings associated with these fields were damaged or on fire. From here they could feel the heat of the burning magazine. When an unexploded barrel of gunpowder went off, they dived for the ground and watched the purplish substance belch into the atmosphere. They spread among the ruined buildings to search.

"Over here!" a man exclaimed. Everyone raced over and then stopped at what they saw. In the courtyard of the largest stone building, the side of which had blown away, were half a dozen bodies burned and torn apart. This was the first slaughter Jane had seen on the campaign created by fire instead of ice. It lacked the beauty of winter death. Instead of bold red on bright white, it was black and gray, the blood like smudges of charcoal. Colors of disgrace, not valor.

To be certain of the outcome, the company went reverentially from one body to the next. Four were dead, the least shocking because they bore the least resemblance to men. Soldiers tossed snow on one of them to sizzle out two spots that smoked. One was shredded, ripped open, but somehow still alive; shock had perhaps delayed the departure of the soul. Mr. Fletcher took another pistol, this time with compassion instead of justice. There is nothing more heartrending than a single, lonely gunshot. Yet the largest and most trepidacious was not to be seen. Had he left? Had he somehow survived? Yet where would he be?

"Ma'am." One of the ensigns touched her on the shoulder, pointing to a set of stairs in the shadow of the building. The group moved as one. At the last, everyone gave way to Jane, who forced herself ahead. There was something leaning against the brickwork. On the way were signs that it had dragged itself several feet through the snow. She was close enough to see now. A large man, shattered. Both legs mangled, one arm gone. *Dear God.* She knelt beside. She touched. Eyes fluttered almost open. Lungs dared to groan.

"We are here," she whispered.

"K-k-k-," he replied. "Ja-Ja-, k-k-."

She kissed him.

Chapter 42

Because of the lull in action, they were able to get Ashton into the surgery immediately. There the doctors sawed off the mangled legs at the knees and made a clean cut of the jagged remnant of his arm, tying up the arteries and cauterizing the stumps with steaming pitch. He was too unaware to receive laudanum or whisky; the amputations brought forth screams to exceed anything that had ever emerged from a birthing room.

A few transports had remained in the bay all these weeks, and the British were loading as many of the sick and wounded as possible, along with the healthiest of the officers' horses. Ashton, however, was too weak to be moved. Jane stayed with him, talking nonstop, reminding him of their life, recounting interesting anecdotes—anything to keep her occupied and him entertained, though she had no way of knowing whether he comprehended anything she said. That evening she heard exclamations of joy outside and went to check on the cause. The hospital was established in a building just up from the dock, and what she saw took away her breath. The French had not withdrawn, but she returned to tell Ashton the exciting news: The Fleet was beginning to arrive!

Ashton was in and out of consciousness all night long, groaning from time to time but never becoming sensible enough to speak. About two A.M. Mr. Fletcher and some of the men removed Jane insistently to an empty bed to let her sleep, such as she could, and took her watch. By morning, she was back at Ashton's side to report that the bay had filled with sails! "I am certain the *Endymion* is among them," she said, believing that the presence of the old *family* ship would buoy his spirits. Having to take their position in the reserve, Mr. Fletcher and the men, with Jane's consent, said goodbye to Ashton one by one. "They'll remember the 95th, Captain," said the normally stoic Fletcher, holding back tears.

There was no indication of major fighting during the day, but all morning long came the repeated reports of pistols puzzlingly close. Jane went out at midday to refresh her spirits with the sight of their magnificent salvation—the Royal Navy—now two hundred strong. It was then she saw that the pistols were being used to prevent their horses from falling into the hands of the French. As far as the eye could see, the beach was covered with carcasses—hundreds and hundreds of them. Cavalrymen were distraught that—now, at the very end—they must kill the valiant creatures who had in appalling conditions carried them to salvation. Some troopers were so unnerved, their shaking hands were unable to kill their mounts outright with the first shot. Men skilled in the art of butchery were taking over to make the deaths as painless as possible. In her short time there, the dock area became nearly too slick to walk, and the color of the water began to turn red. Some horses were panicking, tearing away and bolting down the beach. The men did not try hard to recapture them.

By late afternoon, all of the injured men and most of the cavalry had loaded. A discreet inquiry had her learn that the cavalry wives were also gone—there would be no need to deal with any immediate repercussions from Kat. The surgeons again cautioned her not to move Ashton. In the evening, Mr. Fletcher came by to check on him. He brought Jane something to eat, and they shared it. There had been skirmishing on and off, and the French had pushed back the British outposts: the usual pre-battle preparations. As best the British could tell, the French had concentrated on moving heavy guns up to the heights. If they succeeded overnight, they would gain a severe advantage. A flash of memory to Diamond Rock, where Ashton had helped haul up the British guns and later suffered his first wound. How many centuries ago was that? Now, the positions were reversed and it would be the French raining down shot from on high. She had little appreciation for the symmetry of history.

With the Fleet here, Mr. Fletcher said, the French would come tomorrow, with or without their artillery. In passing, she apologized for calling him by *Mr.* instead of by his rank for all these weeks. "You distinguished yourself. You served the men and my husband. It is this: You have been good Mr. Fletcher to me for so long, I am unable to form another title. I do not mean to disrespect your service."

"I prefer it. My loyalty is to the family and the House."

"Thank you for what you did at the formation. For Ashton's sake. It was deserved. More than that. As God is my witness, it was an act of honor."

Mr. Fletcher nodded and said nothing. He left a little while later.

At daybreak, with Ashton still largely unresponsive, Jane went out to the city walls, joining other nervous denizens. Everyone was afraid of what the battle would bring but everyone was also ready for resolution to the conflict. The front was quiet. She knew roughly where the Rifles would be but could not see anything of their men. She returned to the recovery area, put fresh dressings on her husband's wounds and salve on his many burns, and brought him (oblivious or not) up to date on events. The morning remained uneventful; the occasional person coming through had no knowledge of why the French were delaying an attack. At mid-afternoon, Jane heard a stirring outside the building and all the indications of a mass of military men on the move. She learned that Sir John had had two divisions withdraw and begin to embark. Shortly after, the French attacked. No one knew whether this was a coincidence or whether Soult believed he might carry the day once the British forces were reduced. Very shortly, the noise of battle rose and filled the air. There was the distant sweeping rattle of muskets and the occasional sound of smaller cannons on one side or the other. What troubled her, however, was a deep-throated roar that could mean only that the French heavy artillery was in place and taking the British measure.

Within the hour, wounded began to come in. Jane rallied to help the inadequately staffed hospital cope when the trickle became a flood. She apologized to Ashton for having to leave his side but knew he would understand. She had no skills, but the last month had inured her to what she saw, and she was fully capable of stanching a wound or applying a dressing. The role that was most appreciated was that of angel, when she smiled to a man, told him everything would be all right, and held his hand while he died. By nightfall, the building was full and the injured were spread out in small nearby buildings or lying and sitting in the street. As night progressed, she saw that more and more soldiers were hastening to the harbor to leave. Everything was done in utmost silence; she understood that the British were disguising the extent of their evacuation. Because the troop barges were being warped out by cable, they could move quietly; no oars or sails were required. Nor were torches needed to light their paths out to the marshaling area offshore. The occasional fog and mist helped to obscure the movements and muffle the sounds.

With the wounded came news. General Sir John Moore had been killed. General Sir David Baird had been seriously injured. General Sir John Hope had taken charge and held the British firm. With every wave of soldiers—wounded or departing—Jane looked for the 95th. There was no sign. Finally, she began to ask about them and heard from one officer—a major, who was injured but not enough to keep him from boarding—that they had come up to repulse the final French attack at the end of day. "They're still out there," he yelled to her. "They've lit fires and are making a hubbub—the French don't realize we've gone! They'll be the last ones down."

Rearguard, again.

She knew what this would mean in the morning. Somehow, they would have to withdraw at full speed and board the ships without the French overwhelming them on the field or at the docks. Yet, as the flow of injured ebbed with the cessation of battle, Jane raced to tell her silent husband the good news that she could: His men had fought like Richard the Lionheart on his behalf. They had turned the tide—blunted the last assault. Buonaparte's best were no match for the men of Hants! To herself she thought—as she knew Ashton would think if he were alert enough to understand—how many of his farmers and workers had bled? How many more would bleed tomorrow?

For the rest of the night she helped organize the evacuation of these fresh ranks of the wounded. She was the one who wrote the note in French asking the victors to spare the men too badly injured to be moved. The doctors told her it was her decision whether to take Ashton. There was no chance she would leave him behind, and she agreed for him to be put upon a stretcher for quick removal. But she would not go without the 95th, and she knew the same on behalf of her husband. They would all get off, or none.

At first light, the men were there.

At the same time, the guns of the Spanish citadel opened up in the direction of the French. They were all astonished. Were the Spanish, who with very few exceptions had done little to aid their would-be liberators, actually going to protect them as they left?

"This means the French have discovered our ruse, that our lines are empty," Mr. Fletcher said. "Hurry!"

They were on two of the last dozen barges. As they were boarding, she met Mrs. Stout and three other women, all that had survived of the females of Hants. All that would depart, that is. Another dozen Spanish wives learned as the Rifles scrambled aboard that they were not allowed to go with their husbands. Jane became aware that the entire dock was full of wailing foreign women who had never been told the regulations. (Of which she herself had been unaware.)

They were just getting away from shore when a battery of French guns opened fire from the hill that housed the barracks where the Rifles had first stayed in-country. The first barrage sailed over their heads, but the second and third fell among the transports. Some of the masters of these vessels panicked, cutting the cables that were pulling them to sea to try to maneuver away from the attack. Instead, they began to drift back to the shore, where they would be easier targets and subject to capture. Immediately, longboats from the warships sped in to pull off as many people as they could. The artillery kept coming. One shot ripped through a sail; one shell exploded over their heads, spattering them with metal shards. Jane threw herself over Ashton. Dear God, she thought—will it never end? Will we never get away from this benighted country?

Through a light fog that had infiltrated the bay at daylight, a British man-o-war appeared, moving swift and silent. At that moment, the French fired again. As more shot and shell rattled the transports—one tore a chunk out of their deck—she saw on the British ship a small, trim, dark-haired captain looking through the glass, giving orders. *Frank?* Guns from both decks of the ship opened fire, a single massive broadside. Everyone's eyes turned to see the results. *"Kill them! Kill them all!"* Jane screamed. Eight or ten seconds later, they could see a series of plumes of smoke and dust pound the hill. The French guns went silent. The British warship slid back into the fog. All the ships were moving now. Despite being slung across the width of the Channel by storm and gale, the Fleet did not stop until it touched upon the homeland's soil.

Chapter 43

Jane's observation was that hospitals were not where the sick went to mend but to die. En route to Portsmouth, she and Mr. Fletcher had worked out a plan to take Ashton home as rapidly as possible. First, they made the sad pilgrimage up from the harbor, where not only residents, horrified at their state, rushed to their aid but also French prisoners of war from the hulks, marshaled to assist them, who could not believe the sight of soldiers in worse shape than themselves.

As in Spain, the countryside in recent weeks had endured frost, rain, melting, flood. Now the rains were steady but not torrential, the wind out of the south. Jane and Mr. Fletcher resurrected the left-behind balloon to provide the same service to Ashton as it had for the mare—to ease a wagon ride over rough, soggy roads. When they reached the railroad, which now stretched nearly to Southampton, it was the well-prepared rail bed that provided comfort while Mr. Trevithick drove his locomotive beyond its limits. Like one of their steeds at the gates of Corunna, the mechanical beast coughed and shuddered and breathed its last as it deposited Ashton at the northern terminus of Headbourne Worthy. From there it was again the balloon, which rose to the challenge over the last twenty miles or so to Hants.

Halfway up the last hill, a small but persistent leak began to rapidly expand; Mr. Fletcher was able to land with a scary but safe thud just as the fabric on one side gave way with a loud, insistent rip. From there, the stable master brought an extra team of horses, and workers pitched in to push Ashton through the muddiest section of the lane and onto the gravel carriage sweep.

Jane instantly decided to turn the chapel, unused since George's christening, into her husband's convalescent ward. The room was large enough to hold a separate bed for her and any equipment or other necessities for his recovery; it would simplify access by the staff and eliminate stairs during his recovery.

It took nearly a week for her to find a balance to the dosage and timing of the laudanum to minimize the torment of his injuries. She was able to take him off the medicine two or perhaps three times each day. During these periods, she would feed him soup and weak gruel and talk to him. Mostly, he was unresponsive. Often, he groaned despite the laudanum. He did not seem aware of being fed; it was as though his body was accepting the service rather than his mind. Every day she expected to see improvement and every day, except for her establishing the initial equilibrium, she did not. In many ways, his condition was discouraging. There were times at night when he brought her awake with his agony. Some of what happened seemed akin to the convulsions of George; in this case, however, she did not believe his muscles were seizing involuntarily but rather in a desperate effort to crush the pain. He also broke out in sweats, day and night.

Her hope came when his dark eyes showed signs of life. It was like a swimmer coming to the surface for a few minutes before sinking back deep into the depths. It was while he was present, floating close by, that he would stutter his *J, J, J, k-k-k* and she would smother him with kisses.

Dr. Parry came over from Bath for an evaluation. "Most society ladies do not wish to hear the truth," he said. "They treat a medical prognosis as if it were a question of etiquette. I take you differently, Mrs. Dennis. Having little experience with the military, I have seldom seen such injuries. I wonder how he remains alive. In addition to the loss of limbs, the explosion severely damaged his internal organs. Almost any touch causes pain."

"But he will recover?—I will tend him as long as it takes."

"We can always hope for a miracle, but in my opinion—no. Sadly. Sorrowfully. He may linger for some time. Even years. He will always be in pain. He is beyond the scope of medicine. At least today's. He is in God's hands now."

"And mine."

"I am sure you will give him the best care possible. I hope—but cannot declare—that it will be enough. I fear it is only a matter of time. *And suffering.*"

Dr. Parry provided Jane with additional salves for his burns and amputations, along with the strongest forms of opium. "Do not hesitate to send for more. In his state, he must never lack both the *quality* and *quantity* of the medicine *required*."

They agreed that Dr. Parry would come for regular visits and that Jane might summon him for any emergency. The stronger medicines seemed to help. Ashton slept more soundly and suffered less; when he came off them, he seemed to rise somewhat higher and could remain off them for somewhat longer stretches before yielding to the pain. The improvement was such that he could sit up occasionally, and this meant she could add bread and small bits of softened meat to his diet. Mr. Hanrahan found a large wheelchair and took Ashton for an outing on the first nice afternoon. This was as much to give Jane rest as Ashton an airing, for he was awake for only part of the excursion. At the end of that first trip, however, Mr. Hanrahan reported back with great mortification and contrition that while he was distracted by several aggressive geese, Ashton had somehow fallen from the chair and rolled toward the pond a few feet away. The chair was immediately modified with restraints, though the onset of more wet weather ended the sojourns indefinitely.

Shortly after, as she fed Ashton the more substantive fare, he choked. At first it was a momentary thing; then the food lodged solidly in his throat. She called for help. She shook him; she slammed him on the back. His eyes came alive. He wrenched from side to side but not in an effort for air. He was trying to shake her off! *Leave me!* his eyes beseeched. He heaved back and forth, shrugging her off like a cloak. She cried again and heard distant footsteps coming to her aid. She started toward him but saw that his struggle was not to breathe but to *not breathe*. His huge frame twisted in agony as the corporeal part of him fought to stay in this world while the mindful part of him fought to leave. It was like a demon split in two, tearing at itself: The body raged for air while the soul raged for end. Physicality won out; he coughed and sputtered and dislodged the meat. Just before the door opened to the servants and he passed out, he begged of her: *"K-k-kill me, Jane! If you love me, k-k-kill me!"*

Chapter 44

When he floated up, he remained awake long enough to recognize that he was in the chapel rather than their bedroom.

"Reason?" he asked.

"Expedience—but a little prayer might help."

"*Jane—*"

Before he could say more, and as if this were a typical conversation on a typical day, she launched into a discussion of the state of the estate. Though she began with an optimistic survey of all that was good about Hants and its operations, she resolved to tell him, whatever his disability, of matters more pertinent to their situation. If he were alert enough to understand, he would want to know; if he were not, it would not matter.

She related to him their financial difficulties resulting from the Peninsular campaign. The loans they had pledged to the Government had come due. The haste of the evacuation caused the Army to lose or burn the documents written by General Sir John Moore that the loans had been taken at his official behest and need; without it, the expedition would have failed. The death of Sir John meant that there was no one who would or could support that claim. General Baird went no further than to attest his own loans—which position the Government accepted, he being a commanding officer. Ashton murmured some cynicism that Jane entirely supported: "Yes, it was convenient that they saved the loan papers but lost the corroboration."

She continued: "Though we have filed a formal appeal, it is unclear whether the Government will honor it or how long it might take. Mr. Fletcher is coordinating with Henry and Mr. Thornton in London. The bankers are working with the lawyers. In the meantime, they are having Alethea and Mr. Jarrett raise money. This will cause us losses. As I have been attending to these matters—and to you—Mr. Hanrahan has been kind enough to handle our routine financial affairs."

"Stoves—no!" With these and a few other words and anguished expressions, Ashton was able to indicate that, whatever else needed to be done, they were not to touch the finances of the Rumford division—Alethea's business. Jane promised they would not—while also telling him bluntly that all of their forward-looking investments were done. He shrugged as if that decision were inevitable.

"It might not matter too much, anyway. Mr. Trevithick destroyed your locomotive getting you here safely."

"Men?"

Here she hesitated, setting down her work. "Many of our sick and wounded went out early. The rest of us jumped on whichever ship we could. We were all separated. Regiments were mixed up. Transports put in everywhere. Our men are still making their way back."

Ashton's eyes demanded specifics.

"Mr. Fletcher says about a hundred and twenty made it home. Those healthy enough to resume their lives. When so many men took sick beyond Astorga, I never thought it would be a good thing—but they were sent back, and missed the worst of everything—the fighting, the marches. But, dear, we will have lost about eighty men—sixty dead, more or less. The others badly injured."

His harrumph was for himself in that last number. His tears were for the others.

She had been monitoring his rising pain. She gave him enough opium to send him to sleep. His resistance to the vial—he did not want succor—did not subside until she pointed out: "A lack of medicine will not end your life. It will only make it painful."

Still, before he dozed off, he tried again—

"Jane—k-k-kill—"

"I understand your despair," she said. "I understand the temptation to end it all. But we cannot. It is against God's ordinance. And Man's. Even if it were not—I cannot do it. I cannot let you do it. As you told the men—one more step. Every time you feel you cannot go on—persevere. Take one more step."

He snorted—how was a legless man to take another step?

He succumbed to slumber.

———

Their conversations continued, several times a day; the dialogue more one-sided than in their history. As always, the topics ranged to the distant and philosophical as well as to the immediate and practical. Knowing that many skeptics find their faith during a personal or physical crisis, Jane tried to learn whether there had been any evolution in his beliefs. However things might end, her primary concern was that his relationship with God was put aright. Their many discussions of religion had primarily been in the context of its role in society: whether it should support the social order (and order in general: Jane) or encourage change (even at the cost of chaos: Ashton). He remained, even now, a critic of the church as an institution. "A closed organization is a corrupt one," he said. More than that, the institution was the method by which Jesus's teachings were distorted or watered down. If clergymen actually understood Jesus's radical nature, they would nail him to the cross as eagerly as the Pharisees and Romans had.

"He preached peace and love," Jane rejoined.

"When was the last time the English church—or French, or German—preached peace and love and really meant it?" Ashton replied. "Don't they send their baa-ing sheep off to the latest war, while *they* stay home and pray?"

His contempt for those who justified wars had not stopped him from serving in those wars, and she knew he respected her brothers for their lifetimes of dangerous vigil on the sea. For a man full of theoretical arguments, he would act or not as he determined at the moment, and let others worry about philosophy.

His respect for her own religious beliefs had led him to play down his heterodoxy within their social set. He would not have let social approbation come down on her for something she cared so deeply about. His attitude was that of a man watching a family he adored in the middle of an activity he did not care much about. He enjoyed escorting her to church because he knew what it meant to her and liked how her face lit up each Sunday. He listened attentively to the sermons and critiqued their logic. He sang the hymns so ardently off key that it took all the women of the party to drown him out. Yet he did not concede on substance, continuing his airy dismissal of the Bible whenever it contradicted the evidence of the world. Though he spoke of what God inscribed directly in the rocks, she was not certain of his meaning of *God*. The word seemed to be a placeholder for some aspect of reality that humans did not yet understand. He spoke of "Nature, and Nature's God," as if God were the afterthought of the natural world instead of the other way around. Much of his talk seemed a quibble, an effort to provoke her into an angry misstep that would cause her to lose one of their entangled metaphysical arguments.

"If we can believe in gravity, which can be felt but not seen, why can we not believe in a Moral Presence, equally unseen but more powerfully felt?" she argued.

He agreed. "Whether God created it, or Man has projected it, Moral Presence permeates the universe—it is strong enough to bend the stars."

His statement, of course, was not remotely as elaborate as this. His burns, his struggle through pain, his inability to sustain attention for more than a few minutes at a time—all these things muffled and confounded his expression. But he said enough for her to understand. When she looked at the mangled features of her tragic patient, she saw in its place her husband's original face and form; when he spoke, she filled in the words with what he meant instead of what little he was able to say.

Sometimes, after one of these elaborate conversations, she would come to herself at the end of a walk, on her daily respite from care, and realize that this is where the tête-à-tête had occurred. More than once, Cass nudged her about the situation—when, because Ashton was passing in and out of consciousness, it was never quite certain how much he could hear—and also when Jane wandered afield, disputing with the open air as her husband had been wont to do.

"I argue with him in my mind as he has often done with me, to refine a position sharply enough to cut through the other's defenses," Jane said. "But also to fully develop his thoughts—as he would think them—so I might better understand their content."

"It appears a little strange," Cass said, though it did not matter to Jane that her sister, Mr. Hanrahan, Mrs. Lundeen, and Abigail—the only ones allowed in the room—often saw her in deep philosophical discussion with a man whose contribution to the argument consisted of mutters and moans.

"My goal is not to defeat his position but to understand it better," Jane said. "If he has difficulty with thought or expression, it is my duty to make up the difference. What has really changed? Our entire marriage has involved a woman who spoke with too much ease and a man who spoke with too little."

The sum of all these conversations—with him, or at least related to him—was the reinforcement of what she knew after their earliest conversation. Ashton wanted her to expand her mind—to see beyond the limited Creation of a controlling church. She wanted him to expand his soul—to see beyond the limited reality visible to Man.

This philosophizing took her repeatedly to the central question she did not know how to face. How could she reconcile Ashton's desire to kill himself—and her desire to end his pain—with her own belief that life was too precious to end until it ended itself. By keeping him alive, she upheld everything she had been taught—believed—while providentially preserving her own security and that of her family. But the cost to Ashton was excruciating pain—or to remain sedated, floating in a gray moral and mortal limbo—for an indefinite number of appalling years. Letting him die, or helping him to die, would be a mortal sin. But is not the torture of a human being a sin as great? The thought, the logic, the consideration: All these things served to shield her from the clammy feeling in her gut that whatever decision she made would be dreadfully, horrifically, irretrievably wrong.

Because she had no answer, her actions were the same whenever he brought up the forbidden topic, or assaulted her with his *k-k-k*'s. She sent him dreamily away.

More than once, when he believed he was thinking clearly—or at least harshly—Ashton tried to goad her into acting. He mocked her and those precious beliefs of hers. He abused her for not having the courage to kill him, calling her purported morality the easiest path for her, the hardest for him. Trying to provoke her into murder, he told her that he never loved her.

"I know, you married me for my money."

"Nor did I ever find you pretty!"

She laughed. "No, dear love, I was never pretty. The only beauty is what you found in your eyes."

Cassandra added her own bizarre tangent to these trying interactions when, after they had bathed Ashton, she pointed out something rather obvious: under Jane's tender ministrations "his strength still came upon him." When Jane did not understand, Cass gave an indication and added: "You could still have an heir. You know he would wish that more than anything in the world. And you would lessen his suffering, if only for a little while." These comments sent her whirling. Such thoughts, at such a time, were almost blasphemous; that they were objectively rational made them even more insane—to seek an heir, now, in Ashton's situation!

One could not begin or end with her husband's wishes, even if there was any clarity among his agony-crazed judgments. And never mind that she had not been able to conceive since George's birth (though circumstances had rendered opportunity uncommon). What if she had another *defective*? A girl? What if Jane should die—at birth or later—leaving behind a parentless child? She determined on principle that if a woman should not be used as broodmare for a man, then a man should not be used as brood stock for a woman. In addition, "I will not bring a child into the world unless I know I can provide for it." Still further: "My responsibility toward Ashton at this point in our lives is not to take but to give."

Chapter 45

As Jane returned from her walk, she saw the vicar waiting for her in the garden. This visit was exactly what she did not require, but she gave him the sad smile she would give anyone visiting now. His presence added another religious point of view—a rigid, sterile view—she did not wish to intrude upon her cogitation. Yet she took this walk daily; she had these thoughts daily. He was bound to show up after one of them.

He turned and walked with her. He did not speak, using the reticence of his position to encourage any kind of confessional topic his parishioner might wish to bring up. When she offered nothing but bare pleasantries, he came to the subject that brought him to Hants.

"I have heard that Mr. Dennis had a difficult day recently. Several difficult days."

"He is in great pain. Even the medicine cannot entirely soothe it. Some days are worse than others."

"There was talk—in the village—of his nearly choking to death. And nearly drowning."

There was a warning in his voice.

She turned to him. "You understand his grievous wounds. His difficulty eating. One spasm of pain was so severe he was thrown from his chair near the pond before Mr. Hanrahan could intervene.

Even for a village with limited gossip, I am surprised that a man's agony would rise to the level of entertainment."

They walked on, Mr. Collier holding his hands behind his back.

"There was some indication that perhaps Mr. Dennis lunged from his chair. Speaking of the incident at the pond."

"Between the pain and his medicine, he is seldom in his full mind. At times he tries to stand. Rather difficult in his circumstance."

Mr. Collier began to speak but Jane cut him off. "Servants want to tell their friends about *secret* or *special* activities at a grand house, even if nothing secret or special is about. Villagers want to take the most common incident and imbue it with scandal. Ashton and I once went on an innocent excursion. By the time it ended, an entire county was convinced we led a French invasion."

"I have no doubt that what you say is true, Mrs. Dennis. But the reports are disquieting. If there were any evidence of *desire* by Mr. Dennis to act in some *untoward* manner, there would be serious repercussions."

"You may come as often as you wish to observe my husband's actions. You can decide how many *untoward* thoughts a man can entertain when he is out of his mind with pain. Stay as long you like. We can always use someone in the midnight hours. The rest of us would benefit from the sleep. He resides in the chapel; you would find that comforting—or perhaps amusing."

She nodded as if to dismiss him, but before she could turn away, he said with conviction: "I am the vicar, Mrs. Dennis. I speak to you today not as an acquaintance, or a social inferior, but with the authority of my position. You *must* listen."

"You are a toad, Mr. Collier. My hope for salvation—my hope for the world—is that the God you purport to represent is *not* a toad."

He grabbed her by the arm. "It is imperative, Mrs. Dennis."

"Take your hand from me, sir, or I shall forcibly remove it!"

"Please," he said, though he relinquished his hold. "As the moral authority in the area, I must report any ... *suspicious* ... *event* ... should it occur. I have no choice. The news will escape, regardless. Mr. Dennis is too well known. His injuries before the walls of Corunna—*part of that glorious stand!*—have been broadcast far and wide."

His eyes indicated that the meaning of *event* went beyond the word to something neither of them might wish to acknowledge. The tone was one she had never heard from him before, and she waited to understand its meaning.

"Mr. Dennis tolerated me," Mr. Collier said. "For his amusement, and that of your friends. Chubby little rabbit, that was it—a tired joke, here and in the village. Even a dull vicar could not be unaware. I did not have his respect—"

"You will *not* speak of him in the past tense."

"I *do* not have his respect, but he has mine."

She waited: Again, his tone was unusual.

"Even the appearance of self-murder—*felo de se*—will require an inquest. Suicide is a crime. You know that."

"You cannot wait for that to happen, can you? To repay us for our self-importance and superiority? For all we have that you do not?"

"I have been wounded by your attitude. You dismiss me for mindlessly following the traditions of my Church, yet you believe I lack the imagination to do better. What is a chubby little rabbit to do?"

She was taken aback by his insight—his eyes were shrewder than they looked. "Mr. Collier, do not take hubris on my part as a deficiency on yours. Your comment wounds me now—for fear it might be true. Hold me accountable—not my husband."

"Please understand me. I do not wish the downfall of the Dennis family. Nor of you, personally."

"There is no heir, Mr. Collier. We all fall down if Ashton dies."

"Twice he has put his life at risk for England. A man who by wealth and position could have stayed at home. Twice he has been injured, this time severely. I have no idea whether he was a warrior, but he *served*. His courage was not defined by how he performed in battle but by the fact he went at all. That is not all, of course. Despite his reservations about our religion, he has cared for the poor with a generosity that most of our gentry lack. They complain that the poor tax leaves them unable to give voluntarily, but when it is reduced—they give no more. Perhaps he compensates for his deficiency of faith. Perhaps out of a native generosity. I do not need to analyze the reason to appreciate the deed. His contributions, I noticed over the years, took a jump after any engagement in which he used me for his sport. Some emotional adjustment, I suppose. Even a dull vicar can appreciate the benefit to our parish—and recognize an apology by the act. *Dull vicar* is my other title, as you know."

"He was better with acts than words."

"Too many of us are the other way. You are not the first *kind* Dennis, madam, though I fear you may be the last. You brought thoughtfulness to his kindness. And your father—I met him years ago—*kind*. A simple word, a less common description than it should be."

"It is fair to challenge your beliefs," Jane responded, "but I am wrong to abuse your humanity. Where are you going with this line of thought?"

"He must die in his sleep, Mrs. Dennis. In his own bed. That is how we all wish to go, is it not? Quietly, with our soul at rest? He must not be found in some incriminating circumstance."

"I was the one who prevented his choking. That the servants will confirm. If he has had thoughts in that direction, they have not been aided. If—I emphasize *if*—he were to do something, though, there is a possibility we could not prevent it."

"Then you must do whatever else might be necessary. Is it not better for Hants to stay within the family, however distant? Is it not better for everyone involved to avoid the shame?"

"Nothing Ashton has ever done has had *anything* to do with shame."

"Think of his mother, the elder Mrs. Dennis. His sisters. The family reputation. What may not matter to you will matter very deeply to everyone else. And possibly, one day, even to you."

"You have been candid, and fair, today, Mr. Collier. I do not know what to say. His pain overwhelms him from time to time. I cannot say if anything else is involved. We take him outside whenever the weather allows. To give him what small pleasure we can—the sun in his face."

"A mercy. But we must avoid anything that might raise questions."

"If it came to that ... my father was involved in several situations in which the church and the authorities acted with discretion ... *leniency*. It is common now, whenever there is any doubt, for an inquest to issue a ruling of temporary insanity."

"Not when the individual is rich. Not when the country is at war. Given the straitened circumstances of the exchequer, the terrible losses incurred by Moore's campaign—an inquest will find him guilty. The estate will be forfeit to the Crown. *All of it!*"

"They have already taken much of what we have. I cannot believe the Crown would go so far—act so callously—as to snatch the last farthing from a dying man—a soldier—officer!"

"There is more than enough left for the Crown to covet. Do you wish the entire Dennis line to be impoverished?"

"Of course not."

"Do not forget the last—a suicide cannot be buried in the churchyard."

She was staggered; she had to grab his arm—the very one she had just refused. She had never known anyone who had, without any question, taken his own life; therefore, she had long forgotten the burial injunction. Before this final point, she had already been disturbed. Was Collier telling her to better manage Ashton so he had no chance to kill himself; to cover up his suicide, if he succeeded; or something more extreme—?

"Ashton will be buried in the churchyard, Mr. Collier, if I have to dig the grave myself in the middle of the night."

"And I would help you, Mrs. Dennis. But let us avoid any curiosities, any questions—entirely. As vicar, I can say nothing more." He began to turn away; stopped; added this last: "I am a toad, Mrs. Dennis; but in this matter, I am *your* toad. Good day."

Chapter 46

Jane went into the drawing room and sat with conviction before Cassandra. "Dr. Parry confirms it—as does the surgeon he brought."

"So it is—as we feared?"

Jane nodded.

It was Cassandra who had first noticed the inflammation in Ashton's legs. They had doubled the salve and changed the dressings more often while issuing an urgent summons to Bath. Jane had also taken over all the nursing. If matters worsened, it could be only her to bear the burden.

"You are certain?"

"One in three—at least—suffered at Corunna." She was not certain that the fetid smell of the hospital there had ever left her nostrils. "I did not require the doctor's confirmation, but I knew he would bring the best surgeon he had."

"Ashton cannot survive another operation," Cass said quietly.

"He is as strong as a horse!"

"He is not a piece of firewood. You cannot keep sawing off the rotten pieces."

"We cannot leave this untreated!"

"We can accept the inevitable. And ease his pain."

"I am already using as much opium as he can stand."

"But not as much as you might."

Cassandra's face and eyes were as pitiless as a death mask. The coldness was not directed at Ashton's situation—her shaking voice told otherwise—but at the necessity for Jane to consider what she so far had refused to consider.

"Cass, you cannot—"

"Dr. Parry left you enough medicine to dose the village. And brought you more today."

"To ensure there was no danger of exhausting the—" She stopped, having never imagined another purpose.

"You break every rule except the one that matters."

"It is not possible," she said.

"Everything is over but his suffering."

"God can make it stop. I cannot."

"If the God we worship does not practice compassion, then the God we worship is the very Devil."

Jane took several of the vials from her pocket and slammed them on the table. "If it is the right thing," she said to her sister, "then you face the same moral requirement as I."

"Ashton does not belong to me."

"I cannot, sister. I cannot."

"The last face he needs to see is the face of the woman he loves."

Jane returned to the chapel, where Ashton slept. It being late afternoon, she asked the two medical practitioners whether an overnight delay would make any difference. "He is weakest now," she explained. "This is the time of day when he is most exhausted. I would rather you operate first thing in the morning—when he has slept. When he is rested." The surgeon leaned toward immediate action but would not impose his will. "It is not far spread," the doctor said, agreeing that the risk of a postponement might well be balanced by an increase in Ashton's strength. He warned, however, that "no mortal could make a conclusive argument on either side."

"Then be ready at first light," she said, calling Mr. Hanrahan to take them to their rooms and make the necessary arrangements for dinner. She spent the next several hours alternately walking the halls and sitting beside Ashton. There was, in truth, nothing more to think about. She had thought it all before, almost since they first came upon Ashton's shattered body in the smoking ruins near Corunna. Even when one's heart is set upon saving the life of a loved one, one's mind concurrently wanders down the murky corridors of *what if.* ...

Both consciously and unconsciously she had wrestled with the situation. She had argued more with herself than she had with her husband. She had written down the details to make them as plain and direct as possible and to try to achieve some emotional distance from them. The result was that each time she balled up the page and threw it into the fire, for fire was the only place for such a statement of the facts. Barring any other action, Ashton would die an ugly, lingering death. Seeing him in that agony every day, she felt the compulsion of mercy—to end his sufferings. Or was it to end her own experience of them? Had the callousness, the casualness, of death on the battlefield rendered her unable to understand or respect the sanctity of life; or had her experiences taught her that compassion was the greater part of morality?

She saw from time to time that Ashton struggled with the contemplation of death. She saw fear, doubt, anger, fear again—but always, finally, resolve. He would continue to try to kill himself and one day he *would* succeed—she would fall asleep, she would miss a sign, he would do something and her response would be exactly wrong. She believed with all her heart that such an act would condemn his soul to Hell.

Ashton opened his eyes, found Jane through some subtle movement of hers, and focused his gaze. The pain, as always, created a veil of insensibility around his mind through which he had to struggle, a swimmer fighting his way to the surface. He looked at her with a sudden alertness as if thinking: *My love!* His recognition reminded her, at this terrible, tender moment, of the way their baby had looked at her at that transcendent moment he first recognized her as his mother, when he saw her and truly knew her for the first time. The same for both, she thought. They recognize. They love. They leave me in isolation.

"It is time, my love," she said. "To say goodbye."

"Now?"

"If we are to do it—now."

"That bad?"

"Yes."

He nodded, struggling still to come fully alert. She waited, knowing by experience how long it would take for this to happen and how many minutes of clarity he would have before the pain became unbearable.

"Do you really suppose there is an afterlife? That we're not done?" These were words he muttered as much as uttered; an explication of expression as much as articulation of speech.

"I believe so. I pray so."

"Hope so. Still—maybe—goodbye?"

"It may be. But I do not believe so. Remember when you chided me about limiting God's power—making his Creation far too small for his Glory? Do not make the same mistake."

"He created Heaven to annoy philosophers." This is what he meant by: "Heav—annoy—philos—"

"It may be necessary to believe," she said.

"Believe anything—ends pain."

"A soul at peace must have the best opportunity to enter Heaven."

If eyes could speak, Ashton's gave voice to most of his intent; that, and his determination to push through pain: "Peace. Mostly. What wanted to do. What miss. Years without you! Despair. But what we had! Love. Little boy. Enough. Worth it. Only fault—mine. Not to appreciate. Regret unkindness. Regret—every—angry."

She admonished him to relax. "You cannot meet God in full declamation."

"Only meek there—tiny Garden after all."

"He will be the first one you cannot out-argue."

"Answers!"

"Everyone is leaving me."

"Demanding."

"If I were so demanding, you would not behave so badly."

"Not willing. Not father. Not George. Not me."

"I will remain alive. I am not certain I will live."

Being at the peak of clarity, he was also at the peak of his pain. She administered some of the liquid, enough to take off the edge. She was able to put his words, the gesture of his good hand, his facial expressions—everything together like a puzzle into statements she herself might have made. What he asked was for her to tell a story. She had them in her head. Half the time, he said, you're a witty conversationalist, and half the time you're lost in your own little world. Creating a new scene—dreamy look. Rewriting one—squint, nose twitches. Moving words around inside that beautiful head of yours.

"I have no stories. None short enough to tell. Just our own: Man and woman meet. Exasperate each other. Fall in love."

"Funny story."

"Universal. If a man and woman fall in love at first sight, the novel ends on the first page. I have no funny stories. A funny story in itself—neither one of us can tell a joke."

"Collier's sermons—told him, excellent—not original. Offended. Every word himself! Told him—book at home, every word he'd used. Dared me—prove it."

She hid her surprise and alarm at his curious mention of the vicar. "And?"

"Took him dictionary."

"I cannot laugh at anything that ridiculous."

"Time to cry, later."

"Are you sure?" she said, indicating the medicine. He was sinking fast. She had to act now.

He nodded.

"It is now, if at all."

She saw what he intended with his good arm; she moved close so he could stroke her face.

"God, I love you," he said.

"Kiss me, Ashton. If you love me, kiss me."

They kissed.

"Love po—?" he asked.

"A love potion, yes. The finest ma—." Here, she was the one who dropped the word, and he understood: "The finest made."

Fumbling, he tried to take a vial, but she stopped him. "No. This is mine to do." To herself but in an oddly formal way, she said: "You are not the only person in this room who can commit a mortal sin." She gave him the draught, and then more, and then more.

"Not ugly death—beauty life!" he cried, searching her eyes. This was the one thing he was demanding she remember from the last few months, from all that they had experienced together. *Do not let the ugliness of death blind you to the beauty of life.* She did not know now whether she would be able to obey that command.

"Is there anything else you want, my dearest?"

With all that remained of his heart, he answered: "Nothing but—." And could not finish.

She waited for something to happen, but in this case what would happen was the opposite of something. How much time passed, she was not certain, for every fiber of her nerves was engrossed in his response, and in her culpability. She had opened the windows earlier, wanting him to breathe the fresh air and feel whatever breeze God might offer for his going. He looked at her with deep affection, seeming to want to memorize her face. As if the final image in his mind would last throughout Eternity. Slowly his gaze lost focus; despite his struggle, he slowly lost consciousness; one last faint smile. His eyes closed, and he fell back into the deep. He had that slight snore, not enough to complain about but enough sometimes to keep her awake. His breathing slowed and shallowed and remained, ebbing, for some time. Her mind attended to every elusive change. He was slowly moving further and further away. She was becoming more and more alone. At once Ashton sighed heavily. His muscles relaxed, his body lengthened. She recognized how pain had contorted his body and felt gratitude for the end to it. "That is it!" she thought. "The end of his torment. Stop—stop now—no more!" But it did not stop. What was happening continued, measured out in his irregular and subsiding breath. He inhaled once in a full and normal way, as if ready to arise; stopped as if holding his breath; coughed in a strange fashion, as he might before correcting a friend on some matter of consequence; exhaled, and did not inhale again.

Rest, she thought, when it was over. Go in peace, dear husband. Go in peace, my love. She touched his eyes to make sure they would remain closed and kissed him on each of his lids, hoping that if any of the unique energy that was Ashton lingered still, he would detect this last indication of her affection.

"O what a crash and clatter you will make at the Pearly Gates!" she exclaimed. "Do you remember your entrance to the ball? Will St. Peter challenge you as Mr. Shanding did? Will you ask the kindly saint to clean your boots?" She took her pocket coins—tip money for errand-runners—and folded them within his one good hand. "Just in case," she whispered.

She disposed of the excess vials. Believing his soul was free, a butterfly out of a shattered chrysalis, she went over to close the windows. Then she sat in the dark room, alone and less than human; for as Ashton took his soul from his body, he pulled much of hers along.

Chapter 47

It was hours, or days, or weeks later when someone came. The physician and surgeon consulted and handled the necessary medical minutiae. Cassandra and the other women must have tended to her, for at some point she was in her room, ostensibly to sleep. As the corpse no longer contained her husband, she cared no more about its disposal than she would a hulk on the river. This was not true, of course, it was a brutal thought to keep her from confronting the concept of *the corpse*. She recognized Mr. Collier and one or two of her interchangeable brothers who came to attend to the details. Mr. Jarrett led the pallbearers. She could not focus well enough to recognize most of the rest of those who came, though she could tell by the rustling and murmurs that the house was full of saddened people.

Afterward what she remembered most was the random movement of inanimate objects: furniture being moved, chairs scraping floors, luggage lifted and dropped, food being placed before her for the purpose of remaining untouched. One day she came upon the wheelchair in a corner and ran from it as if rebuked. Mostly what she recalled was the rain. Hard rain. Soft rain. Still rain. Blowing rain. All of England cried. She would sit in the bower in the rain until Cassandra or Mrs. Lundeen or Abigail would bring her in. After several times, she was shepherded everywhere.

The inheritor of the estate, a cousin through some complex lineage, arrived with little ceremony. He was young, uncertain, and out of his element—his clothes those of tradespeople, poorly tailored to his form. Yet enough of the chemistry existed, a smaller, more put-together version of the Dennis men, that for a few days it was as though her sight had been restored. She embraced him before he could resist.

"Madam," he said, stepping back.

"You bear a resemblance to my—late—husband," she said. "As my son might have looked."

Everything he said was proper and overly involved, someone trying to speak a dialect in which he was not fluent. Yet he was kind, and truly distressed at having to send her away. He was joined by Henry and Mr. Thornton, who explained to all the parties that Ashton's investments had either failed or died along with him. Without Ashton's leadership, other investors had fled and the banks were unwilling to lend funds necessary for any recovery. Ashton's unreimbursed expenses for the Moore campaign had collapsed what was left of his financial edifice. Everything was being sold for debt—major parcels of the estate, the different businesses, the monetary holdings.

"It is not that Ashton was reckless," Mr. Thornton said. "Aggressive, yes, but not reckless. He always kept a reserve. He planned for a decline, but not a *precipitous* one. Not for his own ... *absence*. Too many things happened at once—the embargo, the overseas expansion, the cost of his Rifle company, the security he posted for Moore."

"The financial structure was like a roof designed for snow," Henry said. "We received double the expected." He added: "The Lovelace estate is in even worse condition, as we had weakened them before the campaign. The Earl may well be thrown down, and the other sons squeezed. ... It is not consolation I am trying to offer, only comparison. The difference to the immediate family is that, unlike you, the Colonel's wife is the one who had the wealth."

The Colonel and his wife: The story that glowed like a halo around Robert Lovelace was that while leading the escort for the team that was to fire the munitions, he had died single-handedly repelling a surprise attack by French pickets. That might in fact have been the only story Kat heard, but regardless she would have already forgotten the Dennises and anyone to do with them. She was the sensation of London, the beautiful, brave, *wealthy* widow of one of Wellesley's finest. A survivor, she would look forward, not back.

In summarizing the finances, Mr. Thornton recommended the pursuit of legal remedies in recovering the Moore debt, but added: "The goal of the government will be to make the cost of the suit greater than the amount owed. Like our inheritance cases in which the legal costs consume the entire estate."

"If the choice was between me in silk here or our men in boots in Spain, I am satisfied with the outcome," Jane said to Ashton's heir. "I saw some of our money—bags of silver—tossed off a cliff. I would have been pleased to bring a bag home for you."

When all was sold—the gas manufactory was already being dismantled for transport to its new owner—the cousin would end up with less than a fortune, but much more than he had ever seen.

"I hope, sir, that you can put your inheritance to the best kind of use, as this family did. May it help you achieve your dreams."

Mrs. Dennis came, partly to cast aspersions and partly to organize her personal possessions. Alethea escorted her. Mrs. Dennis was joining her daughter in London, where the Rumford business—independent of the other holdings and outside the estate—would keep them in comfort. Before they left, Mrs. Dennis grudgingly said: "It was not a bad thing my son was loved." Jane replied: "If I accept your praise now, Mrs. Dennis, then I must accept your censure in the past. Good-bye."

When Alethea left, everything went dim again. Weeks trudged by like the funeral procession of someone important but unbearably dull. She understood that everything of hers was also being packed—she took but little, as lavish wear was not to be of any use anymore. All she remembered from this period was having the staff line up to say goodbye: Her one coherent act was to write letters of recommendation for every one. Mr. Hanrahan, Mrs. Lundeen, and Mrs. Shelley stood with fortitude, though Abigail sobbed. Mr. Fletcher waved goodbye from the stables. Both knew they would not survive a farewell. Later that day, the Austen women were once again on the move—to Steventon and from there to Southampton or perhaps it was to London and Godmersham or perhaps it was to Southampton after all. One day she was walking along the beach at one of half a dozen coastal towns in the south. Yes, it must have been Southampton, at least for a few days, because that was the location written on a letter she had copied out.

Cassandra had put her in front of her writing desk with her pen and papers, though Jane was in no more condition to write than a three-legged dog. She could not conceive of anything new to pen and could not revisit anything old—every page had been written in Sanskrit. When her sister demanded she do *something*, her eyes fell to the manuscripts and she realized the one of *Susan* had already been packed away for still another move. That book led her to think of Ashton's voyage to the West Indies, when she told him with hesitant excitement about it being sold and he asked her with unfeigned interest about her early work. That connection enabled her to achieve the following:

5 April 1809

To Messr. Crosbie & Co.
Stationers' Hall Court
London

Gentlemen
In the Spring of the year 1803 a MS. Novel in 2 vol. en-titled Susan was sold to you by a Gentleman of the name Seymour, & the purchase money £10 recd at the same time. Six years have since passed, & this work of which I avow myself the Authoress, has never to the best of my knowledge, appeared in print, tho' an early publication was stipulated at the time of Sale.

I can only account for such an extraordinary circumstance by supposing the MS by some carelessness to have been lost; & if that was the case, am willing to supply You with another Copy if you are disposed to avail yourselves of it, & will engage for no farther delay when it comes into your hands. —It will not be in my power from particular circumstances to command this Copy before the Month of August, but then, if you accept my proposal, you may depend on receiving it.

Be so good as to send me a Line in answer, as soon as possible, as my stay in this place will not exceed a few days. Should no notice be taken of the Address, I shall feel myself at liberty to secure the publication of my work, by applying elsewhere. I am Gentleman &c &c

MAD.—

Mrs Ashton Dennis
Post office, Southampton

---

8 April 1809

Madam

We have to acknowledge the receipt of your letter of the 5th inst. It is true that at the time mentioned we purchased of Mr. Seymour a MS. Novel entitled Susan and paid him for it in the sum of 10£ for which we have his stamped receipt as a full consideration, but there was not any time stipulated for its publication, neither are we bound to publish it. Should you or anyone else, we shall take proceedings to stop the sale. The MS. shall be yours for the same as we paid for it.

For R. Crosby & Co I am yours etc.

Richard Crosby

Stationers' Hall Court
London

Chapter 48

More furnishings shuffled around, more bags folded themselves up, more coaches rolled up for travel. They were on the highway to whatever relatives and friends would take them in, vagabonds if not for hire then at least for entertainment. The marches of the British Army had nothing on the Austen women. They moved, but then, strangely, they stopped. They were no longer in Southampton (the sea air gone), nor at Godmersham (the aura of wealth dispensed)—though Edward was still busily about, instructing his workers in the disposition of their furniture in a new abode.

At first, Jane did not understand that this was home. Her odd form of blindness remained. She could see but not comprehend. The world was transparent of meaning. Her confusion delayed the onset of grief. And yet: The inability to grieve is sorrow in another form. After less than four years of marriage, she could not now recollect what it had been to live without him; nor could she understand how to proceed alone. It was impossible to believe she would never *touch* another consciousness as she had his: through thoughts, words, deeds, and physical play. It was impossible to believe that she could get through any night alone, never mind the rest of her life. She dreaded the cold empty sheets as she would one day dread the dark dank maw of the grave.

Ashton.

Finding the featureless red-brick cottage by reference to the other house—the grand one, Edward's—she considered the habitation no more than a secondary location for the governess-nurses that she and Cass had always been to their brother's children. The charms of the cottage were manifest in the pond across the road, more mud than water; in the peasant tenements beyond that; in the London coaches pounding by at regular intervals day and night. She slowly became aware that this was what had been discussed the year before, the old bailiff's cottage in Chawton. She was pleasantly surprised, for she had liked the quiet, unassuming village, but she also felt pain: The widow had been taken care of, but the situation reminded her of the dispossession of Mr. Fletcher and her other people—though they would all land on their feet and become the stalwarts in their next employ. In truth, she thought, "once of Hants" would become as much a badge of quality in service as "Broadwood" and "Wedgwood" had become in commerce.

From the first, before the luggage was even unloaded, Cassandra had taken her by the arm and made her walk. From their house at the bottom of the village up through the thatched cottages to Mounters Lane, up Mounters Lane with its steep muddy turn to Alton, and in a great westward loop back through Chawton Park to home. Every Sunday they walked to St. Nicholas Church with Martha and Mrs. Austen. When Edward was in residence, they walked to the Great House almost every day. Jane dressed like her sister in the serviceable, frowsy dresses suited to the work of the lower middling class. They spent three minutes on their hair instead of thirty, for caps were all that women needed who were not intent on men.

As the family of the landed proprietor, they received instant and superficial respect. It did not take long, however, before the sisters' engagement of the locals on their rambles and their mother's respectful demeanor in her shopping expeditions awakened a feeling of harmony among the villagers. The Austens let down their vowels in the day as they let down their hair at night, relaxing the clipped pronunciation of the city for the elongated accents of their native hills. "They're just like us!" Jane heard a woman whisper as they left a farm after buying milk. Indeed, they were: industrious, cheerful beyond politeness, generous when they did not need to be. Chawton did not understand—but did appreciate—that far from feeling superior, the Austens hoped to be good enough to become part of their new community.

This was not Steventon, which suffered the blockade of James and Mary. This was not Hants, gone forever. But it was still the rolling fields of northeast Hampshire. Away from Bath. Away from Southampton. Lands with little to recommend—no mansions, no cliffs, no vistas, no seas. Just gentle swells of wheat and oats and barley away from the noise and stink of city life. Just gentle birds and unassuming vegetation which somehow wrought an effect that scenes of grandeur would never have achieved. At first, nature stubbornly rejected her attentions. The birds were anonymously dull. Red squirrels were gray. The trees shied. She could not tell a butterfly from a moth. Slowly, however, day by day, walk by walk, these creatures and plants began to reveal themselves in their usual detail, in their subtle differences, in shapes and colors that were muted but distinct. They gave her permission to see.

And with that change also came the ability to hear. She understood that Cassandra had been talking to her for all these weeks and weeks.

"What would Ashton have you do?" her sister said.

"Anything. As long as I was productive."

"And what are you doing?"

"Gathering myself." With the ability to see and hear came also the ability, for the first time in many a time, to smile. "I cannot find anything in my work that is new. It repeats what already has been done. That has been the problem all along."

Cassandra urged her to write more deeply about relationships than any author had ever done. "Write about you and Ashton. All that you went through."

"I cannot."

"It would be something different—radically so."

"I cannot relive the end because of his pain. I cannot relive the rest because of mine."

"Think only of the past as its remembrance gives you pleasure."

"A lovely sentiment—truly. Which I shall not hesitate to steal. But I cannot—remember—without the pain. Besides, the world is not ready for a story about our relationship. About the deepest things between a man and woman. About their love, their disagreements, their passion, their bond. Especially not as told by the wife. A woman who speaks the truth will not be heard. A woman who writes the truth will not be published."

"An echo then. A shadow."

Jane laughed. "Do you not remember my husband? Do you believe I can shrink him to fit within my miniatures?"

"Even reduced, he would be formidable."

"From a distance, every love story is identical. The opposite is true up close. It is the details which are unique, and it is only the details that matter. If I change anything, I change all. I could not write about Ashton unless it was about him, not some simulacrum. … And that is what I am beginning to understand. I shall not write anything about him, or our life together. I shall lock that life away. That is the only way I can function—to keep that life within me." The more she thought about it, the more she understood that this was exactly what she needed to do. "I shall remove him from my life, as I removed him from his."

When Cassandra blanched at the characterization, Jane explained: "I cannot hasten his death and then live as the sorrowful widow, receiving condolences today and sympathy on important dates. I cannot reconcile my religious beliefs with what my heart ultimately told me to do. What I did was wrong. My conscience knows—it was a *knowing* wrong. Every memory of him drowns in its own guilt. The *only* decision is not the same thing as the *right* decision. I cannot face the daily reminders of his memory. I must remove all traces of him from my life, or I shall go mad. That is my penalty. And my salvation. I cannot go on as if nothing has changed, but I can go on."

"You cannot erase his memory, or his life."

"We have already begun. No one has mentioned his name since I returned—supposedly out of deference to my grief. Do you believe that is the reason? Considering everything? The *illicit* rendezvouses. The *hasty* marriage. The *indecorous* displays of affection. What the newspapers call a *disgraceful* military campaign. And, of course, the *defective* child along with the rumors he sought to *kill* himself. Unless you or I bring up Mr. Dennis, our generation will keep silent. Our nieces and nephews—most of them are too young to remember anything. We will confuse them utterly. Make up a new history of intrigues, of proposals made and rejected, of opportunities missed and love affairs lost. We will recast a letter or two, misdate others. You can write my hand as well as I can write yours. Change a detail here and there. Destroy the rest. Work whatever subterfuges we must. We shall lose Ashton in the mists. Lovely as our family is, they are more pious than moral. They will forget him faster than last week's sermon."

Before Cass could respond, Jane cut her off. "We are all named Jane, or Cassandra, or George, or James. Misdirection will not be difficult. Thirty years from now, our relatives will not remember, or care, who was married to whom. They will be happy to forget the part of Aunt Jane's life that was wholly out of the norm. They will not only acquiesce in the deception, they will embrace it. Encourage it."

"You are mad."

"Very likely. But consider this: Without trying, we hid two unfortunate relatives for a generation. Surely, with concerted effort, we can hide an inconvenient husband."

"What of another—husband?"

"There will be no other. Any more than there was another for you after Tom."

"On one condition and one condition only. If you are not going to live, you *must* write. That is something Ashton and I both could agree upon."

She began tentatively—not at the writing table, that was too soon and too dramatic. She sat with her piles of mismatched papers at the kitchen or dining room table. She spread pages over the sofa, kept them from flying away in the garden. She read everything she had ever written, in order, early to late. She edited phrases as usual but did nothing she considered final; her survey was more to familiarize and internalize than to do. This took more than a week, the authorial equivalent of limbering the fingers and playing scales. Her stories had been begun and suspended so many times, over so many years, that they shied like abandoned pets. She worked around the edges, making notes, sketching passages, teasing here and there, so that her writing did not know what she was up to. It took time to reestablish trust, but progress edged ahead without resistance. It was the way Ashton worked a horse: ignoring the animal until it came to him, nosing his arm to be involved.

All this time she was thinking strategically about where she wanted to take her novels and tactically in terms of scenes and actions. She would not be detoured or dissuaded or delayed—no more, never again. She was not daunted by the limitations on what a woman could write, for she had ideas on how to circumvent them. However publication might go, she could control nothing except for the effort she put into her work—she did not think of it as *art*, for *art* is a word the mediocre use to puff themselves up. It was work she sought and work she knew how to do.

Her time with manuscripts alternated with her time on foot. Every day she went out to nature. She worked in the morning; walked at noon, when her mind sorted all the changes required to what she had done so far that day; and worked again in the afternoon. She went among the trees and flowers, she wore the fogs of the elms like a familiar cloak, she felt the wind as the smile of a friend and the rain as the patter of an affectionate chat. As her lungs breathed deep the Hampshire air, her mind expanded to construct the scaffolding needed for a major work. (Occasionally regret and sometimes vindication crept in; yet all calmed when she reminded herself that the two most precious people in her life knew at the very end that they were loved. None of us can offer more than that.)

One day she awoke before dawn and went out, dew on her slippers, to watch the sun rise. She closed her eyes and felt the tentative warmth on her skin as permission by all that mattered. The earth turned and the sun came up. The earth turned and she went to her writing desk. She dipped the pen into an ink of her own private formulation. Would her vision of the world flow out, or would she merely scratch out a living? She recognized the author's arrogance. Whether one is brave or foolhardy is a matter of retrospection, when one succeeds—or does not—in creating a world out of scribbles. It did not matter. The sun must rise; she must write. The earth turned. She began to make her mark.

THE END

Epilogue: 'The Sun of My Life'

Along with her mother, sister Cassandra, and their friend Martha Lloyd (sister-in-law of brother James), Jane Austen resided in the brick cottage at Chawton, provided by their brother Edward, from mid-1809 until 1817. Having become seriously ill, she was taken to Winchester for unsuccessful medical treatment. She died and was buried there.

Living frugally on small annuities and the financial support of the men of the family, the women occupied themselves with daily chores, the tending of the gardens, and conversational walks. The roads from Gosport and Winchester came together just in front of the cottage on the way north to London. At mealtimes, post-chaises and carriages barreled through the intersection, carrying travelers along on their busy lives and rattling the ladies' plates. Reading remained the primary intellectual pursuit of the household, in conjunction with occasional travel, the social activities of rural Hampshire, and good deeds for the parish poor.

During those years at Chawton, Austen created or thoroughly revised the works that became the oeuvre known today. She wrote steadily, leaving a squeaking door unrepaired so that she could be alerted to anyone coming her way; she would put her work aside to keep it private. *Sense and Sensibility* was published first, in 1811, through the efforts of brother Henry, who managed all of her publications. *Pride and Prejudice*, a much-revised version of *First Impressions*, came out in 1813. *Mansfield Park* was published in 1814. *Emma* was published in 1815, dedicated to the Prince Regent. This was an honor she could not refuse but that, because of his moral failings, she accepted with great reluctance. *Persuasion* and *Northanger Abbey* were published together in 1817.

Northanger Abbey was the book *Susan*, which Austen had sold to Crosby in 1803 but which the publisher never printed. She bought it back for the original purchase price of £10 in 1816—Crosby never realizing that the book was the work of the now popular author of *Sense and Sensibility* and *Pride and Prejudice*. Austen made minor revisions to *Northanger Abbey*, apologizing to readers for aspects of the novel that were now "obsolete" after thirteen years (though the book contains at least one reference to events as late as 1808). She changed the name of the main character from Susan to Catherine, possibly because another novel named *Susan* had been published in 1809. Henry apparently picked the final title, *Northanger Abbey*. Thus Austen's first mature novel was her last one published.

Sense and Sensibility and *Pride and Prejudice* made her reputation, and all of her books sold reasonably well. In total, Jane earned £640 13s for her writing, compared to the roughly £400 to £450 annual income on which the three Austen women and their friend Martha lived. Having gained financial security, Jane indulged in a few luxuries for herself and Cassandra but generally pooled her resources with those of the other ladies in order that everyone might live comfortably.

The extra income was providential, as Henry's bank failed in March 1816, wiping him out, costing Edward at least £20,000 and James and Frank much of their savings. One reason for the bankruptcy was the post-war economic decline; another was a loan of £6,000 that was never repaid by Lord Moira, an aristocrat who had earlier helped promote Frank's naval career. Undoubtedly, Henry's serious illness in late 1815, through which Jane tended him, hampered his ability to rescue his business. Because of the losses, Henry and Frank were no longer able to help support their mother and sisters. Jane lost only £25; the bulk of her earnings was safely deposited in Navy five percent stock.

When James Leigh-Perrot died in 1817, the same year as Jane, the Austens' hopes for inheritance were dashed again. Their beloved uncle left all of his estate to his wife and nothing to his poorer relations. This lack of inheritance was no doubt influenced by the Leigh-Perrots having also lost £10,000 in Henry's bank collapse. The sticky-fingered Aunt Perrot marched on until 1836, when the remaining Austen offspring—diminished by now to five in number—received £1,000 apiece.

Jane took ill in 1816, shrugging off the early symptoms with Austen-Anglican stoicism but suffering over the next year a long deterioration of health. Several months before her death, she was taken by Cassandra and Henry to Winchester to see a doctor. There, she prayed daily with Cassandra and wrote her will, leaving most of her possessions to her beloved sister. Jane waited for the inevitable outcome with "the patience and the hope of a Christian." She died July 18, 1817, at the age of 41.

In retrospect, the cause of her death has been attributed to everything from Addison's disease, a disorder of the adrenal glands; to bovine tuberculosis, an infection brought by unpasteurized milk; to Hodgkin's lymphoma, a cancer of the white blood cells; to a variant recurrence of the typhus that nearly killed her as a child. Though highly unlikely, arsenic poisoning has also been suggested. Because Addison's can be brought on by tuberculosis, it has been speculated that Henry's illness of late 1815 may have been tuberculosis and that, although he recovered, he may have passed on that disease to Jane. The descriptions of her symptoms are too general to know with any certainty what caused her death. The diagnosis of Addison's is related to references to the darkening of her skin color and general malaise. In any event, none of the likely diseases was curable at that time.

Henry arranged for Jane to be buried at Winchester cathedral, where a plaque was installed to commemorate her benevolence, sweetness, and intellect—but not, curiously, her literary achievement. As her popularity grew over time, officials were baffled by the pilgrims coming to visit the crypt of a woman the church knew only as the daughter of a clergyman.

Surprising to generations of readers who feel that they have a dear and personal relationship with their Jane, most of the contemporary reading public did not know who she was. Never in her life did she publish under her own name. The author of *Sense and Sensibility* was identified simply as "A Lady." Later books were ascribed either to the author of *Sense and Sensibility* or *Pride and Prejudice*. Though the proud Henry blabbed at times about Jane's authorship, the broader public was not aware of her identity until her death. Henry's biographical notice, which was included with the posthumous publication of *Persuasion* and *Northanger Abbey*, provided her name along with the announcement of her death five months earlier. Until then, few outside of her close personal circle knew that the novels that eventually achieved such acclaim were written by a woman named—

Jane Austen.

Cassandra burned most of Jane's private papers, including the vast majority of her letters as well as any diaries or journals she may have kept. Most of the missing materials cover the period 1802-1809. The reason for the destruction is unknown, though their niece Caroline described the letters as "open and confidential." Frank's daughter and other descendants destroyed even more material. Of Jane's letters, estimated to be 3,000 in number, only about 160 remain. Some of these are heavily redacted. Almost all of the remaining correspondence concerns routine domestic matters. Beyond a smattering of her own letters and passing references in the journals and letters of others about her whereabouts, virtually nothing is known of Austen's life in the period covered by this trilogy.

Jane and her brother James died young (he in 1819), along with five of Jane's sisters-in-law, three of complications from childbirth. As recounted here, Elizabeth, Edward's wife, died after her eleventh child. Mary, Frank's wife, died after her eleventh child. (Frank then married Martha Lloyd, which may have been his way of providing for the longtime family friend.) Fanny, Charles's wife, died after her fourth child. Jane's cousin and sister-in-law, Eliza, died in 1813, likely of breast cancer, which had taken Eliza's mother. The rest of the Austen family was long lived. Jane's father was 73 when he died in 1805. Her mother died at the age of 88 in 1827. The unfortunate brother George, who lived away from his family for most of his life, died at the age of 72 in 1838. Jane never mentions him in any of her surviving letters; nor is she ever known to have visited him. Visitation and general responsibility were delegated to the eldest son, and Edward apparently bore the cost of his care.

Cassandra was also 72 when she died in 1845. She had gone to visit Frank and had a stroke just as he, still on active duty as an Admiral at the age of 71, was leaving to take charge of England's North American station. Henry tended to her until her death a few days later. He died at the age of 79 in 1850, having spent his post-entrepreneurial years as a clergyman, close by his family in Chawton and Steventon. Charles, by now a Rear-Admiral, died at the age of 73 in 1852 of cholera while leading a naval expedition in Burma. One of his sons served with him. Edward also died in 1852, at the age of 84, after a lifetime of ease as the heir of the Knight fortune.

Frank was the last surviving member of the generation, living to the age of 91. He died in 1865 after being knighted and becoming Admiral of the Fleet, England's highest naval rank. It was poetic justice for Frank and Charles, both talented junior officers, who were overlooked for most of their careers for lack of personal and political connections. By outliving their contemporaries, both men finally gained the highest ranks of a service in which promotion within the upper ranks was determined by seniority.

———

Globally, the Long War finally ended when Buonaparte's own disastrous winter campaign, in Russia in 1812, gave General Sir Arthur Wellesley—Lord Wellington after 1814—the opening to push up from Spain into France. Buonaparte was deposed for nearly a year; exiled to Elba, an island just off France; came back for a hundred days; was defeated at Waterloo in 1815 and exiled again. This time it was to St. Helena, a British colony in the far south Atlantic from which he could launch no more comebacks. He died six years later.

King George III of England, well into his second madness, gave way in 1811 to his son, the Prince of Wales, who in becoming the Prince Regent assumed most of the monarch's duties and gave the name *Regency* to the era. The Regent's highly regarded patronage of the arts was undermined by his extravagant spending and chronic philandering. Ascending to the throne on his father's death in 1820, the Prince Regent ruled until 1831, when the *Times* remarked upon his death that "there never was an individual less regretted by his fellow-creatures than this deceased king."

William Wilberforce reduced his responsibilities in Parliament in 1812 before retiring in 1825. He invested in his oldest son's business and went broke. Having given away several fortunes to charitable causes, Wilberforce lived out his life with two other sons in near poverty. A month after his death in July 1833, England ended slavery in all its possessions, effective July 31, 1834, and phasing in over six years. Slave owners received £20 million in recompense. The slave trade, however, carried on illegally before petering out in 1860, more than half a century after England's original slave-trade bill.

Henry Thornton and his wife died of tuberculosis in 1815.

Richard Trevithick never succeeded in developing a commercially viable rail-road locomotive. His work in other areas, though, advanced steam science. Humphry Davy's chemistry experiments and inventions led to riches and rewards, including a baronetcy in 1819; his assistant, Michael Faraday, revolutionized the understanding of electricity. Charles Babbage became the inventor of the first modern mechanical computer and, along with Ada Lovelace—Lord Byron's estranged daughter—the first computer programmer. John Herschel, the son of astronomer William, made contributions in astronomy, mathematics, meteorology, and photography. He was a founder of the Royal Astronomical Society in 1820.

Having gone out of print in the 1820s, Jane Austen's novels experienced a revival in 1832, when Henry negotiated a payment of £210 to Cassandra for the copyrights. The books have never been out of print since. Jane's first biography was written by a nephew, James Edward Austen-Leigh, with help from his sister Caroline. The descendants emphasized the sweet, quiet, and religious disposition of their aunt, while downplaying her wit, sharp tongue, and independent nature. Though affection for their aunt comes through, their emphasis on the rectitude that was part of the Austen heritage may have blinded them to what the appreciative Henry recognized as "the extraordinary endowments of her mind."

Cassandra remembered Jane in terms of their deep personal relationship. In a letter to their niece Fanny two days after Jane's death, Cass said: "I have *lost* a treasure, such a Sister, such a friend as can never be surpassed,—She was the sun of my life, the gilder of every pleasure, the soother of every sorrow, I had not a thought concealed from her, & it is as if I have lost a part of myself. ... Never was [a] human being more sincerely mourned ... than this dear creature."

It might also be said of Jane, as she once said of her own creation Elizabeth Bennet, that she was "as delightful a creature as ever appeared in print."

Book Club Questions

The Marriage of Miss Jane Austen has proven to be popular with book clubs. The following is a list of questions designed to stimulate discussion about the trilogy.

How does this trilogy differ from a typical Austen or other Regency novel, and why does the author go in this direction?

Jane Austen described her novels as miniatures. How does this trilogy differ, if at all?

Jane Austen wrote the quintessential woman's novel. Does anything change with a woman as the central character when the book is written by a man rather than a woman? If so, what and how?

As a courtship novel featuring a strong female and male character, the first volume of *The Marriage of Miss Jane Austen* shares similarities with *Pride and Prejudice*. Within the courtship framework, how are they different?

The author describes the second volume of the trilogy as a series of awakenings by the main character. What does he mean by that remark?

How does the relationship between the Dennis family and the Lovelace family evolve over the three volumes? What does this evolution tell us about human nature?

Issues that are in the background in Volume I become front and center in Volumes II and III. What are these issues and how do they contribute to the development of the plot and characters?

Why do you think the author uses Jane Austen as the protagonist instead of a fictional character, which would have given him much more creative freedom?

Don't Miss the Rest of This Exciting Series

The Marriage of Miss Jane Austen trilogy follows the complete arc of a mature relationship between Jane Austen and her beau, Mr. Ashton Dennis. Volume I is a courtship novel with several exciting twists. Beginning with a ball, the novel turns on Jane's critical decision to choose a liberating adventure with Ashton over convention. This action sets in motion a series of events that promises happiness, crushes them both in a separation that takes Ashton off to the West Indies, and brings them together again at the very moment Jane fears he may be lost to her forever.

Volume II covers the first fourteen months of marriage when Jane, who until then has led the sheltered life of a clergyman's daughter, undergoes a series of awakenings in her personal life and her engagement with the outside world. She grows emotionally through her deepening relationship with Ashton, accepts the moral challenge of the biggest issue of the day, contends with a friendship gone terribly awry, and undergoes the shifting emotions of a pregnant woman preparing for the birth of a child. Volume III covers the shocking events that send her to a small village in Hampshire to begin her writing career.

All three volumes of *The Marriage of Miss Jane Austen* are available at www.janeaustenbooks.net and www.amazon.com.

Be sure to visit www.austenmarriage.com for insightful commentary on Jane Austen, her works, and her times, and subscribe to the blog at www.austenmarriage.com/blog.

Acknowledgments

Thanks to Joyce Thompson, friend and teacher, and Tom Hanrahan, friend and colleague, each of whom performed detailed reviews of the text, offering suggestions that improved the structure and content. A thank-you is insufficient to express my gratitude to Susannah Fullerton, Austen expert and author, whose perceptive thoughts and sharp eye, as well as her personal generosity, added immeasurably to the work.

All shortcomings that remain, of course, are those of the Gentleman.

Thanks to Megan McKenzie, Brian Edwards, and the team at McKenzie Worldwide for their support in the marketing of the trilogy.

Many warm thanks to other early readers who offered thoughtful and helpful comments on drafts of various manuscripts: Marianne Allison, Mary Falkenstein, Lynn Fulks, Shelley Hanrahan, Wendy Alden Hemingway, Paula Johanson, Patti Knollman, Claire Lematta, Lorchid Macri, Deb Mathis, Bev Maul, Jerry McConnell, Megan McKenzie, Linda O'Neill, and Susan Priddy; and to those who shared their thoughts and feelings on matters that contributed to the content: Julie Allport, Jacquie Braly, Rebecca Chaulet, Carrine Greason, Mary Falkenstein, Wendy Alden Hemingway, Patti Knollman, Cristina Lamoureux, and Patsy Lewellyn.

Others supported *The Marriage of Miss Jane Austen* in various ways: Reese Mercer, Selah Ewert, and the team at Five Talent; Vicki Magson, Robyn Mawn, and Shaun Wootton of Otto PR. Gordon Frye answered questions about period weaponry and Dr. Cheryl Kinney about medical treatments of the early 1800s.

About the Author

Collins Hemingway was born and raised in Arkansas and has lived most of his adult life in the Pacific Northwest. He has a bachelor's degree in English literature from the University of Arkansas (Phi Beta Kappa) with a minor in science, and a master's degree in English literature from the University of Oregon. His interests range from literature to history; from digital technology to aviation; and from business to writing; these endeavors are reflected in the fiction and nonfiction he has written.

In addition to fiction, Hemingway has worked with thought leaders to produce insightful nonfiction books on topics as diverse as corporate culture and ethics; business, the Internet, and mobile technology; retail branding strategies; and the cognitive potential of the brain. He is best known for partnering with Bill Gates on the #1 best-selling book *Business @ the Speed of Thought*.

His shorter nonfiction has won multiple awards in business, computer technology, and medicine.

Attributions

It should surprise no reader to discover that, in a fictional imagining of Jane Austen's life, her actual words appear on occasion. Several of her letters are used verbatim or with small clarifications. Most of Austen's most memorable lines have been avoided as a distraction that would take the reader outside this story. The Gentleman avoided situations, scenes, descriptions, or other direct extractions from Austen's novels. A few interesting phrases from Austen's juvenilia and unfinished works have been deliberately offered a place in the sun. Other historical or literary tidbits, usually two or three per chapter, await readers who may enjoy discovering secondary stories behind the main story. This literary scavenger hunt will have no effect on the casual reader, while (it is hoped) giving those who are knowledgeable about Austen's life and the Georgian-Regency era an extra pleasure of recognition.

One or two Austen phrases have demonstrated their own wanderlust. Commentary on the tax status of windows, for example, originated with Austen's mother, made its way into *Mansfield Park*, and has found a home in this trilogy. Beyond such tidbits, and the obvious parallels between love stories set in the same time and place and involving the same social conventions and restrictions, the intent was to inhabit the mind of this remarkable woman—not to imitate her, or her novels.

A few things that were said about Austen or attributed by others to her have been redirected here, usually by means of putting the words into the mind or mouth of another character. Mrs.

Dennis, for example, calls Jane a "husband-hunting butterfly," a comment about Jane made by the mother of Mary Russell Mitford: Mary was a literary competitor. Anyone knowing of Austen's appreciation of the poet Cowper will recognize lines from his poems popping into her head on her nature walks. Certain historical events, including those related to slavery and Parliamentary confrontations, were repurposed to involve the characters in this trilogy. Except for the names, the letter from Austen to her mother in Volume III is real—written by Lady Elgin to her mother in an identical heart-rending situation. The letter so perfectly captured the agony of a woman at that time the Gentleman felt it would honor both women to use it verbatim.

Finally, the author has included a few rare specimens of interesting phraseology from a variety of histories, letters, diaries, and memoirs. Coming largely from ordinary rather than literary individuals, such phrases would have been part of the vernacular. They add a little color. Any unusual phrases that did not originate either with the Gentleman or with Austen have been italicized, or the source has been credited indirectly.

Anyone desiring attribution of the events and personalities behind this novel may inquire of same to gentleman@austenmarriage.com.

CPSIA information can be obtained
at www.ICGtesting.com
Printed in the USA
LVHW012312130119
603788LV00001B/63/P

JAN 1 7 2019

9 781979 472760